About t

USA Today bestselling author **Naima Simone** writes romance with heart, humour and heat. Her books have been featured in *The Washington Post* and *Entertainment Weekly*, and described as balancing 'crackling, electric love scenes with exquisitely rendered characters caught in emotional turmoil.' She is wife to Superman, and mum to the most awesome kids ever. They live in perfect, domestically challenged bliss in the southern US.

Born and raised just outside of Toronto, Ontario, **Amy Ruttan** fled the big city to settle down with the country boy of her dreams. After the birth of her second child, Amy was lucky enough to realise her lifelong dream of becoming a romance author. When she's not furiously typing away at her computer, she's a mum to three wonderful children who use her as a personal taxi and chef.

Stefanie London is a *USA Today* bestselling author of contemporary romance. Her books have been called 'genuinely entertaining and memorable' by *Booklist*, and her writing was praised as 'elegant, descriptive and delectable' by *RT Magazine*. Originally from Australia, she now lives in Toronto with her very own hero and is doing her best to travel the world. She frequently indulges her passions for lipstick, good coffee, books and anything zombie related.

Second Chance

Second Chance:
Their Enemy Sparks

NAIMA SIMONE

AMY RUTTAN

STEFANIE LONDON

MILLS & BOON

First Published in Great Britain 2025
by Mills & Boon, an imprint of HarperCollins*Publishers* Ltd
1 London Bridge Street, London, SE1 9GF

www.harpercollins.co.uk

HarperCollins*Publishers*
Macken House, 39/40 Mayor Street Upper,
Dublin 1, D01 C9W8, Ireland

Second Chance: Their Enemy Sparks © 2026 Harlequin Enterprises ULC.

Back in the Texan's Bed © 2021 Naima Simone
Craving Her Ex-Army Doc © 2016 Amy Ruttan
Mr. Dangerously Sexy © 2017 Stefanie London

ISBN: 978-0-263-42106-4

MIX
Paper | Supporting
responsible forestry
FSC™ C007454

This book contains FSC™ certified paper and other controlled sources to ensure responsible forest management.

For more information visit: www.harpercollins.co.uk/green

Printed and Bound in the UK using 100% Renewable Electricity
at CPI Group (UK) Ltd, Croydon, CR0 4YY

BACK IN THE TEXAN'S BED

NAIMA SIMONE

To Gary. 143.

Prologue

Love.

Russell "Ross" Edmond Jr. sipped his scotch, relishing the smoky flavor with hints of caramel, fruit and a bite of salt, while staring out the window of the Texas Cattleman's Club meeting room at the beautiful couple currently wrapped around each other in a passionate embrace.

Ezekiel Holloway and Reagan Sinclair—Reagan Holloway now—had caused quite a scandal in Royal, Texas, some months ago when they'd eloped to Vegas against her family's wishes. Especially since Zeke's own family had been embroiled in a dirty criminal investigation that involved embezzlement and drug smuggling. But that had all been cleared up, their reputation restored, and now the newlyweds were living out their happily-ever-after.

Ross barely contained a derisive snort. Sure, the two appeared enamored and, yes, happy. The married couple kissed as if Ezekiel was heading off to sea for a months-long absence. Ross would say they were in love. Or, at least, they believed they were.

Unfortunately—or fortunately, in his opinion—he wasn't a devout disciple at the altar of the emotion that seemed like a convenient excuse for people to lose control, validate idiotic behavior or justify satisfying any impulsive desire.

What *did* he believe in?

Raising his glass to his mouth again, he turned from the view of the couple and surveyed the elegantly appointed room. Due to recent renovations at the Club, the design was less dark wood and stone, and now boasted brighter colors, larger windows and higher ceilings. Yes, the hunting trophies and historical artifacts still adorned the walls, and the stables remained, as did the pool and tennis courts. Yet, now the Club had a day care and sported painted murals, as well. The whole effect exuded a warmth that had been missing before.

But it all still conveyed wealth. Influence. Exclusivity.

And those ideals he trusted.

Money and power. They could be counted, measured, handled, manipulated, if need be, and were unfailingly consistent.

They'd never let him down.

Unlike people. Unlike *love*.

Hell, he couldn't even keep the sneer out of his inner voice.

"Ross, get over here," Russell Edmond Sr. boomed as if Ross stood farther out in the club's entryway instead of just several feet away from him. "Do that brooding shit on your own time. We have business to attend to."

Rusty. Oil mogul. Texas Cattleman's Club member. Tycoon. All things people called Russell Edmond Sr. Whereas Ross considered him *brilliant, ruthless, domineering.* And, on occasion, *manipulative bastard.*

They all fit.

With his tall, wide-shouldered and athletic build that had only gone a little soft around the middle, dark hair dusted with silver at the temples and intelligent, scalpel-sharp gray eyes, Rusty still possessed a powerful physique and commanded respect. Ross strode over to the long, cedar conference table, his gaze fixed not on his father but on the thin stack of documents in the middle of the table. His heart thumped against his sternum in anticipation. To others, those ordinary sheets of paper might seem innocuous. But to him?

Independence. Autonomy.

Identity.

Yes, this deal included the financial and marketing backing of The Edmond Organization, but this project—the luxury food, art and wine festival called Soiree on the Bay, which was to be held on a small, private island—was his baby. Well, more aptly, it was a baby that belonged to him, his siblings, Gina and Asher, and his best friend, Billy Holmes. But for the first time, he wasn't a figurehead wearing the Edmond name and the ineffectual title of executive. Wasn't a puppet tasked with carrying out Rusty-given orders. Wasn't just the useless playboy son riding the coattails of his daddy's success and reputation.

With this project, this event, he would finally step out from under his father's shadow and show everyone he hadn't just inherited the Edmond name—he'd *earned* it. Ross would play an integral role in raising the bar, in solidifying and expanding their legacy as he elevated The Edmond Organization from the national stage to the international one. Something even Rusty hadn't managed to do in the company's history.

But Ross would.

And in the process, maybe earn that thing that had eluded him the entire twenty-eight years he'd been Rusty's son—approval.

Again, not love. Men like his father believed in that emotion even less than Ross did. Just ask Rusty's four ex-wives.

Just ask his children.

"So this is it? The final contract?" Ross set his tumbler

down on the table, trying not to stare down at the documents as if they were the Holy Grail and he a Texas version of Indiana Jones.

"This is it," Billy Holmes, his college friend and future business partner, said, grinning. "The last step before Soiree on the Bay moves from dreams to reality."

"Dreams," Rusty scoffed. "Dreams are for men who don't have the balls to get out there and pursue what they want."

Ross glanced at his sister, Gina, across the table, arching an eyebrow in her direction. She rolled her eyes, but he noted the ever-present frustration there. Even this throwaway comment reflected Rusty's dismissal of women, especially in regard to business and autonomy. All because they'd had the misfortune of being born with a uterus instead of a penis. Though Gina had become as adept as Ross at masking her emotions, he caught the aggravation in her eyes. The hurt.

"Fortunately, everyone in this room is well equipped with their balls," Billy drawled, slanting a grin at Ross's baby sister. "Except for you, Gina. And thank God for it." His gentle teasing garnered the desired effect, and the shadows in her eyes dimmed, lightening with humor and gratitude. "And once we all sign, no one will ever question the influence and reach of The Edmond Organization."

Rusty grunted and slid the contract over the table toward him. As he scanned through, Billy glanced at Ross and winked. Ross smothered a snort, shaking his head. His pal had been a charmer in college, and since he arrived in Royal two years ago, he hadn't changed a bit. With his impeccable appearance and manners, generosity with his time, acumen and money, Billy had everyone from business associates to the often clique-ish members of Royal society wrapped around his finger.

Including Rusty, which was a feat unto itself.

The older man had even vouched for Billy with the Texas Cattleman's Club, and Ross's friend had scored a much-coveted membership. Billy shared a camaraderie and closeness with Rusty Edmond that even his kids couldn't claim.

But that was Billy. The Billionaire Whisperer, they jokingly called him.

All right, maybe not so jokingly.

"This looks good," Rusty announced, reaching inside his suit coat to remove a thick gold pen. With flourish, he signed his name on the designated line. "You did good, son," he praised Billy.

Picking up his drink, Ross sipped, waiting for the dark slick of jealousy to slide down his throat to his chest along with the liquor. After all, his father had just called another man *son*, and Ross was human. So yes, pinpricks of jealousy did sting him. But relief reigned as the most prevalent emotion.

And if that wasn't a fucked-up indictment on the Edmond family dynamic, he didn't know what was.

But one quick glance at Gina and at Asher, his stepbrother whom Rusty had adopted after marrying Asher's mother—wife number two—verified he wasn't alone in this sentiment. That same relief shone his siblings' gazes, as well. Anytime Rusty leashed in that infamous mercurial temper was a reason to breathe deep and bask in the peaceful, and probably brief, moment.

A knock on the door reverberated in the room, and Billy waved toward the contract. "That's my surprise. I'll get that while you finish up here."

Ross moved forward first, adding his signature to the contract, followed swiftly by Gina and Asher. By the time they all finished, Billy returned, bearing a silver tray laden with a bottle of champagne and five glass flutes. In moments, Billy had the sparkling wine poured and they'd all lifted their glasses to meet high over the table.

"A toast." Billy paused, blue eyes gleaming. "To The Edmond Organization stamping its indelible brand on not just the US, but the world. I think we've all waited for this day to arrive. So, to achieving long-awaited goals. And finally, to all of you, the Edmond family. May you all get what you so richly deserve." He smiled. "Emphasis on the rich."

They clinked glasses and sipped the champagne, celebrating this deal that they'd all put so much time into bringing to fruition.

"Vendors have already been contacting me about the festival, just from rumors alone. They want in. I predict tickets will sell out within hours of going on sale," Asher said. "Soiree on the Bay is going to be wildly successful. For all of us."

"It needs to be," Ross added gruffly. "This is the inaugural launch. The potential to make this a coveted, exclusive and profitable annual event is huge. So the first one needs to go off without a hitch. Besides, vendors and investors are pouring money in with ours, and the charities that will benefit from this are counting on it. On *us*."

"We'll do it," Gina swore, her tone firm. "I have zero doubts about that."

"With the Edmond reputation and money on the line, hell yes, you'll make this a success. You have no choice. I want people talking about this festival for months before and after."

"Oh, they will. Rest assured, Rusty, they will," Billy murmured, a corner of his mouth lifting in a half smile. "I promise you. This will be an event that no one will ever forget."

Once more, excitement stirred in Ross's gut. In just months, vendors, investors, the press and ticketholders would flock to *their* festival. He sipped from the bubbly wine, savoring the light flavor with a smile. It would be business for him, but not *all* business. People from all over the world would be visiting the private island where the event would be held. Which meant hordes of beautiful women. Most specifically, women who wouldn't expect more from him than the temporary, mutually agreed upon use of each other's bodies for the hottest, dirtiest pleasure.

He knew the reputation he'd earned—they called him a playboy. And admittedly, it was a moniker he deserved. Flings, one-night stands—the filthy hot fun without the messy emotional attachments that could wrap around a man, trap him, strangle him until he couldn't think, couldn't function, couldn't fucking *breathe*.

His chest tightened, a vise slowly turning until he could practically hear his ribs creak in protest. A face, faded and nebulous, wavered across his mind's eye like a mirage a dying man glimpsed seconds before his heart and body surrendered. Ross's grip tautened around the glass, his jaw clenching. He wasn't a dying man, but he'd beat the shit out of himself if he ever allowed himself to be that humiliatingly *weak* again. To allow himself to believe fucking was more than that—two people satisfying an itch before going their separate ways. It didn't have anything to do with emotion...with love.

God, why in the hell did that word keep rebounding in his head today?

He mentally shook his head, dislodging the wayward thoughts—and that damn face—from his head. Focus. He needed to focus.

He and his siblings hovered on the precipice of obtaining their individual and collective purposes. Of achieving those *goals* that Billy had toasted about mere moments ago.

And nothing would stand in their way.

One

"Charlotte, can I borrow you for a moment?"

Charlotte Jarrett looked up from plating and double-checking the dishes before sending them out for customers to dine on. This was her kitchen, her baby. And her recipes were her soul. If the food wasn't flawless, she sent it back for another plate to be prepared. Nothing less than perfection went out of here.

"Sure thing," she said to Faith Grisham, the manager of Sheen, the restaurant where Charlotte had been working as head chef for two weeks now. "Give me just a couple of minutes to finish up here and get these out and served."

Faith, a beautiful, no-nonsense woman who could've passed for actress Zoe Saldana's younger sister, nodded with a flick of her fingers. "Of course." Number one rule in this kitchen: the food came first, because the customer did. And though Sheen enjoyed popularity and success, they couldn't afford to become lax. One negative review, one bad write-up, and their status as Royal's newest favorite could quickly spin the other way. Nobody wanted that.

Least of all Charlotte.

Not when she'd sacrificed everything to return to the hometown she'd had no intention of ever stepping foot in again.

Not when she had so much riding on this.

Like expanding her clientele to include more exclusive and influential connections. A possible owning partnership in Sheen. Growing her reputation, to take one more step toward becoming a world-renowned chef. Earning her Michelin stars.

And most important, providing a stable, financially secure future for herself and Ben.

Even as she executed the finishing touches on her signature dish of braised beef over Thai noodles with seared tomatoes and asparagus, that warm rush of joy that only thoughts of her beautiful little boy could conjure slid through her like melted sunshine. He'd saved her, blessed her with a reason to keep pushing forward, instead of lying down and fading away. He was her *everything*, so it seemed only fair that she would be more than willing to give up everything to ensure he had a well-rounded, happy and full life.

Even if it meant swallowing her pride and being the one to try to bridge the divide that had estranged her from her parents after she'd left Royal.

Even if it meant facing the memories—and demons— that continued to plague her three years later.

Smothering a sigh, she refocused on the task at hand. Satisfied that the meals were ready, she quickly cleaned the edge of the plates with a paper towel soaked with white vinegar, then set them on the custom-built warming shelves for servers to come pick up.

"Rachel," Charlotte called to her sous-chef, "fire those plantain burgers. They're up next."

"Yes, Chef, on three," the older woman immediately replied, informing Charlotte that the Kobe beef burger, set between two slices of fried plantain, would be ready for her to plate with her made-from-scratch avocado ranch dressing in three minutes' time.

Wiping her hands on a towel, Charlotte turned to Faith, smiling as the manager typed out a message so fast on her ever-present phone that her thumbs blurred.

"What'd you need?" Charlotte asked.

"You, your effervescent personality and beautiful face."

"Do you want me to clue you in on how pimp-ish that sounds, or are we just going to ignore it?" Charlotte drawled, quirking an eyebrow.

"Ignore it."

Charlotte snickered, then grinned. As she had been headhunted from the California restaurant where she'd been working, so had Faith, from her native San Antonio, to run Sheen.

Faith had created a name for herself as a Jon Taffer in heels. Not that Sheen had been failing and needed rescuing when Faith had been brought on several weeks ago and prior to Charlotte's hiring, but the owners had wanted to make sure their venture hit the ground running from the beginning.

"Okay, give. I have nearly a full restaurant of hungry customers to feed," Charlotte said, crossing her arms. "What's up?"

"What's up is I just heard from a source who shall remain nameless that the food critic from the *New York Voice* magazine will be dropping by Sheen next Tuesday."

Astonishment vibrated through Charlotte, and she rocked back on her nonskid sugar skulls clogs. "What?" she whispered excitedly. "You're *kidding* me!"

The *New York Voice*. Holy… The alternative e-zine had only been around for the last five years, but it had immediately become popular not just within New York, but nationally and internationally, too. With its hard-hitting investigative journalism stories on societal issues, along with its focus on the cultural community of art, music, literature and food, it had already won the National Press Foundation Award as well as the George Polk Award. For Sheen to receive a positive review in their food column would be amazing publicity not only for the restaurant, but also for Charlotte's career.

"Nope, all true. Which means we need to be at our very best next Tuesday. I'll handle the front of the house and make sure it's super clean, all the servers are on point. And you're responsible for the back. I don't think I need to explain what a rave review could do for us."

"You don't." Charlotte shook her head, grinning. "And believe me, we will be better than perfect."

"I know it," Faith said, and for several moments they stood there, grinning at each other like two giddy fools. "We got this," she whispered.

"Oh, we *so* got this," Charlotte whispered back, the excitement still humming inside her joined by a steely resolve.

Yes, a glowing write-up and recommendation would mean great things for Sheen, but it went deeper than that. This restaurant was managed by a black woman. The kitchen was run by a black woman. The staff were women of various ethnicities—but they were all women. When the owner had come up with the concept, maybe it'd been a gimmick to differentiate Sheen from the other new restaurants popping up. But both Charlotte and Faith had vowed that they wouldn't let it remain some publicity ploy. Their restaurant would be one of the most successful establishments known for its sublime service and outstanding food. And so far, they were succeeding at this aim.

"Chef, your presence has been requested at one of the tables. They asked to meet you," Carlie, one of their servers, interrupted.

"Thanks, Carlie." Charlotte nodded at the younger woman. "I'd better get out there," she said to Faith, trying to conceal a grimace.

But apparently, she hadn't been quick or stealthy enough. A smirk curled the other woman's mouth.

"Part of the job, Charlotte," she reminded her.

"I know, I know," Charlotte muttered, unsnapping her baggy white executive chef coat and shrugging out of it, revealing the large T-shirt underneath. She strode over to the hooks near the door that led out of the glass-enclosed kitchen and removed her more formal and fitted turquoise chef coat with three-quarter-length sleeves, black piping and fabric-covered buttons. "It's not that I don't like going tableside," she grumbled, slipping into the coat and quickly fastening it over her chest. "I'd just much rather be cooking. I always feel like I'm on display."

"Well, get used to it. You're not naive enough to not know that these days it's as much about the chef as the food. That face and pinup body is an asset along with your truffle mac 'n' cheese." Faith's matter-of-fact tone stole a bit of the wind out of Charlotte's imminent tirade about the unfairness of her appearance being a factor at all. Mostly because, as unreasonable as it might be, Faith was correct.

It still annoyed her, though.

"Thank you for those words, oh, wise one," Charlotte drawled. Then, turning to Carlie, she smiled. "Lead the way."

As they exited the kitchen, Charlotte couldn't help surveying the restaurant, where she spent nearly as much time at as the home she rented for her and Ben. A sister site to The Bellamy's Glass House restaurant, Sheen was made entirely out of glass. This evening, the low lighting complemented rather than competed with the setting sun's rays that poured through the ceiling-to-floor windows, bathing the tables and patrons in its orange-and-red glow.

Beautiful.

And one day, hopefully, hers. Well, partly.

Carlie led her through the restaurant toward the far corner that boasted one of the best tables because of its gorgeous view of Royal. The table, which sat on a small dais, overlooked the entire restaurant. Which meant one thing—VIP guest.

Charlotte fixed a polite smile to her face as she neared the table. Five minutes, max, then she had to return to—

Oh, God.

Frigid fingers of shock crackled through her veins, and her feet stuttered to a stop. Startled stares swept over her like ants marching over a picnic blanket, prickling her skin. But she couldn't move. Couldn't jerk her gaze away from a pair of icy blue eyes.

Her heart attempted to drill a hole through her rib cage, each beat pumping pain and fear to every artery and organ. Pain, fear and something so much more complicated.

Pain, because for the first time in three years she stared into the beautiful, cold face of the man she'd once loved. A man who had been willing to take her body but not her heart.

The convoluted emotion was a noxious mixture of anger, resentment and—Jesus, she hated herself for this—a residue of the delight that just a glimpse of him used to stir within her.

And fear… Damn, the *fear*, because she wasn't just coming face-to-face with Russell Edmond Jr., the man who'd broken her heart.

She was coming face-to-face with her son's father.

A son he had no idea existed.

Two

Fuck no.

Ross stared at a ghost from his past.

A ghost that, as much as he'd tried to banish with time, work and other women—sometimes alcohol—he'd failed to exorcise.

Charlotte Jarrett.

Former head chef at his family's ranch. Ex-lover. The woman who'd walked away uncaring of the damage she'd left behind.

Another woman who'd abandoned him without a backward glance.

Ice coated his skin, sinking deeper, seeming to freeze the very marrow of his bones.

He hated seeing her again. Hated that she hadn't changed. Hated that her tall, graceful frame still boasted the same gorgeous, deadly curves that his hands could trace from muscle memory. That she remained as beautiful as ever—silken, hickory-brown skin, oval-shaped eyes framed by a thick fringe of dark lashes, regal cheekbones with slightly hollowed cheeks, an elegantly sloped nose and...

He transferred his hands to his thighs so the white table-cloth hid his clenched fists.

And a mouth that should be slapped with an indecency

citation. Those plush lips were so flagrantly sensual he dared any man to glance at them and not imagine them dragging him willingly to the edge of ecstasy. An edge he'd hovered and plummeted over many times with her...

He hated that his cock had hardened the instant his eyes clashed with that startled, wide, espresso gaze. Most of all, he despised the heavy, primal thud of his heart that echoed in his stiffening flesh.

What the hell was Charlotte doing back in Royal?

She'd left him. Discarded him like trash. As if she'd never taken him inside her. Or moaned his name in that sexy whimper he'd become addicted to eliciting from her. As if they'd never curled their sweat-dampened bodies around each other, wrapped in their own private cocoon where the outside world couldn't intrude.

Charlotte Jarrett had completed the lesson Ross's mother had started; he'd earned a well-learned and hard-won degree in the field of emotional desertion. *Be foolish enough to become attached, and they don't stay.* Maybe it was something in him that made it so easy for them to walk away from—his father's four marriages were exhibits A through D. Rusty went through women as often as the change of guard took place at Buckingham Palace. Like father, like son. At least Ross didn't marry them.

No, he'd finally learned, courtesy of Charlotte. Fuck and move on to the next one. No promises. No strings. No entanglements. No feelings. As long as he adhered to those rules, no one would ever play him for a fool again.

Never hurt me. Never leave me.

With a sharp mental slash, Ross incised those ridiculous and too weak words from his head. He hadn't been hurt when Charlotte had up and left Royal. Left *him*. He'd been mad as hell. And that anger continued to simmer inside his chest, kindling lower in his stomach as she neared the table where he and Billy dined.

If he'd known that when his friend requested to meet Sheen's chef he would be confronting Charlotte again, Ross would've stalked right out of this place.

Hell, he still might.

"Good evening," Charlotte greeted, her gaze fixed on Billy. Out of habit, Ross rose from his seat, manners drilled into him from birth. Even as he stood, with his pal following suit, that soft, low voice slipped underneath Ross's suit jacket and his shirt, stroking over his skin. Even before they'd become lovers, that husky tone had reminded him of tangled sheets, throats sore and chafed from pleasure-soaked screams. "I'm Head Chef Charlotte Jarrett here at Sheen. I hope the meal is to your liking and you're enjoying your experience with us tonight." Then, just when Ross believed she wouldn't acknowledge him at all, she peered at him and dipped her chin. "Hello, Ross. It's good to see you again."

Lie.

The word scalded his tongue, roared in his head. She was as happy to see him sitting in her restaurant as he was to be here.

"You two know each other?" Billy asked as they lowered back into their chairs, saving Ross from having to reply to that fake smile and sentiment. His friend glanced back and forth between the two of them, a small frown creasing his brow even as curiosity lit his blue eyes.

"Yes," Ross ground out, then inhaled, deliberately releasing a breath and relaxing his clenched jaw. "Charlotte worked as the head chef at Elegance Ranch several years ago," he said, referring to the Edmond family ranch. Then added, "Before she moved to California for another job."

Damn, why had he added that? Yes, she'd moved; it was in the past, and he no longer gave a damn. But still… What the hell was she doing back in Royal?

"What a small world." Billy did the tennis match back-

and-forth once more. "California?" His buddy arched a dark eyebrow. "What part, if you don't mind me asking?"

"Santa Monica," she replied evenly, still wearing that damn polite smile he detested. He recognized it; her mask, he'd called it. She'd always given it to his father, but never Ross.

Until now.

"I love Santa Monica. It's a wonderful city. Not that Royal isn't just as beautiful. But California's loss is our gain." Billy smiled warmly and rose once more, extending his hand toward Charlotte. "Well, since you and Ross don't need to introduce yourselves, allow me. Billy Holmes, and it's a pleasure to meet such a lovely and talented chef."

"Thank you." Charlotte took his hand into hers, and even though it was just a simple press of palms, Ross had to fight back an inane urge to lurch to his feet and step in between them, to prevent his college friend—whom he trusted as much as his brother and sister—from touching her. But she'd revoked that privilege three years ago, and he didn't want to request it again. "Are you enjoying your meals?"

"Yes," Billy praised. "We had your braised beef signature dish, and it's delicious. I can't say I've tasted better."

"Thank you," she repeated, real warmth entering her smile. "Then I'd suggest trying our signature dessert, as well. A peach meringue torte with chocolate crumbles and a dollop of Chantilly cream."

"We'll take it. How can we say no to that?" Billy chuckled, reclaiming his seat. But clearly, he wasn't ready to let Charlotte go, much to Ross's aggravation.

Shit. How much longer did he have to sit here and pretend as if he couldn't catch her sweet yet sharp scent of sugar and figs. If he'd been blindfolded and set in a room full of people, he could still detect her delectable essence. Still locate *her*.

"I'll place your dessert order myself," she said. "Thank

you both—" for only the second time since she arrived at their table, she quickly glanced at him, then away "—for joining us at Sheen tonight. If you'll excuse me—"

"Wait, Chef, one more moment of your time, please," Billy called out, and Ross narrowed his eyes on him. Jesus, what now? He needed Charlotte away from him before he did something stupid. Like escort her out of this restaurant and demand answers. Or commit the cardinal sin of digging his fingers underneath that neat bun at the back of her head and loosening it, freeing her dark brown hair to see if it still contained that same coarse silk texture. Discover if it still swept her shoulder blades or if she'd cut it. Find out whether she'd emit that same low gasp if he fisted the thick strands and tugged, whether her eyes would darken with desire...

Yeah, she had to go.

"Sure," Charlotte said, her tone even, and if Ross hadn't been studying her so closely, he would've missed the flicker of impatience in her eyes. That, too, he easily remembered about her. Cooking, *creating* had been her number one passion, and she had to be chafing at this dog and pony show when she could be back in her precious kitchen. "What can I do for you?"

"Well, we're—" Billy waved a hand toward Ross and then back at himself "—working on a luxury food, art and wine festival called Soiree on the Bay, to be held late July on Appaloosa Island. Are you familiar with it?"

"Yes." She nodded, her focus fully trained on Billy... and only the rapid beat of her pulse at the base of her neck betrayed her agitation. Right now, she probably wished the collar of her chef's jacket fully covered her neck. Because if it did, he wouldn't guess that she was most likely recalling the time he'd secretly taken her to the small, private island in Trinity Bay that his family owned. He'd escorted her there in her first helicopter ride, though it was also accessible by private ferry and airplane. They'd spent a lazy day and sizzling night at the boutique resort on the pristine beaches that occupied the western side of the island along with several large vacation homes.

Man, the things they'd done to each other in their room...

He shifted in his chair, unbidden lust burning an incendiary path through him at the sultry, hot memories of slick skin sliding against slick skin. Of groans punctuated by greedy whimpers and blissful laughter. Of moonlight streaming across sheets wrapped around tangled limbs.

Her gaze slid toward him, and for a long moment, their eyes clashed. Was she as steeped in the illicit past as he was? Did that sweet, tight flesh, which even now he could feel wrapped around his cock, pulse and dampen with liquid heat from those recollections? His own body throbbed so hard he feared one abrupt move could crack him down the middle.

He glanced away first.

"We're already in plans to develop the eastern side of the island," Billy said. "The festival is going to be huge, and we already have vendors lined up, with tickets projected to sell out within hours. Would you consider hosting a tent for the event? For Sheen?"

Ross jerked in surprise. The hell? They hadn't discussed this. He stared at his friend, but Billy continued aiming the full force of his charm on Charlotte. No. Just...no. Spend more time around his ex-lover? Have her involved in this event that could change the trajectory of his career. His *life*? He couldn't have a split focus; he couldn't afford it. And then... She didn't deserve to be involved in this project that meant so much to him. *She'd* walked away. *She'd* left him. So she didn't get to benefit from what was *his*.

And yes, he acknowledged how fucking petty that made him sound. But he didn't give a damn.

"I—" She frowned, shaking her head. "I'm flattered that

you're asking, but I can't give you an answer without conferring with the owner and the management team."

"Please, do that and let us know your answer. With the thousands of people—both potential customers and clients—attending the festival, it could be advantageous for us and for Sheen. Not to mention you, personally, Chef. You're the magic behind the food, and as beautiful as the design and decor are and professional the service, it's the food that makes or breaks a restaurant. I believe this could be a huge opportunity for you."

Billy paused and tilted his head to the side. "In the meantime, while you're thinking the invitation over, would you also consider something else?" He chuckled, the sound self-deprecating. "I know we just met, and I'm already throwing a lot at you. But we're compiling an advisory board for the festival, and we're seeking the best creative minds in Texas. I've heard you're one of them, and it'd be an honor and asset to have you take part in it."

He'd heard she was creative—where? *When?* Ross had been under the impression that the other man hadn't known of Charlotte until five minutes before he'd asked to meet the chef after raving over their meal. Which, Ross grudgingly had to admit, had been exquisite. But then again, he expected nothing less from a woman who placed her career over everything else. She hadn't even cared that she'd left her parents behind.

Or me.

He locked that irritating and insidious thought down. Because that was in the past. His pride had been hurt. But as his reputation had proven, he was over it—over *her*.

Besides, he'd never give one woman that much sway over him again.

For the first time, unease crept across Charlotte's features, and he damn near felt the tension emanating off her. *Say no*, he silently ordered her.

"I don't—"

"Excuse me, I'm so sorry for interrupting." The server who'd escorted Charlotte to their table appeared, shooting an apologetic glance at Ross and Billy before addressing Charlotte. "Chef, your babysitter called. There's an emergency with Ben. He's running a fever, and she needs to know if she should take him to urgent care. Also—" her voice dropped but not low enough that Ross couldn't catch her next words "—she said he's crying for you."

Charlotte recoiled as if the words had been physical blows, her shoulders actually curling in before she jerked them back. Maybe remembering she had an audience. Because when she turned back to him and Billy, she'd carefully composed her features into a smooth mask.

If only he had the same superpower.

A baby? Charlotte had *a baby*? Shock, bone-deep, chilling and sickening, swam through him, burrowing to the dark soul that he'd believed too jaded to be stunned by anything.

"I'm sorry," she said in a calm tone that belied the worry gleaming in her coffee-colored eyes. Worry and…something else. And that something else had the hair on the nape of his neck prickling, standing at soldier-straight attention. If it had been anyone else, he'd have called that quicksilver emotion in her gaze fear. But he had to be mistaken. Sure, there wasn't any love lost between them, but why in the hell would she be afraid of him? His stomach twisted, clenched. "I need to go, but I'll place your dessert order. I hope the rest of your evening here at Sheen is—"

"You have a son?" he rasped, only the second time he'd spoken to her since she'd arrived at the table.

Again, that flash of something-that-couldn't-be-fear glinted in her eyes. And he wanted to erupt from his seat and demand she either stop looking at him like that or, better yet, explain why just glancing at him caused that reaction.

"Yes," she abruptly answered. Then, nodding, she edged back a step. "Again, thank you for dining with us."

With that, she whirled on her heel and quickly wound a path through the tables toward the rear of the restaurant. Ross stared after her retreating figure, frowning.

Don't even think about going after her. Keep your ass in this chair.

He growled that at his conscience, at the muscles in his thighs that already bunched in preparation of launching him from his seat. This restaurant—and her son—were her business. Not his. She was no longer his concern and hadn't been for three years.

"Did I overstep there?" Billy murmured, picking up his fork and flipping it between his fingers. It had been a nervous gesture of his since college—a small tell in an otherwise confident and self-possessed demeanor. "I should've checked with you first to ensure you were okay with me asking her to be a vendor and a member of the advisory board."

"It's fine," Ross said, waving off his friend's concern.

It wasn't, though. But damn if he would explain to Billy why.

No one knew of his and Charlotte's affair from years ago. They'd kept it secret for the obvious reason—him having sex with his employee had been inappropriate, at best. At worst, it was a power imbalance that he'd been too entitled, too damn infatuated and desperate for her to acknowledge. He'd justified it by convincing himself he'd never be the kind of asshole that would fire her if—no, *when*—their affair ended.

His father was that kind of asshole, though. His son involved with a staff member? Hell no. Rusty Edmond possessed enough good ol' boy in him to rate that sin just under murder but above stealing.

That had been cause enough to keep their…relationship quiet. But he'd harbored another, more private one.

Charlotte had been his. His choice. His beauty. His secret haven from a world where he was judged by his name, his reputation. His entire life, his father had determined his schools, career, even the women he'd dated. But Charlotte? She'd been the one person—the one decision—that had been strictly his own.

She'd been special.

But he couldn't tell Billy that—couldn't tell anyone. And even if he'd been free to, he still wouldn't. Because in some ways, Charlotte still remained the only autonomous decision in his life. And despite everything, he treasured that.

"Are you sure? I—" Billy frowned, his lips snapping closed as he studied Ross.

"What?" he asked, just shy of a snap. He wanted to be done with this conversation, hell, this restaurant that seemed to bear the stamp of Charlotte in its walls, in the decor, even in the scent of its food. Now that he knew she was the chef here—that she was back in Royal—she permeated everything.

"Fine. I'm just going to say it," Billy said, setting the fork down and leaning back in his chair. "I might be out of line here, but there seemed to be…tension between you two. Am I wrong?"

"Yes," Ross clipped out, but then inhaled, forcibly relaxing his jaw. "Yes," he repeated, this time more evenly. "Charlotte was our head chef for a while before she left for another job opportunity. We were amicable, but that's it. Nothing more, nothing less."

"Okay, if you say so. I believe you." But that steady, unwavering stare didn't shift from Ross's face, and he smothered the urge to snap at his friend again. Finally, Billy shrugged a shoulder and picked up his wine. "She's a beautiful woman," he observed before sipping from his glass. "And obviously talented and successful. So you wouldn't have a problem with me asking her out? There wouldn't be an issue because she used to be your employee?"

"Of course not," Ross growled. Yes, honest-to-God *growled*. Because just the thought of Billy's fingers spanning that slender waist or cupping that dramatic flare of hips had him clenching his own wineglass so hard he feared it might shatter under the pressure. "I don't have any claim on her. She was just our chef, for God's sake. Do what you want."

The words, the tone sounded angry to his own ears, so when the other man said nothing but pinned him with a speculative look, Ross didn't challenge him on it. Didn't snarl out another protest. Why bother? He didn't believe his own damn self.

"I'm just going to say this, then leave it alone," Billy murmured. "From one friend to another, whatever is eating at you? Deal with it before it deals with you. Now—" he took another sip of wine and set his glass on the table "—as for the advisory board, I was also thinking about approaching Lila Jones from the Royal Chamber of Commerce…"

Ross went along with the subject change, nodding and replying when appropriate. But his mind had drifted back to the past. To that day when she'd ended their affair. When she'd announced that she was moving to California. He'd been angry. Hurtful. Harsh. Not because he'd been in love—he hadn't believed in that emotion then any more than he did today. Yet, it had shown him that wanting something for himself—believing someone could want him just for him—was a dream better left behind for the boy who'd once believed in superheroes, purple, singing dinosaurs and mothers who stayed.

And he'd stopped dreaming long ago.

Three

There were worse things in life than listening to your mother complain and nag. For instance, volcanoes exploding and drowning whole cities under their molten flow of lava. Wars that left countries devastated and torn. Pandemic viruses infecting the population and turning them into hordes of flesh-eating zombies.

Firefly being canceled.

Yes, so many worse things than having to sit quietly while your mother criticized your parenting.

But right now, Charlotte wouldn't mind a zombie bursting into her house and chasing her around her kitchen. It would definitely be a good excuse to end this phone call.

Smothering a sigh, she pinched the bridge of her nose and prayed for patience. "Mom, I'm sorry I didn't tell you myself about Ben, and that you had to hear about it when you called the restaurant," she apologized. *Again.* "As soon as I got home, I rushed him to the emergency room. But I promise I would've called you this morning."

"It was just so humiliating and hurtful to find out from an employee, instead of my daughter, that my grandson was sick," Cherise Jarrett harped. Only the genuine hurt in her mother's voice kept Charlotte from snapping back in irritation. "I know we've…had our differences in the past few years, Charlotte, but we love Ben, and when we couldn't reach you…"

Had our differences. What a nice way of saying "estranged because you got knocked up and had a kid out of wedlock."

But she clenched her teeth, locking the sarcastic words down. Wasn't this part of the reason she'd returned to Royal? To try to heal the fractured relationship between her and her parents? She'd disappointed them three years ago when she'd called with the news that she was pregnant, but they'd also disappointed her with their reaction.

Brian and Cherise Jarrett had always been strict, conservative but loving parents. Charlotte had expected them to be worried and upset by her news, but not to practically disown her. Nor for them to be relieved that she moved to California so they could avoid gossip about their daughter having an illegitimate child. If not for her sister, brother-in-law and niece in California, Charlotte would've been all alone in the world. Her parents' rejection and disapproval had been like a dagger to the chest, and for months she'd felt adrift, no longer anchored by their love and friendship.

But Charlotte had to give her parents credit. Once Ben was born, their cold demeanor had thawed. Her son and their love for him had helped bridge the divide that had sprung up between them seven months prior. Even if they allowed people to assume that she'd married and divorced while in California, and Ben was the child of that union. Yeah, that continued to sting. Still, now that she'd moved back to Royal with Ben so they could be closer to her parents, she hoped that distance, and the hurt, would disappear altogether.

Then there were days like today…

"They made me shut off my cell phone at the hospital, and it was after 2:00 a.m. when we arrived home. I didn't want to wake you and Dad. Especially when Ben was fine.

If it'd been more serious, I would've found a way to contact you guys. But his fever broke while we were there, and the doctor said it's likely nothing more than a twenty-four-hour bug. So please don't worry."

"Still—"

"What was so important you had to call me at the restaurant?" Charlotte interrupted, hopefully diverting the subject. She had to try before she opened the cabinet where she hid the emergency bourbon and poured it into her coffee.

"Well, it doesn't seem such an emergency now, but…" Her mom paused, and Charlotte's stomach clamped down tight on the unease twisting through her. Silly to feel this way. And at one time in their relationship, she wouldn't have. Instead, she would've teased her mother about being dramatic. But that wasn't their relationship anymore. Now Charlotte tensed, unsure what to expect, bracing herself against what was possibly to come. "But the caterer for the church's Women's Day celebration backed out at the last minute. The event is in two weeks, and I wanted to see if you could step in with small appetizers and finger foods. Nothing too fancy, since I know this is short notice…"

"Sure, Mom," Charlotte murmured, even as *Are you out of your mind?* rang in her head. She already had so much on her plate, yet she didn't rescind her agreement. Her parents had always supported her dream of being a chef even though they'd envisioned her following in the footsteps of her father and sister as an attorney.

And when was the last time her mother had asked anything from her?

No, that part of her that still longed to please her parents, and hungered for their smiles of approval and love, couldn't turn her mom down. "Send me a list of the food you were thinking of, the place and time of the event, and when you need me there to set up."

"Thank you, Charlotte," her mother breathed, relief

flooding through their connection. "You have no idea how much I appreciate your help and jumping in at the last minute."

"You're welcome." And for the first time since she answered the phone, she smiled, a warm glow pulsing in her chest. "I'll get—" She broke off as the doorbell echoed through the house. "I'm sorry, Mom, that's the door. I need to go. But I'll check back in with you later about Ben. Don't forget to send me the information."

"I won't. And give that beautiful boy a huge hug and kiss from his grandma."

"I will," she promised. "Talk to you later."

Ending the call, Charlotte strode from the kitchen down the short hall toward the front door. She glanced down at her smartwatch, noting the time with a frown. Nine twenty. Who would show up at her house so early on a Friday morning? Even Faith didn't call her until after twelve because Charlotte had made it known that her mornings belonged to Ben. And she'd already called and left a message with both Faith and Jeremy Randall, the owner, to inform them she wouldn't be in today because her son was still under the weather.

Her thoughts drifted to Ben as she pushed aside the curtain over the window bracketing the front door. He had still been napping when her mother called, but she needed to check on him—

Jesus.

Her arm dropped like a leaden weight to her side, the curtain drifting back into place as she helplessly stared at the window.

No. It couldn't be. God wasn't that unkind.

But she doubted God had anything to do with who stood on her porch. All that credit belonged to the guy a lot farther south.

She squeezed her eyes shut, and as if of its own volition,

her hand rose to her neck, fingers lightly stroking the necklace underneath her long-sleeved shirt. As soon as she realized what her wayward fingers were doing, she jerked her arm back down. *Dammit.* As much as she fervently wished otherwise, nothing could change the fact that he stood on the other side of her door.

The thunderous pounding of her heart and the rush of her pulse in her head only validated it.

She could pretend not to be home. Avoid him. After all, he'd shown up at her house unannounced and definitely uninvited. This wasn't Sheen, and she didn't have to speak to him. Or look at him. Drown in those eyes that both threatened frostbite and to consign her to flames. Inhale his masculine, earthy, *raw* scent that carried notes of sandalwood, man and sex. Burn in the contempt that leaped from him in rolling waves of heat.

She owed it to herself, and especially to Ben, to protect her son at all costs. Because the alternative was…unthinkable.

Fear fissured through her, its impact stealing her breath. Ross believed she'd "gotten rid of him," as he and Rusty had ordered her to, three years ago. What would he do if he found out she hadn't obeyed his command…

The doorbell pealed again.

Dammit. Her fingers curled into her palms, the short fingernails digging into her flesh.

She wasn't a coward. Ross Edmond no longer wielded any power over her. He was a nonfactor, and to not answer that door and hide would mean he affected her emotions, her life. And she refused to grant that to him.

Before she could talk herself out of it, she twisted the lock and doorknob, flinging the door open.

Maybe she should've taken a few extra minutes…

Yes, she'd just seen Ross last night, but those hours hadn't inoculated her against the force of his presence.

Three years and over a thousand miles' distance should've been enough. But that had been wishful thinking on her part.

Silently, she shuffled backward, and his ice-blue gaze didn't shift from her face as he stepped inside her home. Which was fair, she supposed, since she couldn't remove hers from his.

It wasn't fair.

Someone who led the dissolute lifestyle of a playboy should wear the corruption of it on his skin, his body. Like a masochist, she'd occasionally done a Google search of Ross's name over the years. And every time, an image of him with a different woman as they emerged from this party or that club had popped into the feed.

But no. His golden skin remained as unblemished and smooth as ever. His lean, broad-shouldered body stood as straight and powerful as before. The wide, carnal curves of his mouth still promised sex and sin. Those penetrating, bright blue eyes were as clear and incisive as she remembered.

Not that she could ever forget the arrogant slashes of his cheekbones or the patrician slope of his nose or the strong, bold facial structure. Every day she looked into her son's features, she saw Ross. Was reminded of the man who'd fathered her beautiful little boy and rejected them both.

She couldn't escape him.

Couldn't forgive him.

The reminder of his unpardonable offense—not wanting her or the baby they'd created together—wrenched her from the dazzling tapestry he'd always been capable of weaving around her. He might have the appearance of an archangel, but he possessed the morals and heart of one of the fallen brethren.

"Ross," she greeted flatly, closing the door with a soft, definitive click. "This is a surprise." *What are you doing here? How did you know where I lived? When are you leaving?* She slid a surreptitious glance down the hall toward Ben's room. He needed to go before her son woke from his nap. "What can I do for you?"

He didn't immediately answer but surveyed the postage-stamp-sized foyer with its generic paintings and cherry wood mantel that had come with the home. The living room opened up off to the left, with the large bay windows, small gas fireplace, overstuffed couch and love seat, and the glass coffee table visible. From his vantage point, he couldn't glimpse the connecting dining room with its long, cedar table and chairs that seated eight people, or the pretty chandelier that hung from the tall ceiling.

Her home couldn't compare to the palatial Elegance Ranch where his family lived and where she'd once ruled the dream of a kitchen that could compete with any restaurant's commercial space. But this single-level, two-bedroom, two-bath house was comfortable, cozy and more than enough for her and Ben.

"You have a nice place," he finally said, his glacial gaze resting on her once more.

"Thank you," she replied, refusing to shiver under that stare. "That's not why you're here, though, is it?"

A corner of his mouth lifted in a just-short-of-humorous half smile. "Still direct, I see," he murmured.

No, she'd never been that direct with him. Not that honest, either.

If she had been honest—if she'd trusted him enough to be—she would've confessed how she hadn't felt safe at Elegance Ranch in those last couple of months she worked there. How his father had been steadily hitting on her. Rusty Edmond hadn't touched her, but the flirting, the sly compliments and innuendos…those, in a way, had been more insidious. Because if she confided in others, they could wave it off as harmless, warning her she didn't have concrete evidence to complain. And complain to whom? Her boss? The very man who made her feel uncomfortable and threatened?

Threatened, because if she dared called Rusty on his actions, he would've fired her. And he probably wouldn't have just stopped here. With his power and privilege, he could've destroyed her career as easily as he ordered a rare T-bone steak for dinner. She'd felt trapped, cornered. Defenseless. And the only way out that she'd seen was leaving.

She'd could've told Ross about the situation with his father; she'd been tempted to confess all. But every time she gathered the courage, something held her back. No, not something. *Fear*.

Fear that he wouldn't believe her.

Fear that he would believe her and still side with his father over her.

He was an Edmond first. And his family took precedence over everything—and everyone.

"I have things to take care of before I leave for the restaurant, so…" She trailed off, letting her not-so-subtle hint to get on with it linger in the air between them. The most important subject she hadn't been direct or honest with him about lay sleeping down the hall. She needed Ross out of the house. Five minutes ago.

He nodded, sliding his hands into the front pockets of his pants, the motion opening his suit jacket. And she tried to convince herself that she didn't remember how wide and strong his chest had been. How that divot in the middle of his pecs had been perfect for resting her cheek. How hard and muscled that delicious ladder of abs had been between her thighs when she straddled him.

Tried and failed.

"Two reasons. First, I wanted to check on your baby. How is he feeling this morning?" he murmured.

"He's fine. Better," she amended, hesitant.

Why would he care? No hint of anger threaded through his voice... Oh, God, wait. He'd said *baby*. How old did he think Ben was? Did he assume she'd had a child with another man? Relief trickled through her. But underneath, winding through like a silver thread, lurked an irrational fury. He hadn't wanted their baby, so how dare he show concern over another man's.

Fucking great. Now she was getting all fired up over an imaginary partner who'd supposedly fathered her child.

This was what being around Ross Edmond for five minutes did to her.

"The father," he hedged, his voice slightly deepening even as his words confirmed her suspicion. "Where is he?" Once more he scanned her home. "Did he move back with you?"

She barely smothered her snort. "His father isn't in the picture." Not a lie. "It's just us," she added, skirting him and heading into the living room.

Not because she relished the idea of him having more access to her house, her private sanctuary. She would be a fool not to guard her life, her secret against him. But she also needed to be free of that tiny space where his scent filled her nostrils, sat on her tongue, clung to her clothes, her skin. She just craved a breath that didn't carry *him*.

Ross stared at her, his crystalline gaze unreadable before he glanced away, a muscle ticking along his jaw. "Charlotte, I—" he ground out, thrusting a hand through the longer strands of dirty blond hair that waved away from his face.

"What else, Ross?" she interrupted him, not bothering to prevent the edge from creeping into her voice. She tried not to glance down at her watch, but the minutes steadily ticking by before Ben woke drummed against her skin like impatient fingertips. "You said there were two reasons you stopped by."

For a moment he studied her, flint in his eyes and the

sculpted length of his jaw still tight. "Last night, Billy asked you about joining the advisory board for the festival. It was awkward as hell for him to put you on the spot like that, and I understand if you decide against it. But I wanted to see if you'd made a decision."

"You couldn't have called and asked me this?"

"I don't have your number."

"No," she shot back. "But somehow you found out where I lived, so unearthing my phone number probably wouldn't have been that much of a leap."

"Touché," he murmured, his lips quirking in that maddening—and damn sexy—half smile that had never failed to tempt her into stroking her fingers across his mouth. Three years ago, she could, and did, submit to that urge. Now she curled her fingers into her palms, convincing herself that the itch tingling in her fingertips and palms had zero to do with that old impulse. "You've been away from Royal three years, but surely you haven't forgotten how not much remains secret around here. It didn't take but asking the right question of the right person to find out where you'd moved to. Just making that clear so you don't think I took up a second career as a stalker in your absence."

She snorted, crossing her arms over her chest. He spoke the truth. And she hadn't missed the "everybody knows your name and your business" mentality of this small Texas town.

Of course, she and Ross had achieved the miraculous. Their affair had been one of the best-kept secrets in Royal.

Until she'd outed them to Rusty, that is.

"Right. About that." She shook her head, loosening her arms to hold her palms up. "I'm sure your friend meant well, but given our…past, it's probably not a good idea for me to be on your advisory board."

"Last night, I agreed with you. But I've been thinking…"

His gaze narrowed on her, and she resisted falling into that storm of ice and heat.

"Thinking what?" she prodded.

"That the success of this festival, Soiree on the Bay, is important to a lot of people. With that in mind, I'm willing to put aside our *past*—" his lips twisted as he mimicked her word "—to achieve that goal. And this advisory board is part of that. We need the best creative and forward-thinking minds in this group. And whatever happened between us, I remember you were a brilliant, innovative chef. You can bring that originality, imagination as well as your business sense to the board. It can only benefit all of us."

What had that silent but deafening pause been about? What was he *not* saying? She gave her head a hard, mental shake. None of her business. She couldn't afford to get bogged down in anything Ross. In anything Edmond.

Been there, done that. Had the stretch marks to prove it.

"I'll consider what you're saying, Ross." She absolutely would *not*. "But I can't make any pro—"

"Mama."

A light patter of rapid footsteps followed the plaintive, soft and utterly sweet voice calling out to her. Chubby arms wrapped around her lower calf, and in spite of the dread pumping through her veins like a freight train and flooding her mouth with the metallic taste of fear, she knelt to the floor and pulled her son into her arms. His arms wound around her neck, and he burrowed close. Her heart hammered against her ribs, threatening to break each of them, but she still placed a gentle kiss on top of Ben's thick, light brown curls, breathing in his precious scent. She squeezed her eyes against the sting of tears that suddenly pricked her eyes. Not just because one day he would lose that sweet baby smell.

The abrupt rush of overwhelming sadness and dismay was due to the silent man who loomed several feet away from them. The man whose gaze seared her like a flaming hot brand.

The Sword of Damocles that had hung over her life—over Ben's life—had suddenly fallen.

And there was nothing she could do to sweep them out from under its crashing, lethal weight.

"How're you feeling, baby boy?" she asked, pressing the back of her hand to his forehead and then to his cheek. Relief was a soothing balm inside her at the coolness of his skin. No fever. Thank God. No mother ever felt as helpless as when her child was sick.

"Good," he mumbled, crowding closer to her, his arms tightening as he notched his head under her chin and tried to crawl up her torso. In spite of the bile churning in her belly and burning an acidic path toward her throat, she smiled. Ben was a friendly, bubbly child with seemingly endless energy—except when he fell ill. Then he clung to her, not wanting to let her out of his sight. Not that she minded. Holding him, having his small, sturdy body pressed close, and listening to him breathe were just small things to reassure her that her baby was okay. "Eat," he demanded. "Hungry." Even though the order sounded more like "hungwy," she fully understood it.

"You want banana pancakes?" she asked, suggesting his favorite breakfast. Okay, so sue her. She was spoiling him this morning.

He nodded, his tawny curls brushing her chin. "'Nana 'cakes. Juice."

"You got it." She pressed another kiss to the top of his head. "Can you go play with your trucks for a minute while I finish talking to this nice man?" She fought to maintain her soft, even tone, but with her heart lodged in her throat, it was becoming more of a struggle.

For the first time, Ben turned his head and looked at Ross. Shy with strangers, he didn't say anything, but the panic crackling inside her, dancing over her skin like a live wire, ratcheted to a higher, dissonant level. Her son stared at his father for the first time, although he didn't know it. It was a surreal moment. Father and son studying one another... Especially Ross, with that narrowed, enigmatic scrutiny...

Part of her wanted to thrust Ben behind her, shield him from Ross. Protect him and yell that she wouldn't allow him to hurt her son.

But the other half... That proud, almost smug half yearned to stand Ben before him, let Ross get a good, long look and brag that this was the precious, brilliant and perfect boy that he'd wanted her to get rid of. That he'd wanted nothing to do with.

That vindictive, ugly part of her wanted him to soak, fucking *drown* in regret.

Did that make her a bitch? Probably. Still, the primal need to protect Ben superseded any petty desires.

"You play for a few, then we'll eat banana pancakes." She stood and, taking his tiny hand in hers, led him to the corner of the living room with a trunk full of his toys. After removing a couple of trucks and making sure he was entertained, she inhaled a deep breath that did absolutely nothing for her nerves and turned to face Ross. Jerking her head toward the foyer, she said, "Over here."

She didn't wait for him to agree but strode out of the living room and returned to the small entryway. There would be questions; one glance in his glacial gaze and she could practically see the suspicion crowded there. But she wouldn't have this conversation within earshot of her son.

"I thought he was a baby," Ross murmured, but she didn't mistake that low tone for calm. Not when she noted the thunder rumbling underneath. "And you let me think that."

She didn't wilt under the dark accusation in his voice.

Didn't flinch from it. It wasn't *her* fault that he'd assumed she had an infant instead of a toddler.

Ross shifted his stare away from her and back to the living room. Silence descended between them, and in the cramped foyer, the weight of it threatened to crush her. Again, she fought the urge to jump in between them, guard her son from that razor-sharp speculation, that ice-cold face. She silently ordered her arms to remain by her sides instead of wrapping around her torso in a telltale, too vulnerable gesture of self-preservation.

"How old is he?" he snapped, the frost melting under the steam of the heat throbbing in that deep, raw timbre.

"Ben is two," she replied, reaching for and clinging to a calm that was as fake as the flowers in the vase behind her.

"Two," Ross rasped, still not removing his eyes from the little boy who crashed trucks together, complete with sound effects. Blissfully ignorant to the jarring tension that hissed and popped just feet away from him. "The eyes," he continued in that same hoarse voice that almost hurt her ears. "They're you. The hair, the skin, they're…" *They're both of us*, she silently finished for him. Skin just a shade darker than his light brown curls—curls that were softer than hers but a little coarser than Ross's hair. Ben was a beautiful melding of his genetics and hers. "But his face, his features… It's like looking at a picture of me as a kid."

She still didn't say anything as he sussed out who Ben was to him. Instead, she stood silent as he swung his attention back to her, stoically witnessing the succession of emotions that marched through his expression. Shock. Disbelief. Rage. And something not as simple, but just as dark and powerful. But then the rage returned, capsizing everything else until lightning flashed in the sky blue of his eyes. The fury tautened the skin over his cheekbones, his jaw, until the bones seemed ready to slice through. His sensual mouth flattened, tightened until only a cruel slant remained.

"Is he my son?" he growled. "And think carefully before you answer me, Charlotte. Especially since the evidence is staring me in the face. Don't lie to me."

"Why would I need to lie to you?" She notched up her chin, defiant, but unable to quell the shiver jetting down her spine, vibrating through her. "Ben is yours."

If possible, his eyes brightened, so hot with fury that her skin bore the brunt of that heat.

"You didn't think I had a right to know? If I hadn't shown up here today, would you even have deigned to inform me that the son *I didn't know existed* lived in the same goddamn town as me?"

"Lower your voice and watch your mouth," she snapped, and even though every self-protective instinct in her roared a warning to keep her distance, she shifted closer to avoid even the chance of Ben overhearing them. "And the answer is no, I wouldn't have told you. Don't try to turn this around on me," she hissed, her own hurt and anger burning through the coolness of her tone to leave it trembling. God, she hated that it trembled. She hated any sign of weakness in front of this man. The last time she'd betrayed her vulnerability with him, he'd shut her down. *Rejected* her. He would never get the chance again. "You decided you didn't want him, didn't want to upset your life with the inconvenience of a baby. So I don't owe you a damn thing, nor do we need anything from you. I made the decision to become both mother and father to him, so you don't get to act the victim now."

"What the hell are you talking about? You never—" He shook his head, his hand slashing between them. "Not here. And not now. I don't give a fuck what you believe your reasons were to lie and keep my son away from me. Just so it's clear, there *isn't* a good enough reason," he snarled.

"To protect my son from being hurt is a damn excellent reason. The best," she hurled back.

"Protect him from his father?" A quicksilver emotion flashed in his eyes, and if she'd believed Ross capable of feeling anything beyond lust, pride and self-gratification, she might've called it pain. His face hardened further, and he shifted backward. As if being in such close contact with her disgusted him.

Screw. Him.

And screw herself for that thin sliver of pain that slid between her ribs and buried right in her heart.

"I want a DNA test done."

She tilted her head to the side, arching an eyebrow. "I thought he was the image of you as a child. Now you're questioning his paternity. That turnaround was quick," she drawled, offended that he would dare doubt Ben.

Dare doubt me.

The shifty, taunting whisper brushed across her mind before she could smother it. No, she didn't care if he doubted her. She didn't care how he thought about her at all, because he didn't matter.

Only Ben did.

His lip curled into a derisive sneer. "I don't question whether he's mine. It's you and your motives that I have zero trust in. So before I can make my next move, I need concrete, *legal* proof that he's mine so you can't deny me access to him."

Her breath stalled in her throat, and she stumbled back. On a low curse, Ross moved, reaching for her, but she batted away his hands, forcing her knees to strengthen, willing every ounce of the meager strength she retained to her legs.

Though so much fear poured through her that she ached with it, she managed to speak the dreaded words. "What is that supposed to mean?" she pressed. "Before you make your next move?"

His gaze crystallized, and his big, lean body straightened so he seemed to loom larger. More intimidating. "I'll be in touch, Charlotte. Word of advice—don't even consider pulling another vanishing act like you did three years ago. This time I will follow."

With those ominous words echoing in the foyer and ringing in her ears, he crossed the short space to the door, jerked it open and exited through it.

She didn't move—couldn't, even though Ben waited on her. Ross's statement rooted her to the floor.

His next move.

What was he planning? Custody? Taking Ben from her? With the full weight of the Edmond name and the power of their money and connections behind him, he could. He might—

No.

The objection slammed into her head, and she fisted her fingers. No, she wouldn't allow him to rip her baby from her arms. Not when Ross had been the first one to walk away, to abandon them both.

She shoved away from the wall, resolve gelling inside her, fortifying her.

She was no longer that lonely, needy girl who'd left Royal and nearly begged him not to turn his back on her and their baby. Motherhood had made her a warrior.

If Ross wanted a battle, then a battle was what he would get.

Four

He had a son.

Ross stared at the paternity report that had been emailed to him a couple of hours earlier. For what could've been the hundredth time, he scanned it, his gaze settling on the line at the bottom that changed his life forever.

"The alleged father is not excluded as the biological father of the tested child. The probability of paternity is 99.9998 percent."

His pulse roared in his head, the thunderous crash of sound a sonorous backdrop for the seething cauldron of emotion boiling over in his chest. Shock. Fear. Pain. Joy.

God, so much joy.

Until the moment three days ago when he'd stared down into a tiny face that could've been a replica of his twenty-five years ago... Until he'd met familiar brown eyes brimming with curiosity and shyness... Until then, children had been a "someday" notion that bore no place in his hedonistic life. But the moment Ross met his son, someday had become now, in an instant.

He'd wanted those brown eyes to reflect delight and love when they looked at him. Wanted those arms to lift to him in a show of faith and confidence.

Ross just longed to call that beautiful boy son. To claim him as his own. And to be claimed as father in return.

The intensity of that need burned so fiercely that his skin and bones almost couldn't contain the strength and power of that yearning.

His gaze scanned the report once more, passing over the name at the top. Benjamin Jarrett. *Ben*.

For some reason, he hadn't been able to say his son's name aloud at Charlotte's home. As if it were some kind of talisman that would make this too real. Real, only to be stolen from him with greedy, vicious hands.

But not now. Not with these paternity test results.

"Ben," he whispered, finally giving his newest but deepest hope voice, a name.

Even as a now recognizable and intimate anger stirred within him like a flickering, dancing flame. He'd been denied the first two years of his son's life, and Charlotte had denied their son his last name. She hadn't even given Ben that—given Ross that.

Did she really hate him that much? His fingers curled into a fist on top of his desk, the skin over his knuckles blanching before he deliberately relaxed his hand, extending each finger one by one. He inhaled, held the air in his lungs, then slowly released it, attempting to blow a cooling breath over his rage.

It didn't matter if she hated him or not. Or what her trumped-up reasons were. *She* had chosen to leave Royal. *She* had chosen not to tell him she was pregnant. *She* had chosen to rob him of his son. Every step of the way, Charlotte had made the decisions for all three of them, uncaring of the repercussions. Ben deserved both of them—a mother *and* a father.

And Ross was through letting her have all the power in their lives.

His desk phone intercom buzzed, interrupting his

thoughts. "Ross." His assistant's voice echoed through the console speaker. "There's a Charlotte Jarrett here to see you."

Pressing the button, he ordered, "Send her in, please."

Rising from his office chair, he rounded the desk. Grim satisfaction thrummed within him. As soon as he received the paternity report, he'd texted Charlotte and asked her to come by his office so they could speak.

Those dots had bubbled for a while before she actually replied. But she'd agreed, and now that she stood on the other side of his office door, the anticipation of getting answers, of demanding his rights as a father to their baby coiled inside him like an agitated rattlesnake ready to strike.

The knock came a second before the door opened, revealing his assistant and Charlotte. But all he saw was *her*. It was that goddamn superpower of hers, that ability to dominate a man's attention so all else faded to blurred nothingness. Today she wore a short black leather jacket in deference to the February morning. A simple but formfitting white shirt emphasized the full curves of her breasts, and dark blue skinny jeans clung to her sensual, rounded hips and thick thighs. Camel-colored ankle boots elongated legs that already seemed to stretch for eternity.

She might as well have been wearing a couture ball gown with miles of skin revealed by strategic cutouts. Or nothing at all. She commanded every bit of his full, undivided attention. And even unwillingly, he complied.

With her, he'd never been able to do anything but be attuned to her.

To *want* her.

She'd left him, lied to him, kept his son from him. And yet, his dick didn't give a damn.

Yeah, if only it were that simple.

His cock had gotten hard for plenty of women over the years. But none had elicited this visceral, nearly primal hunger like Charlotte Jarrett had from the very first time he'd seen her in his father's study when Rusty had hired her.

If he could, he'd claw that traitorous part of him out of his body, his soul, wherever it hid inside him.

He tore his gaze away from Charlotte to nod at his assistant. "Thank you, Sandra. No interruptions for the next hour, please."

She nodded and left the office, closing the door behind her.

"Do you want to put your things down?" He gestured toward the large purse slung over her shoulder that was more akin to a messenger bag. "Can I take your coat?"

"No, thanks. I have to be at the restaurant soon, so can we get this over with?" she asked. The belligerent words belied the calm tone. The same calm tone she'd employed at her home before her temper had flared and she'd lit into him. "I assume you received the DNA results."

"I did," he said and waved a hand toward the couch and chairs in the sitting area. "Please sit."

"Really, Ross." Her lips twisted into what could've been called—incorrectly—a smile. "Pleasantries? We're past that, aren't we?" She shook her head and crossed her arms over her chest. Then, as if thinking better of the gesture, slowly lowered her arms to her sides. "I'd rather stand. And get to the point of this."

"The *point*, Charlotte? Okay, we'll do this your way. For the last time," he murmured, moving toward her.

He halted when several inches separated them. Far enough away that he couldn't accidentally touch her, but close enough that he could read the flash of apprehension in her eyes.

Did it make him an asshole that a dark gratification filled him at the sight of it?

Probably.

Fuck it. He owned it.

"The report confirmed that I'm Ben's father," he said, uttering those words aloud for the first time. Absorbing that punch of joy, shock and fear again.

"So now you know for certain." She notched her chin up, and in spite of the anger swirling through him like combustible fuel, he had to battle the need to grip that stubborn chin and cup the vulnerable nape of her neck and drag her closer. Had to smother the urge to slam his mouth to hers until she melted under him, until her lips parted for him… until all those soft, dangerous curves pressed to his frame, surrendering. He wanted to fuck the insolence out of her. Clenching his jaw, he resisted the lust, the grinding lure to conquer, to dominate. "What now?" she continued. "Because we both also know you have no interest in being a father—you didn't three years ago, and you didn't right up until you found out about Ben."

"You have no idea what I want. You've never *asked* me what I want," he snapped, bitterness coating his voice. "Every decision has been yours without thought or care to the consequences or who you were hurting."

"Because I've had to," she shouted back at him, the words bouncing off the walls, echoing in the room. A breath shuddered out from between her lips and, visibly shaken, she swept a hand over her thick brown hair. Straightening her shoulders, she sucked in a breath and glanced away from him.

Several seconds passed before she faced him again, and a mask had dropped over her features. Composed, she said, "You can't revise history to suit your narration, Ross. I did what I had to in order to care for my son. I've provided for him, and I'll continue to do so. I don't need or want your money, but this isn't about me. Child support is about Ben. So if you want to contribute, I'll set up an account for him, and the money can go toward his college education or whatever he decides to do with it when he's of age."

"How magnanimous of you to allow me to provide for *our* son," Ross drawled. "I hate to break it to you, Charlotte, but you can't keep me out of his life any longer. And if you would for just a second put your love for him ahead of your hate for me, you would see that he needs me, *his father*, in his."

"How fucking dare you?" she whispered, her eyes narrowing, but it was the telltale glistening in those brown depths that relayed the level of her anger. Charlotte only cried when her rage reached a level that it was either explode or crumble.

And Charlotte Jarrett never crumbled. She might cut bait and run, but collapse?

Not possible.

"All I've ever done from the moment I found out I was pregnant with Ben was put him first. I almost lost my relationship with my parents. I left my old life. I started over in a new city. I worked long hours. I put my goals on the back burner. *For. Him.* Always for him. And I don't regret a single one of those choices. So, hell no. You don't get to sit in judgment of me with your righteous indignation. Where were you, Ross? Playing the international playboy hopping from party to party, woman to woman, while I sacrificed and cared for Ben. *Loved* him."

"You didn't give me that choice, Charlotte. Didn't even grant me the damn option of deciding if I wanted to put aside that lifestyle and be in his life. So now you don't get to be a martyr and cast me in the role of devil because you made decisions all on your own without anyone else's input," he snarled.

"Please." She slashed a hand through the air. "You believe donating your DNA grants you some rights to him? You're wrong. An absentee father is better than one who will play with him like a shiny new toy, then abandon him as soon as something important like a social event, gala or business prospect pops up. Or better yet, a father who didn't want him in the first place."

"What the hell are you talking about…that I didn't want him in the first place?" he growled, latching on to the last accusation because trying to unpack the others lanced him to the core. Was that how she really saw him? A self-indulgent player who didn't give a damn about anything but the next good time and his dick? Was that the real reason she'd kept Ben from him? The pain bloomed in his chest, radiating outward in a toxic, blazing red mushroom. "You said that before, and I call bullshit. Because it implies that you gave me a choice. When you didn't, Charlotte. You stole two years of my son's life from me that I can never get back," he finished, voice hoarse with fury, hurt…grief.

He'd missed his son's first smile. His first word. His first step. Ross knew nothing about Ben. Not his favorite food or toy. Not how cranky he could be when he was tired. Not his laugh.

The hole that yawned wide inside him spread big enough for him to plummet into and never hit the bottom.

"Are you serious, Ross?" She speared him with a look of such disgust it rolled over his skin, polluting him. "Is this the game you're going to play? You don't remember telling me to get rid of our son?" She snorted. "Plausible deniability doesn't become you. Neither does playing dumb."

He almost lashed out with a reply designed to strike and hurt. But then her words penetrated his skull. *You don't remember telling me to get rid of our son?* The question ricocheted inside his head, and he almost stumbled back from the vileness of it. The acidic horror that crowded into his throat and spilled onto his tongue.

"Charlotte, please," he rasped. When she parted her lips, no doubt to blast him with more contempt, he held up a hand, palm out. "Just…pretend I don't know, and tell me. What do you mean I told you to get rid of Ben?"

She glared at him, her chest rising and falling on loud, staccato bursts of breath. For a moment he didn't believe she would grant him that. But then she shook her head, huffing out a hard chuckle. "This is crazy," she muttered but then waved a hand. "Fine. Where should I start this trip down memory lane?"

"The beginning. And leave nothing out."

"Right." Another abbreviated laugh that wasn't a laugh, and she said, "A few weeks after I left Royal, I realized I was late. I called you. Do you remember that?"

"Yes," he ground out. How could he forget? For four weeks, his pulse had leaped every time his phone rang. Only for his stomach to drop and his anger to rise when it turned out not to be her. So when her name had appeared on his screen, and her voice had caressed his ear, taunting him with its sultriness and sweetness that he could no longer have, he hadn't been welcoming. Hadn't been kind. "You mentioned nothing about being pregnant."

"No, but I tried. You didn't give me a chance to, because you had to go. A date that you couldn't be late for," she reminded him.

He'd lied; his ass had been planted on the couch in his sitting room at the ranch while he treated himself to his father's eighteen-year-old scotch. But his pride hadn't allowed him to admit that to her. He'd made up the date so she didn't know he hadn't been with a woman since she'd left him.

"Here's how you should've gone about that, Charlotte. 'Before you go, Ross, I'm pregnant.' Which, I repeat, you *didn't* do."

"No, I didn't," she replied, an edge honing her tone until it could slice clean through his sarcasm. "But I did try again. And when the call went straight to voice mail, I tried the ranch. The housekeeper told me you weren't home, but before I could hang up, she transferred me to Rusty. He demanded to know why I was attempting to contact you when

I'd quit. I think…" She faltered, and this time, she did wrap her arms around herself and her gaze slid over his shoulder to the large window behind him. "I was so stunned that I just blurted out the truth about the pregnancy. He ordered me to get rid of the baby. That his son, an *Edmond*, would not end up raising a child with 'the help.'" Her lips twisted into a grim caricature of a smile, and his fingertips itched to rub those lips, smudge that ill-fitting smile from her mouth like faded lipstick. "He also told me he knew about our… relationship. Courtesy of you. And you'd assured him that you were done with me."

"That's a lie," he snarled, and her gaze jerked back to him. "I've never said anything to my father about us. I've never told anyone."

"Of course you haven't," she murmured, and those four words sent a slick, sour glide into his stomach.

"Dammit, Charlotte," he said, thrusting a hand through his dark blond hair, gripping the strands tight. "That's not how I meant it. I—"

"It was a long time ago, Ross," she interrupted, then flicked a hand. "And whether or not he lied about that, he didn't about you moving on, did he?" She didn't wait for his answer but continued, "Anyway, he promised to have you contact me, but not before warning me that if I didn't go through with the termination of the pregnancy and breathed a word of it to anyone, he'd ruin me. And he wouldn't stop with just me, but he'd harm my parents, as well. I believed him."

"I can't believe…" But yeah…he did. His father would've been—was still—capable of doing all she'd relayed. He wouldn't have been above threatening an ex-employee to protect the precious Edmond name.

"Don't bother, Ross," she murmured, that bitter note making a reappearance. "You might be able to deny knowing about the phone call with Rusty, but you can't ignore the letter."

The letter. What letter?

Maybe she glimpsed the confusion in his eyes, because she scoffed, tipping her head back and muttering something toward the ceiling. Then she tugged her bag open and rummaged inside. Seconds later, she emerged with a worn, brown leather wallet. Opening it, she removed a folded piece of paper from the billfold and, crossing the short distance between them, slammed it onto his chest.

On reflex, he lifted his hand, covered hers. And that small contact—the first time he touched her in three years—nearly knocked him on his ass. Pleasure crashed into him, an anvil that had his fingers clasping hers, as if she were the one thing anchoring him to this world. His fingers flexed, starting to tighten around hers, needing to trap the burn from her palm that seemed to sear straight through to his skin.

But she snatched her hand back, retreating a step, leaving him clutching the paper. She cupped her palm, rubbing a thumb over it. Then, noticing that he caught the betraying action, she dropped her arms to her side.

"Do you want to read that aloud, Ross?" she asked, the rough silk of her voice a stroke over his chest, abdomen... lower. "Maybe it will jog your faulty memory."

He studied her closed-off expression but couldn't forget that telling gesture of hers...as if she were trying to erase the imprint of his touch. Not until the pointy edges of the paper bit into his fist did he glance down and slowly unfold it.

"Charlotte, you were intended to be a fling, not the mother of my child. Get rid of it. Use the enclosed check to pay for the procedure and your trouble. Then move on with your life, because I've moved on with mine. Russell Edmond Jr.," she recited the letter as he read it. "Russell

Edmond Jr.," she repeated on a chuckle. "Like I no longer had the right to call you Ross. Nice touch."

Shock blasted him in an icy deluge. He damn near shattered with it.

"No," he breathed, rereading the paper for a second time. A third. Though typed, it was his signature. What *looked* like his signature. Because he damn sure hadn't written this, signed it or mailed it. "How…"

He knew the how. His father. Rusty had never mentioned a call with Charlotte, and he'd sent the letter, forged it.

Charlotte hadn't robbed him of the first two years of his son's life. Rusty had. Fury raged through him, an uncontrollable inferno desperate to destroy, to consume. And if his father had been in the building instead of attending an out-of-town meeting, Ross would've stormed down to his office and unleashed hell on him.

What a goddamn joke. He'd accused Charlotte of placing her needs above her son. Ross should've known better. After all, his father had been a prime example of a parent doing just that for years.

"You have no reason to believe me, Charlotte, but—" He cleared his throat of the thick snarl of emotion—the anger, the betrayal, the sadness—that lodged in his throat, and tried again. "But I didn't write this. I didn't even know where you lived in California to send it."

"It was mailed to my parents, who forwarded it to my sister, where I was staying. I kept the check, by the way," she supplied, her scrutiny like a magnifying glass determined to analyze every detail and nuance of his expression.

And he held nothing back—not the devastation over his father's lies. Not the grief over what they'd cost him. Not the pain of knowing she'd believed the worst of him. Yes, he might be guilty of being a man-whore, but not a deadbeat father. Not a poor excuse for a man, who would walk away from his responsibilities and ignore the existence of his child.

"I don't give a fuck about a check," he ground out, mind whirling a thousand miles a minute. "Why did you keep the letter?" he asked, holding it out to her, studying its perfectly folded edges that seemed permanently creased into the paper—as if it'd been opened and reread dozens of times. "Why are you carrying it around with you in your wallet?"

"As a reminder." She tugged the paper from his fingers and carefully refolded it, stowing it away in her purse before lifting her head and meeting his eyes. Resolved hardened her gaze. "Whenever I start to doubt myself, or am so tired I don't think I can go on, I pull this out and reread it. Remind myself that I did it once before, and I can do it again. Also, to remember that the only person I can truly count on is myself. Others might have failed me, but I refuse to do the same to myself."

"I didn't know, Charlotte," he murmured, that quiet but fierce statement a brutal blow to his chest. "I didn't know you were pregnant, and I never wrote you a letter telling you to get rid of my baby. I wouldn't..." He scrubbed a rough hand down his face. *I wouldn't abandon you, or my child.* Not after he'd been on the receiving end of that by his own mother. He understood the pain, the confusion, the sense of unworthiness. No, he wouldn't ever inflict that on another child, much less his own. "Give me a chance to prove to you that I can be a good father to Ben. A co-parent with you. I understand you don't owe me or my family anything, but I need you to give me a chance. Please, Charlotte."

She shook her head, and for the first time, indecision flickered across her face. "I—"

The door to his office swung open, and his sister strode in, frowning down at the tablet she held in her hand. "Ross, Valencia Donovan with Donovan Horse Rescue called.

We need to send over—" She finally lifted her head, and spotting Charlotte first, jerked to a stop. "I didn't…" Gina glanced at Ross, then back at their ex-employee. "I'm sorry, Ross. Your assistant wasn't at her desk, so I just…" Her voice trailed off again, but with a small shake of her head, she gathered the poise and manners that had been instilled in her from the cradle. "Charlotte Jarrett. It's been a while," she greeted, walking toward Charlotte with her hand extended. "It's wonderful to see you again."

"Thank you," Charlotte enfolded Gina's hand in hers for a quick shake, before dropping it. The smile she summoned for his sister was small, weak. "It's good to be back home."

"Not to be nosy…" Gina grinned, shrugging a shoulder. "Forget that, I'm *definitely* being nosy. What're you doing here? Is your family okay?"

"Billy and I ran into her at Sheen a few nights ago. Charlotte's the new head chef there. I asked her to stop by and talk about hosting a tent at Soiree on the Bay, and possibly serving on the advisory board."

Gina smiled, nodding. "Wonderful. I've heard so many great things about Sheen and its new chef. I can't believe I didn't know it was you, Charlotte." She glanced down at her tablet again. "This can wait a little while, then. Could you find me after your meeting, Ross?"

"I can. Give me a few more minutes, and I'll come to your office."

"No need," Charlotte interrupted, and the desperation in her voice might not have been clear to his sister, but Ross caught it. "I need to get going anyway."

He almost objected; they weren't finished with their conversation, not by a long shot. But at the last moment, he swallowed the vehement protest, unwilling to draw undue attention to them. He wasn't ashamed of Ben—even now, he wanted to rent a billboard, post it on top of the Texas Cattleman's Club and declare to the world that he had a son.

But this decision wouldn't affect just him, but also Charlotte and especially Ben. Until they hashed out details and he digested these new, earth-shattering revelations of the past, the information had to remain private.

"Oh, no. You don't have to leave on my account," Gina said, frowning.

"I'm not," Charlotte countered, though clearly she lied. Someone who'd just been pulled into a lifeboat off the sinking *Titanic* wouldn't have appeared more relieved than her. "It was nice seeing you again."

Gina crossed the short space separating them to grasp her elbow and give it a warm squeeze. "Same. And I'm so glad you're going to join us at Soiree on the Bay. You were a brilliant chef, and we'll be lucky to have you there. Welcome home, Charlotte."

"Thank you," she murmured. Barely sparing Ross a glance, she lifted a hand in a wave as she turned toward the office door. Her escape hatch. "Ross, I'll let you know about the advisory board position."

"I'll call you," he vowed, and they both knew he wasn't referring to the advisory board or the festival. He didn't care if it sounded ominous. If she tried to hide from him, or attempted to keep Ben from him, there were no lengths he wouldn't go to, to be in his son's life.

She nodded, then exited his office, pulling the door closed behind her.

"Are you sure I wasn't interrupting something more… personal?" Gina asked, her dark eyebrow arched high. Only his father failed to see and appreciate his sister's insightfulness and intelligence. Rarely did anything skate by her. Including the undercurrents of tension that fairly vibrated between him and Charlotte.

"No," he said, voice flat, inviting no further discussion on the topic. "Now what's going on with Valencia Donovan?"

Gina treated him to one last narrow-eyed scrutiny before diving into the reason behind her impromptu visit.

And Ross offered up a silent promise.

Charlotte might have escaped him for now.

But unlike three years ago, wherever she decided to go, he would damn well follow.

Five

"Well, the Hudsons can't stop raving about your food," Faith praised, strolling into Sheen's private dining room, from where Candice Hudson, her mother, aunt and several of their friends had just left, taking their excited chatter and laughter with them.

A glow of pleasure and satisfaction bloomed in Charlotte's chest as the restaurant manager sprawled in one of the chairs that Candice, the happy bride-to-be, and her party had just abandoned. Hearing that her food had been enjoyed never got old. Gathering up the last of the cards where the guests had scored the selection of food, she shot Faith a narrowed glance.

"Why are you so tired? I'm the one who did all the cooking, and the staff did the serving," she drawled.

The other woman waved a hand, flicking away her tart words. "I had to talk. Do you know how exhausting it is to entertain and be *on*?" She sighed. "It's not a job for the weak."

Charlotte snorted, slipping the cards in the pocket of her chef's coat. "You poor, fragile thing."

"I know, right? But one must do what one must." Snickering, Faith jabbed a finger in Charlotte's direction. "But enough about me. The Hudsons just laid down a five-thousand-dollar catering deposit, and all because of your food. Not that I had any doubts that they wouldn't love your menu. Who could possibly resist grilled oysters with sweet basil, pesto and Parmesan? I swear, I just orgasmed saying that…"

"Oh, God, you're awful." Charlotte laughed, heading out of the private room and making a beeline for the kitchen. Faith followed, hot on her heels.

"What? They're aphrodisiacs. You're doing both the bride and groom a service for their wedding night."

"Stop it," Charlotte chided, even though she swallowed another burst of laughter. The first time Faith's naughty sense of humor had made an appearance, Charlotte had been in the middle of sampling a Parmesan lobster bisque. It hadn't been pretty. "I'm just glad they enjoyed what I put together."

The menu included additional food items for those guests who didn't like oysters or the balsamic and rosemary steak options. Coordinating the menu for the high-society wedding that would include nearly five hundred guests had been a challenge requiring hours of work. But the clients' obvious pleasure had been well worth the effort.

"*Loved* it," Faith corrected, trailing behind Charlotte into the bustling kitchen. "And the proud mother of the bride mentioned recommending us to all of her wealthy, connected friends for their wedding receptions and events. Now I have to speak with Jeremy about possibly printing out new brochures that focus on weddings and receptions. If the Hudsons are open to it, we could possibly hire a photographer to take some shots of their wedding and reception to spotlight in the pamphlets," she mumbled to herself, tapping away on her phone.

Switching her formal chef coat out for her work one, she washed her hands and left Faith to her notes and emails. Just as she moved to the stove to begin preparing the creamy wine sauce for her signature dish, the kitchen door opened and Jeremy Randall poked his head inside.

"Charlotte," he called, a tiny frown etching his brow. "Can I speak to you out here for a moment?"

"Sure." Inwardly sighing, she tossed a pining look at the stove and her ingredients. Faith hadn't been wrong. Entertaining people was exhausting, and after presenting each dish to the Hudsons and their guests, and explaining the ingredients in each one, all she longed for was to return to the kitchen and get lost in cooking. It was her happy place. But when the owner of the restaurant requested her presence, she couldn't refuse.

Seconds later, after instructions to her sous-chef to take over in her absence, she pushed through the kitchen door. It swung closed behind her and she joined Jeremy in the hall between the main dining area, the kitchen and prep area. "What can I do for you, Jeremy?"

The handsome older man ran a hand over his salt-and-pepper hair. With his smooth, unlined brown skin and tall, fit frame, Sheen's owner could've been anywhere between forty and sixty. The gray hair only lent a distinguished, composed air to his appearance. But right now, with his frown and the anxious gesture, he appeared more agitated than composed.

"Ah, Ross Edmond is here to see you."

Damn.

She should be surprised…but she wasn't. Ever since she'd left—okay, *bolted* out of—his office yesterday, she'd been expecting him to call her or turn up at her house as he'd done before. But not here at Sheen. She wasn't ready to field curious questions as to why the eldest son and heir to the Edmond Organization had an interest in her.

Out of habit, she reached for the necklace beneath her chef coat. She'd sent up so many prayers since her first and last encounter with Ross that he hadn't noticed its presence.

How did she explain to him that she didn't want anything to do with him, wanted to erase him from her life, but she still wore the one gift from him that she'd allowed herself to keep? She'd thought she'd left it behind along with the other bracelets, earrings and clothes he'd purchased for her during their affair. And when she'd discovered it among her things in California, she'd almost thrown it out. But... she couldn't. Not when memories were attached to the gold chain and diamond-encrusted heart pendant like ghosts connected to an old house.

"I showed him into my office to give you a little privacy. But uh—" he cocked his head to the side, that dreaded curiosity glinting in his hazel gaze "—is there something I should know? Do you need me to stay with you?"

She shook her head, appreciative of his willingness to be her protective shield. But this battle was between her and Ross. "Not necessary. It's probably just about the tent for the Soiree on the Bay festival that I was telling you about," she said. "Nothing to worry about. But I shouldn't keep him waiting."

Although she wanted nothing more than to do just that.

"Okay, if you're sure," he said with a note of hesitation. "I'll be at the bar if you need me."

She nodded, and moments later, she twisted the knob to Jeremy's office and pushed it open. Ross's back faced the door, but as soon as she entered the room, he turned around, his startlingly blue gaze falling on her.

For a second, she froze. Because his crystal eyes, which were usually shuttered and guarded, were awash with anger and pain. God help her, but in that instant, she believed him about not writing the letter. And if she accepted that truth, then she also had to admit that he hadn't known about Ben, either. Those eyes...they didn't lie.

Where did that leave her? Well, she'd been trying to figure that out for the past twenty-four hours. Because three years of hurt and betrayal didn't just disappear overnight. She still didn't trust him—didn't trust that he would put Ben first over his family, put aside his lifestyle and make Ben a priority or take care not to trifle with her son's feelings.

Or her own.

She shut that thought down with a hard, open-handed slap. This wasn't about her; she had no claim on Ross other than him being Ben's father. Nor did she want one. Because he had shown her long ago that settling down with one woman wasn't what he desired. Especially not with her, a woman his father would never approve of. She wasn't rich enough. Her parents weren't connected enough. Her pedigree didn't reach far back enough.

And she'd rebuffed Rusty's advances.

No, she was through hoping for the impossible with Ross. She was done three years ago, when he hadn't fought for her before she left Royal. It'd been her fault that she'd fallen in love with him knowing he could never offer that love in return.

She wouldn't be guilty of such blind devotion again.

"Ross," she said, shutting the door behind her. "What are you doing here at my job?"

"Tomorrow morning, I'm headed to Dallas for the next few days for meetings," he replied, his scrutiny flicking over her body before returning to her face. She convinced herself that her breasts didn't feel heavier, her belly didn't tighten and her sex didn't pulse from that cursory glance. She didn't feel *anything*. "I needed to settle things between us before I left. Charlotte—" the full, sensual curves of his mouth flattened before he continued, voice deepening "—I don't want any more time than necessary to pass by without me being in Ben's life or getting to know him. I've already lost so much of it."

"I—" She sighed, briefly closing her eyes. "I don't want you to, either, Ross."

"Then you believe me?" he pressed, shifting forward, his intense gaze hot on her face. "You believe that I didn't know about the phone call, the letter. About *Ben*."

"Yes," she murmured. "I do. But it doesn't change the fact that he doesn't know you. All he's ever known is me. We have to introduce you to him with care. I'm not going to disrupt his life or upset him."

Ross nodded. "I agree… Which is why I want him to live with me."

Horror and shock punched the breath from her lungs, and she could only stare at him. He intended to sue her for custody? Anger surged through her, a backdraft of emotion. And not just at him for planning to take her baby away from her. But at herself for actually believing he'd changed, that he wasn't selfish and self-absorbed any longer.

"I'm leaving," she said, turning away. There was nothing else for them to discuss—

"Dammit, wait," Ross growled, long fingers wrapping around her upper arm, drawing her to a halt. She tensed under his hand, hating the heat that radiated out from that firm grip. Hating that it seemed to brand every part of her. "I'm sorry. That came out wrong. Shit, Charlotte. I'm so far out of my depth here. Just… Just give me a minute."

Ross. *Apologizing?* She froze for an entirely different reason now. It was the apology and that frustrated, helpless note in his voice. Two things she'd never heard before from this confident, arrogant, charismatic man. It astonished her enough that she slowly pivoted, facing him again.

He released her, but her skin under her chef coat continued to throb as if his hand still clasped her.

"I don't want just Ben to live with me, Charlotte. I want you to move in with me, too."

Jesus, would he stop throwing verbal punches today?

Just when she recovered from one, he opened his mouth and another plowed into her, pilfering her equilibrium.

"That's your idea of easing into this change?" she rasped, incredulous.

"Yes," he said. "Live together platonically as co-parents. So Ben can have you and me under one roof, raising him together."

"So, basically shacking up," she scoffed, shaking her head. "No, thank you."

"Charlotte—"

"No," she interrupted him. "Do you know what finding out I was pregnant and unmarried did to my relationship with my parents? Almost wrecked it. Healing that rift is part of the reason I returned to Royal. Now you want me to just obliterate all the progress we made by telling them I'm moving in with a man—with *you*? I won't do it."

Informing them that the heir to the Edmond Organization was the father of their grandson already promised to be one hell of an uncomfortable conversation.

"So we're supposed to live according to other people's views or opinions?" he challenged. "This is our son, not theirs."

"That's easy for you to say," she slung back. "You're Ross Edmond, Rusty's son. Heir to a fortune. No one would dare criticize or ostracize you. I can't live for myself, Ross. I have other people I'm responsible for, indebted to. And yes, I care about my parents' opinion. I'm not willing to lose them again."

"Fuck," he growled, thrusting a hand through his hair, tousling the ruthlessly styled strands. He paced away from her, halting in front of the far wall and staring at it for several long moments before whirling back around. "Charlotte, I feel like I'm clutching a handful of sand and it's steadily slipping through my fingers, no matter how tightly I hold on to it." He stretched his arm out, thrusting his fist forward, then peeling his fingers open, spreading them wide. "That's the years I've missed. The milestones I've lost. I can't get those back, and I'm trying so hard to grab on to the ones ahead of me. Every day that passes without me there is another day, another minute where something else could happen that I'll miss."

She blinked, taken aback by the vehemence, the *passion* in that plea. This man wanted his son. Wanted to be a part of his life. As a mother, as a woman with a heart, she couldn't deny him. Couldn't deny Ben, either. Because the truth was, although single mothers raised children all the time and did a damn fine job of it, there were things she couldn't teach Ben about manhood. There were things only his father or a male role model could. And while she loved having her father and brother-in-law in his life, they couldn't replace Ben's father.

She owed it to her baby boy to give Ross a chance to be a real father.

But move in with him?

She couldn't.

"I don't want to take that away from you, Ross," she murmured. "You should have every one of those moments, but..."

I can't compromise one more standard for you.

At one time in her life, she'd dreamed of living with Ross as his wife. Even when she'd called him three years ago, she'd still naively clung to that hope of being a family. Now what he offered was practically a marriage of convenience—without the benefit of marriage. She was a single mother, and proud of it. But in the eyes of society, she would be the "baby mama" whom Ross screwed and knocked up. She refused to be the live-in woman who accepted his handout of a home but wasn't good enough to be "blessed" with his last name.

She had a line and couldn't cross it. Even though a part

of her—that woman from three years ago who still clung to daydreams and impossible hope—yearned to not just cross it but leap over it.

"Don't say no just yet," Ross urged, erasing the distance between them with his sensual prowl. "Think about it for the couple of days I'm gone, and we can discuss it again."

She hesitated, then shrugged. "Okay, fine. I'll do that." Not that a couple of days would change her mind.

"Thank you."

He moved even closer, his arm lifting, that big hand hovering between them. Her breath snagged in her throat, and she stared at that so-damn-familiar hand with its short, buffed nails, long, elegant fingers and incongruously calloused palm. Ross might be a businessman and have possessed no interest in cattle ranching, but he'd loved horses. Sometimes it had seemed like he'd enjoyed their company more than people. That abraded palm appeared to testify that he still did. She also recalled how that skin used to feel against hers, that sensual contrast of rough and gentle, coarse and soft. A molten, sinuous warmth coiled around a jagged-edged lust, settling low in her belly. That was also how it had been between them.

Tender with teeth.

Just when she thought he would touch her, bring past and present colliding together, he lowered his arm back to his side. Then slid that hand into his pants pocket as if he didn't trust it to behave if not landlocked.

"I'll call you tomorrow morning, if that's okay. Check in on Ben, at least say hi to him so he can start to become familiar with my voice."

She nodded. "That's fine."

Silence settled between them, as fragile and volatile as an undetonated bomb.

This is about Ben. This is about Ben.

The mantra marched through her mind, and she clung to

it. Even as his sandalwood-and-earth scent embraced her, teasing her with the temptation of his big, powerful, sensually charged body. There'd been a time when she would've surrendered to that lure, cuddled against that tall frame and just inhaled his fragrance straight from the source of his sun-warmed skin. Let him cup her hip and the nape of her neck, press himself against her. Felt his cock nudge her stomach, promising her exquisite pleasure unlike anything she'd ever known.

Stifling a full-body shiver, she shifted backward, injecting desperately needed space between them. Space that didn't contain the memory of sex. Amazing, bone-melting, screaming-until-your-throat-was-raw sex.

"Talk to you soon," he said in that deep rumble of his that added more sensation to her imminent sensory overload.

She moved back and away, granting him room to exit the office. And only once the door closed did she exhale hard and loud.

Ross Edmond was trouble for her.

Some things never changed.

Six

Ross pulled his Aston Martin DBS to a stop in front of Elegance Ranch's scrolled, black iron gate. Pressing the automatic opener on his dashboard, he waited for it to part before driving through to the circular drive. He paused, his nearly soundless engine idling while he stole a moment to stare beyond the palatial Palladian-style villa to the setting sun. Beams of gold, deep orange and brilliant red streamed across the rich ranchland and rolling fields, transforming the estate into a beautiful world that appeared to be on fire.

This was his favorite time of day. For some, it was morning when the day loomed rich with possibilities. But for him, it was evening. It meant a day of hard work, accomplishments and completed goals. It meant a sense of satisfaction that he'd pulled his weight, been a man, not just an Edmond. And the beauty of the sunset congratulated him.

Sighing, he slowly drove into the air-conditioned multicar garage, and after switching the ignition off, just sat there inside the car's plush interior. A quiet peace filled him at being back home after three days in Dallas. Meetings and dinners had filled those hours, for both the Edmond Organization and the festival business. Everything had gone well, and pride filtered through him. Even his father couldn't complain about the connections and headway he'd made. Well, Rusty Edmond actually could find something to criticize, because that was what he did.

Speaking of Rusty…

Clenching his jaw, Ross shoved the car door open. For days he'd put off this conversation with his father because it wasn't one he'd wanted to have over the phone. He needed to look into Rusty's eyes, see each nuance and tick of his expression as Ross confronted his father about lying to him for three years about Charlotte.

Rage that had simmered at times, but never fully extinguished, flared to a flash fire as he exited the garage. Each step through the sprawling and luxurious home stoked those flames. This time of evening, his father would be in one place—his study. Sipping on a tumbler of whiskey before settling in to continue the work he hadn't finished at the office.

For as long as Ross remembered, work had been his father's obsession. Well, work and women. A man couldn't marry four times and not make room for play. But each marriage had ended because he treated his wives the same way he did his children. Like employees. There for his instruction, censure and disposal. And very rarely his praise.

When any of those wives dared complain, he'd sweep an arm out as if inviting them to look around them. Telling them that the work they nagged about had bought the estate, with its many rooms for entertaining, bedrooms and private baths, resort-style pool, stables, several guesthouses and miles and miles of ranchland. Moreover, his many hours at the office paid for the designer clothes, purses and jewelry in their walk-in closets and the extravagant parties they threw on the entertainment pavilion.

Yes, Rusty Edmond could be an arrogant, sarcastic dick.

Which, again, explained the four ex-wives.

On his way to Rusty's study, Ross passed the state-of-the-art kitchen with its separate service kitchen, butler's pantry and wine cellar. It didn't require exerting too much imagination to remember Charlotte rushing around in there, owning the area like the pro she was. That was how she'd first nabbed his attention. That confidence. That cool poise in the midst of controlled chaos. That wild beauty.

And those quick, clever hands.

Shit, did it make him a pervert that those hands so easily and assuredly chopping vegetables, stirring sauces, flipping meat or skillfully plating exquisite dishes had hardened his cock so it resembled the marble floor in the entryway? So delicate, so fine-boned, but strong and capable. He couldn't watch her sauté food and not visualize those fingers wrapped with the same dexterity and talent around his dick.

It hadn't just been her flagrant curves and gorgeous face that had drawn him to her like a moth to a flame. He'd been surrounded by beautiful women since before his balls dropped. But Charlotte had possessed...something more. To this day, he couldn't put his finger on it. But whatever that "something" was, it'd captured him...hell, *enraptured* him. Whereas other women had been transient, he returned time and again to her. Unable to stay away. Unable to satisfy that hungry hole that only being with her had seemed to fill.

Then she'd left.

But it had been his father who'd kept her out of his life. His father who had prevented him from knowing his son. His father who *owed* him.

Ross didn't knock on the closed door of Rusty's study but twisted the knob and entered. His father, still in a light gray dress shirt, barely glanced up from his desk, sparing Ross a narrowed look before returning his focus to the computer.

"You're back," he said in that booming, deep voice that could issue curt orders and deliver charming compliments whenever the occasion warranted. "Sometime between when you left and now, did you leave your manners in Dallas? A closed door usually means you knock and wait to be admitted."

"Sorry," Ross said, without the faintest hint of sincerity. Which his father must've noted, because he shifted his wintry gaze away from the monitor to settle on him. "I need to talk to you."

"I'm in the middle of something. It'll have to wait."

"No. Now."

His father's big frame stiffened, and for several seconds they stared at one another, adversaries engaged in a visual battle. Usually, Ross would be the first to look away, to end the pissing contest that always struck him as macho bullshit.

But not today.

Maybe his father sensed this, because the corner of his mouth lifted in a smirk as he leaned back in his massive black leather chair that more resembled a throne than office furniture.

"Well, if you insist, son," Rusty drawled, arching an eyebrow and sweeping a hand toward the visitor chairs in front of his desk. "Sit."

Like a dog.

But with fury rumbling and festering inside him like an angry, infected wound that needed to be lanced, he wasn't in the mood to heel.

He strode closer to his father, ignoring the chairs and coming to a halt directly in front of the massive glass desk. "Have you been to Sheen yet?"

"The restaurant?" He frowned. "No. What's this shit? You have your balls in a sling over food?"

That was his father. All class.

"Then you don't know who the owner hired as executive chef?" Ross pressed, ignoring the vulgar question.

"No, Ross, I don't know," his father growled. "Since it's

not putting money in my pocket, I don't really give a damn who the cook is."

"Chef," Ross corrected. "And it's Charlotte Jarrett, Dad. Charlotte is the new chef."

An emotion too quick to identify flickered in his father's gaze before it shuttered. Rusty had created and patented the poker face. He only displayed what he desired anyone to see. And right now his expression was as shut tight as one of the infamous NDA clauses he demanded of his lovers.

"Charlotte Jarrett," he repeated, voice cold and flat. "I had no idea she'd returned to town."

"Yes, she has."

"So? What does that have to do with either of us? She was an employee years ago. Staff has come and gone from this place before, and I never made it my business to keep track of them. Why should it interest me?"

"Is this the game you want to play?" Ross murmured, not surprised in the least. He hadn't expected his father to admit what he'd done. Rusty considered himself a master chess player, and not just on the board, but in life. He would allow his opponent to make their move so he could counter, evade or trap. "Okay, fine. Have it your way." He cleared his throat, then prepared for battle. "Well, three years ago, after Charlotte quit, she called here looking for me but got you instead."

Rusty didn't respond, just continued to stare at him with that unwavering gray stare. Silently daring him to proceed.

Ross shoved down the rage, covering it with a sheet of ice. He refused to hand his father ammunition to use against him, to turn around and accuse him of being irrational. "She told you about her relationship with me."

"You mean, she told me you two were fucking."

Those red-and-orange-tinged flames licked at his gut. Enticing him to let this consuming anger loose. *It's what he wants. I'm not giving him what he wants.*

"But that wasn't the only thing, was it?"

Again, no answer from Rusty. But the slight flare of his nostrils, the even slighter thinning of his mouth telegraphed his annoyance.

"She was pregnant. And you told her to get rid of it. Get rid of my baby," Ross ground out.

"So?"

You can't hit your father. You can't hit your father.

The mantra spilled through his head, and Ross silently repeated it several more times before he was fully convinced that he couldn't take that course of action.

"So," he echoed coldly. "You told her to get rid of *my* baby. *Not yours.* You had no right."

Rusty snorted. "The hell I didn't. You're my son, and I wasn't allowing some random girl to trap you."

"And that baby is *my son*," Ross threw back. "You didn't even tell me about him, didn't give me the opportunity to make a choice that was mine, not yours."

"What the fuck do you mean—*is my son*?" Rusty asked, voice soft, dangerous, eyes narrowing.

"Yeah, Dad." Ross nodded, scalding satisfaction flooding him. "*Is*. As in Charlotte didn't do what you ordered her to do in that phone call or that phony-ass letter you sent with my forged signature." Disgust churned inside him. "Despite all your manipulations, she had my baby. My son."

"How do you know, Ross?" Rusty demanded, slowly rising from his chair. He planted his fists on his desk, leaning forward.

"Because I've seen him. Met him."

"You're fucking lying," his father snarled, pounding a fist on the glass desktop. "She didn't have that baby."

"Yes, she did." Ross smiled, and not with a small amount of pride. Charlotte had done what he, himself, had found difficult to do. Stood up to and defied the great and mighty

Russell Edmond Sr. "For once, someone didn't obey your edicts. And he's absolutely mine."

"Why? Because some loose-legged girl who you fucked says so? If she opened her legs so easily for you, Ross, who else did she give it up for? Use your head, not your dick."

"Watch yourself," Ross growled. "You don't get to talk about her like that."

"What? She's your supposed 'baby mama' and now you're her champion?" Rusty chuckled, the sound mean, dirty. Because his father didn't know how to fight any other way but down in the mud. "She was the *help*, son. And if you think she didn't see you as a ripe opportunity to climb into a world she has no business in, then you're a goddamn idiot. She was a user then, and she's one now if she's showing up out of the blue with a kid and trying to pawn it off on you. Do you really believe you were the first one she tried to get under? I promise, you weren't."

"Last time, Dad," he warned, steel threading his voice. "Keep your mouth shut about her. And Ben is mine. I had a DNA test done. And despite your best intentions, I'm claiming my son and intend to get to know him."

"The hell you are," Rusty snarled. "I refuse to allow you to tarnish this family's name by having anything to do with this woman and her baby."

"Get used to it." Ross mimicked his father's pose, flattening his hands on the desk and leaning forward so only inches separated them. "Because I've asked Charlotte to move into the ranch with me. Her and Ben. I'm going to be a father to my son whether you like it or not."

"I forbid it, Ross. This is what she wants, what she wanted when she called up here looking for you years ago. Don't you see that? You're upset about the letter I sent her? Well, did she happen to mention the check I included? Ten thousand dollars, son. And she cashed the check. Wake up, Ross, she's just a gold digger."

Ross barked out a harsh crack of laughter. "Is that supposed to mean something? Am I supposed to look down on her for that? She was a soon-to-be single mother who'd left everything behind—her family, her home, her job. You really believe I begrudge her using that check for whatever she needed to care for herself and our son?" He shook his head. "And gold digger? That name doesn't exactly apply since she hasn't asked me for a damn cent in three years."

She's not my mother, hovered on the tip of his tongue. She hadn't abandoned her child, taken the money and ghosted out of his life. Charlotte might have walked away from Ross, but not their son. He granted her major points for that. "It's happening, Dad. She hasn't agreed yet, but it's only a matter of time."

"Not under my roof. And let's not pretend that this house, this land, this company, hell, your *life*, aren't mine. I own all of it. The lifestyle of cavorting off to different cities around the world to do whatever the hell you want without a care? That's courtesy of me. The expensive suits and watches you like to flash? Me. All me. And if you go through with this…idiocy of claiming this woman's son, of trying to move her in here, there will be repercussions. Repercussions you literally can't afford to deal with. Don't force my hand on this, Ross. Cut ties with her and this boy. And cut ties *now*."

"Two years," Ross whispered, deliberately straightening, his gaze never leaving his father's.

"What?" Rusty snapped.

"Two years. That's how old my son is. Two years of not knowing he existed. Two years of firsts. Two years of his life that you stole from me. From us. Do your worst, Dad. Issue your threats. But you don't get another day, another hour."

"Goddammit, Ross—"

"Hey, fellas." Ross turned around in time to see Billy

shut the study door behind him and walk farther into the room frowning. "I could hear you two all the way down the hall. And so can the staff. What's going on?" He cast a look from Ross to Rusty, then back to Ross, concern darkening his eyes. "Is everything okay?"

"Hell no, everything isn't okay," Rusty growled. "Talk to your friend, Billy. See if you can pound some sense into him, because I can't seem to. But somebody better," he threatened.

"Ross—" Billy said.

"Later," he threw at his friend before tossing a look at his father over his shoulder. "We'll finish this later."

"No, we won't. Don't push this, Ross."

"No, don't push *me*, Dad."

Stalking across the study, he jerked the door open and left, the anger, disappointment and, yes, sadness, propelling him down the hall toward the steps that led to the second level and his wing of the house. He'd expected his father's reaction. But he hadn't been prepared for Rusty to deny a child—to urge Rusty to desert a child—that was their blood. All Ross's life, Rusty had preached about teaching his son to "be a man." But a man took care of his responsibilities, provided for his children. A man protected the vulnerable.

Though Ross and his father had their differences, he'd always seen his father as a man upholding those values.

Now the sadness inside him threatened to capsize the anger. The sadness for who he'd believed his father to be. For the death of that belief.

"Ross, what the hell?" A hard grip surrounded his upper arm, drawing him to an abrupt halt. Billy appeared in front of him, blocking his path to the staircase. "What's going on?" Before Ross could answer, his friend guided him through the formal living room on their left and out the glass French doors that led to one of the terraces facing the stables. Once they were several feet away from the house and on the lighted, pebbled path, he stopped, thrusting his hands over his black hair. "Talk to me. What the hell happened in there with Rusty?"

Initially, Ross hadn't any intention of talking about Charlotte and Ben with anyone. At least not until his temper cooled. But the story burst out of him on a ragged, streaming torrent. When he finished, his chest rose and fell on his harsh breaths and the maelstrom of emotions that continued to roil through him.

"Well, damn," Billy murmured. "I wasn't expecting all that."

For the first time since entering his father's study, Ross snorted with true humor. "Yeah, when it comes to drama, I'm all go big or go home." But in the next instant, he sobered. "Just tell me what you're thinking, Billy."

His friend sighed. "I don't agree with how your father handled the situation those years ago. Lies always end up hurting everyone in the end. But trying to see it from his point of view, I can understand his motives—"

"Are you *serious*?" Ross barked. "He kept this—"

"Hold up." Billy thrust up a hand. "I said I could understand his motives, not that I agree with them. Ben is your son, and no man should ever walk away from his child. I like your father, respect him, but I can't back him on this. You're my friend, and whatever you need, I got you."

Love and gratitude for this man, who was as close to him as his brother, Asher, filled Ross, soothing the jagged edges left behind by the argument with his father.

"I appreciate it, Billy," he said, then exhaled roughly. "I'm going to need all the moral support I can get. Especially when this comes out. Because I refuse to hide Ben or Charlotte."

"You mean you're going to need all the support because of Rusty."

"Yes," Ross murmured. "Why does it feel like I'm about to go to war with my father?"

"He'll calm down," Billy assured him, clapping a hand to his shoulder. "Right now he's upset, but once he calms down, he'll see reason."

Ross chuckled sadly. "You don't know Rusty Edmond at all, do you?"

Because *he* did. Rusty didn't forgive or forget. And Ross had openly defied him, when in the past all he'd had was his son's obedience.

No, this wouldn't blow over. Not when neither of them were ready to back down.

But this was one battle Ross couldn't afford to lose.

Seven

This time as Ross approached the small house in the older but cozy section of Royal, he was expected. He'd called Charlotte as soon as he'd hit the city limits last evening to let her know he was back in town. And asked if he could drop by the following morning to see Ben.

Over the three days that he'd been in Dallas, he'd called and talked to her, and had even video-chatted with Ben over his phone. Not that a two-year-old could chat. But he had been able to coax a *hi* out of him. Those moments had carried him through the long, interminable three days. And one day, hopefully sooner rather than later, his son would smile when he saw Ross's face and heard his voice. Would run to Ross when he saw him.

God, he lived for that day.

Butterflies. He'd never experienced butterflies in his stomach before. The closest had been the tightening and twisting of his gut when he'd known he would be with Charlotte. But that had been about anticipation, desire. Not nerves. No, these were honest-to-God nerves. And not over a woman, but for a boy. A toddler who had the power to squeeze his heart so hard that the ache throbbed in his chest.

Climbing the shallow steps to the front door, he dragged in a breath, then knocked. Within seconds, the door opened as if the person on the other side had just been waiting on him.

Charlotte stood in the entryway, her dark hair hanging in a long braid over her shoulder. A long-sleeved, emerald dress clung to her full breasts before the soft material fell to the floor. She looked casual, even comfortable. But there was nothing comfortable about how his cock thumped against his zipper, stretching, hardening. Dammit. The woman could make a nun's habit sexy as fuck.

"Hi, Ross," she greeted, stepping back, granting him room to enter. "Come on in."

"Thanks." Instead of studying the elegant slant of her cheekbone or the sensual curve of her mouth or—hell—the lush rise of her breasts, he surveyed her home. As if it were his first time there. As if he hadn't memorized every square footage of the place that he'd seen. Anything was better than staring at her like a starved animal.

Hell, he shouldn't find her sexy. Shouldn't want her. Shouldn't fucking *feel* around her.

He accepted she hadn't lied to him or kept his son away from him out of spite or malice, but he still didn't trust her. Didn't trust her not to disappear—she'd done it once before. He also didn't trust her not to renege on allowing him access to Ben.

But while he might be angry—an *understatement*—with his father, Rusty Edmond had still raised him. And one thing he'd taught Ross was to understand what your opponent needed and find a way to supply it. It might seem inherently wrong that he viewed Charlotte as his adversary, but right now he wanted her and Ben to live with him, and she was opposed to the idea. So he'd found her weakness and was prepared to lean on it until she surrendered. She'd shown him that he wasn't enough for her to stick around for. Maybe his incentive *would* be.

Fighting fair? No. Was he being his father's son at the moment? Probably.

Did he care? Not even a little bit.

"Where's Ben?" he asked, glancing toward the living room.

"My parents have him. I usually run later than usual on Friday nights, and they offered to keep him until this morning. They're bringing him home shortly."

Disappointment coalesced inside his chest, tight and hot.

"I texted you last night to let you know, just in case you wanted to drop by later this morning," she said, her tone apologetic.

"Yeah, I didn't see it." In his haste to confront his father as soon as he got back, he'd forgotten his phone in the car, and hadn't checked it for messages yet when he'd retrieved it today. "Maybe this works out better. We can talk over some things before he gets here."

She stared at him, then slowly dipped her head. "Fine." Without waiting for him, she strode toward the living room, and he followed. She didn't sit on the couch or love seat but turned and faced him. The resolute jut of her chin and the thrust of her hip relayed that he didn't have an easy battle ahead of him.

He hadn't expected it to be.

"I spoke with Billy while I was in Dallas," he said, starting with a more innocuous subject. "He told me you agreed to serve on the festival advisory board."

"Yes. I brought it to Jeremy, Sheen's owner, and Faith Grisham, the manager, and they both agreed it would be in the restaurant's best interest to host a tent and for the head chef to be on the board. Billy assured me the meetings wouldn't interfere with my work schedule. And as long as they don't take up too much of my time with Ben, I'm willing to do it."

"We appreciate it. Whatever input and ideas you can add will be valuable. Thank you for doing this, Charlotte."

She shrugged a shoulder and unfolded her arms. Skimming a hand over her braid, she huffed out a breath. "We'll see how it works out," she said, and then added, "Rip the Band-Aid off, Ross. You want my answer about moving in with you, and it's still the same as it was before. No, I can't."

"Hear me out first, Charlotte," he requested, shifting closer to her, and after a second, slid his hands in his suit pockets. That was becoming a habit when around her. Occupying or trapping his hands so they didn't rebel and do something heinous like run the backs of his fingers over the delicate but stubborn line of her jaw. Trail his fingertips over the lush curve of her bottom lip. Grab that braid, fist it and tug her head back...

Fuck.

Refocusing, he gazed into her brown eyes and proposed the arrangement that he'd been formulating over the last three days.

"I understand your reservations about moving in with me. Especially given our...past. But I have a counteroffer." The rough thudding of his heart belied the calm of his voice. He *needed* her to agree. But pride kept him from letting her know that. In his experience, voicing what you wanted, *begging for it*, had zero effect. The one time he had, his mother had walked away and left him and Gina anyway. It'd been the best and the cruelest lesson he'd learned. "Commit to one year of you and Ben living with me. Just one so I can get to know my son, and we can work out how to co-parent. Then if, at the end of the year, you decide it's not working, you can leave."

When she didn't say anything, he risked moving closer, and that sharp and sweet scent teased him with a heavier, spicier fragrance. One that had to do less with figs and sugar and was more raw, pure woman.

Fuck if he didn't hunger to lap it off her smooth hickory skin.

"Also, at the end of the year," he continued, centering his attention once more on the conversation and not how delicious she used to taste, "I'll gift you with five hundred thousand dollars to go toward anything you desire—like maybe opening your own restaurant. I remember that was your dream."

He'd anticipated surprise or even a token resistance before quick capitulation. But he hadn't predicted the indignation simmering in her dark eyes.

"A bribe?" she bit out. "That's your counteroffer? Your solution to the problem I represent? Throw money at me?"

"It's not a bribe—"

"Right," she drawled, her tone so sharp it sliced through the thick tension crowding the room. "It's a *gift*. Like the ones you used to leave in the guesthouse for me to find. Or the ones you undoubtedly give all the other women you sleep with and don't bother to call. Same sentiment, different dollar amount. No, thanks. I don't need your guilt gifts."

Anger surged inside him, joined by a scalding hot retort to her unfair accusation. Hell, he'd been trying to give her what she wanted, and she was...damn, she was *right*. Realization doused the flames. He blinked at her, and for the first time, he glimpsed himself in her eyes.

It was true. While they were together, he'd think nothing of having his secretary purchase the latest, most expensive purse or shoes. Or have his jeweler send over a glittering pair of earrings, ring or bracelet. The gifts had been an afterthought, nothing to him. And after her, he'd done the same with the parade of women who'd graced his arm, his bed. None of them had ever complained when he sent jewelry and a note of thanks for a wonderful night.

It wasn't meant as a demeaning or dismissive gesture; it was...what he knew. He'd witnessed his father do it time and time again with his wives and girlfriends, and it'd appeased them, momentarily healing the rift between them and Rusty.

Even his mother had taken a hefty divorce settlement and left, happy to go about her way without her family in her daily life.

Yet the explanation lodged in his throat. At one time in their relationship, he might have been able to share this with Charlotte. Like after the scent of sex perfumed the air of her bedroom, the sheets tangled around their sweat-dampened bodies as she lay sprawled over him, her breath tickling his chest. Back then, in those quiet soul-baring moments when they'd shared their hopes and dreams, disillusionments and disappointments, he could've admitted this revelation of how he used money as emotional currency.

But not now.

"I'm sorry," he said, his mind whirring to find the words to convey his sincerity while struggling to convince her not to abandon this plan. "I didn't mean to offend you, Charlotte. I was only thinking that other than your job at Sheen, you would be rearranging your life for an entire year for me, the least I could do was help you achieve what you've always wanted. It's only a gift. Whether you stay or you leave, the money is yours."

She didn't immediately reply but simply stared at him. Finally, she glanced away, murmuring something he couldn't catch under her breath.

"And after a year, Ross?" she asked quietly, returning her scrutiny to him. "What then? Do we just walk away from the little experiment as if it didn't happen? Do we pretend we haven't let Ben become accustomed to a certain living arrangement where he has both parents every day in his life to separate houses again with biweekly visits?" She sighed, shaking her head, her gaze sad. "What about you? After being a father every day, how do you handle going to only seeing him a few times a week? Have you thought about how that will affect you?"

Again, she stunned him.

By broaching another aspect he hadn't considered, but also because she was concerned…about him.

"I hadn't thought about that," he admitted gruffly. Narrowing his gaze on the neat stack of toys across the room, he swallowed past his suddenly constricted throat. "For me, I'd rather have that year where I wake up to Ben and have the privilege of putting him to bed. Where I can feed him breakfast, can experience his good and bad moods, his smiles and frowns…hear him call me Daddy. I'd rather have twelve months of that even knowing there's a possibility that I might not have it in exactly that way afterward."

She glanced away from him, and her slender throat worked before she returned her attention back to him. "And what about Ben?" she whispered.

Ross studied her for a long moment. "You're a wonderful mother—I can tell that from being with him those ten minutes. Hopefully, you can teach me to be an equally great father. And between the two of us, I know we can help him navigate and adapt to any change. He needs to know me, Charlotte," he said, voice lower, rawer, exposing the depths of his emotion. "And I need to know him."

He didn't voice it, but he assumed that at the end of the twelve months, she would want to leave. But what if she *didn't*? What if she discovered she enjoyed a more luxurious life at the ranch where she didn't have to worry about bills, expenses or day care? They could go on indefinitely with the living arrangement. Hell, even a…marriage, maybe. Bottom line? They could essentially live separate lives but still be a family for Ben.

But he needed her to say yes first before bringing that option to the table.

"Jesus, I can't believe I'm actually considering this,"

she muttered, and the low grumble most likely not meant for his ears had a cautious joy and sweet satisfaction pulsing through his veins. "*If* I agree to this, I have a couple of conditions."

He risked a nod.

"One, I'm not moving to your family's estate." When he frowned, she shook her head. Hard. "No. I'm not compromising on that. I won't be under your father's roof. I've worked too hard to be independent, and I won't give that up to be reliant on you or Rusty."

"Where would we stay then?" he asked, glancing around her living room. What he'd seen of her home was nice, but the house was small. "How many bedrooms do you have?"

"Two."

He shook his head. "I'm not saying no to this condition. But would you concede to us looking for another place together? I don't want to confiscate Ben's room, and then he'll have to move into your room. That's not fair to either of you."

She studied him for a moment, then finally, she nodded. "Okay, I can concede to that."

"And you're renting, right?" When she dipped her head again, he said, "I'll cover the rest of the rent that's left on your lease. No, Charlotte, I'm *insisting* on that," he growled as her lips parted, undoubtedly to object. "It's because of me and what I'm asking you to do that you're moving in the first place. It's the least I could do."

She sighed and grudgingly muttered, "Fine."

"What's your second condition?" he asked, anxious to get all her concerns out there so he could tackle them one by one.

"I'm not accepting your money or *gift*," she added.

"No." This time he shook his head, vehemently. "For two years, you've provided for Ben on your own without any financial help from me. If I'd known about him, I would've gladly paid child support. Consider this a lump sum of back payments. The money is yours and Ben's, Charlotte. I'm not negotiating on this."

Again she hesitated, but eventually nodded. "Okay. That's fair."

"Good. Now *I* have one last condition." He paused. "I want Ben to have my last name."

He braced himself for her argument, had his reasons ready—he was, after all, Ben's father; if he'd been at the birth, he would've signed the birth certificate; and he wanted to claim his son.

But shock erupted inside him, stealing those words and his breath when she whispered, "Okay."

"Thank you," he said softly.

They stared at one another, and the tension vibrating between them thickened, tightened to the point of bursting. As if of its own volition, his gaze dropped to her mouth, and he could practically feel the softness of it. The tender give of it. The gut-twisting greediness of it.

Fuck, he wanted it. Wanted it all. That uninhibited response to him that held no artifice. That needy moan he remembered so well he could hear a faint echo of it now. That sultry, addictive taste that'd had him counting down the hours until he could see her again. Indulge in her again. *Devour* her again.

He'd never been one to deny himself. And he didn't now.

Lust throbbing in his veins, he edged closer, eliminating the space between them. Immediately, the heat from her body and the rich, heady perfume from her skin inundated him, and he inhaled. It was visceral. Intoxicating. Borderline…sexual. Taking a part of her into him, just as he'd once slid so hard and deep inside her.

He granted her time to move, to avoid him—at least he convinced himself he did. And when she didn't, just stared up at him with those lovely, bottomless eyes, he surrendered to the urge that had been riding him since the moment he'd seen her cross that restaurant floor, her sexy, confident stride carrying her to his table.

Need was a growling, straining animal inside him, but he didn't pounce on her like that beast demanded. Not when it had been three years of deprivation, of starving for the touch that taunted him in his most secret, dirtiest dreams.

Because it had been that long, he intended to *savor*.

Dragging his fingertips up the elegant column of her neck, he relished the softness of her skin before tunneling his fingers under her braid and over her scalp. Her low, soft gasp bathed his lips as he lowered his head, and when he took her mouth, he took that small, hungry sound, as well.

He groaned as his lips closed over hers, unable to restrain it. Not when her lips parted for him so sweetly, as if she didn't resent every breath he drew. As if this need wasn't one-sided. As if she'd been dying for a taste of him, too.

He slid his tongue over that overripe bottom lip, sucking on it for good measure before slipping between. Slipping into heaven. Into *her*. With another moan, he pressed closer, aligning his larger frame against her curvier one. God, she was made for him. Even as the thought prowled through his head, he hated it, shoved it aside so hard it ricocheted off his skull. Sentimental drivel had no place here. Not when her tongue greeted his, lapped at his, tangled with his.

This. He lifted his other hand, cupping her cheek, holding her for a deeper, harder possession. *This* was what he'd been searching for the last three years with the nameless, faceless parade of women. This hit, like an unhealthy combination of dopamine and alcohol, arrowed straight to his system. That lethal mix pumped through his arteries, aided by his wildly hammering heart, and pounded in the erect thickness of his cock.

One kiss. She had him on the verge of coming with *one* kiss.

He angled her head, positioning her so he could take more. No, to hell with that. *Conquer* more. He wanted to brand her with his kiss so she would remember clearly how he made her body convulse with pleasure, made her throat raw by eliciting scream after scream.

He could do that for her now. Fuck, he *needed* to do that for her now. For him, too.

She released a whimper then leaned her head back, turning to the side. "Ross," she rasped.

He trailed his damp lips over her cheek to her ear. There, he pressed a kiss to the tip and murmured, "Come away with me this weekend."

The invitation tumbled from his lips before the idea had fully formed. A warning alarm blared in his head, loud and screaming, What the fuck? But he didn't rescind the offer. Though she stiffened against him, he didn't release her, just shifted his hand from her face to her hip, steadying her.

"I have a cabin in Colorado. You, Ben, me—we can fly there tonight after you're finished at the restaurant, spend tomorrow there, and I'll have you back Monday in time for work. We can talk over the details of the move and how we're going to proceed with our families. I want to spend time getting to know my son with his mother. Take a risk and a day off work, Charlotte."

"I don't have to take a day off," she murmured, almost absently. "One of my conditions when I accepted the job at Sheen was that I have Sundays off to be with Ben."

Whether she realized it or not, she was halfway to agreeing to go with him. He pushed his advantage, because the invite might've been spontaneous, but he wanted this. Wanted her and Ben alone.

"Say yes, Charlotte," he said, finally stepping back even

though his body screamed in rebellion and promised swift retribution. Even though his palms tingled with the need to cup that rounded, firm hip again. To squeeze it. Mark it. "This is about Ben. What happens afterward—*if* something happens—is up to you."

Her eyes darkened, and the thick fringe of her lashes lowered. But not before he caught the gleam of arousal in her eyes. The uncertainty, too. Yes, she'd understood his meaning. He hadn't been referring to their co-parenting plan or how they intended to break the news to her parents that he was Ben's father.

He'd meant that kiss.

And the hot, raw sex that followed.

When he'd proposed their...cohabitation, he'd stipulated it would be platonic. And that had been his plan. Up until she'd moaned into his mouth.

Now he was leaving it up to her; the ball was in her court. And if she wanted to play, he was all in. A year with free access to her body, to her pleasure?

He wanted it. He wanted *her.*

Trust her? No. Dying to be buried inside her? Hell. Yes.

"Come away with me." The offer, roughened by the lust tearing at him, still hung between them.

Her lips parted, moved, but nothing emerged. She bowed her head, pinching the bridge of her nose. Anticipation and the need to press for an answer whipped inside him like a gathering summer storm, but he held back. Granting her space and time to come to her decision. Because it had to be hers, freely given.

Finally, she lifted her head, met his gaze. Desire still simmered in her eyes as did the doubt. But so did resolve. He had his answer even before she murmured, "Yes."

He exhaled. "Good," he said. "Call me when you're about to leave work. I'll come by to pick up you and Ben tonight."

"Okay." She sighed. Then whispered, "I hope we're not making a mistake, Ross."

The assurance that they were doing the right thing hovered on his tongue, but he couldn't utter it. Because it would be a lie.

He didn't know.

And right now, he didn't care.

Eight

A cabin, he said.

Charlotte shook her head, smiling wryly down into the steaming cup of coffee she cradled between her palms.

Only Ross Edmond would call this luxurious four-story chalet in exclusive Telluride, Colorado, a cabin. She scoffed. *Right*. And Godzilla was a cute little lizard with anger issues.

Leaning on the wood railing, she studied the beauty of Mount Wilson and sipped the fragrant brew. Somehow the coffee tasted better up here in the mountains, with the crisp air biting at her cheeks. It should've been too cold to stand outside, but bundled up in her oversize sweater and a coat Ross provided from one of the cabin's fully stocked closets, and with the freestanding fireplace at her back, she was warm enough.

And even if she'd been in danger of frostbite, she still would've remained out here on this ridiculously gorgeous terrace, watching her son and his father play together.

Ben had gone a little crazy at the sight of snow; he'd never experienced it in California, and though it did fall in Texas, none had fallen since they'd returned to Royal. His excited squeal had filled her chest with joy, and even if she was questioning her wisdom in agreeing to this impromptu trip, that delighted and wondrous sound had silenced every misgiving.

Ross had always appeared to her as self-confident. Arrogant. So sure of himself. But from the moment he had picked them up from her house, through the drive to the airport and the trip here in the Edmonds' private jet, he'd been different. Uncertain. Even a little bit…nervous. And she knew the reason why.

Ben.

The small, three-foot-tall boy had humbled Ross Edmond.

He was in awe of Ben, and the fascination seemed mutual. Between the phone calls over the days Ross had been in Dallas and the trip here, Ben had lost most of his shyness, and had been stuck like glue to Ross. Falling asleep in his arms on the flight here. Climbing on his lap and contentedly eating with his father. And now building a really abysmal-looking snow fort in the huge yard behind the chalet.

They had a real bromance going on.

One of Ross's reasons for this trip had been to bond with his son. Well, she snorted, that could be checked off the list. The other reason—hammering out the details of their arrangement—had yet to be accomplished.

God, she still couldn't believe she'd agreed to moving in with him. Before he'd arrived at her house, she'd been firmly entrenched on #TeamSeparateHouseholds. But Ross always had possessed a silver tongue—and a gifted one. No, dammit. Don't think of *that*.

But once that floodgate was opened, the waters rushed in, tugging her under.

That kiss. His mouth had brushed hers, and she'd gone up in lust-driven-pride-abandoning flames. Had he guessed from her reaction that she hadn't been with another man since him? That would be utterly humiliating. Especially as he'd been with countless women if the gossip magazines and sites were to be believed.

It hadn't been for lack of opportunity, but her priorities had been Ben and working. They'd left no time for dating or even casual hookups. Besides, the last time she'd trusted a man with her body, he'd let her down in the most spectacular of ways.

Obviously, her libido couldn't give a damn about that. Even now heat pooled and thickened, beading her nipples under her multiple layers and swelling the flesh between her legs. She shifted, her thighs sliding against each other, doing nothing to assuage the ache deep inside her. The man had always been able to turn her inside out with need. With him, she threw away every rule and expectation, stripped off every inhibition and became…his. His to use, to corrupt, to imprison in a world of pleasure that she never wanted to be free of.

His to cast aside when he was finished.

She sucked in a breath, the truth of that slamming into her like a solid punch.

Because he would do it. Just as he hadn't asked her to stay three years ago or come after her. Just as his arrangement already wore a predetermined expiration date.

Ross Edmond might be able to make her burn hotter than the sun, but he wasn't dependable. He wasn't a man for the long haul.

He wasn't *her* man.

"Mama!"

Her son's cry yanked her from her sobering thoughts, and when she lowered the cup to the railing and smiled, the warmth in the gesture was real despite the heaviness of her reality. Ben perched on Ross's shoulders, his chubby, short legs wrapped around his father's neck, his hands spread like little starfish on Ross's cheeks.

"Me!" Ben shouted, which she interpreted as "Look at me!" He patted Ross's face, ordering, "Daddy, go!"

Ross smiled, and cupping Ben's arms, he started slowly spinning around. The way their son screamed in glee, he might as well as have been on a roller coaster. Charlotte laughed at Ben's antics, but the warm joy lighting Ross's face? She pressed her hands to her chest and exhaled a long, shaky breath. Telling Ben that Ross was his "daddy" had been a spontaneous decision for her this morning. And in the face of Ross's happiness at being claimed—and ordered around—by his son, she could set any doubts aside that she'd made the right decision.

On that, at least.

"Are you hungry?" Ross called up to her.

When Ben yelled, "Eat!" in reply, his grin widened and softened at once.

"Ben cast his vote. How about you?"

"I could eat." She picked up her cup and jerked a thumb over her shoulder. "Let me go see what's in the refrigerator, and I can cook us something."

"No need." Ross tumbled Ben down into his arms, earning another delighted squeal of approval from their son. "This is supposed to be a rest for you, too. I already had dishes prepared. I got it."

And he certainly did.

A half hour later, she sat at the huge marble island in the middle of a kitchen that made her chef's soul weep with its top-of-the-line appliances. But could she expect less from a place with five bedrooms and bathrooms, a media room, a library, enough windows that a person could enjoy stellar views from each room and an elevator? An *elevator*, for God's sake. She shook her head.

"What?" Ross glanced at her over his shoulder, a glass baking dish in one hand and the other curled around the open stove door. "I think I can handle warming up a pre-cooked meal," he drawled, eyebrow arched high.

She held up her hands, palms out. "I didn't say a word about your culinary skills," she swore. "Actually, I was thinking, how many TVs are needed in a place like this? I get having the theater-sized one in the living room and in the bedrooms. But there's one out by the hot tub *and* in each bathroom. The. Bathroom."

He snorted. "That you even have to ask that question has me questioning your reasoning. Seriously, Charlotte. What happens when nature calls and the Rangers are playing the Mariners? Am I supposed to just miss out on an important play? I think not."

"No." She smirked. "You just pause the game on one of your fifty DVRs and go like a big boy."

Ross chuckled. "Touché." He slid the dish in the oven and closed the door. "Ben is having a good time," he murmured, his gaze shifting to the toddler, who sat in front of the huge, dark brown sectional couch. Ben babbled to himself as he happily played with the mountain of toys that'd been waiting for him when they arrived at the cabin.

"How could he not?" she drawled. "It's like Christmas came early."

A corner of Ross's mouth kicked up as he shrugged a shoulder. "I might've gone a little overboard." At her snort, he held up his hands. "Fine. A *lot* overboard. But I have birthdays, Christmases and all the other gift-giving holidays to make up for." He paused and cocked his head to the side, studying her. "Do your parents know that you two are here with me?"

She shook her head. "I told them I was going on a business trip and that my manager's husband was coming along to watch Ben and their kids."

He nodded but his face had settled into an inscrutable

mask that betrayed none of his thoughts. "When do you plan on telling them the truth about me?"

"Soon." She laughed softly, but nothing about this situation was remotely humorous. "Especially since we're apparently moving in together. My parents and I... As I mentioned before, we're in the process of rebuilding our relationship. And I'm more than a little worried about how this news is going to affect it."

"Yes, you told me a little bit about what happened with them," Ross said, leaning a hip against the counter behind him, crossing his arms over his chest. She tried—and failed—not to notice how the muscles flexed underneath his long-sleeved white Henley. The man could make arm porn a multi-million-dollar industry. "From what I remember, you and your parents used to be close."

"That was before I embarrassed them by getting pregnant out of wedlock. They were incredibly disappointed and disagreed with me raising the baby as a single mother. And they were very vocal about it."

Vestiges of the hurt echoed in her chest even though she'd forgiven her parents long ago.

"Needless to say, our relationship was strained for a while. It started to heal when Ben was born. They fell in love with him at first sight." She glanced over at her son, love swelling so hard it brushed away those whispers from the past like a broom sweeping out dirt from dark corners. "But I still never told them who his father was—and they never asked." She huffed, shaking her head. "They're going to have some explaining to do with their friends, though. People assumed I got married and divorced while I was in California, and they didn't disabuse anyone of that assumption. When it becomes known that you're Ben's father and that we've never been married, they're going to be scrambling."

"Are you angry with them?"

She didn't immediately answer. *What are you doing?* a small inner voice yelled at her. The last time she'd allowed herself to confide in this man, to trust in him, she'd set herself up for a heartbreak that had nearly broken her. Letting him in again would be a foolish mistake, and she'd promised herself long ago that she'd never be a fool for any man again. Particularly *this* man.

Yet… In a short time, they would be living together again. Co-parenting. They needed to have some sort of cordial relationship—some level of trust—to ensure Ben flourished in a healthy, calm environment. And that required her opening the door to Ross, even if only a little.

Sighing, she dipped her chin. "I was. They emotionally abandoned me just because I did something they didn't approve of. And I can't lie, there are moments when I still have a hard time wrapping my brain around the fact that I've forgiven them. But for the most part, I've let the anger go."

"For Ben's sake, are you going to be able to do the same with me?"

Her breath caught in her lungs, and she stared at him. At the electrifying blue eyes that smoldered with an intensity that simultaneously stirred the embers of desire inside her and set her veins racing with an inexplicable fear.

Discovering he hadn't known about her pregnancy and hadn't callously tossed her aside had gone a long way toward soothing her anger and resentment toward him. But a part of her clutched at the slick shards of bitterness that were embedded in her soul. Because that part hadn't forgiven him for not loving her, not needing her, for letting her go when all she'd wanted was to be his.

Before she could answer, Ben raced from the living room and up to her. He wrapped his arms around her legs and tipped his head back. "Mama, potty!" he announced.

Relief poured through her. Lord, she'd never been so

happy to potty train her son. "Let's go," she said, grasping his chubby little hand in hers.

Ross's gaze seared her as she escaped his question and presence. A temporary reprieve. But one she was grateful for.

She needed the time to shore up her defenses against the force that was Ross Edmond.

"Is he finally down?" Charlotte glanced up from her glass of wine to smirk at Ross. He'd left the living room earlier to put Ben to bed.

A half hour ago.

"Yes." He sprawled at the end of the couch she sat curled up on, his long, muscled legs spread out before her. "Just out of curiosity—" he rolled his head toward her, eyes narrowed "—do you usually read three books to him before he goes to sleep?"

She snickered into her wine. "Not. Even. Close."

A grin flirted with his mouth. "I had a feeling I was being suckered. That kid's lucky he's so adorable."

"Here." She leaned forward and picked up the second wineglass on the coffee table in front of her. Offering it to Ross, she chuckled. "I thought you might need this when you eventually came out."

"I appreciate it." He accepted the glass, sipping the Moscato.

Her belly dipped at the sight of those firm but soft lips pressed to the rim and the up-and-down glide of the Adam's apple in his strong throat. Damn. She couldn't even look at Ross drink without getting hot. She needed an intervention. And more wine. Grabbing the bottle off the table, she topped off her drink.

"Maybe we should talk over how we're going to make the living arrangements work," she suggested, desperate to concentrate on anything other than Ross, his lush mouth and his sexy throat muscles.

"Right," he agreed, taking another sip. "When we return, we can start looking for a house. But until we find one—" he set the wineglass on an end table "—staying at the ranch makes the most sense."

"I said no," Charlotte said, her answer automatic and adamant. "I'm not staying there, Ross. I thought we were through discussing that."

"I'm trying to understand why you're so against it. Is it because you used to work there, and that makes you uncomfortable? Or is it because it's where you and I—"

"No," she interrupted, not wanting him to finish that sentence. Not wanting to hear him describe what they used to do. Meet up? Fuck? Make love? "Like I said before, I've been independent for a long time. And you know how your father operates, Ross. He will try to run our lives if we're under his roof."

It was as close to the truth as she could come.

How could she explain to him that she dreaded being back under Rusty's thumb? Because if Rusty chose to pick up where he'd left off flirting with her, hitting on her, then he wouldn't find the same vulnerable girl; she wouldn't run scared. He would force her hand in telling Ross the real reason she'd been so eager to leave his father's employ. That Rusty couldn't keep his inappropriate comments to himself, and she feared that one day he wouldn't let it go at just talk. From the few times Ross had confided in her—and from her own two eyes—she could tell father and son didn't share a close, affectionate relationship. But Ross wanted more from his father...yearned for more. She refused to be responsible for torpedoing whatever chances they had of achieving that.

But deep inside her resided another reason. A reason that walked hand-in-hand with her insecurities. Just as she hadn't trusted Ross three years ago to have her back with his father, to stand up to him, she couldn't say with certainty that he would today, if he had to choose between Rusty and her and Ben. Rusty was a powerful, charismatic and domineering force. And for a son who looked up to his father, hungered for his acceptance and love… Ross might want to have her and Ben in his life, but if it came down to it, would he fight for them?

She didn't know.

And didn't want to find out.

Therefore, living at Elegance Ranch remained out of the question.

"I need you to just accept my decision."

Ross studied her, and she silently ordered herself not to flinch, not to betray any reaction to that blue, piercing stare. "Fine," he murmured. "But I am asking one thing."

She dipped her chin, indicating for him to continue.

"When we return back to Royal, come with me to introduce Ben to my family. We don't have to stay at the ranch, but I would like you there."

Though a barb-tipped unease clung to her ribs like burrs, she nodded again. "Okay," she conceded. "I can do that."

Even if she'd rather eat a plate of boiled okra first. With hot sauce.

But if he met her halfway with not forcing the issue of the ranch, then she could do this. As long as she didn't have to spend too much time in Rusty's company.

"What is your work schedule like?" he asked, picking up his glass again.

"Monday through Saturday. I go in at about twelve thirty to help with food prep and then I don't leave until after closing. It's long hours, but it's also why I insisted on Sundays off so I could spend a whole day with Ben. I was taking a chance including that demand in my contract, since most chefs work seven days a week, including holidays. But Jeremy agreed, and I have a wonderful sous-chef as well as an excellent staff to cover me."

"Those are long hours," he murmured. "How did you juggle the job and a new baby in California?"

"Let's just say I haven't slept a full night for over two years," she replied dryly. "But I leaned a lot from my sister and her family. They were invaluable. Now I have a babysitter for Ben, and my parents take him often, as well."

"I have another proposition for you to consider. Let me take Ben while you're at work." He shifted toward her, forestalling her instinctive objection. "My schedule is more flexible than yours. When you leave for work, you can drop him off to me. The office has a day care for all of our employees. So I can visit him throughout the day. And after I leave, we can come over to the restaurant and have dinner with you on your break."

She blinked, stunned into silence.

How many times had she wished that her parents would offer to bring Ben by her job so she could see him? Being a single mother with a very demanding job, she constantly battled the guilt of not being there enough for her son. Of missing out on so many little things—like his giggle at a TV show or cuddling with him at bedtime. Building her career wasn't just for her success or fame; it was for Ben, too. She not only desired to provide for him, but to show him that no dream, no goal was too far or big for him to achieve. Even more than being a master chef, she hoped to be her child's inspiration.

But being his inspiration sometimes cost her time with him. *Precious* time.

"I—" She cleared her throat. "If you're sure it wouldn't be an inconvenience…"

"My son could never be an inconvenience."

His son. Not her.

Good. She was glad he said that. It served as a reminder that their sole connection was the child they had together.

"Thank you, then." She wrapped both hands around the bowl of her wineglass. "We can do that." Lowering her gaze, she studied the ruby depths as if it were a scrying glass. "I'm afraid to trust in this," she whispered, the confession slipping from her without her conscious permission.

"In this...or in me?"

She jerked her gaze up, meeting his shuttered scrutiny. *Retreat*, a voice hissed. *Retreat into casual chitchat and surface topics.* Because those subjects didn't tread on ground she'd burned long ago.

"Both." *Dammit.*

"I asked you before, but you didn't answer." He swirled the wine in his glass, but his unwavering stare remained on her. "You let your anger go with your parents, for Ben's sake. Have you done the same with me?"

"Have *you*?" she shot back, yes, avoiding that question. It was too loaded...too dangerous. Pitted with minefields she dreaded maneuvering.

Several seconds ticked by where only the crackle of logs burning in the cavernous fireplace filled the space. She waited with bated breath, every part of her clamoring for his reply.

"Yes," he said. "Knowing the circumstances and knowing you didn't intentionally keep me from Ben, I'm not angry anymore."

"Liar." Good Lord, her mouth had launched a rebellion, and she couldn't bring it back under control.

Ross arched an eyebrow. Didn't speak. But his eyes... No longer shadowed, they gleamed with—what? Surprise? Anger? Something darker...hunger?

"A part of you will always blame me for missing the first couple of years with Ben. But that's not even what you're lying about."

"Really? Enlighten me then, Charlotte."

"You still haven't forgiven me for leaving in the first place," she said brazenly. "Before you knew about Ben, you seethed with that anger, Ross. And it didn't just disappear."

Deliberately, Ross set the glass down on the end table. He stretched an arm out along the back of the couch, and the other settled on his thick thigh, long fingers splayed wide. But he didn't look at her, his attention seemingly transfixed on the fireplace's dancing orange-and-red flames.

"You think you know me? That's presumptuous of you, isn't it?" he murmured, no rancor in his low voice, but she caught the edge. Sharp enough to leave stinging cuts.

"I knew you better than most," she said, and at her words his head turned toward her, and the icy shock of his wintry blue gaze slicked over her skin like sleet.

"We fucked, Charlotte," he stated bluntly.

Though he spoke the truth, it still drove a fist into her stomach, leaving her winded and hurting. Because he said what she'd always known but had mourned. For him, it had been just sex with the family chef. For her, it had been so much more. And that was her fault, not his. But wisdom didn't mean shit when the heart became involved. Lucky for her, she'd stopped being that foolish, naive girl three years earlier.

"And yet, you still resent me. Come on, Ross, get it off your chest now that you have the chance. Want to tell me why?" She taunted him, and fire leaped in his eyes as if she'd poked those flames.

Did she want to be burned?

Yes.

The word vaulted, unbidden, to her mind. And she wanted to deny that need, but her actions belied it.

"What are you doing?" His hooded scrutiny dipped to her mouth, then lower. Over her suddenly sensitive breasts, down to her thighs…to the aching space between them.

When his gaze met hers again, the heat from it licked at her skin.

God, she wanted to lean into it. Bask in its warmth. Let it consume her.

Even though every self-preserving instinct screamed at her to protect herself.

"I don't know what you mean," she said, the rasp of the tone making a mockery of the statement.

His sensual lips curved at one corner, lending it a carnal, almost cruel cast. "Don't you? Do you want a fight, baby? Is that it?" he murmured. "Or do you just want to use it as an excuse to get your mouth on me?" He cocked his head, and his teeth briefly sank into his bottom lip as if he were nipping her mouth instead of his own. "You don't need that charade, Charlotte. If you want to taste me without having to feel guilty afterward, it can be our little secret."

Little secret. The words clanged in her head, a warning bell.

That's all you are to him. All you've ever been.

Truth. She *knew this*. Yet…lust pumped through her like an engine with greased, faulty brakes—fast, screaming, out of control.

Maybe he was right; she did want his anger to take the decision out of her hands so she could give in. So she could blame emotion instead of accepting that she wanted his mouth again. Craved his tongue licking at her, sucking on her.

A kiss. That was all she'd allow herself. Another kiss. Then she could sate this need that had been teasing and taunting her since yesterday. For three years, she'd been sacrificing—for her career, for her son.

Tonight, she could take for herself. Just once.

One little taste. Who could it hurt?

You.

Bullshit. Because she wouldn't let it.

"That's nothing new for us, is it?" she whispered. Rising from the couch, she slowly moved across the short distance separating them. "Secrets. We're made of them. So what's one more, right?" She pressed a knee into the cushion along his outer thigh. "Except this time, you're mine. I'm not yours."

"Charlotte." A faint frown marred his brow as she lifted her other leg, straddling him, caging him between her thighs. His hands shot up to cradle her hips. "What're you—"

"Taking."

Without breaking his gaze, she lifted her glass, sipped. Then, turning it around so his lips would close over the same spot, offered it to him. He accepted the drink, and the intimacy of the gesture had her sex clenching, an empty ache pulsing deep inside her.

The moment he lifted his head, she dipped a fingertip in the wine, swirling it. Setting the glass on the end table next to his, she turned back to him and slowly, sensually painted first his top and then the fuller bottom one with the wine. She stared at his stained mouth, her breath a ragged, heated thing in her chest.

Lowering her head, she hovered above him, halfway expecting him to tilt his head back and confiscate this kiss. But with his blue eyes like crystal flames in a face of harsh, almost severe angles, he didn't move. Just watched her. Waited. And for a man accustomed to control in the bedroom and out, this show of temporary submission was unusual…and hot as hell.

A moan caressed her throat, but she trapped it, not willing to betray the erotic storm that whipped and howled through her body. And she hadn't even kissed him yet. But she'd rectify that.

Now.

Curling her fingers around the back of the couch, she

closed the scant distance between them. Swept her tongue over his plush bottom lip. Tasted Moscato and him. Again, she locked down that telltale moan. She repeated the stroke over his top lip, drawing the flesh between her teeth, sucking every bit of the wine from him.

His grip on her hips tightened, his fingers digging into her skin. What did it say about her that she secretly hoped he would mark her, leave a souvenir from this taboo and unwise pocket of time? Either that she was desperate or sad, or a total sucker for this man's possession.

Probably all three.

Shoving the distressing thought aside, she sank into the kiss, stroking her tongue between his lips, tangling with him, sliding against him, licking at him. That raw sandalwood, rain and Texas wind scent that clung to his skin was stronger here inside his mouth. Richer. Even more delicious. She could drown in his taste. Drown in this almost overwhelming sensation of heat, liquid lust and pleasure.

The moan she'd been so determined to rein in broke free, and she released the sound into his mouth. His tongue curled around it, claimed it as his own, and with a tilt of his head and a hard thrust, demanded another. And God help her, but she gave it to him. Surrendered it, along with the control she'd wielded but now wanted him to seize.

As if sensing the shift, he grabbed her ponytail, tugged hard on it, jerking her head back. Smoking lightning bolts of need struck her, and the whimper that escaped her would probably bring the sting of humiliation later, but not right now. Now she closed her eyes, relishing the sting across her scalp, dwelling in the sense of vulnerability from her exposed throat.

"If you're going to be sorry for this later," Ross murmured against her skin, his breath a hot, damp caress, "then I'm going to give you something to really regret."

Then he dragged his teeth down her neck, the slight burn

vibrating through her so it reverberated in her nipples, down her spine, in her sex. And when he clamped a firm, possessive bite on the crook where her neck and shoulder met…

"Ross," she groaned, loosening her clutch on the couch to burrow her fingers through his thick, dark blond hair, fisting it. Holding him to her.

"Missed that," he growled, rubbing his lips over the spot that had just received his teeth. "Missed the sound of my name when I'm about to give you what you need. And you need this, don't you, baby?"

She shuddered, her grasp on him tightening. The scraps of reason that still remained forbade her to answer, to give him this ammunition against her. But those remnants didn't stand a chance against the lust coursing swollen and unchecked through her body.

"Yes," she gasped. "Give it to me."

His dark chuckle tickled her skin, a faintly menacing warning wrapped in seductive, rough silk. "Ask for it. Nicely."

For real? She ground her teeth together, trapping the order to "get on with it." Because past experience had taught her that when he was in this kind of mood, a taunting mood where anger roiled just below the hunger, he could—would—drag out this pleasurable torture until she begged for what only he could deliver. An ecstasy that would break her.

"Ross, I need—" The word *you* lodged in her throat. But she didn't need *him*; she needed what he did to her body. Two different things as he'd so expertly shown her. "I need you to make me come."

"Damn right you do," he rasped, and hauling her head down, he crushed his mouth to hers.

This kiss was fire and ice. Gasoline and cooling water. A reunion and searing loss.

He ate at her lips, and she tilted her head, serving herself up. Leaving her mouth tender and wet, he dragged stinging kisses down her chin, lower to her neck and lower still to her collarbone. He paused, sucking the thin skin there between his lips, marking her. And she loved it. Silently urged him to suck harder, *longer*.

Impatient fingers gripped the bottom of her sweater and yanked it up and over her head. For a moment, panic flared bright inside her, and she almost lifted her hand to her neck. But then, she barely managed not going limp in relief. She'd removed the necklace and pendant before leaving the house. *Thank God.* What would his reaction be if he saw she'd kept it? She shook her head as if that could erase even the possibility.

"What's wrong? Where'd you go?" he murmured, tossing her top to the couch, leaving her clad in only a thin tank top and a black, scalloped lace bra. Being a chef who worked long hours, most of the time her body only knew chef coats, T-shirts and black pants. As a concession to the woman who loved fashion, she had an addiction for pretty underwear. And the desire flaring in those light eyes telegraphed his approval.

"Nothing," she replied, skimming her fingers over his shoulders and avoiding his gaze. "Nowhere."

He didn't call her on her bullshit; instead he slowly slid a hand up her side, rucking the tank top so the fire-warmed air brushed her exposed skin. She held her breath, her chest lifting and falling on her deep, labored breaths. Oh, God. It'd been so long. And she ached so much. *Touch me.* The words screamed in her head like a pissed-off banshee. *I need. I need. I need.*

The chant exploded in her head like pop rockets, quick, loud and bright.

His lips closed over her nipple. And she cried out. Jerked in his hold. Melted against him.

"Shh," he soothed, sweeping his lips over the tip through her thin top and bra.

They proved to be an insubstantial barrier to his tongue, his teeth, his passion. He drew on her, alternating with a quick lash and a lush lick. Big, capable hands cupped her, molded her, lifted her to his lips and plucked at the peak that hadn't received his mouth yet.

She sank onto his lap, her sex grinding against the steely length of his cock. With a ragged groan, she tipped her head back on her shoulders, clinging to his head and working his erection. Lust had a way of burning away good sense, shame and inhibition. And as she rode him, circling her hips, bucking against him, racing toward an ending that she would gladly fly into, she shed all of them.

With an impatient growl, Ross tugged down the top of her tank and her bra cup. That needy sound roughened as he bared her to his gaze and his mouth. He switched to her neglected breast, drawing it deep to grant it the same erotic attention, and she trembled, unable to tear her enraptured gaze from the sight of him loving her body. His hand slipped down her belly, not stopping at the waistband of her black leggings, but sliding underneath. Drifting lower... Until he stroked a caress over wet, aching flesh.

"Ross," she breathed, stiffening as pleasure arced through her, momentarily stunning her. His attention on her breasts—God, yes, it was good. But this? This light but firm strumming of the taut nerves cresting her sex? The delicious stroke between her swollen folds? This defied "good" and rammed straight into "exquisite."

"I need it," she pleaded, hips jerking and rolling in an uncontrolled rhythm. "I need it so badly. Please."

Hunger reduced pride to smoldering cinders. Desperation razed caution to the ground. She wanted this man with a desire that should've scared her. Maybe later, when lust didn't cloud her mind, it would. But not at this moment, with those elegant fingers swirling a diabolical caress around that sensitive nub. Not when she hovered on the verge of coming apart with him for the first time in three long years.

He hushed her, freeing her breast with a soft pop then reclaiming her mouth again. The indulgent thrust of his tongue, the luxurious tangle reflected his touch down below. He glided through her sex, fingers flirting with her entrance before slowly, deliberately pumping into her.

She cried into his mouth, and he greedily took it. On a rumble of pleasure, of approval, he withdrew, then stroked back into her, burying one then two fingers inside her grasping core. Pleasure spun, a crazy, blinding storm that built and built, threatening to sweep her away and never return her to who she'd been before she made the impulsive decision to start this.

Her fingers scrabbled at his shoulders, clutching at his head, as she held on for the inevitable climax. Yet, even as her hips bucked and ground against his hand, her body demanding more, she fought that ending. She feared never feeling this again, never *having* this again.

Pushing the thought aside, she buried her face in his throat and chanted soundless words against his skin. But maybe he heard them, because he thrust harder. Curled his fingertips against that high, soft-and-hard place so deep inside her.

And she surrendered.

To the pleasure. To the power. To the lust.

She shattered, and as his low, insistent and ragged voice urged her to fuck his fingers, to take everything, she threw herself into the fire, knowing she would emerge scarred, marked…

Changed.

And not for the better.

Nine

"Thank you for leaving work early to do this with me." Ross glanced across the middle console of his Aston Martin toward the silent woman perched on the passenger seat.

Charlotte stared out the window, her hands folded on top of her thighs, her spine poker straight. His gaze trailed over the tight bun of her hair, the almost fragile beauty of her profile and the sensual pout of her mouth. Clenching his jaw, he dragged his perusal back to the road where it belonged. Where it was safer for a number of reasons.

Aside from the obvious, with his attention focused squarely on driving, he couldn't stare at her and reminisce on how good that mouth had softened against his. How the flavor of her still lingered nearly two days later. How he could still feel the tight grip and flutter of her silken, hot sex on his fingers.

Jesus, she'd nearly burned him alive. The memories of how they'd been together hadn't compared to the reality of Charlotte in his arms, twisting on his lap, screaming in release. A shiver rippled through him, and he shifted on his seat, his body stirring, hardening. This was what she did to him. And it scared him what he'd do—what he'd give up— just for another chance to have her over him. Under him.

To be inside her.

"I agreed to go to the ranch with you and introduce Ben to your family," she murmured, yanking him from his thoughts. Thankful for the distraction, Ross checked the rearview mirror to see their son asleep in his car seat.

It was nine o'clock at night, which was past his bedtime. But when they returned from Telluride the day before, Rusty hadn't been in town. He'd just arrived this afternoon, and Ross didn't want to put this introduction off any longer. His father, Gina and Asher needed to meet his son, so they could all start on this road to being family. He didn't worry about his sister and brother as much as Rusty. But Ross clung to the hope that once his father laid eyes on this beautiful little boy, he would set aside his stubbornness and anger and embrace him as his grandson. Embrace Ben's mother, as well.

"Does Rusty know that we're coming?" she asked in that same even, flat tone that contained no emotion.

He tossed another glance in her direction. That note in her voice. It rubbed him the wrong way. As did her reluctance to even *visit* the ranch. He accepted her reasons for not wanting to live at his home, even if he still didn't agree with them. But something small, almost undecipherable continued to needle him like an irritating bee sting. Like there was more to her objection than she was telling him…

"Ross?"

He gave his head an abrupt shake. "Yes," he replied, his fingers curling around the steering wheel in a tighter grip. "I spoke with him earlier and told him we were coming over. And why."

"I hope this turns out the way you want," she said. "For your sake, I really do."

He didn't reply because the turnoff to Elegance Ranch appeared before him. Yet, it didn't prevent an ominous trickle from tripping down his spine. Shaking it off, he slowly drove to the big gate with its elegant scrolls of *E* and

R worked into the black iron, and lowered his visor. He and Rusty had experienced their difficulties and disagreements, but when it came down to it, family and the Edmond name meant more to his father than anything else. Rusty might threaten, but he'd never abandoned him like Ross's mother had. Grim assurance rolled through him as he pressed the button on the automatic gate opener. No, Rusty was guilty of a lot of things but he wouldn't—

"Son of a bitch," he growled. He jabbed the button again. But the gate remained shut. "He did it," he whispered, shock crackling through him on an electrified, discordant wave. "The bastard really did it."

Grief and anger crashed fast on the heels of the astonishment. Hadn't he just thought his father, who claimed family to be more important than everything, wouldn't cut him loose? Had Gina and Asher known what he'd planned? Would they abandon him, too?

A yawning vacuum opened inside his chest. *Alone.* He was alone, and the emptiness threatened to swallow him whole. In an instant of time, he was swept back to that ten year-old boy who watched his mother walk out of their house. This void had swamped him then, too, and he'd tried to fill it with the stingy love and approval of the only consistent parent he'd had left. And now he didn't even have that.

He'd been rejected, discarded.

Again.

"Ross, what's wrong?" A hand settled on his taut forearm, and only then did he realize that he had such a stranglehold on the steering wheel that his knuckles had blanched white. Peeling his hand free, he flexed the fingers, the blood rushing back into them with a tingle. He turned to Charlotte, who studied him in the deepening darkness, with a slight frown.

"I can't open the gate," he murmured, still staring at it as if at any moment it would belatedly swing open. He laughed, and the bitterness of it filled the interior. "He essentially changed the locks on me so I can't enter the property. My father kicked me out." Out of the house. Out of the family.

"Damn," she whispered. Her fingers curled around his arm, squeezing gently. "I'm sorry, Ross. I'm—"

"Doesn't matter," he cut her off, shifting the gear into Reverse and then hooking his arm over the back of her seat so he could turn the car around. At the same time, shaking off her touch. He couldn't handle her sympathy—her pity—right now.

Not when the betrayal, the fucking hurt, of the person who was supposed to love him, support him, *accept* him, tore at him with greedy, poisonous claws. The temptation to pull over, call Rusty and try to convince him to reconsider tugged at Ross. Hard. But Rusty had not only passed down his name to him. He'd bequeathed to Ross his stubbornness, as well. And Ross refused to beg his father for anything. Especially to let him come home.

He hadn't run after his mother.

He hadn't run after Charlotte.

Damned if he would with his father, either.

"Ross," Charlotte said, and her soft voice with its hint of worry scraped over his senses, leaving emotional welts.

"Sorry about needlessly taking you away from work. I'll drop you two back off at your house," he interrupted her again.

"Where will you go?"

He shrugged a shoulder, the gesture deliberately nonchalant. "I'll grab a hotel room for now. Doesn't matter." Goddamn, he was getting tired of saying those two words. Of *needing* to say them. "We planned on looking for a house together anyway."

Silence hummed in the car for several moments, and he could feel the weight of her speculation.

"We're going with you."

He whipped his head to the side, spearing her with a quick glance before returning his attention to the road. But that look had been enough to glimpse the resolve in her expression.

"No, that's not necessary," he said with a shake of his head.

"Maybe not, but we're still doing it."

"Charlotte—" he snapped.

"I'm not leaving you alone tonight," she murmured. "You were just cut off from your family several minutes ago. I know what that's like. To feel alone. Without the anchor you always counted on to be there." Her voice trailed off. But a second later, she cleared her throat. "So no, Ben and I are going with you. And tomorrow morning, we start the house search."

"I don't need your pity," he ground out.

Another beat of silence. "How about my friendship?"

The objection welled in his throat again and pushed onto his tongue. But that part of him…the part of him that constantly surrounded himself with people, parties, with *noise* because he hated the deafening and crushing silence of loneliness, smothered the prideful rejection.

"Okay."

Ross paced the sunken living room of the luxurious hotel suite, his fingers clasping the tumbler of scotch ferociously tight. Either as a desperate lifeline or a potential weapon, he couldn't decide at the moment. Maybe after several more sips, he could weigh in more decisively.

Thrusting his other hand through his hair, he stalked to the floor-to-ceiling glass wall and stared out over the lavish gardens that The Bellamy, Royal's five-star resort, boasted. Usually, when he had occasion to visit The Silver Saddle bar or enjoy fine farm-to-table dining at The Glass

House, both housed within the luxury hotel, he paused to appreciate its beauty. Inspired by George Vanderbilt's iconic French Renaissance chateau in North Carolina, Deacon Price and Shane Delgado had built its newer, hipper cousin. With over fifty acres of gorgeous gardens, a spa, two hundred and fifty richly appointed en suites that included the latest in technology and amenities, The Bellamy was a crown jewel in Royal.

And for the first time since stepping foot in the resort, his corporate credit card had been declined.

He downed another swallow of alcohol, the burn of it mingling with the fury that still seethed in his chest. Not only had his father banned him from the only home he'd ever known, but he'd cut him off financially. Trying to break him. To make him heel like a naughty puppy.

But he wasn't anyone's pet.

And he had resources and investments his father couldn't touch. He'd use those to purchase a home for him, his son and Charlotte.

And he also had the name Rusty had given him. Ross had used *that* to place this stay on his own tab.

Turned out the one thing that was so important to Rusty, he couldn't snatch away from Ross. He smirked down into the drink. The irony didn't escape him.

"Ben is asleep." Charlotte's voice reached him, wrapping around his chest, sinking into him. With his back to her, he briefly closed his eyes, savoring that low, husky tone. "Considering it's late, he didn't put up much of a fight." A small hand settled just below his shoulder blade. "Ross, are you okay?"

"I'm fine," he replied, not removing his stare from the amber alcohol.

She released an impatient sound that landed somewhere between a scoff and a tsk. "You're *not* fine. How could you be?" She moved in front of him, and he lifted his head, meeting the concern in her brown eyes. "Listen, I know we're feeling our way through being co-parents and possibly friends, but you can talk to me. Like you used to."

"That's when we were naked and sex had loosened my mouth," he drawled. Yes, he was being an asshole. But agreeing to her staying with him had been a bad decision. He was too on edge. Too angry. Too raw. And with her scent teasing his nose, her beautiful eyes on him and that gorgeous body close, he was too reckless.

She had every right to snap at him for his crass reply. Instead, she silently studied him. And like a coward, he turned away, striding back over to the bar to refresh his drink. And avoid that piercing scrutiny.

"Now who's spoiling for a fight?" she murmured, lobbing a variation of his words from the cabin back at him. "Classic Ross Edmond move," she taunted.

Bile churned in his gut, but he shoved it back down, nursing the bitterness. Anger was better than the emasculating need to curl his arms around her and lean on her, until not every breath he took carried the ache of loneliness. "Lash out. Hurt before they can hurt you. Push away so no one can see that you actually feel. You told me it was presumptuous of me to claim I knew you. But some things haven't changed in three years."

He didn't see her approach him again, but the thick, cream carpet couldn't muffle her footsteps. And the hand that, once more, rested on his shoulder blade seemed to singe him through his shirt, branding him.

His movements turned jerky, and a little of the scotch spilled over the rim of the glass as he splashed the alcohol into the tumbler. Quickly recapping the decanter and smacking it back down on the bar, he seized the drink and downed a big swallow.

Only then did he step away from her—from her and the

hand that he didn't want on his back. No, he wanted those delicate, skillful fingers farther south. Wrapped around him. Squeezing him and trading one pain for another.

"I don't want to fight, Charlotte. But I'm beginning to suspect maybe there's another reason you're out here pushing me. Maybe there's something you want from me other than…honesty," he said, sipping slower as he faced her. Making a show of scanning her from head to toe, his eyes drifted down the blue-and-white ruffled shirt and slim navy pants she'd changed into for the meeting with his family and to the tips of her black stilettos.

On the deliberate path back up all those delicious curves and dips, he struggled not to reveal how she affected him. Had him damn near trembling inside with the flare of heat and a need that burrowed deeper than simple lust. Fuck, what was he doing? What danger was he courting? In his current state, she was kindling thrown on an already simmering fire. It wouldn't require much for the flames to rage higher, hotter and out of control.

"You used to do that, too," she said, tilting her head to the side. If his words or perusal had offended her, she did an admirable job of concealing it.

"Do what?" he asked, interjecting a boredom into his voice that he hoped covered the razor-thin shards of panic cutting into him.

"Use sex to avoid a conversation."

"Oh, baby, if I were using sex you would know it." He rubbed his thumb over his bottom lip, smothering a groan as her gaze tracked the motion with a fascination that she would undoubtedly hate him for noticing. "Did you forget so easily? Do you need a refresher course? First, there wouldn't be a need for conversation. Not with that greedy little tongue of yours seeking mine out, tangling with me. Getting wild with me. The second hint would be those pretty but inconvenient clothes sliding off, revealing that dick tease of a body. Third would be the needy sound you make at the back of your throat when I kiss the tops of your breasts, suck on those hard nipples or cup that beautiful ass. Fourth would be the shiver that never fails to telegraph how close you are to coming. All it would take is a touch, a stroke over that tight, wet—"

"Stop," she rasped.

It should've been triumph that crackled through him as his gaze dropped to the rapid rise and fall of her chest. But the dark thing with claws tearing at him wasn't victory.

It was lust.

Hunger.

His plan to shut her up, to drive her away, had backfired.

Big-time.

"That's not a word you would be uttering," he rumbled, mimicking her previous action and cocking his head. "Not unless 'don't' preceded it. Don't stop. More. Harder," he recited. "That's the only conversation we'd have."

"Ross, you think I can't see you're upset? That you're hurting?" she stubbornly continued, even though those expressive brown eyes gleamed, and the tight points of her nipples jutted against her shirt.

"I never claimed I wasn't hurting," he drawled, setting the glass on the bar. He then shifted forward so close she tipped her head back to maintain eye contact. "Let me show you where."

He grasped her wrist and drew her hand forward, slowly enough that she had more than enough time to glean his intention. And that same amount of time to yank her arm back. But she didn't stop him as he pressed her palm to his cock. Didn't hiss an objection when he instinctively ground against it.

No, it was his curse that assaulted the air, his hand that threw hers off.

He who wheeled around and stalked across the room.

"Go to bed, Charlotte," he ordered, voice shredded, control not too far behind. "It's been a long day for both of us."

He needed her gone, preferably tucked away behind a locked door. With the imprint of her palm branded on his dick, he couldn't guarantee he could keep his hands off her. And nothing good would come of that. Not with desire and anger roiling inside him, urging him to wreck the tentative truce they'd forged with hot, filthy sex. Because there would be nothing cleansing about what he'd do to her. *Take her. Conquer her. Corrupt her.* That was the kind of fucking he'd indulge in and demand from her to sublimate this rage, this pain.

"Not until you talk to me."

He snarled, sharply pivoting and charging back across the room. *Calm. Keep your distance.* The judicious warnings whispered through his mind, but they were reduced to ash underneath the burning riot of emotions. He didn't stop when he approached her. Didn't halt until her back pressed against the window and his palms slapped on either side of her head, caging her between glass and his body.

"Why are you pushing this?" he growled, lowering his head until his lips grazed the curve of her ear. "What do you want to hear from me? That my father is a bastard? That he evicted me like some random tenant? That he cut me off, and I'm angry as hell? Yes, dammit. Are you happy? I'm shocked, furious and even a little scared. All of that. But he isn't the first person to walk away from me, Charlotte. I'm a fucking pro at this. So save the sympathy, the pity. I don't need them. What I *do* need is for you to take your sweet ass into that bedroom, lie down next to our son and leave me alone. For both our sakes."

He shoved off the window, air plowing out of his lungs. Dammit. He hadn't meant to say any of that. But her nearness, this unrelenting need and his hurt had propelled the words off his tongue, and not even God could turn back time to erase the too-revealing confession. Slowly he backed away from her, his narrowed gaze fixed on her face. A face that betrayed her surprise and, heaven help him, resolve.

He walked away. Again. Hell, if she wouldn't leave, he would. His pride had disintegrated and littered the floor around his feet. What was one more retreat?

Her hand circled his wrist.

And the last, tattered scraps of his control crumbled.

Turning, he simultaneously lunged for her, cupping her face between his hands, tilting her head back. Her fingers curled into his shirt, holding on. Probably to maintain her balance, since he leaned over her so far that her back arched, her full breasts pressing to his chest.

He shuddered.

"Goddammit, Charlotte," he bit out, lips moving over hers. "Leave now or stay and let me use you to pound out this…thing inside me. I won't be gentle—I can't be. I'll take from you, and I can't promise to give anything back. I want to feast on you and not stop until we're too broken to even breathe." He crushed a hard kiss to her mouth, thrusting between her lips in a quick taste-and-tangle that did nothing to satisfy the craving for her. "This is your chance to walk away now, baby. Because I can't."

Harsh puffs of air bathed his lips as her fingers encircled his wrists. But not to haul them away from her face. This brave, beautiful and *foolish* woman rose on her toes and took the next kiss. Opened wide for him. Allowed him entrance. Invited him to devour.

And on a groan heavy with desire, with demand—with gratitude—he accepted.

From the onset, the kiss consumed. Raw. Carnal. Ravenous. He went wild at her taste, diving back for more, always for more. Each lick, each slide of tongues, each rub of lips and bite of teeth ratcheted the desire consuming him to combustible levels. What was it about her that could transform him into this insatiable animal that was ready to snarl, claw and maul to keep her for himself?

Tonight, the last shred of reason interjected. This was just about here and now. Getting through the night. The only "forever" between him and Charlotte was Ben.

On the tail end of that thought, Ross sidestepped, maneuvering her so she backpedaled toward the couch. Without breaking the mating of their mouths, he guided her down to the cushion. As soon as she sat, he pushed between her legs, cupping her knees and spreading her wider to accommodate his torso.

He broke off the kiss, leaned back and watched his hands stroke up her toned, sexy legs, his fingertips skirting the crease where her thigh and upper body met. Didn't matter that she still wore her clothes. Her warmth seeped past the material to his skin, and he swore her rich fig-and-sugar scent was deeper, denser...headier. His gaze shifted higher, focusing on the cloth-covered flesh between her legs, and he slicked the tip of his tongue over his bottom lip. The source of that scent, that flavor emanated from right there.

And he wanted to gorge on it.

"If you really care about this shirt, you need to take it off now. I won't be as careful with it," he advised, raising his gaze from her sex to her face.

Her lips, swollen and damp from his kiss, parted, and a soft gust of breath eased past them. He almost leaned forward to feel that puff of air on his mouth, but he didn't. Couldn't risk missing her unveil herself for him.

Silence pulsed in the room, a thunderous heartbeat that nearly drowned out his own as he studied those elegant fingers move to the hidden buttons behind the ruffle that stretched from her throat to her waist. Quickly, she undid her shirt and peeled the two sides apart, revealing another of those sexy-as-hell confections others would call a bra.

Pale green this time. Silk and lace molded to her luscious breasts. His mouth watered for a taste. And he didn't wait for her to shrug completely free of it before bowing over her and sucking a nipple deep into his mouth.

With a hushed curse, she battled the cuffs of her shirt, and he took advantage of her bound hands, cupping one breast, pinching the tip, rolling it while tonguing the other. Her tortured whimper mingled with his groan, and then her fingernails were scraping across his scalp, and he was popping the bra's front closure and freeing her.

Jesus. She was too fucking beautiful for words.

Switching breasts, he nuzzled the other mound, licking a path toward the peak. She arched into him, urging him on with whispered chants of his name, pressing his head to her, lowering a hand and closing it over his, so they squeezed and caressed together.

"Damn, I can't get enough of you," he muttered, brushing his lips over her wet nipple, then trailing a path punctuated by stinging kisses down her softly rounded stomach, pausing to trace the faint stretch marks over her skin. Marks that gave testimony to the precious life she'd brought into this world.

"Ross," she breathed, her fingers massaging his scalp, tugging at his hair. Trying to get him to look at her.

But he refused, couldn't. To do that, to gaze into those chocolate eyes, might trick him into believing this wasn't just a physical release. No, he wanted to get lost in her body, in the pleasure, not silly, deceptive notions of *more*. He skimmed one more caress over the light lines on her stomach, then continued lower. And when his lips bumped the waistband of her pants, he didn't hesitate to pop the closure, unzip and tug them down and off her.

For a moment, he froze. Drinking her in. All that smooth, silken almond skin clad in only green lace. And then, with one yank, not even that.

"Baby," he growled, raking his teeth across her hip. She jerked, a low cry escaping her. "Easy," he soothed, sweeping his tongue across the same path. "Hold on to me."

He issued the command, palming her inner thighs and spreading her wider. On a dark, hungry snarl, he dove into her. He barely heard her sharp scream, almost didn't feel the bite of her nails in his shoulders. Everything in him focused on her concentrated scent, the addictive taste and her slick flesh. God, he tried to slow down, to invoke the control he was known for. But that proved impossible. With each lap, suckle and swirl of his tongue and lips, he lost more of himself. And in that moment, his sole purpose became bringing her pleasure. Hearing her voice break on his name. Feeling that flutter of her muscles around the fingers he slid inside her.

Her hands grabbed his head, her hips undulating in a wild rhythm that seemed to demand and beg for the release she hovered on the verge of. With a purse of his lips over the stiff nub of flesh cresting the top of her sex and two hard thrusts into her, she toppled into that release. Trembling thighs squeezed his head. Pleasure-thick cries spilled into the room. Her flavor flowed onto his tongue.

This was heaven, his place of sanctuary.

Nothing could touch him here while he was between her legs.

Hunger surged hotter, fiercer inside him, churning in his gut, pounding in his cock. In lightning-quick movements, he stripped his clothes off, only pausing to grab his wallet and remove a condom from it.

He palmed the protection, and though his body roared for relief, to be buried deep inside the flesh his mouth and fingers had just enjoyed, he didn't rip the foil open. Lifting his gaze to hers, he cupped her cheek and rubbed his thumb over her bottom lip. God, he couldn't get enough of her mouth. To prove it, he leaned forward and, as gently as the lust raging through him would allow, kissed her.

"You can get up and leave if this isn't what you want," he offered, though if she backed out, he might just lose his mind.

"I want this," she whispered, shifting her hand to his dick. Giving him a tight, hard squeeze that propelled the breath from his lungs. He briefly closed his eyes and ground his teeth, giving himself over to the pleasure that careened through him at the long strokes of her hand. "I want you inside me."

He carefully nudged her hand aside and tore open the condom wrapper, swiftly sheathing himself. Weaving their fingers together and nabbing a pillow, he guided her off the couch to the floor. The plush carpet cushioned his knees as he crouched over her. Brown eyes steadily met his, and he didn't look away as he fisted his cock and notched himself at her entrance. He watched her, studying her features for any sign of discomfort, of pain. But she didn't flinch as he pressed deeper, surging forward. No, it was he who closed his eyes as the wet, tight heat of her parted for him, embraced him. *Broke* him.

He shuddered, fighting not to plunge inside her, to rut over her like a beast concerned with only his own gratification. Jesus, he wasn't even all the way inside her, and he shook with the need to come.

"Ross." Charlotte slid a hand over his tense shoulder, up the side of his neck and cradled his jaw. "Look at me." He lifted his lashes, and the sight of her damp lips, flushed cheeks and glazed eyes worsened the struggle for control. "I'm not fragile. Take what you need from me. I can handle it."

He blew out a hard, ragged breath, buried his face in the crook of her neck—and slammed inside her.

Twin moans filled the room, his dark rumble and her

lighter whimper. Fuck, she… A tremble worked over him. She was so damn perfect. Strong. Delicate. Wet. Hot. She was *everything*.

With a growl he couldn't contain, he drew his hips back and thrust forward, powering into her in a greedy stroke. She rose to meet him, her legs wrapping around his hips, and he burrowed impossibly deeper. Palming her ass, he lifted her into him, riding her, grinding into her, burying himself over and over because he couldn't bear not being balls deep inside the heart of her.

She chanted his name, her nails digging into his back, scratching him. *Marking* him. Yes. God, yes. He wanted that physical claim of ownership—

He shook his head, his mind rebelling at the thought even as he owned her body. Not ownership. Pleasure. He wanted the physical evidence that he could render her mindless with his touch, his cock. Nothing else mattered.

Gritting his teeth, he levered off her, sliding his arms underneath her thighs and hiking them higher, spreading her wider. He pistoned into her, the sound of damp skin slapping together, of his grunts and her moans littering the air. Electric currents sizzled and snapped up and down his spine, even the soles of his feet. But he held on, fought the surge of ecstasy that heralded an orgasm that might take him out of here. Not without her, though.

Reaching between them, he swept his thumb over the top of her sex, circling the little nub of flesh. Circling, then pressing. Hard.

Charlotte stiffened, her back arching hard, her beautiful breasts pointed toward the ceiling. Unable to resist the lure of them, he bowed over her, sucking a nipple deep, thrusting and riding out the orgasm that clutched her in its powerful grasp. A strangled cry escaped her, and she shook, her sex clamping down on him in a bruising grip.

Yes, dammit. He wanted to be bruised, to still feel that steel-and-silk clasp tomorrow.

As her tremors started to subside, he gave his own needs free rein. Releasing her breast with a soft pop, he reared back and let go. Each thrust shoved him closer to that crumbling, death-defying edge. Until he just leaped. Bone-cracking pleasure punched into him, and as the orgasm barreled over him, he didn't fight it.

Didn't fight the rapture.

Didn't fight her.

Didn't fight himself.

He surrendered, and for tonight—for this moment—it was all right.

Ten

Ross stood at the window of the Texas Cattleman's Club meeting room, and a sense of déjà vu whispered over him. Hell, had it only been a few weeks since he'd stood here with his father, siblings and Billy, signing the contract for Soiree on the Bay? So much had happened since then. He'd bumped into the woman who'd haunted him for three years, had discovered he was a father and had been disinherited. He shook his head. And to think, when he'd been finalizing those documents, all he'd seen ahead of him was money, success and partying.

Scoffing lightly, he turned and headed to the serving set the club staff had laid out on the small conference table. He poured himself a cup of coffee and sipped, glancing down at his watch. A couple of minutes before one. His stomach twisted, and he clenched his jaw. Another thing that had changed. Never had nerves attacked him at the thought of seeing his sister and brother. They were his best friends— no, more than that. When people survived wars together, that made them closer than blood because their relationship was forged in conflict, battle and grief. Rusty's marriages and divorces had been combat they'd endured, their childhood the battlefield where the three of them had bonded.

But in the week since Rusty had disinherited Ross, he

hadn't heard much from his brother and sister. Most of that distance could be placed on his own shoulders. He'd been so busy finding a home for Charlotte, Ben and himself as well as shoring up his own financial resources that he hadn't prioritized sitting down and talking with them. Also, a part of him had subconsciously put off this meeting. Because that part feared where they stood in this face-off between him and Rusty. Gina and Asher had always been his allies, but at the risk of incurring Rusty's wrath?

He didn't know. And he dreaded finding out.

The door to the room opened, and Gina and Asher walked in. Ross stood at the end of the table, tension drawing him tight, unfamiliar indecision humming through him. He studied their faces, searching for…what? Anger? Sadness? Resignation? Did they resent him for making them choose a side…

"Dammit, Ross," Gina snapped, striding forward and not stopping until she threw her arms around him and held on. Relief poured out of him like a geyser, almost sapping his strength. He wrapped his sister in an embrace that was probably too tight, but he couldn't ease up. Not when he'd never been so grateful for a hug. "Where the hell have you been?" A smile curved his mouth at her muffled scolding. "We've been worried sick about how you've been doing, and all we can get out of you is a 'fine' or an 'I'll call you back.' Which you don't do, by the way."

Gina tilted her head back, glaring at him. "Good thing you arranged this meeting because I was ready to storm The Bellamy." She lightly punched him in the arm. "And thank goodness for the Royal gossip hotline or I wouldn't even have known where you were staying."

"She was actually ready to barge in five days ago," Asher added, voice dry but holding an unmistakable affection for their sister. "I convinced her to wait since you had a lot going on—you know, new family and being disinherited—but we didn't intend on waiting too much longer."

Asher clapped Ross on the shoulder, giving it a brief squeeze. His tone might have been amused, but concern darkened his brown eyes. Ross gave him a small nod, which his brother returned before picking up a cup and pouring coffee into it.

"Gina, quit making like a clingy octopus and release Ross. Here." He passed her the cup and fixed another for himself, a brief grin flashing across his face as she switched the glare from Ross to him. "Okay, Ross. Tell us what the hell is going on. We've heard Dad's rant about your ungratefulness, stupidity, disloyalty to family and being led around by your dick." He sipped the fragrant brew. "Now, what's the truth?"

Ross arched an eyebrow, that vise around his chest loosening at his brother's sardonic words. "How do you know that's not the truth?"

Asher snorted. "When Rusty starts trying to curry favor with me instead of treating me like the unwanted, red-headed stepchild, then I know he's full of shit. And he wants something. That something being getting me on his side to pressure you into caving and falling back into line. Which, even if you weren't my brother, would've put me firmly in your camp."

"Same here. Since you've been banned from the office, he's acting like he actually cares about my input on business decisions. When we both know he doesn't respect my opinions—never has. He's in full-on bribe mode." Gina shook her head, disgust curling her mouth. "As if we're so stupid we can't see right through his manipulations."

Or desperate enough for his attention and his approval that they would turn on him. That was how Rusty Edmond operated in business and with his children.

"So give," Gina prodded. "And start from why we're just finding out we're an aunt and uncle."

Ross did as they requested. And with the two people he trusted most in the world, he confessed everything that had happened since that moment he and Billy had spotted Charlotte in Sheen. By the time he finished with discovering he'd been locked out of the ranch, his credit canceled and then being swiftly tossed out of the family business, they'd all sunk onto the couch in the meeting room's small sitting area.

"If I doubted Dad's seriousness, the package he had delivered to The Bellamy would've confirmed it. It included a letter stating I was not welcome at Elegance Ranch and fired from The Edmond Organization, along with the newest copy of his will with me cut out of it. Congratulations, by the way." He shifted his gaze from the empty coffee cup to shoot his sister a wry smile. "You're now the recipient of the majority shares of the company and his estate."

"Awesome," she drawled. But no humor lightened her troubled gaze. "A son, Ross. You have a little boy," she whispered. "How are you handling that?"

He inhaled a breath, then slowly released it, leaning back against the chair. "Gina, Ben is…" He shook his head, his first real smile of the day curving his mouth. "He's beautiful. And amazing. At two, he's so smart and funny. I didn't think I could love someone so quick and so much. But…" He swallowed. "I do. Crazy, I know."

"No, not crazy." Gina covered his hand with hers, eyes gleaming. "You just sound like a father. And I'm so happy for you."

"I am, too," Asher said, leaning forward in his chair and perching his forearms on his thighs. "And what about Charlotte? How do you feel about her?"

Ross didn't reply; instead, he stood and crossed the room back to the table and the serving set. Yes, he freely admitted to stalling a reply to his brother's question. Because while his love for his son was uncomplicated and easy, his feelings toward Charlotte weren't nearly as cut and dried. Did he love her? No, because in order to love someone, to make a commitment to them, you had to trust them. And as much as his dick hardened for her, he didn't trust her.

But the need for her, the lust that hadn't abated just because he'd been inside her again... That muddied what should've been a simple co-parenting arrangement. Instead of satisfying his craving for her, that night at The Bellamy had only intensified it. And though he could list a thousand reasons why he should maintain a platonic relationship with Charlotte, he hadn't heeded them. Neither of them had. They hadn't discussed the ramifications of continuing a co-parenting-with-benefits arrangement, but each night that he stayed at the house with her and Ben or they came to him at the resort, they gave in to the need.

If he was a better man, he wouldn't take advantage. If he was a prouder man, he would demand more of himself. But when it came to Charlotte Jarrett, he was neither.

"She's Ben's mother," he finally said, staring at the dark stream of brew as it flowed into his cup. "We've come to an arrangement that works for both of us. For the next year, we're going to give living together a try. After that, we'll see."

"Now you know that's not what he was asking." Gina snorted. "But that nonanswer was answer enough." Moments later, she appeared at his elbow, cupping it. "What about Dad? Do you plan on trying to approach him again? In case we haven't made it clear, Asher and I are on your side. Just tell us what you need from us."

Ross encircled his sister's shoulder, giving her a small hug of gratitude. "Thank you for that. Both of you," he added, glancing over his shoulder at Asher, who rose from his chair. "But I don't want you to get involved. This is between me and Dad. I don't want you to be casualties in the fallout."

"How are you doing moneywise?" Asher interjected when Gina frowned and parted her lips, prepared to object to Ross's request. He joined them at the table and shot their sister a look, gently shaking his head. "Can we help you there?"

"No, I'm good," Ross said, grateful for his brother's intervention. He meant it; he didn't want his brother and sister's lives affected by his decisions. Rusty could be vindictive, and though Asher was older than Ross, he had to protect him and Gina from their father's possible retaliation. "I have investments in several companies, stock and connections that aren't tangled up in The Edmond Organization. And I still have Soiree on the Bay. The contracts have been signed. Dad can't kick me out of that like he did from the company."

If anything, being fired had forced Ross to rely only on himself. Thank God, he'd diversified his own funds years ago, not living completely off the family business. He wasn't a pauper by any stretch of the imagination. Hell, according to his financial portfolio, he was still a millionaire in his own right. But... Unease coiled inside his chest. But he might not have enough on-hand cash to pay Charlotte the five hundred thousand he'd promised her.

"I hate that you're going through this," Gina hissed, crossing her arms over her chest. "While I'm pissed at Dad, I can't say I'm surprised. Just look how he treated Mom when she dared to defy him."

Ross stiffened, an old but very familiar anger kindling in his veins. "This situation is completely different from that."

"Not by much," his sister argued. "She asked Dad for a divorce, and he went after her with everything he had. Forget that she was the mother of his children. He kicked her out of her house, changed the locks, made it difficult for her to see her children. He took everything that was important from her."

"She chose a big settlement over her children," he snapped. "No one forced her to leave Royal, to leave us. She divorced Dad, not us. I've only had Ben in my life for a matter of weeks, but I would do anything for that little boy. Destroy anyone who tried to hurt him. You fight for those you love. *Sarabeth*," he uttered her name on a mocking sneer, because she hadn't been Mom to him a long time, "chose to walk away. To not be in our lives except for the occasional visit or phone call. If she truly wanted to be there for us, no power in this world, including the long arm of Rusty Edmond, could've kept her away. So no, it's not similar at all."

Asher edged closer to their sister, clasping her hand in his, and Ross pivoted away, suddenly feeling like an ogre. His issues with his mother were just that—his issues. He had no right to jump down Gina's throat because she chose to see the woman who'd essentially abandoned them in a kinder light.

"When was the last time you saw her, Ross? Spoke to her?" Gina asked softly.

"Years. And I'm fine with maintaining the status quo."

"You should call her. Talk to her. I think you would be surprised with the answers she could give you."

Answers? Could her *answers* turn back time and give him her much-needed presence in his life? Could they make up for her absence? For her rejection of him? For making him question his own self-worth? How could he be worthy of anything when the two people who were supposed to love him unconditionally had rejected him at every turn? His mother had chosen freedom over him, and his father— fuck, Rusty was Rusty. Everything had come before Ross, Gina and Asher. Business, women, a goddamn prize bull.

The man had missed Ross's college graduation because of a cattle sale. And now, he put his pride before his son.

No. He didn't need to ask Sarabeth anything. Her absence and Rusty's emotional deprivation had been enough of a very thorough explanation.

"I'm through talking about her," Ross said, a sudden bone-deep weariness creeping into his voice. "Do you two want to meet your nephew?"

He'd brought Ben with him to the clubhouse and left him in the day care while he met with Gina and Asher.

"Of course." Gina crossed over to him and wrapped him in a hug. "I'm sorry for bringing up Mom and pressuring you," she murmured.

"No worries." He pressed a kiss to the top of her head.

"Let's go," Asher said. "I want to officially meet my nephew. You said he's beautiful. So that means he must take after his mother."

Ross met his brother's smirk and grinned. "Asshole."

Asher laughed, pulling the meeting room door open. "Well, that's a family trait, so let's *really* hope he takes after his mother."

Gina gasped in mock outrage. "I beg your pardon," she objected as she swept past Asher into the hallway. "Speak for yourself. I merely know my own mind and am not afraid to let others know it, as well."

Asher tilted his head. "Huh. When I do that, I'm always called an asshole."

Ross chuckled, following his brother and sister—his family—toward the front of the building.

God, he loved them.

Eleven

"This is ridiculous," Charlotte grumbled, staring at herself in the closet mirror.

Hah. As if the space that was bigger than her bedroom in her former home could be called something as simple as a *closet*. She didn't even have enough clothes to fill all the drawers, racks and hangers. Not to mention the stacks of mini cases meant to store jewelry. Besides the pair of diamond studs that was a graduation gift from her parents and the necklace Ross had given her, she only owned costume jewelry that would look laughable in those boxes.

Speaking of the necklace… She grazed fingertips over the heart-shaped pendant, then removed it, laying it on the island behind her. So far, she'd done a good job of keeping it hidden from Ross even though they now lived together.

And slept together.

No, that wasn't exactly correct.

They had sex and then went their separate ways to their separate bedrooms.

Then, in the morning, they pretended they were nothing more than Ben's parents. Cordial strangers who happened to share the same space. Sometime between his meeting with his brother and sister at the TCC clubhouse and that evening when she'd returned home from work, he'd grown distant, unfailingly polite—colder. But just with her.

With Ben, he was simply wonderful. After Ben was born, and Charlotte had faced those nights of midnight feedings, crying, explosive diapers and runny noses alone, she'd wondered how different things could've been if Ross were there. If she'd had someone to share the load. And now she didn't have to imagine. As aloof as he was with her, Ross poured all of his affection into their son. Even her parents, who'd been understandably shocked and confused when she'd confessed about Ross being Ben's father, respected Ross for how he'd stepped up and taken to parenthood with an obvious enthusiasm. Though Charlotte's unease about forever being connected in some way to Rusty and her fear of his retaliation hadn't faded, she couldn't deny Ben adored his father.

She also couldn't deny her growing feelings for Ross.

Stupid. Stupid. Stupid.

She mentally slapped her palm to her forehead over and over. As if that could shake some latent sense of self-preservation loose.

What was it with her continually falling for the same unavailable and totally inappropriate man? What did that say about her? What was it about herself that made her believe she wasn't worthy of a man who would put her first, be proud to claim her as his own, be fully committed to her?

For most of her life, she'd longed for a relationship like her parents. Total devotion. Yet, the first time she'd fallen in love, it was with a man who'd been okay with keeping her a secret from his family, his friends, the world. Yes, she'd had her reasons for agreeing to the clandestine affair, too. But deep inside, where the most vulnerable desires of her heart hid, she'd longed for him to say, "fuck that," and shout his delight in being with her to anyone who would listen. Just as she'd longed for him to stop her from going to California, to ask her to stay for him. For *them*.

She'd promised herself she'd never place herself in that predicament again. But now, here she stood. In a gorgeous home she could never afford on her own, in the exclusive, gated community of Pine Valley, living with Ross Edmond as his baby's mother. Falling for the same man again.

And her love for him was still a secret.

"You look beautiful."

Her head jerked up, heart pounding a double-time cadence. Ross leaned against the doorway, a shoulder propped against the jamb, hands in the pockets of his black tuxedo pants. As if her body had a "clap on" switch, just the sight of him had her belly clenching, lust lighting up her veins like the Vegas strip, and her sex pulsing.

Dammit. She returned her gaze to her reflection in the mirror, but that didn't eradicate the image of him from her brain. Dirty blond hair tamed and waving away from his stunning face erected of strong, arrogant angles and carnal curves. Tall, big body clothed in a white shirt, bow tie and pants that showcased the lean, muscular perfection of his frame. She intimately knew the strength of that body. Knew how he could restrain and unleash its power.

A curl of heat spiraled through her, whispering over her nipples and winding down to the empty, aching flesh between her thighs. Deliberately, she reminded herself that he'd probably uttered those same words to hundreds of women.

The compliment wasn't anything special to him—and neither was she.

"Thank you," she said, giving herself a mental fist pump when her voice emerged even, unaffected. "Although that has more to do with the dress—which you would know since you had it sent over," she added dryly.

The deep purple, sequin-embellished, floor-length gown

skimmed over her curves like a lover's caress. The wide dolman-style sleeves cuffed at her wrists, and the neckline plunged to a point beneath her breasts. A skinny belt of the same material cinched her middle, emphasizing the indent of her waist.

It was the most beautiful, expensive thing she'd ever owned besides the necklace he'd given her.

He moved fully into the closet and appeared behind her in the mirror. At five foot eight, she wasn't a short woman, but he dwarfed her. And then quickly, a visual of them from the night before flashed in her head. Her, on her hands and knees. Him, behind her, covering her...

She briefly closed her eyes, but the image burned brighter, hotter. When she opened her eyes, they clashed with Ross's hooded, ice-blue gaze. No, not ice. Heat and smoke.

Tension filled the closet, winding around them, and she could feel the stroke of his perusal over the skin bared by the daring neckline. She tried to smother the shiver working its way through her body. Tried and failed.

Apprehension that was purely feminine flared inside her, and she could do nothing but watch him. Wait for his next move. Half hope, half dread he would strip her of the dress and take her down to the closet floor and ease the sensual pain spasming in her sex.

Strip her of her dignity while he was at it.

"What's ridiculous?" he asked.

She blinked. Relief and disappointment cascaded through her, and she quickly recovered, running their conversation back in her head and realizing he must've been standing in the closet doorway longer than she'd noticed.

"All of this." She waved a hand from the top of her hair, which the stylist had fashioned into an elegant yet edgy Mohawk, and down her body, encompassing the gown. "I'm a chef. Not a socialite. I should be at my restaurant, cooking on a Saturday night, not attending some party. The most talking I do is giving orders in the kitchen and meeting customers tableside. And even then, I try to keep it as short as possible. This—" she once more flicked a hand up and down her frame "—isn't me."

"How do you know?" he countered, shifting closer so his chest brushed her spine. "Maybe this is just an aspect of who you are. Your dream is to become a master chef. That could take you around the world, to television, to endorsements. And all of that requires socializing with people, selling yourself. Consider this a training ground for the future." His words painted a picture she'd dreamed of, craved. She lifted her gaze from her neckline to meet his eyes. Did he believe she could obtain that future? Did he believe in…her? A merciless hand squeezed her heart, and she silently cursed herself for even caring about his opinion—caring about his esteem. She *was* enough, dammit!

"And Jeremy obviously thinks the same, since he approved and fully supported you attending this *party*." His lips twisted into a sardonic smile around her terminology for the swank event scheduled for this evening. "He understands you are the face of Sheen and the connection with Soiree on the Bay will only increase his profile in Royal as well as nationally, perhaps internationally."

He skimmed the backs of his fingers down her cheek, dropping to caress her throat before lowering his arm back to his side. Her skin pulsed and tingled from the contact as if it'd been sunburned.

"Besides, Brett Harston, Lila Jones and Valencia Donovan will be there," he added, referring to the other members of the advisory board.

Since joining the board, Charlotte had become friends with the other members. She snorted. If anyone had told her just a month ago that she could claim a self-made millionaire, a Chamber of Commerce employee and the founder of a charity as friends, she would've escorted them to a waiting Uber with an admonition about drinking too much.

But here she was, chummy with members of Royal high society, wearing a gown that probably cost more than her car down payment, and getting ready to attend an event at the famed Texas Cattleman's Club.

She sighed, about to rub her damp palms down her thighs, but catching herself at the last minute. *This dress isn't your food-splattered chef jacket*, she silently scolded.

"Well, I'm as ready as I'll ev—"

"What's this?"

She turned at Ross's harsh bark, and her throat spasmed, trapping her breath. Seemingly of their own accord, her fingers drifted to her bare neck, where the necklace currently clenched in his fist had rested minutes earlier.

"I—" She couldn't squeeze anything else past her constricted throat.

God, she'd been so careful. Hadn't expected him to show up in her room or her closet. But none of her intentions mattered now. Not with that arctic glare pinning her to the spot and his body so taut he practically vibrated with the blast of frigid rage rolling off him.

"Why do you still have this?" he demanded in a low, dark tone that rumbled with…emotion. Not just anger. Something else—something almost raw—threaded through it. And though she couldn't identify it, she trembled underneath it. "Charlotte," Ross growled.

She jerked at the sound of her name, dragging her gaze from the dangling pendant and chain to once more meet his stare. And try not to flinch from it.

"It's mine," she said. "You gave it to me."

"I know that, dammit," he snapped. "I remember everything I ever gave you. *Everything*. And when you ran away to California, you left it all. I went into the guesthouse afterward. It was empty except for all of the earrings, bracelets, clothes I'd given you. Like they were a message you wanted to make sure I received. That they—like me—meant nothing. Just trash to throw away once you were done with them."

With me.

He didn't utter those two words, but they echoed between them as if they'd been shouted at the top of his lungs.

"That's not true," she whispered. Leaving those things behind had been a desperate act of self-protection. It had been her survival instinct kicking in. She couldn't take any reminder of him with her to California. Because they would've been torture, constant souvenirs from a time when she'd been at her happiest—when she'd been fatalistically and foolishly in love. She couldn't keep those pieces of him and make a new life for herself absent of him.

Little had she known that she'd left with the most permanent of reminders inside her.

"Then what is the truth? Did this accidentally make the journey to California?" He chuckled, the serrated edge of it pricking her skin, her heart.

"Actually, yes," she admitted. "I didn't know it was in my suitcase until I arrived there." She clearly remembered that moment when she'd found the jewelry in her carry-on. Remembered how she'd broken down, curled on the bed, clutching it to her chest. How ironic that the pendant was heart-shaped, when hers had been shattered so completely.

"And yet you kept it? Why not pawn it? Believe me, it would've brought you a pretty penny. Several hundred thousand of them," he scoffed, the corner of his mouth pulling into a cruel smile. "Why, Charlotte? For once, give me a straight answer."

"What are you angry at, Ross?" she asked, forcing herself to face that stare that both froze her blood and heated it. "Why do you care?"

"You left," he accused in a low roar.

And there it was. The crux of why he would never for-give her. Not for having a baby he'd known nothing about. Not for missing out on two years of his son's life. No, she'd had the audacity to walk away from him before he could do the honors. To take his favorite toy of the moment away from him when he hadn't been finished playing.

If her heart hadn't already been battered, scarred and calcified, it might've broken all over again.

"I'm sorry," she replied, and surprise flickered in his narrowed stare. "I apologize for not remaining in Royal as your dirty secret. Please forgive me for being exhausted with remaining here as someone you hid out of shame."

She drew her shoulders back and tilted her chin higher, desperately grasping for an aloof mask that concealed the pain throbbing inside her like an open wound.

"You want a straight answer? Okay. You're right. I could've thrown the necklace away or pawned it. God knows the money I could've gotten for it would've helped. But I didn't. I kept it because every time I saw it, touched it, I remembered that for almost a year I allowed myself to be involved in an affair that demeaned me. That I lowered my personal standards to become the plaything of a man who deemed me good enough for a fuck but not to escort past the kitchen. Every time I wear that necklace it's a reminder to myself to never repeat that mistake. A reminder that I'm worth more than being a receptacle for a rich man's lust."

The air crackled with their fury, her hurt, her pain. The bitterness of her words lay acrid on her tongue, leaving a grimy residue that no amount of mouthwash—or apolo-gies—could rinse clean.

I didn't mean it.

The cry screamed inside her like a banshee. It wailed in her head, begging her to say it. But she couldn't. Be-cause part of her—that lonely, pregnant woman who'd felt betrayed by the man she'd loved—had meant every festering word.

"At least we know where we stand with each other," Ross finally said into the thick, deafening silence. "Here." He dropped the necklace on the island, the pendant clacking against the marble top. "I wouldn't want you to lose it." Turning on his heel, he strode toward the closet door. And she curled her fingers into her palms, convincing herself she didn't want to stroke the rigid line of his spine. Or brush a caress over the perfectly cut hair above the collar of his shirt. "Let me know when you're ready. We can't be late," he instructed without glancing back at her.

Then he disappeared through the door, leaving her alone.

Except for the echo of her cruel words.

Twelve

"How're you enjoying yourself, Charlotte?" Billy Holmes appeared at her elbow, holding two glasses of wine.

Giving Ross's friend and business partner a smile, she accepted one of the flutes and immediately sipped. Alcoholic fortification was an absolute must to get through this night.

"What's not to enjoy?" she replied, glancing around the crowded, cavernous great room.

Whoever Ross and Billy hired to decorate needed a fat tip. The designer had turned what could've been an austere room with its cross-beamed cathedral ceiling and dark wood floors into a winter wonderland. White lights and flowers with boughs of greenery wound around tall pillars and along the massive fireplace. Crystal centerpieces adorned the round tables and mini trees painted white, and entwined with more lights, added an almost fairy-tale air. And strategically placed in all that ethereal beauty were brochures, pamphlets and even samples from Soiree on the Bay's attending vendors, sponsors and the charities benefiting from the donations. Before she'd left work earlier, she'd overseen the samples from Sheen—an Alaskan king crab cake with a sweet and spicy roulade sauce and squares of ham, feta and sweet potato quiche.

Last time she'd checked, there'd only been a few dishes left of each.

As if reading her mind, Billy murmured, "Great wine. Great food." He cocked his head. "Your samples have disappeared, and dinner hasn't even been served yet. I'd claim that as a ringing endorsement of Sheen and its chef. Congratulations." He toasted her with his glass and grinned, his blue eyes gleaming. "Far be it from me to brag, but I unashamedly accept full credit for bringing you into the fold."

Charlotte chuckled. "Well, I'm so glad you're above an 'I told you so,'" she drawled. "I admit, I had my reservations about joining the festival, but they've mostly been laid to rest. This is a great move for Sheen."

"And for you, Charlotte," Billy added, briefly cupping her elbow before dropping his arm back to his side. "A restaurant is only as strong as its chef, and your reputation as an extraordinary culinary artist precedes you. So thank you for taking a leap with us."

She nodded, unsure how to respond to the outpouring of praise. Ross's words from earlier floated through her head. *Consider this a training ground for the future.* According to him, she belonged here, receiving compliments as her due.

Of course, that had been before the blowup that had decimated all the ground they'd recovered.

Billy cleared his throat, and stared down into his glass, lightly swirling the wine. "Charlotte," he murmured, lifting his head to meet her gaze. "I don't mean to pry, but Ross is my best friend. And I can't help but notice there seems to be some—" he hesitated "—*distance* between you two tonight. Is everything okay?"

The "We're fine" danced on her tongue, but it lodged in her throat, the lie refusing to be uttered. Instead, she avoided that concerned scrutiny under the pretense of surveying the room. And inevitably, her perusal landed on Ross. Surrounded by his brother, sister and a small crowd, he appeared to be the charming, charismatic playboy she'd always known. Not a care in the world. As she watched, a beautiful brunette in a slinky gold dress inched up to his side and laid a hand on his arm. He bowed his head over her, and—

Nope. She turned away, raising her glass for a healthy gulp of wine. Not even going to do it to herself.

"That's the daughter of one of our largest investors besides The Edmond Organization. Believe me, there's nothing inappropriate going on between them," Billy said, his gentle tone almost painful.

Was she that obvious?

How could Ross's friend see what she tried so hard to hide?

"Doesn't matter," she replied, and the smile she forced felt brittle to her own self. "Ross and I are just co-parents. He's free to do whatever—or whomever—he wants."

"As long as I've known Ross, things have seemed to come easy to him. Most definitely because of his last name and family. Then add in his looks, which would make a lesser man completely insecure," he said, flashing her a smile, "and a magnetism that just seems to draw people to him, and he hasn't had to struggle. Not that I'm implying he isn't a hard worker, because he is. But it hasn't been until you came back to Royal and he learned about Ben that he's been truly challenged for the first time in his life. And he's risen to it. Being a father has given him new purpose, and yet, I can't imagine how scary all of this must be for him. So please, as his friend, I'm asking you not to give up on him. You and Ben, you're good for him."

"Yes, we're so good for Ross that his father disinherited him because of us," she said, battling back the warmth that skated too close to hope. "Did you see the two of them tonight? Rusty barely spared Ross a glance."

Billy sighed, slipping a hand in his front pocket. "I admire Rusty. He's a brilliant businessman, and no one can deny that. But the personality that makes him a force to be reckoned with in the industry is also the same personality that he brings to his family. C'mon, Charlotte, you worked in that house, you've been around the family enough to know there were issues way before now. They'll get through this—they're strong, and underneath the stubbornness is an abundance of love. But I don't know if Ross will make it without you and Ben. You two were the catalyst for this change, and he needs you."

He shrugged a shoulder. "Like I said, I don't know what happened between you two before tonight, but my friend is more focused and happier than he's been in a long time. So again, please hang in there with him. Don't give up."

Billy squeezed her hand, then walked away, his plea echoing in her head.

My friend is more focused and happier than he's been in a long time... Don't give up.

There was so much between her and Ross—too much. Mistrust. Hurt. Resentment. Insecurity. As their argument earlier in the closet proved.

And yet… She glanced across the room and unerringly sought him out. Though still surrounded by people, for once, a smile didn't curve his mouth. Someone wasn't commanding his attention. He stood there, an island in a sea of admirers, hangers-on and wannabe lovers. Alone. Untouchable. Lonely. Did any of them truly see the real man behind the tuxedo, the magnetism, the playboy exterior? The man who longed for a domineering father's approval and concealed a wounded heart behind an indifferent demeanor? The man who'd unconditionally accepted a son he hadn't known about and loved him without reserve.

No, none of them saw *that* man. But she'd been gifted with glimpses of him. And those glimpses only made her crave more of him. Made her yearn for the impossible.

That he would someday give her the same uninhibited love he so freely offered Ben.

What would it be like to love him without fear of rejection, without baggage from the past, without dread that outside forces would come between them? With the security that she was enough?

It would be the kind of dream that slowly faded when morning arrived, but which she desperately tried to cling to even if only for a few sacred moments.

As if he felt her gaze on him, Ross glanced up, and their eyes met. And even though a room separated them, she reeled from the intensity of that stare. In spite of the harmful words she'd hurled at him earlier, she needed to feel connected to him. Needed to somehow work toward erasing the distance that she'd placed between them.

God, she just needed him.

Heart thumping against her sternum, she tipped her head to the side, hoping he understood her message to follow her. Not waiting lest she lose her nerve to go through with this, she turned and slipped out one of the side doors. She walked past several closed doors, and randomly choosing one that was far enough away from the great room, she twisted the knob and entered. A large and curtainless picture window dominated one wall, allowing moonlight to stream through and illuminate what appeared to be a private and informal meeting room. A stone fireplace, several big armchairs, a small couch and a couple of coffee tables filled the space.

She didn't make it past the first chair when the door opened behind her and clicked shut. Inhaling a breath, she held it for several seconds, and then slowly released it, pivoting to face Ross. In the semidark, his large frame loomed larger, and her belly fluttered. With his impassive expression, he betrayed nothing of his thoughts or emotions. But he was here. And she'd take that as a positive sign.

"Ross," she began, then stopped. Because she had no

idea what to say. *I just needed you to look* at *me and not* through *me* didn't seem like a good opener. She shook her head, tried again. "Ross, I wanted to apologize. About earlier. This night is important to you, and what happened between us threw a pall over it that doesn't belong. I'm sorry for that."

"Is that what you and Billy were talking about?"

She blinked, taken aback by the abrupt question. "No," she said. "Well, not really…"

"Which is it?" he pressed in the low, quiet tone that still set her instinctive alarm system clanging. "Because it looked like a serious conversation, given the way you two were cozied up together."

She frowned, lifting her hands. "Wait. What the hell is going on here?"

"He asked would I mind if he asked you out. Did I ever tell you that?" He stepped away from the door, stalking closer to her. "After he first met you at Sheen," he continued, not granting her the chance to reply. "He called you beautiful and wanted you."

"What did you tell him?" she breathed, still unsure of what was happening but rapidly getting tugged down by the undertow of desire swirling around them.

Ross might appear the epitome of cool composure, but his eyes… They burned bright. Anger? Lust? Didn't matter, because both caused the air to snag in her lungs, dampened her palms and beaded her nipples into tight points, setting off a pulsing throb in her sex.

Jesus, what did that say about her?

Nothing flattering.

"I told him to go for it." He moved even closer. And closer still, until the lapels of his tuxedo jacket grazed the tips of her breasts. She just managed to swallow a gasp. "I didn't know you were the mother of my son then, but the reason still stands. We're sometimes acquaintances, sometimes enemies. Co-parents who want nothing from each other but the best for our son. We're a mistake that are now connected for the next sixteen years, right?"

"Ross," she whispered, voice breaking. "I'm—"

"Sorry," he finished, flicking a hand, the gold of his watch glinting in the shadowed room. "You said that. Did Billy flirt with you? Ask you how we were doing?"

"Yes, but not how you're insinuating," she objected, frowning.

He arched an eyebrow, and the mocking gesture sparked a flame of irritation. "Really? And what am I insinuating?" he drawled.

"If I didn't know better—and believe me, I do—I'd swear you were jealous. Which is ridiculous considering you were just out there with women not just hanging from your every word, but from *you*," she snapped.

Shit.

She didn't lose her temper often, but dammit, when she did, her mouth ran like a swollen spring river—fast, babbling and all over the place.

"And if I didn't know better, I'd think that was jealousy," he taunted, cocking his head and peering down at her through a thick fringe of lashes. "Fortunately, I know better, too. But just in case you need clarification, other than how they can benefit the festival, I don't give a damn about those women. And I definitely don't want to fuck them. You're the only one I need to be inside of. The only one who can get me hard just by breathing." He tunneled his fingers through the fall of her hair and tugged, yanking her head back so his mouth hovered over hers. "And you're wrong, Charlotte." He pulled harder, and she sank her teeth into her bottom lip, trapping the groan that almost slipped free at the corresponding tingle across her scalp. "I am jealous. Two times Billy touched you. And both times

I battled back the urge to rush across the room and shove him against the wall and away from you."

Shock crackled through her, the static of it convincing her she'd misheard. She slowly shook her head. "You don't—"

"Mean it?" he interrupted her once more, completing her sentence. "Yes, I do. To you, I might be a mistake," he repeated what she'd called him again for the second time in as many minutes, and it shredded her. "But to all of them out there, including my friend, you're mine. At night, when you're under me, moaning my name, coming around my dick, you're mine. Aren't you?" He rolled his hips, his erection, thick and hard, grinding against her belly. "Aren't you, baby?"

She squeezed her eyes closed. Trembled. And rasped, "Yes."

His mouth crushed down on hers, consuming the echo of the word and robbing her breath. Hard, rough, hot. Nothing gentle about this kiss. It was pure lust and aggression. Pure need. She shoved her fingers through his hair, fisting the cool strands, her ravenous desire rising to match his.

She didn't give a damn that just down the hallway, hundreds of people congregated. Didn't care that anyone could easily open that door—just as easily as she'd done. No, she didn't spare one more thought on any of that. Everything in her focused on this man devouring her mouth like he'd been on a hunger strike, and she was his first meal.

His arm wrapped around her waist, hauling her tighter to him, and his big frame surrounded her. Protecting her. Even as she tumbled headlong into the wild sexual chaos he never failed to stir within her, she didn't fight or fear it. Not when she had utter confidence that he would be her anchor.

"Put your legs around me," he ordered seconds before hiking her into the air.

She obeyed, wrapping herself around him, trusting his

strength, his power. In several long strides, he had her back pressed to the wall. One glance over his shoulder assured her they were steeped in shadow, the pale moonbeams not reaching them in their corner. Of course, Ross would've considered their privacy and her modesty. Even if by chance someone passed by the window that looked out over the lawn and stable, they wouldn't glimpse her and Ross. The knowledge allowed her to sink further into him, under his spell.

With the wall behind her and his body aligned against her front, she was trapped. And didn't want to escape. Cupping his jaw, she settled her thumbs on his chin and tugged. Demanding he open wider for her. Triumph and satisfaction sang through her when he complied, cocking his head so she could thrust deeper, help herself to more of him.

God help her, but she would never get enough of this man. She acknowledged that fact with a fatalistic certainty. She could no more change it than she could who fathered her baby. Ross had imprinted himself on her so long ago, branding her with his special mark of passion, of possession. Maybe it hadn't been time, work and motherhood that had prevented her from becoming romantically involved again in these past three years. Maybe it had been the knowledge that no one else could make her fly and die at the same time.

"Touch me," she pleaded, unashamed in her need. Peppering fevered kisses across his cheek and jaw, she whispered, "Please, touch me."

The night at The Bellamy, it'd been she who'd sought to help him forget with passion. Now she needed him to do the same for her. Help her forget she'd hurt him with her angry words. Help her forget she'd hurt herself.

"Where?" He cupped her breast in his big hand, his thumb rubbing her nipple over her dress. She whimpered, arching into the caress. "Here?"

"No." She wrapped her fingers around his, and with the other hand, tugged the neckline to the side, exposing her bra and flesh. Still not satisfied, she yanked down the cup, freeing herself. "Here."

He bent his head over her, his growl of approval humming against her skin as he sucked her deep. Pulling on her. Licking her. Tormenting her. She rasped nonsensical words as he worked her over. They could've been praise or pleas, she didn't know. Didn't care. Just as long as he kept hauling her to the brink. Here they let down their guards, their swords, and loved.

Or at least she did.

Biting her lip, she clutched his head, lifted it and brought it to the neglected breast. Together, they bared her, and together they offered her up to his voracious mouth. She shook in his arms, undulating wildly, rubbing her sex against his dick. Yes, layers of clothing separated them, but it didn't prevent each stroke and glide from sending more and more pleasure streaking through her. She could come from just this. From just his mouth and fingers and riding his cock.

"Back pocket," he snapped, abandoning her breasts to capture her mouth again. "Get my wallet and take the condom out." Impatient fingers dropped to her thighs, gathering her dress around her hips. "Now, Charlotte."

"No," she breathed, flattening her palms against his chest and pushing. He jerked his head up, his eyes blazing down into hers. She shoved again, and he stepped back, and in spite of the disbelief flaring in his gaze, gently lowered her to the floor. "Not yet."

And she dropped to her knees.

"Fuck." His groan reverberated in the room, and he didn't stop her as she loosened the tab on his pants. Instead he slapped his hands to the wall, looming over her. She tipped her head back, meeting his narrowed stare as she lowered the zipper, dipped her hand inside his black boxer briefs and pulled him free. "Baby, you don't have to do this."

"Yes, I do," she murmured, rubbing a thumb over the swollen and already slick head. "I need this. And so do you."

Without hesitation, she took him inside her. Their twin moans filtered through the air, followed by his sharp bark of pleasure. Or was it pain?

Closing her eyes, she lost herself in the earthy taste, the soft and steely texture, the heavy density of him. How he filled her mouth to overflowing. She fisted the bottom half of his cock, pumping it in a steady rhythm, her lips bumping her fingers on the tail end of each stroke.

"So good," she whispered, dragging her tongue up his length. "I'd forgotten how good you taste."

"Are you trying to make me come right here in this pretty mouth, baby?" He cupped her cheek, the tender gesture belying the roughness of his voice. "Keep talking like that, and I will."

"I want all of you," she confessed on a low rasp before sucking him back in. He probably assumed she meant his sex, his body, the rapture they gave each other. But she didn't. She yearned for *everything*. His body. His touch. His time. His laughter.

His heart.

Even as she pleasured him, tears glinted her eyes. Because part of her knew this would probably be all they could have. Too many words, bruises and wounds stood between them. Too many secrets.

Desperation plowed into her, and to battle it, she swallowed him deeper, his tip hitting the back of her throat.

"Enough," he snarled, jerking free, and cuffing her upper arms he hauled her to her feet. "I want inside you," he muttered, hurriedly removing his wallet and a condom. In moments, he sheathed himself and lifted her back in his arms, his hands cupping her ass. "Take me inside, baby."

Breath blasting in and out of her swollen lips, she reached between them, encircled his erect flesh, pulled the wet panel of her panties aside and guided it to her entrance. Wrapping her arms around his neck, she lifted herself and sank down. Until all of him was firmly surrounded by her.

Oh, God. She buried her face against his throat. As often as they'd had sex since that first time at The Bellamy, she'd become used to him. But she'd never become used to how completely he filled her. Branded her. *Completed* her.

"Move," she ordered. Begged. "Please, move."

Pressing her harder against the wall, Ross grabbed her hair and tugged her head up. "I want to watch it," he said, his gaze roaming over her face.

She didn't need to ask the definition of "it." Because when his hips drew back, then thrust into her, and she cried out, lips parting, eyes closing, he murmured, "That's it."

He didn't grant her any mercy. Using the leverage of the wall, he slammed into her over and over again, alternating between slow, dirty grinds and hard, abrupt strokes. Each time he buried himself in the core of her, the base of his cock massaged the top of her sex, agitating the bundle of nerves there. The slap of skin punctuated the air along with his grunts and her hoarse cries. He dragged her to the edge of the abyss, and she fought it, then willingly went.

She couldn't breathe. Couldn't think. Couldn't do anything but break.

And God, did she.

She erupted, shaking and seizing in his arms, flinging herself into ecstasy with no care of how she landed. *If* she landed. Her sex clamped down on his cock, and his growl echoed in her ear as he drove past her quivering flesh, pursuing his own end. She held on, and though exhaustion pulled at her, she bucked her hips, giving him the same measure he'd gifted her.

Her name, shouted in his raw voice, rebounded off the walls of the room, and she finally wilted against him, confident he wouldn't let her fall.

At least not physically.

Because for her heart, it was too little, too late.

Thirteen

Ross sat in his car in the same parking space that had been his since he'd officially started working for The Edmond Organization six years ago. He snorted. He might've been disinherited and fired, but at least his father hadn't gotten around to reassigning his spot.

Drumming his fingers against the steering wheel, he stared at the building that had been his home away from home. And now he had neither. He sighed, scrubbing a hand down his face.

What the hell was he doing here?

What did he hope to accomplish with this visit?

Immediately, Ben's face drifted across his mind's eye. Before he'd dropped his son off at his grandparents' house for an afternoon visit, Ben had wrapped his arms around his legs, beaming up at him. No hesitation. No uncertainty. His son was so secure and confident in his father's love that he'd demanded, "Daddy, kiss bye!" without any fear of rejection. Certain he'd receive the affection that was his due.

Ross huffed out a soft chuckle, the sound somehow foreign to him in the silence of the car. As was the prickle of heat behind his rib cage. That free display of love had triggered a yearning in him—a yearning that had driven him here instead of his meeting with Billy. Ben deserved to know all of his family. Especially his grandfather. Maybe he and Rusty hadn't enjoyed a loving relationship, but that didn't mean Ross's son couldn't have that with Rusty.

Though it meant swallowing his pride, he had to try.

Not just for his son. But for himself, too.

Resolute, he climbed out the car and headed into the Edmond building. Security had every right to stop him and force him to sign in as a visitor. But the guard on duty only greeted him as Ross walked toward the elevators. Even the pass that only certain personnel possessed to access the executive floor worked. It hadn't been deactivated, as he'd expected.

Frowning, but not questioning his luck—accepting it as fate—he emerged from the elevator onto the hushed floor housing his family's offices. More than a few people did a double take as he strode toward his father's assistant's desk. But he ignored them, focusing instead on the task at hand. Because getting in to see his father without an appointment would be the hugest hurdle.

"Good afternoon, Lisa," he said, smiling at the pretty blonde. "Does Dad have a few minutes available in his schedule for me?"

"Hi, Ross." She offered him a smile in return, though curiosity gleamed in her brown eyes. No doubt wondering what business the disinherited heir could possibly have with his father. She tapped on her keyboard and glanced at her monitor. "He doesn't have a meeting until two, so there's about a half hour free, but—"

"Thanks." He strode past the desk toward the closed double doors. "I'll just go in. No need to announce me."

"But—"

Inside he cringed as he gripped the knob and pushed the door open. That had been an asshole move worthy of a spoiled child, but if he'd allowed her to give Rusty a headsup that his son wanted to see him, Ross would've spent the

BACK IN THE TEXAN'S BED

rest of the afternoon sitting on one of the couches in the waiting area.

Rusty could carry petty to a whole new level.

His father glanced up at the opening of the door, then scowled. "Ross, what are you doing here?"

Shutting the door behind him, he crossed the huge office, coming to a halt in front of Rusty's desk. He didn't bother taking a seat in one of the visitors' chairs since he most likely wouldn't be here long enough to become comfortable.

"I'm here to see you, Dad. We didn't have a chance to talk Saturday night."

Rusty snorted, tossing down his pen onto his desk. "Is that right? Could be because the rest of us were working while you were up that woman's skirts." His mouth curled into a hard, mocking smile. "Think no one noticed you two disappear? Or that before then, something was off between you? Christ, son, you looked like someone had shot your goddamn dog. Whether you're fucking them or arguing with them, you shouldn't let a woman interfere with business. And you failed on both accounts Saturday."

Heat bloomed beneath his collar, and he slowly dragged in a breath. *You're here to heal the rift, not widen it. You can't tell the old bastard to go to hell.*

The reminder drifted through his head, and after several seconds he could inhale air that wasn't singed by his anger.

"I'm not here to discuss Charlotte," he said.

"What else is there to discuss?" Rusty snapped, slapping his palms to the desk and surging to his feet. "She's at the root of all of this. First, she disrespected my employment and my home by sleeping with my son. Then, she gets pregnant, no doubt on purpose, and when I tell her to get rid of it, she lied about doing that. And then, she has the gall to show up here in Royal again, looking to hook you, an Edmond, with a kid that's her responsibility, not yours, since she made the decision to keep it."

"What kind of man would it make me if I denied my child, abandoned him? That wouldn't make me any better than Sarabeth," he countered.

"Don't bring up that woman's name to me. Your mother was another one who used her children for a big payday and then disappeared. And you can damn well bet that's going to happen with Charlotte," he fumed, jabbing a finger at Ross. "You think you have this happy little family? What happens when she realizes I'm serious about not giving you one red cent, Ross? Do you really believe she's going to stick around? You're being led around by your dick, and I'm not going to stand by and watch it happen. And when she leaves with that boy, I'll be damned if you come crawling back to me."

Each insult barreled into him, delivering strikes to every insecurity and doubt that hid in his subconscious. He was far from penniless, but even with the home he provided for her and Ben, Ross worried it wouldn't be enough. Especially since last week, he'd gone over his finances with his accountant, and as he'd suspected and feared, though he possessed stocks, investments and property, he wouldn't have enough liquid wealth to give her the five-hundred-thousand-dollar payment at the end of their year together. Once he told her the truth, would she pack up Ben and leave? After all, she'd held up her end of the bargain—leaving her home, moving in with him, completing the paperwork to change their son's last name—and the one thing he'd promised her, he couldn't come through on.

I lowered my personal standards to become the plaything of a man who deemed me good enough for a fuck but not to escort past the kitchen. Every time I wear that necklace it's a reminder to myself to never repeat that mistake.

He locked his knees, steadying himself as Charlotte's words threatened to knock him back into the chair. Yes, they'd disappeared during the event and had sex. And later that night, after they returned home, he'd lost himself in her again. But he couldn't eject those words from his head. Couldn't convince himself that, although she'd apologized, she hadn't meant them.

She'd called him a mistake and it was nothing he hadn't thought before. A mistake to her, to his parents, even to the women he'd fucked and forgotten. Which made sense in a screwed-up but logical way. Because if he was truly important to them, how could they so easily walk away from him?

So while he'd had Charlotte's body, he didn't have her loyalty. Definitely not her love, not that he'd asked for that, and not since she'd made it clear he was an error she'd never repeat. The bottom line was he had no hold on her, except their son, that would compel her to stay with him. And Charlotte had proven her capability in raising Ben as a single parent.

No.

The objection blasted through his head, loud and furious. Ben was his son. And regardless of whether she left or not, he wouldn't allow her to take Ben away from him.

"Don't worry, Dad," Ross said, arching an eyebrow and forcing an indifference that was a lie. "I won't come crawling back. And I'll make sure to use you as an example. Both you and Sarabeth."

With that, he spun on his heel and left Rusty's office. His every good intention in this visit had backfired. But he'd emerged crystal clear on one thing.

He couldn't count on his father to be there.

Couldn't depend on Charlotte, either.

The only person who would never fail him was himself.

Fourteen

Charlotte sighed, sliding the key into the front door. Usually, Mondays were a slow night, but for some reason, it seemed as if every person in Royal had decided to drop by Sheen tonight. Jeremy had credited the unprecedented influx with her presence at the Soiree on the Bay fundraising event over the weekend as well as the samples of their dishes. Possibly. She'd shared his opinion with Ross when he'd brought Ben by the restaurant to see her, and he'd managed not to throw an "I told you so" at her.

She frowned, unlocking the door and twisting the knob. Actually, Ross had been distant and aloof tonight. Since Saturday, they'd formed a tenuous truce, but he'd reverted to being that cold, reserved man she'd met at Sheen weeks ago. A tight ball of dread had settled in the pit of her stomach and remained there for the rest of the evening like a pebble she couldn't shake from her shoe. It had been a relief when the night ended, because she'd come to a decision sometime between preparing the sauce for her signature dish and plating dishes for a party of twelve—she needed to be honest with Ross.

She had to tell him that as hard as she'd tried, as angry as she'd been, she'd never stopped loving him.

Fear trickled through her as she entered the house. But

intertwined with those dark tendrils was excitement, too. He'd been jealous, possessive on Saturday. And there was no denying he'd been hurt by her. That had to mean he felt *something* more for her than he would for a tolerable person to co-parent with… God, she hoped so. Because she'd been here before, three years ago. Uncertain. Scared. Hopeful.

Only to end up broken, devastated and alone.

Would she survive that kind of agony again?

Would she have to?

It was those two questions that had her wavering back and forth. She didn't know if her heart could stand losing him again…but what if she didn't lose him?

That damn hope. It was both a blessing and a curse.

Still, she couldn't just continue to exist in this torturous limbo. Tonight, she'd have her answer. Tonight, she'd—

"Dammit." She stumbled to a halt, her toe throbbing in protest at whatever she'd just stubbed it on. Frowning, she glanced down. "What the hell?" she murmured, spotting the set of black luggage in the foyer. The smallest of the two listed to the side from the kick she'd inadvertently delivered to it.

"Charlotte, I need to speak to you."

She shifted her gaze from the suitcases to Ross, who stood just inside the entryway to the living room. It was a little after twelve, and most nights when she arrived home, worn jeans or loose-fitting sleep pants adorned his tall frame. But tonight, a dark gray suit had replaced the pajamas and T-shirt.

Her frown deepened. "Hey." She set her bag and purse down on the table beside the door. "Did I forget you had a business trip or were headed out of town?"

"No," he said, both his voice and face shuttered. That knot in her stomach pulled taut, and dread crept inside her, an unwelcome intruder. "Can we talk in here?"

He turned, but she didn't move. "No," she whispered. He

halted and slowly pivoted back to face her, and she shook her head. "No," she repeated, stronger, louder. "Whatever you have to say, we can do it right here. Especially since you'll be leaving directly afterward, right?" His expression remained a mask of stone, but she caught the flicker in his eyes, and she let loose a low, jagged chuckle that abraded her throat. A heavy, suffocating weight settled on her chest, shortening her breath, causing an echo in her ears. She recognized this feeling. The forerunner of panic, of an onslaught of fear. But she shoved it back, focusing on the silent, brooding and cruelly beautiful man before her. "Let's just get this over with so you have easy access to the door."

"Fine." He nodded, sliding his hands into the front pockets of his suit. How could he be so cold? So unfeeling when she was shattering into pieces? "I haven't been honest with you. After a meeting with my financial advisor, I can't afford to pay you the half-million dollars that I promised. It wouldn't be fair of me to expect you to hold up your end of our agreement when I can't. Of course, you and Ben can continue to stay here—"

"Liar."

Ross's head jerked back as if her accusation had delivered a verbal punch.

"I never asked for that money in the first place, so don't try to place the blame for you leaving on it. You saw your father today, didn't you?"

"I don't know how you found out about it—and not that it matters—but, yes," he said, eyes narrowing on her.

"Gina called me because she was trying to get in touch with you, and you weren't answering your phone. Apparently, your father was on the warpath today because you showed up at the office. She wanted to make sure you were okay." Charlotte shook her head, a bone-deep weariness and ache invading her. "And to think I felt that this time, maybe, just maybe, things would be different."

Ross sliced a hand through the air. "I don't know what conclusions you've drawn in your head, Charlotte, but like I said, this has nothing to do with Rusty. I'm trying to do what's right here. What's fair."

"I don't know if you truly believe that or if you're really trying to convince yourself of it." She wrapped her arms around herself. "When I left for California, I so desperately wanted you to fight for me. To ask me to stay. To stand up to your father and tell him you and I were together and nothing he could do would change your mind. But you didn't. And I resented you for a long time because of it. But this time, you did exactly that. Maybe not for me, but for Ben. Still, you defied Rusty, and it made me hopeful. It made me foolish," she added with a self-deprecating chuckle. "Because all it took was one visit with Rusty and you fell right back in line. Same result, just took a bit longer."

"That's bullshit," he snapped, eyes bright with anger. "I'm not abandoning you or Ben. I still want joint custody. Or are you trying to tell me that because I don't want to live in this house, I can't continue to see my son on a regular basis? Because I won't allow you to cut me out of his life."

"Wow," she whispered. "For a moment, I could've sworn Rusty Edmond stood before me instead of Ross." He flinched, paling at her direct hit, but she didn't back down. "Contrary to whatever nonsense your father might've spouted about me only wanting you for your money and withholding Ben to get it, I would never do that to Ben. He adores you. But I'd also never do that to you."

She tunneled her fingers through her hair and briefly closed her eyes. Ordering herself not to shed one damn tear in front of him. He didn't deserve to see her pain. "You just don't get it, Ross," she rasped. "Three years ago, I fell in love with you. You. An Edmond. A man I should've run far away from. But I couldn't, because under the bravado was a unique, vulnerable, funny, sweet, *good* man who made me feel more special than I'd ever felt in my life. You weren't your father, no matter how hard Rusty tried to make you conform to be the image of him. And I loved that about you."

"You never said…" Ross stared at her, eyes dark with surprise, body unnaturally stiff. "Why didn't you…"

"Because you didn't want that from me. I knew what I was to you even if I hoped for different. Your father would never accept me, and when you surrendered to that and ended things with me because Rusty didn't see me as worthy enough, I knew it would break me. So I left before it could happen. I ran from here, but I couldn't outrun my heart. And then I found out I was pregnant. I accepted then, even after the phone call and letter, that you would always be a part of me. So when you appeared back in my life, in Ben's life, I convinced myself I could be happy with our co-parenting-with-benefits arrangement. But I lied. That's what I planned to tell you tonight. I want all of you or nothing. Seems like you'd already made that decision for both of us, though."

Not giving him a chance to reply—because really, what could he say when he literally had his bags packed?—she crossed the foyer for the staircase. But she paused at the bottom step, hand on the newel.

She didn't look at him as she offered him one last confession.

"Do you remember when you gave me the diamond heart necklace?" she murmured. "You'd taken me to the resort on Appaloosa Island, and one night after making love, you surprised me with it. You'd bought it at one of the shops because it reminded you of me. You said the heart reminded you of mine—beautiful and precious. That's why I kept the necklace, Ross. Because of all the gifts you'd given me, this one meant the most. No motive behind it. You bought it simply because you'd been thinking of me. And my heart."

She climbed the steps and didn't look back.

Fifteen

"Ross? A word."

Ross froze at his father's request. Request, hell. Rusty had issued the order and expected to be obeyed. He glanced at the door to the meeting room, debating whether he wanted to give his father the "word" he wanted. But in the end, he remained in place, curiosity momentarily overriding animosity and bitterness.

"You okay?" Asher murmured, pausing beside him. His brother, sister, Billy and Rusty had met at the clubhouse for a meeting about the festival, since Ross refused to return to the family's office building. He wasn't a fan of going where he wasn't wanted. "I can stay."

"No," Ross said, studying Rusty's face as his father tossed Asher an irritated glance. "I'm fine. I'll call you later."

His brother clapped him on the shoulder, and Gina squeezed his hand as she passed by him. Billy patted him on the back, and then moments later, the door closed, leaving him alone with his father.

"What's this about?" Ross asked, crossing his arms.

Rusty took his time answering, rounding the table and hiking a hip on the edge of it. For several long moments, he studied Ross, and he steadily met his father's stare. If

Rusty expected him to fidget like a kid called on the carpet, then he'd have a long wait.

"I heard you're no longer shacking up with that woman and her kid," his father finally said, the smug note in his voice raking over Ross's skin.

"I have to commend the Royal grapevine," Ross drawled. "It's only been three days."

Three interminable, hollow, gray days since he'd walked out of the Pine Valley home he'd bought for his family. Three days since he'd woken up to Ben's laughter and demands for banana pancakes.

Three days since he'd last seen Charlotte. Heard her voice. Inhaled her scent. Touched her body.

He clenched his jaw, fisting the hands in his pockets.

Three days since she'd lobbed her bomb about being in love with him years ago and wanting all of him now.

It was also that long since he'd been able to draw a breath that didn't have razors attached to it. God, why couldn't he carve this Charlotte-sized ache out of his chest? Evict her voice from his head? Only working on the various projects he'd thrown himself into had kept him sane. The projects and Ben.

"News like that travels fast, son," Rusty said.

"I'm *son* now?" Ross chuckled. "Since when? Let me guess. Three days ago."

"You did the right thing, Ross." Rusty nodded, mouth flattening into a grim line. "I hate that I had to take such drastic measures to make you see what a mistake you were making, but if the end result was you coming to your senses, then I'll live with my actions. You deserve someone who adds to your wealth, social standing and reputation, not some faithless, disloyal *cook*," he sneered. "Just tell me the situation has been handled and we can move on from here."

Ross stared at Rusty, shocked by the venom that seemed

directed at Charlotte. Yes, she'd been their employee, but she was also a successful, gifted chef. What the hell had she ever done to deserve Rusty's enmity?

He slashed a hand through the air. Fuck it. His father took classism and snobbery to a whole new level, but he was through allowing his father to run his life like it was one of his subsidiaries.

"Is that what you assumed? That I left Charlotte because of you disinheriting me?" He shook his head, his bark of laughter drawing a fierce frown from his father. "Sorry, Dad, but I regret to inform you that I'm still as much of a disappointment as I was when I left your office. This has nothing to do with you. It was my choice because I was trying to do what was best for her. And Charlotte and Ben aren't a *situation* to be *handled*," he snapped. "He's my son, and she's the mother of my son. She and I aren't living together—" weren't together *at all* "—but I'm not abandoning my son. So your praise might've been a tad premature."

Rusty slid off the edge of the table, standing to his full, intimidating height. Well, it used to be intimidating. Not any longer. Somewhere between watching Charlotte strip herself emotionally bare before walking away and leaving him broken, and checking into The Bellamy, his father's approval and acceptance had stopped being the driving force in his life. There were only two people whose esteem mattered. One loved him unconditionally. And the other? Well, the other, he'd hurt so badly that there was no coming back from it.

"Ross, I don't know what this is, but you need to get your shit together," Rusty thundered. "You will not have any association with that woman or child. This is nonnegotiable."

Ross studied his father as if it were the first time he was truly seeing him. "You want me to choose you over Charlotte, over my son. Which is so damn ironic because in every situation you never offered me the same courtesy.

Business first. Women first. Yourself first. But never me, my happiness, my well-being. No," he stated flatly, with a finality that resonated through him. "I won't do it. Keep your money, your inheritance, your business empire. And if you're stubborn enough to demand it, your title as my father. When my son looks at me with love and respect, knowing I'll always be there for him, that's worth more than anything you could possibly hold over my head. Goodbye, Dad."

He turned and strode toward the door, the crushing weight of guilt, sadness and anger on his chest a little bit lighter.

"Don't you walk away from me, Ross. We're not finished here," Rusty bellowed. Like a child throwing a temper tantrum.

"Yes, Dad, we are."

He opened the door, stepped through and closed it behind him.

Closing it on his past.

Ross handed his car keys to The Bellamy's valet and entered the hotel's entrance. His cell phone jangled in his pocket, and like the last three times his sister had called since he'd left his confrontation with Rusty, he ignored it. He loved Gina, but right now his emotions huddled too close to the surface. They were too raw, and he couldn't hold a conversation with her.

He strode across the lobby toward the elevators, but as he passed the sitting area, a woman rose from one of the chairs. Shock barreled into him, jerking him to a sudden halt.

No. Not today. All the anger, pain and sadness simmering inside him ratcheted to a boil and flowed over him, singing him with memories, bitterness and a little boy's betrayal and love.

"Sarabeth."

His mother's smile wavered but then rallied. Probably all that beauty pageant training. Oh, how Rusty used to go on about that. How he'd found her on the pageant circuit and lifted her out of her lower-middle-class life to rarefied Royal society. And all he'd received in return was a cold-hearted gold digger more concerned with what he could do for her, instead of the wife and mother he'd wanted.

Ross hadn't cared about any of that at the time. At ten, all he'd wanted was his mother.

He studied the tall, willowy blonde as she approached him. Though nearing fifty years old, his mother appeared ten or fifteen years younger. All that free living without the baggage of children could do that to a person, he mused.

"Ross, I'm sorry to ambush you like this," Sarabeth apologized, the blue eyes he'd inherited from her meeting his. She chuckled, and it struck him as nervous. Of course, cornering the son she hadn't seen or talked to in years had to be stressful. "God, in some ways you look exactly the same. I would've recognized you anywhere." When he didn't reply to that, she shook her head, that smile finally fading. "I understand if you'd rather not see me, but if you could give me just a few minutes, I'd really appreciate it."

He smothered his initial instinct to tell her no, and dipped his chin. Pivoting on his heel, he stalked toward The Silver Saddle, trusting her to follow. At two o'clock, most of the tables remained empty, a stark contrast to how it would be jumping with patrons in just three more hours. But for now, he snagged one in a corner that would afford them privacy.

Once they were seated and had placed their orders with their waitress—a beer for him and a white wine for her—she folded her slim hands on the table and gazed at him.

"I'm sorry for staring," she apologized after an awkward silence. "It's just that… It's been a long time. I've missed you."

"I've been in the same town, at the same address all this time," he said brusquely. "If you missed me so much, you knew where to find me."

"I deserve that," she whispered, hooking a strand of hair behind her ear. "There's so much I want to say to you…" She cleared her throat, momentarily dropping her eyes to the table before lifting them to him. "Will you hear me out? Please? And at the end if you still want to walk out of here and have nothing to do with me, then I'll understand."

"Fine." He leaned back in his chair as the waitress set their drinks on the table. Twisting the cap off his beer, he tipped it toward her. "I'm listening."

"Thank you." Her inhale of breath echoed between them, as did the long exhale. "I want to preface this by saying I'm not excusing my absence from your life. I just want to explain my side of it and hope that maybe you can forgive me."

She sipped from her wineglass. For courage? Because that was the reason he gulped down his beer. To try to bolster the bravado to sit here and listen to his mother explain why he hadn't been important enough for her to stay in his life.

"I married your father when I was young—nineteen. Like a fairy tale, he whisked me away to this beautiful home, provided a life I'd only dreamed about. I guess you could say Rusty pampered me, because he did. Beautiful children, a home, clothes, jewelry, cars, vacations abroad— everything I could ever ask for. Except for a faithful husband."

She lifted her glass for another sip, this one a little longer than her last. And when she lowered her arm, her slim fingers slightly trembled around the long stem.

"I couldn't stay in a loveless marriage any longer," she continued, her voice a shade huskier. "Not when I walked in on Rusty with another woman. Asking him for a divorce was terrifying, but at least I had you and your sister. Or at least, I naively believed. As punishment for daring to leave him, Rusty used all his power, including a judge who knew him, to ensure he got custody of you and Gina. I might have received a financial settlement, but what mattered most to me—my children—I lost."

Ross tried to steel his heart against her tale; he'd heard some of it through Rusty. But the cheating, the judge in Rusty's pocket? No, his father had left those details out. Not that either shocked him. When Rusty played to win, he refused to lose at all costs.

Still, she'd left his father. Why had she then divorced her children?

As if she read his mind, she continued, her voice low, pained, "I tried to maintain a relationship with you and Gina. God, I tried. But you two were growing older and preferred to be with your friends rather than a woman who was increasingly becoming a stranger to you. I got it. And Rusty didn't help matters, either. He didn't try to enforce our custody arrangement. Then I couldn't find work here in Royal, and everyone treated me like the scorned ex-wife. I had to leave town simply to survive."

As someone who'd recently been on the receiving end of Rusty's hardhanded tactics, an unprecedented empathy he'd never offered his mother swelled within him. He understood survival.

He understood trying to escape the steel, booby-trapped box Rusty could trap a person in.

"Now, in hindsight, I wish I'd fought harder to get you back. To try another court if one didn't listen. The Edmond name and power extends beyond Royal, and I didn't have the financial resources to fight. But if I'd known divorcing him would mean losing you and your sister, I would've stayed married to him, regardless of his mistreatment and cheating."

She stretched her arms across the table, hesitated, but

then carefully clasped his hands in hers. "Ross, I have so many regrets. And the main one is allowing fear of your rejection to keep me from reaching out to you in all this time. As your mother, it was up to me to connect with you, not place that burden on you. I just ask for your forgiveness." A tear slipped down her cheek, and she swiped at it before clasping his hand again. "Like I said, I have many regrets. But in spite of the hell I went through with your father, I'd do it again in a heartbeat, because it brought me you and Gina."

A quaking started in Ross's chest, and then a loud crack he was surprised no one could hear crashed in his head and through his heart. He was so damn tired of being bitter. It had eaten away at him for so long that sometimes he didn't recognize the man he'd become. He'd been punishing everyone because of this anger—his father, Charlotte, himself.

God, *Charlotte*.

Three years ago, he hadn't allowed himself to love her because he'd been so afraid she would leave him. And when she had, it had been a self-fulfilling prophecy. Then, after she'd come back in his life, offering him a second chance with her, a chance to have a family, he'd again fallen back on fear. Walking out on her before she could.

He was tired of being afraid. Tired of being bitter and angry.

He just wanted to be loved, to be…happy.

He blinked against the sting of tears as he stared at the woman he'd always just wanted to love him, to accept him.

To stay for him.

Maybe she hadn't then, but she was here now.

Just as Charlotte had wanted to be.

Oh, Christ, he'd screwed up so bad. So *goddamn* bad. But he could start fixing it now. And that healing had to start with Sarabeth—with his mother.

"I've blamed a lot of my actions and behavior on you and your leaving me. I've hurt the mother of my son, the woman I...love—" his throat closed around the word, at admitting it for the first time aloud "—because I couldn't grow up and accept accountability. I'm sorry for all that you went through, and that when I was old enough, I chose to wallow in resentment than ask you why. I needed you when I was younger, and you weren't there. So I can't say that I can magically let go of that hurt, but I do forgive you. Because forgiving you means forgiving myself."

"Oh, honey," Sarabeth whispered, more tears streaming down her face. She cupped his cheek, and he savored it. Cherished the affection from his mom that he'd craved for so long. "I can't make up for the past. If only I could. But if you'll let me, I'll be here for you now. And the woman you love? Don't make the same mistakes I did, Ross. Go after her. Fight for her."

I so desperately wanted you to fight for me. To ask me to stay.

Charlotte's voice echoed in his head, and he silently vowed that he wouldn't fail her now like he had in the past.

He would go to war for both her and Ben, and this was one he couldn't lose.

Because he was battling for the woman he loved and his child.

He was battling for his life.

Sixteen

"I need the braised beef," Charlotte called out from the warming shelves as she finished plating a Tomahawk steak entrée. "It's up next."

"Yes, Chef, on two," her sous-chef replied.

Satisfied, Charlotte returned to the dishes waiting for her to check and send out. Sheen had been packed since the Soiree on the Bay party, and this Friday night, they had a line out the building, of customers waiting to dine. The knowledge should've filled her with happiness at their success, but for the past week—since Ross had left—everything had been shrouded in a layer of gray, dulling her emotions. Which she appreciated. Because she feared feeling *anything*. Feared that if she allowed even a sliver to surface, then the pain, disappointment and grief would surge through that opening like scavengers, to feed on her.

No, this coat of numbness was saving her at the moment, and she clung to it.

"Chef, you have a guest who'd like to see you tableside."

Dammit.

Forcing a smile that probably resembled a grimace, Charlotte glanced over at Carlie, who stood in the kitchen doorway.

"Okay, I'll be out in just a minute."

Switching out her jackets, she hurried from the kitchen with instructions to her sous-chef to take over for her. The sooner she got this over with, the quicker she could return to the kitchen, her sanctuary. Where she could lose herself in work and think about nothing else. No *one* else.

"Right over here, Chef," Carlie said, guiding her toward the back of the restaurant.

Charlotte followed, threading through the tables, pausing to greet diners but steadily moving forward. Hopefully, this guest wasn't chatty. She couldn't abide a talker right now...

"Hello, Charlotte."

She slammed to a halt, the air pummeling from her lungs at the sight of the man who hadn't left her mind in a week. Her knees locked, preventing her from crumbling to the floor. What the hell? Why was Ross here?

She glanced at Carlie, but the server had already disappeared. There had to be some mistake...

"No mistake," Ross murmured, because she'd obviously said the thought aloud. He rose from his chair, his tall frame towering over her. Reminding her of how well his body sheltered her.

No. *Hell no.* Not going there.

"What are you doing here, Ross?" she rasped. God, the gazes on them crawled under her jacket, skating over her skin. She *hated* it. No doubt this little visit would be the new topic of gossip.

"I came to see you." As if that were enough explanation. He cocked his head, his blue eyes gleaming with...what? Nope, she didn't care. "You look beautiful."

"Seriously?" she hissed. "After walking out of our house, leaving a home you bought for a family you claimed you wanted, that's what you come to my place of business to tell me?" She glared at him. "I don't know what game you're playing, but I quit."

"No game, baby," he murmured, causing her heart to

shudder and twist at the endearment. He had *no* right to call her that. None. "I forfeited my privilege to come and go in the house, so I didn't want to ambush you there. Because that's what this is. An ambush. I freely admit that."

"What? You don't believe I'll cause a scene and kick you out of the restaurant with all these witnesses?" He was correct, damn him. But he didn't have to know that.

"I hoped you wouldn't," he said. Sighing, he threaded his fingers through his hair, disheveling the thick strands. That gesture of nerves from him, especially in front of a restaurant full of people took her aback. Again, what the hell was going on? "Two minutes, Charlotte. Can you give me two minutes?"

He lifted his arm, and it hovered between them for an instant before he gently brushed the back of his fingers down her cheek. A gasp lodged in her throat, and she stiffened, despising her body's programmed response. Lush desire flowed through her, as if only needing his touch to once again stir to life.

She stepped back.

His head dipped in a nod, his eyes dimming. "I came here to apologize, to *beg* if I have to, for your forgiveness. I don't deserve it, but it's not stopping me from asking for it. Charlotte—" he held his hands up in the age-old sign of surrender "—I walked away for one reason. I was terrified of losing you. I figured I'd do it first before you could do it to me. Because I believed you eventually would. Whether it was in a week, a month or when the year was up, you would leave. Especially after I was disinherited and didn't even have wealth or connections to offer you." His mouth twisted, but the disgust in it seemed self-directed. "I was so fucking scared to let you in that I convinced myself it was better to end things sooner before I became used to a life with you and Ben. Before I let myself believe the idea of having both of you could be forever. Before I fell in love with you. But it was too late. I'd fallen back in love with you the moment you approached this table weeks ago. I was just too much of a stubborn coward to admit it."

He balled his fingers into fists and stared down at them. "I was so determined to hold on to the past—of you leaving me years ago, of missing that time with Ben, of not believing you could possibly want me for myself—that I lost my future. And if that's true, if you can't forgive me, then that's on me, and I'll have to live with it. But I can't let another moment go by with you not knowing that I love you. I've never loved any other woman *but* you. For three years, you've haunted me, never left me. And finally, having you back, it's a miracle that I callously threw away."

"Ross," she whispered, stunned speechless. Pressing her hands to her chest, she stared at him, afraid to trust. Afraid to take that step toward him.

Afraid he would devastate her again.

"I broke us, baby," he said. Swallowing hard, he paused, then shifted forward, claiming the space she'd placed between them. "I'm begging for the chance to put us back together. Let me prove to you that I am the man you need. Let me give you and Ben my last name. Let me love you. I don't need an inheritance if I have you and Ben. You're all I need. And, baby, I do need you."

Pride could have her reject him in front of all these people. Teach him a lesson. But she didn't care about other people. Didn't care about punishing him. Punishing them.

All she cared about was *him*.

She loved him.

"I never cared about your money," she said, meeting his bright gaze. "I was in love with the man—still am in love with him. If you come to us penniless, it's okay. You and Ben… If I have you two, I have everything."

"Baby," he breathed, then lunged forward, cupping her face, tipping it back and taking her mouth in a blistering kiss that leveled her. Pulling back, he pressed his forehead to hers, swiping his thumbs over her cheeks. "There's so much I have to tell you. Will you sit with me? Have dinner with me?"

"I wish I could—"

He chuckled, brushing another kiss over her lips. "On the hope that you would give me another chance, I cleared it with Jeremy for you to take a break from the kitchen and have a romantic dinner with me."

"Well, didn't you think of everything?" She grinned, and stepping back, encircled his wrist and led him back to the table. "I would love to."

Once they were seated, Carlie appeared with a wide grin and set down two plates of her signature dish before Charlotte and Ross.

"You'll never believe what happened…"

Over dinner, Ross told her about the confrontation with his father and the surprise visit from his mother. She held his hand as he relayed how they tentatively started the process of healing their relationship, which had culminated in Sarabeth urging Ross to go after Charlotte.

"Wow. I owe your mother a debt of gratitude for her advice," she said, caressing the back of his hand. "I'm sorry I didn't have the opportunity to meet her."

"She's actually planning to move back to Royal so she can get to know her new grandson." He smiled, and joy for him burned like the sun in her heart.

"That's amazing, Ross." She straightened in her chair and exhaled a breath, keeping a hold of his hand. If they were going to start their relationship anew, then he deserved the whole truth. It was time for it. "I don't want to begin our foundation on secrets, so I have something to tell you. I haven't been completely honest about why I left three years ago." God, she didn't want to hurt him. "Rusty had started hitting on me."

Anger darkened Ross's face, his narrowed eyes flaring bright.

"Did he touch you?" he growled.

"No," she assured him, even as she almost sagged in her chair. Because he believed her. That had been one of her fears back then. But he accepted her word as truth. If possible, she loved him more. "He didn't get physical, but he was insistent, and I grew uncomfortable. Especially with us being involved and knowing the power Rusty wielded. I didn't tell you earlier because you love your father, and a relationship with him was important to you. And I didn't want to taint that in any way. But if we're starting over, we need a clean slate. No secrets. And also—" she briefly closed her eyes before meeting his unwavering gaze "—I want to apologize for putting all the blame on you for leaving back then. I had a part in it. And not just because of Rusty and his connections. I was afraid that if we went public, you would see how others looked at us together and not want me anymore. That had nothing to do with you and everything to do with my own sense of self-esteem."

"Baby, you have nothing to apologize for. Nothing at all." He stood, rounded the table and gently pulled her from her seat. Cradling her cheek, he smiled, his love for her so brilliant she would never doubt it again. "Right here, right now, is where we begin. The past is over with and you are my future. I need you, Charlotte Jarrett-soon-to-be-Edmond. I love you."

She turned into his palm, placing a tender kiss to the center. "I love you, too, Ross. You've always been my forever. You always will be."

* * * * *

CRAVING HER EX-ARMY DOC

AMY RUTTAN

For my boys. For the times you have fun together and the times you drive each other crazy. Remember this, Aidan, James *will* grow bigger than you.

Love you both.

PROLOGUE

"Get out of my OR!"

"Not on your life." Luke stood his ground. He wasn't about to be pushed out of the OR by the arrogant upstart trauma surgeon at the hospital. "I got him off the mountain and I'm not going to let him die on my watch. So if you want me out of your OR you're going to have to physically remove me."

Those blue-green eyes behind the surgical mask glittered with barely concealed rage and Luke smiled behind his own mask, knowing he'd pushed the surgeon's buttons. She was some hotshot surgeon from out east. One who had been teaching a workshop in Missoula and got called in when Shane was brought in, because Missoula was slammed.

There had been several landslides after a small earthquake rocked the area. All hospitals in a hundred-mile radius were overflowing with the injured. If Luke had the supplies he could've set up a mobile OR in Crater Lake. He'd worked in worse conditions in Afghanistan.

Only, he hadn't practiced surgery since his honorable discharge and he certainly wasn't going to start on Shane Draven. He did surgery when needed, but he preferred practicing in the wilderness. So in this situation he'd rather this trauma surgeon work on Shane.

Still, she needed to know he was just as capable as her. He would have done the surgery another way. That was why he was questioning her.

She was cocky and full of herself. She definitely needed to be taken down a peg or two and he was just the guy to do it.

He might not practice as a traditional doctor, but he was just as much a surgeon as this woman. He had spent time on the front line, patching up soldiers in the midst of fire. How many lives had he saved? He wasn't sure, because he didn't keep score. All that mattered was saving lives. That was why he'd joined the army, it was what he'd wanted for so long, but he'd given it up for another.

Don't think about that now.

This surgeon had sized him up the moment he'd rushed in with Shane Draven's stretcher. She thought he was nothing but a first responder or a paramedic. Obviously a surgeon who didn't know any better. Paramedics were on the front line.

Usually he wouldn't question another surgeon in the OR, unless the patient was at serious risk, but the moment he walked into the OR with Shane she'd been treating him like a second-class citizen. Which was why he decided two could play at that game. So he questioned her every move.

She wanted a fight? Oh, he'd give her a fight.

"I will physically remove you," she snapped.

"I'd prefer you focus on my patient, Doctor, rather than argue over my presence here."

Her angry gaze met his. "You're questioning my skill, Mr.…."

Luke grinned smugly. "It's Dr. Ralston."

Her eyes widened in obvious surprise. "Doctor? I thought you were a paramedic."

"Looks can be deceiving, I guess, but I am a doctor. Though I'm not insulted you thought I was a paramedic, but I suppose that's the reason why you feel I should be kicked out of your OR."

She cursed under her breath. "Doctor or paramedic, it doesn't matter. I won't have you undermining my authority in my OR."

"This isn't your OR. You're not from around here."

"When I'm operating it's my OR, whether or not I'm from here."

Luke had to admire her spunk. And she was right. Perhaps he'd been undermining her a touch, but this was a man he'd pulled off the mountain and Dr. Eli Draven was this patient's father. He had made it clear that he was going to hold Luke responsible if Shane died, because Luke had allowed Dr. Petersen to place the chest tube.

Luke didn't know what Dr. Draven had against Dr. Petersen and he didn't really care. He'd pulled Shane down off the mountain. He was responsible for Shane's life. Dr. Draven had been throwing his weight around in the Missoula hospital, because the chief of surgery was one of his former students.

Besides, Shane was also the nephew of Silas Draven, who was sending Luke the most work up on the mountain, and Silas Draven was someone he didn't want to mess with. Luke appreciated all the work, but still he felt responsible for taking care of Shane. Luke, his brother,

Carson, and Dr. Petersen were all instrumental in getting Shane Draven to Missoula alive.

Luke hadn't left Shane's side since they were airlifted off the mountain and he wasn't going to leave him now.

No man gets left behind. Every life gets saved.

Luke's commanding officer's words rang true to the credo he lived by and it wasn't going to change now. He'd served two tours of duty as an army medic. Even when he couldn't live by that credo, when life couldn't be saved, it still drove him.

Don't think about losing patients now. Not with Shane on the table.

He shook those thoughts away. There was no place for them here.

"I got this man down off the mountain. He's my patient whether this is *your* OR or not."

"If you stay, Doctor, keep your opinions to yourself, then." She looked away and continued to work on Shane. A true hardened trauma surgeon, as he'd been once.

Damn, she's a spitfire.

He admired that about her and if circumstances had been different, meaning if he had any interest in pursuing a relationship again, he'd go after a strong-willed spitfire woman like her, but she was off-limits.

All women were.

He wanted to say more, but he knew when it was best to keep his mouth shut. As long as Shane's life was saved, and then he could get Eli Draven off his back, but he still watched the surgeon like a hawk.

"Yes, Doctor." And he gave her a little salute.

The surgeon mumbled a few choice words under her breath, but continued working on Shane.

Luke tried not to move toward the side of the table, where the lead surgeon stood, because if he did that then she would have grounds to throw him out of her OR.

He might be a bit of a control freak when it came to his patients, but there was no way he'd push it any further. He wasn't leaving this OR. He wasn't going to leave Shane Draven behind.

He didn't even know her name and he didn't care; she seemed to be competent. That was all that mattered.

When the surgery was over and they were wheeling Shane to the ICU, Luke gave up his perch in the OR. He planned to be on that ICU floor and personally monitoring Shane until he came out of the woods, as it were.

Dr. Ralston is a fine surgeon and a heck of an officer.

Only that wasn't entirely true. Not anymore. He wasn't an officer anymore. He'd given it all up. He didn't renew his commission because his wife was done being an army wife, but then Christine had left him. He did it all for her and for nothing.

Luke shook that thought from his head. Nope. He wasn't going there, because he wasn't going to let that happen again.

No one was going to dictate how his life should be again. Which was why he wouldn't settle down into a practice with Carson. It had been Christine's wish after he finished his tours of duty. He'd partner with Carson, raise a family with Christine and do what he loved, practicing medicine. He'd been planning to do that. Luke was going to give up the army for his wife to make her happy. At least that had been the plan.

Then it all went to hell in a handbasket.

Christine left him when he finished his second tour, for his best friend, Anthony.

He cursed under his breath as he walked down the hall to the ICU. He was angry at himself for allowing those thoughts to creep into his head again. To let her creep into his thoughts again. It was because he was in a hospital again.

Surrounded by people.

On his mountain it was just the sky, the wind, the trees and the majestic behemoths rising from the earth toward the clouds.

On his mountain he was himself and he had no one to answer to. No one but him controlled his life, his fate, his destiny.

"Hey!"

Luke spun around and saw a woman in surgical scrubs and cap approach him. The physical attraction was immediate. Full red lips, which were slightly pouty. White-blond hair peeked out from under the scrub cap and big blue-green eyes sparkled with annoyance.

Oh. No.

It was the spitfire surgeon. He'd only seen her over the surgical mask. Now seeing that she was a gorgeous woman with a strong personality to boot, well, that was a dangerous combination for Luke.

"Can I help you?" he asked.

She crossed her arms and sized him up. "I'm looking for a Dr. Ralston. Do you happen to know where he is?"

Luke took a step back, in case she started swinging, but then the words sank in and he realized she didn't know who he was. But then, he'd been wearing a surgical mask, cap and gown when he'd been in the OR with Shane. And this surgeon wasn't a local surgeon. She was visiting. She wouldn't recognize one person from another behind a surgical mask, because not being at this hospital every day he certainly didn't.

This could be fun, one part of him thought. While the other part told him to walk away and not entangle himself with her, because he knew she spelled danger.

"Why do you need him?"

She huffed. "If you see him tell him Dr. Ledet is looking for him." She turned to walk away and for a brief moment, one fraction of a second, he saw himself grabbing Dr. Ledet and pulling her into his arms, kissing her. Forcing the image away, he overcame the urge to taste those soft, moist lips, running his hands through her blond hair.

Maybe doing a little bit more than that.

Definitely dangerous.

"Where can he find you?" Luke asked.

She glanced at her watch. "After eight he can't. I'm flying back to New York."

"New York?"

"Yeah, I was here on business and decided to lend a hand for an old teacher. A fat lot of good that did me when I had to deal with an arrogant jerk like Dr. Ralston."

"Well, if I see him before eight I'll tell him."

She didn't thank him, just nodded curtly and walked away.

A New York surgeon, eh? Well, that was too bad, but it was for the best.

He'd never see her again.

It would've never worked anyway and not because of the distance, but because he would never let it.

CHAPTER ONE

Six months later, mid-January,
Crater Lake, Montana

I HATE THE COLD. I hate the cold.

Sarah thought coming from New York she'd be used to the frigid temperatures of northwest Montana. New York State bordered Canada, too; it should be the same, but it wasn't. Not at all. This was a different kind of cold. There was no moisture in the air and as she tried to shake the remnants of bone-chilling frigidity from her brand-new office, she couldn't remember why she'd decided to take this job in Crater Lake, Montana.

Dr. Draven.

Right. Her teacher from medical school. Dr. Eli Draven. She didn't study under him, because she didn't have an interest in becoming a cardio-thoracic surgeon, but she remembered him clearly from her days at Stanford.

He was a good teacher, if not a bit full of himself. He'd taken a shine to her until she'd decided not to pursue cardio; then she was no longer his star, but he still spoke highly of her and when this job was offered to her by Dr. Draven's brother, she couldn't pass up the opportunity, because she was more than ready to get out of New York and out of her father's iron grip.

No matter what she did, nothing was good enough for her parents.

They still saw her as their baby.

And they wouldn't be happy until she was living a pampered life in a Central Park West penthouse, married to an investment banker or a lawyer or even a doctor.

She couldn't be the doctor, however.

That was unacceptable.

Why do you need to work, pumpkin? Your husband, if you marry well, can take care of you.

Her mother's archaic way of thinking made her shake her head. Sarah peeled off the thick parka she'd bought when she moved out to Montana and hung it on the coat rack in her office. There were no cabs in Crater Lake, unless you counted the very unreliable Bob's Taxi, and she didn't.

At least she'd bought a car when she first landed in Missoula and had snow tires put on it. She was well versed in the rugged country living she was immersing herself in, even if she did complain about the cold just a bit.

Why do you want to go work out in the wilderness?

Sarah's sister, who was married to a very prominent surgeon and occupied one of those coveted penthouse suites on Central Park West, couldn't understand what was driving her to do this.

Sometimes Sarah wasn't even sure herself.

Because your dad got you your prestigious appointment in that Manhattan hospital. It wasn't you.

Sarah sighed when she remembered. After a summer

of touring around different hospitals in each state, presenting her Attending's research and teaching different surgeons on using the newest model of robotic surgery, she came home to New York to accept one of the most prestigious positions offered to a trauma surgeon at Manhattan Grace, only to find out that the only reason she was chosen to tour the country and work with Dr. Carroll was that her father was friends with Dr. Carroll. They played a few rounds of golf in the Hamptons. Even her brother-in-law pulled strings for her as if she couldn't make it on her own.

It just shook the foundation of everything Sarah had thought she knew.

It had knocked her confidence completely. Perhaps she wasn't the surgeon that she'd thought she was? So she'd turned down the position, much to her father's chagrin.

This was why she distanced herself from people. So many people trying to control the course of her life. She just couldn't trust anyone.

Not even herself.

Do you know how many strings I've had to pull for you over the years? Just so you can play doctor? Come to your senses, Sarah.

Sarah came to her senses all right. She threw the job back in her father's face, sold her apartment on the Upper West Side and took the job offer from Silas Draven to be the general practitioner and general surgeon at his newly opened ski lodge.

The ski lodge was set to open in one month, on Valentine's Day, and Sarah couldn't wait to get started. It would be a slower pace of life, but at least she would be able to help people here. She could be a doctor and not worry that her father was pulling strings to get her whatever she wanted. She was burned-out and really didn't know who she was or what she wanted anymore. She didn't even know if she wanted to be a surgeon and that thought terrified her, because for so long surgery had been her life.

For now a general practitioner sounded good. She could practice medicine and figure out where to go next. It sounded almost too good to be true.

Yeah. She could do this.

She smiled to herself and picked up her diploma from Stanford, in its frame, which was looking so forlorn on her desk. In fact her whole office was a complete disaster, with boxes and supplies scattered everywhere.

This was not an office yet. She couldn't see patients in a place that looked as if a storage unit had exploded. It wasn't very professional.

"Time to make this place my own." She spied the stepladder that had been left by the painters in the corner. She grabbed a hammer and a nail. She'd never hammered anything in her life, but there was always a first time for everything.

"I can do this," she said, as if trying to reassure herself. How hard could it be to hammer a nail into a wall? She had this. Except where she wanted to put the nail in was a little out of her reach for the stepladder. So she climbed to the very top of the ladder and held the wall for a bit of balance. Her perch was precarious, but all she was doing was hammering in one nail and it wasn't that big of a drop down to the carpet.

She lined up the nail and held the hammer, ready to drive the nail home.

"Did you check for a stud?" a male voice asked from behind.

"What…?" Sarah turned, surprised that someone had snuck into her office and she hadn't heard them, but in the process of turning around she forgot what a precarious perch she had on the top of the stepladder and lost her footing.

Sarah closed her eyes and waited for her backside to hit the floor, but instead she found herself landing in two very strong arms and being held against a broad, muscular chest.

"You shouldn't stand on the top of a…" He trailed off.

"Who are you to tell me…?" Sarah opened her eyes and bit back a gasp as she stared up at the most stunningly handsome man she'd ever seen. Brown hair, with just a bit of curl, deep blue eyes and a neat beard, which just added to the ruggedness of his face.

Those blue eyes of his were wide with surprise and then she had the niggling sensation that she'd seen this face before, but couldn't recall when or where.

"What in the name of all that's good and holy were you doing up there with a hammer?" he demanded as he quickly set her down on her feet and took a step back from her as if she were on fire.

"Excuse me?" she asked. Who did this guy think he was?

"I'm telling you that wasn't a smart move climbing up on that ladder. You could've killed yourself if I hadn't showed up."

"Why did you show up? Who are you?"

His blue eyes flashed and he crossed his arms, fixing

her with a stare that was meant to frighten her. Well, it didn't scare her.

"I'm here to take you out."

"Out? I don't believe I made any dates with anyone since I arrived in town."

He smirked. "Not on a date, darling. Though if I were to go on a date with someone, you're quite the fetching thing."

"Fetching? Darling?"

He held up his hands. "Look, I was teasing. I'm not interested in dating coworkers, let alone headstrong doctors from out east. I'm to take you out on the skis to show you some of the private residences being built and how to access them."

"Oh." She was slightly disappointed. Not that she had any interest in dating a mountain man, but a fling might've been fun. Especially since this mountain man was deliciously handsome.

Don't think like that. You're here to prove yourself, not date.

Sarah didn't date.

Her parents had tried over and over, setting her up with the *right* sort of man. Well, in their eyes anyway. It was just easier to concentrate on work and not bother with dating, romance or sex.

All the right kind of men Sarah had dated briefly in her early twenties were all wrong. It never felt right. There was never that spark or connection one was supposed to feel when falling in love with someone, but then again, since she'd never experienced it, maybe it was just a myth.

Men seemed to gravitate to her because she was a socialite and came from money. It was all about status for them, and as she was too focused on her career, she never pursued a man on her own and she never made the time to look for a man beyond her parents' circles.

Single life was so much easier.

And lonely.

"Do you know how to ski?" he asked disparagingly, breaking her chain of thoughts.

"No." Then she groaned inwardly at the thought of going back outside in the cold.

"I thought as much," he said condescendingly. "Well, I'll give you a few minutes to suit up so we can head out."

It was the tone that sparked a vivid memory for her suddenly. She could see those dark blue eyes glittering above a surgical mask. Defying her.

Get out of my OR!

Not on your life.

No way. It couldn't be him. It just couldn't be him.

"What's wrong?" he asked. "Don't like the cold?"

"It's not that. I think I know you."

He smiled. "Do you?"

"What's your name?" she asked.

Don't be him. Don't be him.

Then he grinned like the cat who'd got the cream. "Dr. Luke Ralston."

Damn, but then she was ticked. She'd put that memory of her time in Missoula far from her mind, not giving it much of a second thought because, really, what did it matter? She was in New York, let Luke Ralston have Montana.

Besides, Shane Draven had pulled through.

It was all trivial. Except now she was in Montana, working on their patient's uncle's resort and Dr. Luke

Ralston was her coworker? This was a totally messed-up situation. Something she was not comfortable with.

"You knew exactly who I was."

Luke shrugged. "Not at first, but when you fell into my arms it all came back to me."

"And you didn't say anything? Like, maybe, 'Hey, we know each other, we've worked together before' or something like that?"

He shrugged again and then hooked his thumbs into the belt loops on the waist of his tight, tight jeans. "What does it matter?"

"It matters a lot. You're a jerk!"

"Why am I a jerk? I mean, I did save you from probably concussing yourself or something."

"You were the guy I talked to in the hallway in Missoula. When I asked who Dr. Ralston was, you said you didn't know where he was. You lied to me."

"I didn't really want to argue with you in the hallway. I was on my way to the ICU to check on my patient. To make sure he pulled through surgery."

"He was my patient."

He grinned, smugly. "I brought him down off that mountain. He was my patient. You were just a locum surgeon. You didn't stay to make sure he made it through the night. You headed back east, to wherever you came from. I knew nothing about you and I didn't trust you. Of course, now you're going to be a regular here in town."

"Had I known there was a Ralston in Crater Lake I would've turned the job down."

Luke chuckled. "You must've taken this job on an impulse, then."

"Why do you say that?"

"If you'd researched Crater Lake you'd realize the

family practice in town is run by a Ralston. I wasn't really hiding my identity. Not in my town."

Damn. He was right. She hadn't really looked to see what physicians were in town. She'd taken the job so quickly. She'd just been so eager to get out of New York City and away from her father's control. Crater Lake had sounded like a nice small town, and a job catering to the rich and famous in a resort had sounded perfect. It was a chance to prove herself to those who moved in her parents' circles.

Then maybe she could step out of her father's shadow. She wouldn't be Sarah Ledet, New York heiress and daughter of Vin Ledet, one of the wealthiest men on the eastern seaboard. She'd be Dr. Ledet, physician.

"You're regretting your decision to take this job, aren't you?" Luke asked. "I can see it on your face. You look absolutely horrified."

"Not the job, just who I have to work with."

He grinned and then laughed. "You're still a spitfire."

"Spitfire?"

"It's a compliment."

Sarah tried not to smile. She didn't want to smile. He was the jerk who'd disrupted her OR, given her a hard time and then lied to her. He was the one who'd questioned her surgical procedure and every move she'd made on that patient until she'd snapped. Only his smile had been infectious and she couldn't remember the last time she'd laughed, even though she was ticked off that it was him. The thorn in her side from last summer, standing right there in her office.

She should just throw him out. As she should have done from her OR.

When she glanced back up at him the lighthearted

mood had changed. He looked annoyed and uncomfortable.

"What?" she asked.

"Nothing."

"Something changed. Just a moment ago you were complimenting me and joking. Now you look annoyed."

"I'm annoyed we're wasting the light standing around pointing fingers."

"Okay, you're right. I'm sorry."

"Well, I would gear up. I don't have all day to wait around for you." He walked out of her office leaving her standing there absolutely confused.

What had just happened?

Sarah wasn't sure, but she knew it would be best to keep her distance from Luke Ralston, though that was going to be tricky seeing how she was about to be dragged out on the mountain in the bitter cold with a man who was a little bit dangerous.

Not just a little bit dangerous.

A lot.

CHAPTER TWO

DAMN. IT HAD to be the spitfire.

Luke had forgotten all about her when he'd returned to Crater Lake after Shane Draven had pulled through. For a while he'd thought of that trauma surgeon he'd butted heads with in Missoula, but as he'd dealt with the last messy stages of his divorce, he'd put her from his mind.

Dealing with his ex just reminded him of all the reasons why he didn't trust women or romantic entanglements.

It hurt too much, but Christine wasn't the only reason. Hurt went both ways. He liked his life too much and part of that was doing risky things to save lives up on the mountain.

He'd given up his life in the army for a woman he loved and look how that turned out.

To live the life he'd made for himself since leaving the army, he couldn't have love. He wouldn't give up his life for anyone.

He threw himself completely into his work and avoided hanging around the town of Crater Lake as much as possible. It was bad enough being divorced, but having your ex-wife and former best friend, who was now your ex's husband, living and working in the town you grew up in was a little too much for him.

The problem was, his former best friend was the town sheriff. That was why they were staying in Crater Lake, but Luke wouldn't be driven out of town.

He'd grown up here. He was going to stay here.

And an injury to his leg during an avalanche last winter prevented him from returning to active duty, even after giving up his commission.

Besides, he preferred being up on the mountain.

He liked being alone in his cabin. He liked the work; though he missed surgery and envied Carson just a bit for seeing patients every day, there was no way he could've chained himself to a desk, to an office or a hospital. He would suffocate, but he'd been willing to do it for Christine.

Maybe if you hadn't joined the army Christine wouldn't have left. Maybe you could've been happy.

Only his call of duty had been strong. He'd always wanted to serve and further his medical education in the army. And Christine had known that when they'd got together.

Luke cursed under his breath.

No, she would've left. Just as he hadn't wanted to change the course of his career, Christine hadn't wanted to be his wife. Of course now he wasn't a soldier, but by the time his career in the army was over Christine was over him.

No, he wasn't going to think about her. She'd broken his heart and he wouldn't let her or anyone else make him feel that way again.

Why did it have to be her? Why did it have to be the spitfire?

Silas hadn't told him the name of the physician who would be working at the resort. All he'd said was that she was from out east and had asked if Luke could train her on mountain survival and survival medicine.

She's from money, Ralston. I'm sure she's been on skis, but probably not in a way that would satisfy your sensibilities.

Which was why Luke was here. It was just fate was a bit sick and twisted by making that physician Dr. Ledet, the surgeon he'd butted heads with.

As if dealing with her in the summer wasn't enough? Maybe it was karma? He'd teased Carson when Esme Petersen had come to town. Perhaps this was retribution?

The only difference was Carson had found love with Esme and Luke was not looking for that at all.

Carson hadn't been looking, either.

"Is this okay?"

Luke shook that little voice from his head and glanced over at Sarah. She had a good parka on, waterproof mitts, a hat with ear flaps, boots, but nothing on her legs except black stretchy pants that fit her curves like a glove. His blood heated.

Think about something else.

"Where are your snow pants?" Luke asked, tearing his gaze away from her. He didn't want to look at her at the moment. He had to regain control.

"Snow pants?"

"Don't you ski?"

"I told you before, no. I've never skied."

"Doesn't every eastern WASP rich girl ski? Isn't that what the Poconos are for?"

Her stare was icy cold and she put her hands on those

curvy hips. Hips he'd thought about touching himself. "Excuse me?"

Luke groaned. He wasn't going to get in an argument with her. "You need snow pants. If you fall out there and your pants get wet there's no way we're turning around so you can change. I'm here to teach you survival skills. If you were out there on your own, there would be no option to change. You'd freeze to death."

Sarah still looked as if she were going to skewer him alive. "Fine. I'll find some snow pants, but, really, stereotyping me, that was so not cool."

"If the shoe fits."

She cocked her eyebrows and smirked. "Oh, really? Didn't we have this argument in the summer? I seem to recall bits and pieces of it…"

He groaned. "Fine. You're right. I did accuse you of stereotyping me. I apologize, but, really, put on some snow pants before we lose the light."

"Fine and, for your information, not all of us 'rich girls' ski. Some of us prefer yachts and sailing." She winked and then disappeared into her office again.

Luke rolled his eyes, but couldn't help but laugh to himself. He still admired her spunk.

When she came out of her office again, she was properly attired.

"Good, now let's get down to the ski shack and get geared up. I'm going to take you up the first of the four main trails at this resort."

Sarah fell into step behind him; the only sound was the swishing of the nylon fabric rubbing together as they walked down the hall and outside. Luke tried not to laugh, because just under that sound was some muttering. And maybe some bad words, but he couldn't quite tell.

"I feel like a marshmallow," she mumbled. "Do I look like one?"

"Yes. You do, but it will keep you warm." He helped open the door to outside. "Ms. Marshmallow."

With a huff Sarah pushed past him out into the snow. "You're a bit of a jerk. Has anyone ever told you that?"

"Several people."

There was a twinkle to her eye and she smiled slightly. "Good."

"Well, now that's all settled. Let's get the skis on and head out." He led the way to the ski shack, which was closed up. It would open on more regular hours when the resort had its official grand opening on Valentine's Day. Right now, Luke had full run of it and of all the equipment.

It was one of the perks he liked about working for Silas Draven. He wasn't a huge fan of skiing, but cross-country skiing on the mountain trails was the only way to access some of the remote residents of Crater Lake. His horse just couldn't handle the deep snow that collected on the side of the mountain in the winter.

And he would never put his horse in the way of a possible avalanche.

He glanced over to the southern peak, to the forest that was thick, before it disappeared into the alpine zone of the mountain. Old Nestor lived up in that dense forest.

Nestor was a hermit. He liked to live off the grid and away from everyone else. Luke admired him and went to check on him often. Nestor was the one who'd taught him many things about surviving on the mountain, since Nestor had been living up on the mountain for as long as Luke could remember and before that.

Only, Nestor was getting old and in the winter the cold bothered him something fierce. So Luke was thankful for access to skis and snowshoes. It made checking on Nestor that much easier.

He unlocked the door and headed over to the rack.

"Oh, cool! Snowshoes," Sarah remarked. "I've always wanted to try them."

"Really?" he asked, surprised.

She nodded. "Anything to make walking on snow easier."

"Snowshoeing is just as much work as skiing. Skis can move you faster."

"Yeah, but cross-country skis don't go uphill. You said you wanted me to learn how to access trails and stuff. Shouldn't I be snowshoeing?"

She's got a point. Skiing will only get you so far.

"You're right," Luke admitted. "Okay. We'll add snowshoes to our pack."

"Pack?"

Luke picked up the large rucksack that he'd stuffed full of emergency and survival gear. The pack was probably half the size of Sarah and when he held it up to her, her eyes widened and her mouth opened for a moment in surprise.

Then she shrugged. "Sure. That's reasonable. Just out of curiosity, though, what's in it?"

"Don't you know?"

She glared at him. "Really?"

"You should know."

"I don't. I've never lived near a mountain. I'm from Manhattan."

Luke shook his head. "Hey, I was trying not to stereotype you."

"I ought to slug you."

He laughed at that. He couldn't help himself; it was easy to tease her. He was enjoying the banter. "I'm sorry. I'll stop."

She crossed her arms. "Fine or I could start talking about mountain men."

"What do you know about mountain men?" he asked.

Sarah shook her head. "Tell me what's in the bag."

Luke knelt down and unzipped it. "This is a standard pack to help you survive in a winter climate on the mountain."

"So I'll only need to carry around this stuff in the winter?"

"No," Luke said. "Some things can be left behind, but if you're working up near the Alpine zone or higher, you'd be surprised how cold it can get even in the heat of summer."

"Okay, so always be prepared for snow?"

He nodded. "Yep. So in this pack you have your essentials like first-aid kit. The only thing I haven't packed in here is a change of clothes for you so I just packed some of my old clothes. If worse comes to worst you can always wear those."

Her cheeks reddened slightly, as if she was blushing, but Luke could've been wrong. It could've been the wind.

She cleared her throat. "Go on."

"Canteen for water."

"What about melting snow?"

Luke cocked an eyebrow. "You're going to need something to carry it in. I also have a pot, ice pick, rope, matches, GPS, topographical map of the area, one day's worth of rations, sleeping bag and an axe."

"It's like you're camping."

"If you get lost out there, yeah, you'll be 'camping' until help arrives." Then he held out something he was sure she'd never seen before. "This is one of the most important things."

"A compass?"

"Close. It's an altimeter."

"A what?" she asked.

"It's a barometric altimeter. It measures changes in atmosphere. The higher you go, the lower the pressure is. If your GPS or compass isn't working, this can be used along with the map to determine where you are. I'll show you how to use it."

"Good, because seriously my eyes were glazing over there for a second." She laughed nervously and he handed her the altimeter to look at. "Though, really, won't you know if you're at the top of the mountain? How can you get lost if you're up there?"

"You can get lost all right and if you're not used to high altitude you can get acute mountain sickness. Dr. Petersen in town suffered from it last year. Just ask her."

"Dr. Petersen? There's a female doctor in town? I thought the other doctor was your brother."

"Dr. Petersen is a cardio surgeon. She's opened a clinic in partnership with my brother. She sees a lot of heart patients from around this area."

"Huh, I wonder what would make a cardio-thoracic surgeon settle down in a place like this," Sarah wondered out loud. "I mean, the nearest hospital is quite a bit away."

"Why did you?" Luke asked.

The question caught her off guard, because she blushed again and quickly started examining the altimeter.

Did it really matter?

It shouldn't matter to him, but he couldn't help but wonder why. There weren't many single people in Crater Lake. It was small. When they'd first got together, Christine had wanted to stay in Crater Lake, and when he got his posting to Germany she wouldn't go with him. She didn't want to live on a base. She didn't want to be an army wife. So she'd decided to stay and start a family with Anthony.

A family he wanted so desperately.

A family he was never going to have.

Don't think about it.

"Come on, I'll pack the snowshoes, as well. We have some distance to travel and some more stuff I have to show you before it gets too dark, and it gets dark here early." He took the altimeter back from her and packed it in the knapsack.

He didn't have time to focus on the past. To focus on his past hurts or the things he would never have.

He was here to do a job and that was to show Dr. Sarah Ledet how to survive on the mountain. That was all. Once he'd done that, he never had to see her again and he was going to make sure that happened.

Sarah thought her lungs were going to burst. She was sweaty and exhausted. Parts of her that she hadn't even known existed ached and each breath was harder to take.

At least I'm not cold.

She just shook her head and leaned up against a tree as Luke set their skis against a fence line that ran on one side of the trail. He glanced over at her.

"You okay? You look tired."

Of course I'm tired, but she wasn't going to tell him that. All her life she'd been labelled and she'd had enough of it.

"I'm fine. Just catching my breath."

He frowned. "If you get a headache or feel ill, let me know right away. That's a sign of mountain sickness."

"Will do." She didn't feel sick and didn't have a headache. All she was was sweaty and tired. "You said Dr. Petersen had this? How did she get over it?"

"You get off the mountain."

"I live on the mountain."

Luke chuckled. "You don't live that far up the mountain, though."

"I thought it was pretty high up, considering I used to live pretty close to sea level."

"Never thought about it that way." Luke pulled out the snowshoes that had been strapped to the back of the enormous pack Sarah had had on her back, which was now resting under a fir tree on a bed of needles so as not to get wet.

Maybe she was picking up mountain survival a bit.

"You ready for snowshoeing?"

Sarah groaned. "How about we head for home? I'm sure it will be faster downhill on our skis."

Luke chuckled. "We'll head down soon enough. I

want to see you practice on these. Just up the trail the snow gets pretty deep. Too deep for skis."

"No one lives up that trail."

"Right, not now, but when this trail is groomed regularly and a lone cross-country skier or snowshoer gets injured or lost up there, you're going to have to know how to get to them."

Sarah sighed, but then took the snowshoes and strapped them on. They were quite easy and didn't look like she'd expected them to. They were made of aluminum and nylon.

"Take a step and tell me what you think," he said as he moved back and then clamped his on.

Sarah began to walk up the trail and it took her a few times to really find her stride, but it wasn't all that bad.

"I think this is easier than the skiing, to be honest." She bounced in her step. "I could get used to these."

"Just be careful," Luke called out over his shoulder.

"Of wha…?" She spoke too soon as she lost her footing and toppled face-first into a large snowdrift. Snow shot up her nose and into her mouth, burning.

I hate winter. I hate winter.

"Are you okay?" Luke was beside her and she could hear the amusement in his voice.

"Fine," she said as she wiped her face. "I really wasn't expecting to do a face-plant with snowshoes on. Skis for sure, but snowshoes. I know I'm klutzy."

"Well, at least this time I didn't have to catch you." He rubbed some of the snow from her face and a rush of butterflies invaded her stomach as she looked up into his eyes. He was smiling at her, but it was tender, as if he really cared that she'd done a horrible face-plant in the snow.

Of course the butterflies could be from that mountain sickness, but somehow she didn't think so.

"Thanks," she said, looking away and glad the snow had made her cheeks red, because if it hadn't he would surely see her blush.

"You should've been wearing your goggles to protect your eyes. Goggles don't belong on your forehead."

"I forgot to put them back on after my break. I was wearing them when we were skiing."

Luke helped her to her feet, his strong arms around her waist as he righted her. She liked the feeling of his arms around her, steadying her. It was comforting.

You don't date. You can't date.

Her mother would set her up on the occasional date, but those were all with men who would take care of her. Who just wanted her to be this pretty, well-dressed society wife. None of them were really interested in her and she'd been burned too many times.

And she never had time to find men on her own, because she was working so darn hard to show her parents that she could have it all, that she didn't need a man to take care of her. That she was old enough to take care of herself.

Men were off-limits.

Of course, her father admitting that he'd had a hand in almost every aspect of her career made her think that all that hard work, all those hours she'd put in weren't worth it. Maybe she should've been out there partying, being seen in all the right places with all the right people, just like her older sister.

Really?

She shook her head. That was all in the past, though. She was in Crater Lake now. In a job of her own choosing and she planned to make the most of it. Even if it meant traipsing around in the snow with the sexiest mountain man she'd ever laid eyes on.

A man that also drove her a bit crazy.

"You ready to try again?" Luke asked.

"Sure. The sooner we get this done, the sooner I can head back to my apartment in the resort and curl up in front of a fire."

"Glad to see you're on board." Luke went over and picked up the knapsack. "You're going to need this."

Sarah moaned as it was placed over her shoulders again. "Thanks. I almost forgot."

"It's your lifeline up here. You can't forget. We'll do a half-mile hike up this trail through the snow, we'll triage a fake patient I have up there and then head back down to the resort. That's after we build a makeshift stretcher."

"You have a patient up there?" Sarah asked. "Who in their right mind would wait out in the cold for hours for you?"

Luke winked. "It's a dummy."

"Clearly."

He rolled his eyes. "It's a simulation. A mannequin. It's not a real person, but it's simulating a very real situation."

Sarah sighed. "Okay. Lead on."

Luke nodded and pulled on his own pack. She watched him for a few moments as he broke a path ahead of her. Even though he was wearing thick snow pants you could still make out the outline of his strong, muscular thighs and his tight butt.

Sarah shook her head. It was apparent she was suffering from altitude sickness, because she was think-ing about the strangest things.

Dr. Luke Ralston was off-limits.

He worked for Silas Draven as well, so that meant it was a no go for her. She didn't mix business with pleasure.

So she couldn't think about Luke that way.

She just couldn't.

CHAPTER THREE

IT HAD BEEN three days since she last saw Dr. Luke Ralston and that was a good thing after the torment he'd put her through up on that high mountain trail. He hadn't been kidding about a simulation. When they'd got to the mannequin, it had been half-buried in ice and under a tree trunk. There had been broken skis and fake blood.

Sarah had never picked up an axe before, but she did that day. She had the blister and the splinters to prove it.

Even though she'd wanted to tell Luke his simulation was cracked, she hadn't backed down. She knew that he thought of her as some kind of spoiled rich girl and that was far from the truth. So she'd learned quite quickly how to use an axe. She'd shown him a thing or two.

She'd also learned how to make a makeshift gurney out of broken skis, rope, a tarp and duct tape. After assessing the mannequin's ABCs, they'd got him on their gurney and down off the mountain.

There had been quite a few stares as she'd come down to the lodge with a mannequin on a stretcher splattered with craft-store paint. Still, she'd done it and he'd grudgingly admitted that she'd done a good job and that was the last she'd seen of him.

She thought she was going to be put through some more training, but so far she hadn't seen him. She should be happy about that and she was, but she wasn't totally. She looked for him everywhere, as if he were going to pop out of the shadows and frighten her. The thought of seeing him actually made her excited, as if she were some young girl with a crush.

There was no denying Luke was handsome. She'd thought that the first moment she saw him. But there was something else about him. A lone wolf quality. He was a man who didn't want or need anyone else. The kind of man who was completely untamed.

He was a challenge, and she'd always liked a challenge.

Focus.

She couldn't think about him that way. Distance. That was what she needed. Right now this time was about her. Career was her life.

If she got together with someone, her parents would never believe she could function on her own. That she was a surgeon.

Even then, she wasn't sure of anything. Everything she'd thought she earned had really come because she was Vin Ledet's daughter. Her father knew people on the admissions board at college. She'd fought so hard for her MCAT scores, achieving one of the highest that year, which should've been enough to get her into medical school, but apparently not enough for her father. Then her residency and her fellowship, her father had had a hand in that. Everything she'd pursued in her medical career her father had had a hand in.

No wonder her belief in herself was fleeting.

Except this place.

She'd earned this on her own by saving Silas Draven's nephew Shane in Missoula.

Silas and her father moved in the same circles and never saw eye to eye.

Sarah knew it wasn't because of who her father was. This job was because of her own merit.

Someone believed in her abilities and she wasn't going to let them down.

She could do this.

This was her focus and she was going to prove to everyone she was up to the task. This clinic was going to be her pride and joy.

Her clinic had opened a bit earlier than she'd planned, but Silas Draven had had a large party of tourists coming in and he'd wanted to make sure that it was up and running. He wanted his resort to be all-inclusive, and didn't want his guests having to go into town and wait at the local clinic.

Even though the resort hadn't officially opened, the large party of skiers was certainly giving her a run for her money. Her clinic had been full the two days she'd been open. It was usually just minor stuff, cuts and sunburns, but she was enjoying the work and, the best part, it was honest work. Though, she missed surgery, the rush of the hospital, but this job she'd got on her own.

Her parents didn't have a hand in it.

Really, Sarah? Sunburns? The only sun you should think about is evening out your tan.

She cursed under her breath, trying to shake away her sister's annoying voice. Her sister had never said those exact words, but she could almost picture her, standing in the waiting room and saying them, because her sister had nagged her about similar things before.

"Patient ten?" Sarah briefly looked up from her chart, to the busy waiting room at her clinic. "Patient number ten?"

A man with a very red face stood up and walked toward her. He nodded and winced. "I am Mr. Fontblanc."

Sarah smiled. "I know, we just use a numbering system here to keep anonymity."

"Ah, oui. Merci beaucoup."

"You can have a seat in exam room one. I'll be with you momentarily."

Mr. Fontblanc nodded again, shuffling off down the hall. She looked at her chart one more time and was about to call the next victim of a really bad sunburn when the door to her clinic burst open. Luke strode into her pristine clinic, dirty and breathless.

"What're you doing?" he asked.

"I'm seeing patients," Sarah said, trying not to look at him. Distance was the key.

"Good, I have a patient for you."

"What? Where?"

"He's in the lobby."

"In the lobby? Why is he in the lobby?"

Luke rolled his eyes and crossed his arms. "Would you stop giving me the third degree and just come to the lobby?"

"I have a patient waiting in my exam room. I can't leave him there."

"Is your patient bleeding profusely with a head injury?"

"That's confidential."

Luke shook his head and pushed past her into the exam room.

"Dr. Ralston!" Sarah tried to stop him, but he was in the exam room. Mr. Fontblanc looked a bit stunned.

"Sorry to keep you waiting…" Luke peered at the man. "Too much sun?"

"*Oui*…uh, yes."

"*Vous êtes Français?*" Luke inquired in perfect French.

"*Oui.*"

Sarah stood back, stunned. She didn't know French at all. Spanish, she knew quite a bit, but French, she was at a loss. Luke seemed to know it. He questioned the man briefly and then pulled out a tube of topical cream from her medicine cupboard, handing it to her patient and then patting him on the back.

The patient still seemed shell-shocked, but overall was happy.

"*Merci.*"

"*Pas de problème,*" Luke said.

The patient left the room and Luke turned back to her. "You ready to go and help the patient in the lobby now?"

"What just happened here?" She watched as Luke began to grab suturing trays, gauze and a bolus for an IV. "What's going on? Why are you stealing my supplies?"

He groaned and grabbed her hand. "Come on. I need another doctor's help with this."

Sarah didn't really have much of a choice as she was dragged from her clinic. The other patients watched her leave, just as confused as she was at the moment.

"If this patient needs another doctor, why didn't you get your brother to help you?" Sarah asked.

"There was no time to take this man to town." Luke pushed the button on the elevator, not looking at her, but watching for the door to light up and open.

"What's wrong with the patient?" she asked.

"Have you ever seen a mauling?"

Sarah gasped. "Did you just say a mauling? By what?"

Luke glanced at her. "A bear."

She shook her head. She'd seen pictures in textbooks when she was a resident. As a trauma surgeon you had to be prepared for everything, but she'd never actually encountered one personally. She was aware of the damage that could be done. Her stomach twisted in a knot at the very idea, but they were in bear country. It was to be expected.

The elevator arrived and they got on. It was a quick ride down to the lobby. When the doors opened everything was in chaos and Sarah could see a trail of blood from the door to a boardroom down a darkened hall.

"I don't get it," Sarah remarked as she fell into step beside Luke.

"What don't you get?" he asked.

"Bears hibernate. It's January."

Luke sighed. "No, not really. It's called torpor. It's like hibernation—they can be woken. This idiot was fool enough to stumble on a bear's den and, instead of leaving the bear well enough alone, he crawled inside to get a picture. Thankfully, people were with him."

"Idiot is right."

He nodded. "If you haven't seen a mauling before, prepare yourself."

She nodded. "I've seen worse stuff in the ER."

"Possible disembowelment and bite marks?"

"Yeah. A car can do damage to a patient, too. I'm ready."

A small smile played on his lips, but just briefly. It was almost as if he was impressed that she didn't shy away or that she wasn't squeamish at the prospect. It scared her. It was something she was completely unfamiliar with. It was something she was a little terrified about herself since moving from Manhattan to a remote town in northwest Montana, but this was her job. She was going to help Luke any way that she could. It was the trauma surgeon in her.

"Did you bring enough supplies down?" she asked.

"We've got enough supplies in here. We have to get him stabilized before the air ambulance gets here."

Sarah nodded. "Okay."

She walked into the room and tried not to gasp. The man was in bad shape. There were deep lacerations to his arm, his legs and torso, but his face was really bad. She could see teeth marks, deep gouging all over; she could see bone on his arm and the bandages on his abdomen were already soaked through, which tipped Sarah off that this guy would need packing if he was going to survive the trip to the nearest hospital. The way his abdomen was distended, she knew from her trained eye he would suffer from compartment syndrome sooner rather than later and that could be fatal if not controlled.

"Buddy, I've brought another doctor here to help me." Luke spoke to the man. "Just take it easy."

The man just moaned.

"I'm surprised he's lucid."

"Me, too," Luke said. "I did give him a shot of morphine in the field when I found him, but he's lost a lot of blood."

Sarah nodded and pulled off her white lab coat. "Gloves?"

Luke gestured in the direction of the sideboard, where a box of rubber gloves was waiting. She slipped on a pair and then grabbed a pack of gauze.

"I need you to hold him down—I'm going to put in a central line," Luke told her.

"You're going to put in a central line here?"

He nodded. "No choice. Look at his arms, and his veins are chunky. The bear did damage. Lots of damage."

"Sure." Sarah leaned over and held the man down. She looked down into his dark eyes, full of confusion and fear. "Don't worry, sir. We're going to get you patched up in no time. Soon you won't be in so much pain. I promise."

"Hold him now for me," Luke said.

"I've got him. Just do it."

Luke inserted the central line quickly and efficiently. She couldn't remember the last time she'd seen someone put in a central line so fast before. She was impressed. The patient barely flinched, but that could be because maybe some of the fight had gone out of him, or it could've been the morphine.

Once he was hooked up to a drip, he passed out and Luke went about stitching what they could to help control the bleeding. Sarah packed his face and set a broken bone in his arm. They didn't say much to each other; there wasn't much to say, really. They were both totally focused on their patient.

The last time they'd worked on a patient together,

they were at each other's throats. This was different. It was nice. Comforting almost, as if she'd been doing this with him for a long, long time, and she couldn't remember the last time she'd felt such a familiarity with another surgeon before.

"He has extensive damage to his abdomen. There is nothing I can do here."

"Pack him?" Luke asked.

She nodded. "No choice. If I start poking around to find the source of the bleeders I could do more damage. His body needs to rest before repairs. Does bear saliva have an envenomation? You know, like the wolverine or Komodo dragon?"

"No, but the saliva often carries staph or strep, which can lead to infections and organ shutdown." He frowned and seemed upset for a brief moment. "Either way he'll need a good course of antibiotics, tetanus and rabies. Though rabies from bear bites are rare."

"Why is that?"

"The injury rate from bear attacks in North America is like one person per couple million. Of course, that report by S. Herrero is from 1970. It could be different now."

"Wow."

"The more we encroach on their territory, the worse it gets. I read a lot on animal attacks for obvious reasons."

"Makes sense."

She would have never thought about reading medical papers on animal attacks before coming here. It wasn't something that happened a lot in Manhattan. She'd dealt with dog, cat and human bites in the city.

It was time to broaden her reading if she was going to stay here.

Luke impressed her with his knowledge and that was a hard thing to do. She liked working with him. They could work on the patient seamlessly and still chat easily. She'd never had that kind of rapport with another surgeon before.

It felt so right working with him. It was just sad that this poor man had to suffer and Sarah decided right then and there: she didn't want to mess with a bear in any way, shape or form.

When they had done all they could do, they just monitored him and waited for the air ambulance to come. Nothing but the sound of the portable monitors between them.

"How long do you think it will be before the air ambulance comes?" Sarah asked, breaking the silence.

"Should be here soon, though there was a storm rolling in from the southwest. I hope that didn't hinder the flight in from Missoula."

"If it does?" she asked.

"Great Falls will send one. Missoula is bigger, though."

She nodded and there was a knock at the door. A paramedic stood there. "Someone call an air ambulance?"

They worked with the paramedics to get the patient onto the stretcher and then out into the cold to the waiting ambulance, which would take him down to the airport. The ambulance had landed on Silas Draven's private airstrip.

Once the patient was loaded up the ambulance flicked on its sirens and headed down the long windy road to Crater Lake. Sarah didn't stand outside for too long because it was cold and she didn't have her coat on.

Luke followed her back inside.

"I hope he makes it," Sarah remarked.

"He will. Death is rare. Although compartment syndrome worries me."

"Me, too," Sarah said. "Glad you caught that, as well."

"I've seen compartment syndrome many a time as an army medic. The bowels inflating, then the liver and kidneys begin to shut down. It's a domino effect."

"It is. I thought you would've followed him. Didn't you get him down off the mountain?" she teased, as that had been the reason why he'd stood in her OR last summer questioning her every move.

"I usually would, but he woke a bear up. The bear just didn't go back to sleep. I have to track it and…" He trailed off.

"What?"

"I have to make sure it goes back to its den, but, since the bear has been fully woken up from its torpor, it's going to be looking for food. I don't want to have to destroy it."

She frowned. "Oh. I hope you don't have to do that."

"Me, too. It's not the bear's fault that moron decided it would be a good selfie. Me with a bear."

Sarah chuckled. "A tourist?"

"Close, a surveyor. A new one. The surveyors I train to work up in these mountains know better than that."

"I'm sure they do, but I didn't see his pack."

Luke chuckled. "I think he left it up there on the mountain."

"How are his friends?"

"Shaken up. I should go talk to them."

"Do you want me to?"

"No. It's okay. I can. Thanks for helping me," he said.

"I really didn't have a choice." She smiled at him.

"I'm sorry about that. I overstep my boundaries in emergency situations."

"It's no problem. That's what I'm here for. To help patients."

And then it hit her.

Oh. No.

"Darn it," she cursed out loud. "Darn it."

"What?" he asked.

"My patients in the clinic. How long was I gone for?"

Luke glanced at his wrist. "About forty minutes."

Sarah groaned. "If they complain to Mr. Draven..."

"If they complain I will tell him you helped one of his employees who was dumb enough to stick his face in a bear's den."

"I think Mr. Draven will be more ticked about the patients in my clinic, though."

Luke frowned. "Come on. We'll tell them why."

"Are you serious? We have to protect privacy rights."

"They won't know him. These are tourists. Tourists like bear stories."

Sarah looked at him as if he were crazy. Maybe he was. Maybe he'd spent too many winters up on that mountain and he'd lost his mind. Her patients were going to be mad that she'd left them up there for that long.

Mr. Draven had made it pretty clear that he wanted patients to be seen within twenty minutes of their arrival and registration at the clinic. Not forty.

"I don't know. I don't think that's a good idea."

Luke rolled his eyes and then took her hand. It shocked her. It was calloused, warm and strong. It sent a tingle of electricity through her and she could feel the heat flooding her cheeks at just the simple act of a touch from him, but then she wasn't used to physical intimacy. It had been so long and her parents weren't exactly huggers. So that simple touch threw her for a loop.

"Come on, we don't have to tell the particulars, but you can bet when I warn that group of European tourists off the mountain trails because of a bear being at large, that will get them talking."

"Or send them packing." Sarah grudgingly let him lead her back to her clinic. "If it were me and I heard that about a bear, I would be packing my bags and leaving the general vicinity. Bears are beautiful animals, but I never want to encounter one in the wild."

He shook his head. "That's because you haven't been properly trained on how to deal with a bear in the wild."

"Please don't show me."

He laughed and pushed the button to the elevator, the doors opening instantly. "If you're living in bear country, Sarah, you really don't have a choice in the matter. Everyone in Crater Lake needs to know what to do in case of a bear. Do you have bear deterrent?"

Sarah shook her head and pinched the bridge of her nose. "Oh, God."

"I take it you don't."

Sarah glanced up at him and could see he was enjoying her torment. "I have a spray can of something in my office, but I didn't buy it. It was just there when I took over."

"I know. I bought it and put it there. Most offices of the permanent staff have a can. It's better to be prepared and, since most of you aren't from Montana, I thought it would be the best."

"You're really enjoying this, aren't you?"

"Enjoying what?" A small smile played across his lips. It was a devious smile, even if it was partially hidden behind his beard. It was the kind that made her a bit weak in the knees and she fought the urge to kiss him. Even though she couldn't remember the last time she'd kissed a man. She resisted the urge to kiss him and gave him a playful shove instead.

"Hey, what was that for?"

"For enjoying my torment and for teasing me." Sarah shook her head. "What am I going to say?"

"Sorry would be a start."

"Not to you. The patients."

"I'll handle it. Besides you don't speak French."

She chuckled. "This is true."

The elevator dinged open and her stomach knotted. She hoped word wouldn't get back to Silas Draven that she'd left a big group of VIP tourists by themselves. She didn't need him to think she couldn't handle her job and she definitely didn't want this to get back to her father.

"Don't be nervous. It will be fine." Luke took her hand and she tried not to gasp at his familiarity. "Come on, you have to face the music."

She took her hand back and marched ahead of him, trying to put some distance between them. "Okay, we can do this."

Facing all those tourists was better than having him touch her. Not exactly better, but safer. Actually she'd rather face a bear over being alone with Luke. Luke was dangerous. He was the kind of dangerous she secretly yearned for. It was electric, intense and was, oh, so wrong.

The patients left in the waiting room were pacing and looked none too pleased when she walked in.

"I'm sorry," she began, but as the words came out the din of French was overwhelming.

Luke stepped into the fray and shouted over the noise. A few choice words and the noise ebbed and the patients sat down again.

"Do you have enough exam rooms for five people?" Luke asked out of the corner of his mouth.

"No, I have two."

Luke made a face. "I guess Mr. Draven didn't really think you'd be this busy on any given day."

"Or maybe he thought two would be enough. I'm sure he didn't expect me to be called away for a mauling."

"I'd call your next patient. I'll help you. We'll get them in and out fast.

"Really? You're going to help me."

"Of course."

Sarah nodded and picked up the discarded patient charts, handing Luke three and keeping two for herself.

"Hey, how come I get the majority?"

"You speak the language." She winked at him and then walked away. Pleased that she was tormenting him just as much as he was her, but most importantly she had to put distance between them.

"Patient eleven?" she called out.

Luke put the last of the files on Sarah's desk. She was typing away on her computer and didn't even bother to look up at him.

"There. All done. Two more sunburns. The French have mountains, don't they? Surely they ski."

"These guests are from an island in the Caribbean called Marie-Galante. It's tropical."

"That doesn't explain sunburns. They should know how to use sunblock."

"Snow sunburns. One of them told me they'd never seen snow before—they didn't think they could get a sunburn in the winter. Actually, I'm glad they spoke French and not Creole."

Luke grinned. "Me, too. I knew a Cajun man once in my unit."

"Right, you were a medic in the army."

"Yeah. Right." Luke should leave, the conversation was turning in a direction he wasn't comfortable with, but he couldn't pry himself away from her and he didn't know why. He was drawn to her. This was why he'd gone out into the woods for a few days.

He'd had to get out of temptation's way.

"Thanks again for helping me," she said. "It's been a while since I've been in a clinic."

"No problem. You helped me with the mauling, but honestly I'm surprised you're in a clinic. I thought you were a surgeon."

"I am a surgeon."

"So why did you leave the OR?"

Sarah's lips pursed together and he was wondering if maybe now he was making her uncomfortable, just as he'd felt moments ago when he'd unthinkingly mentioned his time in the army. Something he was not ready to talk about, because he did miss it and it reminded him of his failed marriage, which was something he wanted to forget.

So what had made Sarah leave surgery?

None of your business.

Only he couldn't help himself. She'd been such a bulldog in the OR last summer. Surgeons with that kind of drive and passion didn't just walk away.

You did.

"I wanted a change of pace," she said.

"A change of pace?"

She shrugged. "Sure, why not? The city was getting to me."

"Somehow I don't believe that."

"You want to talk about truths? Why did you leave the army?"

Luke's spine stiffened. "My tour of duty ended. Well, I better go. Thanks again."

"You're welcome."

He left her office, without so much as a look back. It was for the best. If he looked back, he might stay. The way that she'd looked at him, he knew that she didn't believe him. Heck, he wasn't even sure if he had convinced himself of that fact. This was why Sarah was dangerous. She affected him like no one else had. Not even Christine. Sarah got under his skin. She actually made him yearn for things he used to want. Things that he'd thought were long gone.

He didn't need that.

He didn't want that.

Didn't he?

CHAPTER FOUR

"She did what?"

"She signed out a pair of snowshoes and headed up the lake trail," said the equipment-rental guy. He looked a bit scared, which was good. Luke wanted to strike fear into the guy's heart. Didn't they know there was a bear loose? A bear that had mauled a guy two days ago. A bear that hadn't been tracked down yet.

What was she thinking? Clearly she wasn't. He had to find her before the bear did.

"What trail did she take?"

"The Lakeview trail."

"When did she leave?"

The rental guy looked confused and shrugged. "Like twenty minutes ago?"

"Why did you let her go out?"

The young man just stuttered. "I didn't know I wasn't supposed to. Besides, I just started my shift. She was heading out just as I came in."

Luke cursed under his breath. "Don't let anyone else out. There's a bear on the loose."

"Aren't bears supposed to be hibernating?"

Luke just shook his head and walked away from the

rental guy. He couldn't believe she'd gone out there. Why would she head out on her own?

You haven't seen her for a couple days. Maybe she thinks the bear has gone by now.

It was a foolish assumption. Anyone from around here would know to wait for the all-clear, or at least find out the areas the bear had been seen in.

She's not from around here. It was his fault. He should have explained it to her. Instead he'd kept his distance.

He'd avoided her because she was getting too close for him. Since he'd come home expecting to start a life with his wife and realized his life wasn't going to be how he'd pictured it, he'd been keeping people at a distance.

Less chance of getting hurt that way.

Except, he enjoyed being around Sarah. The back and forth with her was refreshing and it totally caught him off guard. He couldn't be around her, yet here he was, worried about her.

She most likely would be fine on the Lakeview trail as the bear's den was nowhere near that, but, still, she didn't know anything about the mountains.

Luke returned to the rental chalet. "Give me a pair of snowshoes, please."

Once he had the snowshoes secured to his knapsack, he climbed on his snowmobile and headed up to the Lakeview trail. When he got to the edge of the trail, he parked his snowmobile, strapped on his snowshoes, pulled on his rucksack and unstrapped the tranquilizer gun.

He could see Sarah's fresh tracks in the snow. She couldn't be too far off. He'd taken her out once; she was good, but she wasn't that good. He was confident that he could catch up with her in no time.

As he headed up the path, he soon saw her. She had stopped not that far into the trail, at a lookout. She was holding her camera and was taking pictures.

Luke watched her for a few moments. She had a really fancy camera. He didn't know much about cameras, but it looked high-tech. Sarah was completely immersed in what she was doing. She was very unaware of everything around her.

Her cheeks were flushed from the cold and the exercise, but she was smiling as she held up her camera and then he couldn't help but smile, too, watching her. It was enchanting.

She's so beautiful.

And he shook his head, because he couldn't think about her like that. She was off-limits to him. It was a beautiful vista; he couldn't really blame her for that. Crater Lake was a beautiful place. This was home.

There had been so many times when he was serving overseas, in the heat and the desert, trying to patch up wounded soldiers who were flown in from the front lines, that all he'd been able to think about was the mountain with the snow cap. The blue, blue water.

And of Christine. Only she'd never seemed to miss him. Maybe that should have been an indicator that rushing into marriage with her hadn't been the best idea. That was her reasoning when he'd come home and found out that she wanted a divorce.

We were too young, Luke. You were going to medical school and you were my first. You were safe. Anthony understands me. We don't have anything in common,

Luke. When you were gone he was here. He was always here. I can rely on him...

His smile instantly vanished. Just thinking about Christine and the heartache that she and Anthony caused him ruined the moment.

This was why he couldn't get involved with someone. This was why he was single and kept people at a distance. You couldn't trust people. It was too painful.

"You know, there's a bear on the loose still and you're on a trail that is an avalanche risk."

Sarah lowered her camera and stared at him in shock and there was a touch of annoyance there, as well.

"What're you doing here?" she asked.

"Didn't you hear me? There's a bear out there on the loose."

She paled. "Wait, I thought you caught it."

"Who told you that?"

"The woman at the rental chalet. She said, and I quote, 'I think he caught him or something. Yeah, yeah, he caught it.'"

Luke rolled his eyes. "Well, that explains it. I spoke to a clueless guy. He really doesn't know much."

"Apparently so. I would've never come out here had I known. I really thought the bear issue was a moot point. I figured since I hadn't seen you for a couple days that you'd dealt with it. I thought you'd gone back up into the woods like you do all the time."

"I understand the woods. I'm used to them. I live in the woods."

She cocked an eyebrow. "Really?"

He nodded. "I have a cabin in the woods. It's on the edge of my parents' property. I built it myself."

"Wow, I'm impressed. I mean, I figured you were a

bit of a hands-on guy, but I had no idea that you could build a home with your own hands. That's amazing."

"Thanks. Well, when I got back from my tour of duty I had a bit of free time." Then he cursed inwardly, because again just a simple twist in the conversation and he was opening up to her again. How did she manage to do that? He was worried that she would try to turn the conversation back to his time overseas. Something that was off-limits.

"Well, it's quite impressive. Most surgeons I know wouldn't risk damaging their hands by doing something like that."

"I'm not like most surgeons. I'm not traditional in any sense of the word." Besides, he didn't practice much surgery anymore. He missed it, but he loved this more. He loved what he did in Crater Lake.

"That's for sure." She smiled and then looked away, aiming her camera at the mountains.

"Didn't you hear me say there's a bear on the loose?"

"I did, but I just want a couple more shots."

A couple more shots? The woman was infuriating.

"So why are you up here?"

"Taking pictures."

"I thought you didn't like the cold?" Luke asked.

"I don't, but it was a beautiful day."

"So what do you do with the pictures?"

She grinned. "I paint a bit."

She paints?

Now it was his turn to be impressed. He hadn't thought she had any hobbies beyond what he'd seen, and that hadn't been much. He'd thought she was a career-focused surgeon. Usually young surgeons didn't have the time for much else—they were too focused on honing their craft.

It pleasantly surprised him.

"Paint?"

Sarah nodded. "I have hidden depths, too."

Luke laughed. "I guess you do. I build homes and you paint."

"I wouldn't mind seeing it sometime."

His blood heated at her suggestion. The thought of her in his home was definitely a dangerous idea, but not all that unpleasant. Luke cleared his throat. "Maybe sometime, but really we have to get down off the trail. Until I find that bear, I really can't authorize people being out here alone and unarmed."

"I brought that can of deterrent."

He smiled at her briefly. "That won't be enough to dissuade a hungry bear just fresh out of torpor."

Sarah sighed. "You're right."

"Come on, I brought my snowmobile, so at least you don't have to hike the entire way back. Even if it would be good practice for you."

She glared at him as she packed her camera carefully back in its case and into her knapsack. "Ha-ha."

"Glad to see you were taking my advice about the backpack."

"Good advice is good advice. Though I'm a bit worried about avalanches. Do those happen a lot up here?"

Luke nodded. "They do. We can do a little simulation if you'd like?"

Sarah groaned. "Fine, but as long as it's inside."

"I promise. I wouldn't want to risk causing an avalanche out here."

* * *

Sarah had been surprised to hear Luke's voice from behind her. She hadn't seen him in a couple of days since the mauling. Every time she seemed to get a little bit closer to him, he turned tail and ran into the woods. Of course, she didn't mind. It was better they had that separation.

She barely knew anything about him and really she shouldn't care all that much, but she wanted to get to know him. Maybe because she was alone here in Crater Lake. She didn't know anyone apart from Luke and a few employees that she greeted in passing at the resort. Then again, when had she really had any friends?

Her whole medical career, heck, her whole life, she hadn't had much time to form any interactions or friendships. And that was the way she wanted it. Her parents had tried to put Sarah into the same activities as her sister. It was just Sarah never really was social. She'd preferred science camp or painting class over tennis camp. She'd been so focused trying to prove to her parents she could do the things she wanted to do, she hadn't made many friends.

Or at least friends who were interested in the same things as she was.

The last date she'd been on the previous year had been so unremarkable. The guy had been handsome, well-to-do, but boring and very full of himself.

Luke was cocky, confident, but there was a difference. He didn't think he was a god. He didn't think he was better than anyone else. He actually tried to help people around him, even if he didn't want people to know that he cared, which she didn't get.

And most of all, he didn't date her because of who her father was.

"You ready?" Luke asked as he straddled the snowmobile.

"I don't have a helmet."

He reached into his knapsack and tossed her one. "There you go. Now get on."

"Do you have furniture in there? Is it like a bottomless bag?"

He chuckled. "Perhaps. You know my motto is be ready for anything."

Sarah laughed and put on her helmet, climbing on the snowmobile behind him. Suddenly she was very nervous about being so close to Luke. Which was ridiculous. They were just coworkers. They weren't even friends.

He's the closest thing you have to a friend.

Which was true and that thought scared her.

"You need to hold on," Luke said over his shoulder.

"Right." Her heart was pounding and she was very aware about how close she was to him. Though she couldn't feel his skin, she was pressed against him enough to feel the hard muscles under all the thick layers of his snowsuit.

At least that was something. There was a wall of protection between the two of them, but for one brief moment she wished there weren't and she couldn't help but wonder what it would be like to be wrapped up in his arms.

Where did that come from?

She shook that thought away, because she couldn't think like that.

Luke was off-limits.

She just held on tight and tried not to think about it. She had to shake the idea of Luke out of her mind. This was her chance to prove to her parents that she didn't need their help to survive. She didn't need anyone's help. She was here because of her own merit. She'd earned the right to be here and she was going to prove to everyone she had the right to be here.

Nothing was going to get in her way.

This was her chance and she had to focus on making this clinic the best. She had to be the best, so there was no time to think about Luke or what might be.

She didn't have time for romance. She couldn't lose her focus and if she got involved with Luke, she probably would. He was so gorgeous, so delicious and so very distracting.

This job was too important to her. Her parents had scoffed when she'd turned down the job her father had got for her and taken this one. They believed she would fail and come back to them with her proverbial tail between her legs.

This job won't wait for you, Sarah. I pulled a lot of strings for you.

She couldn't let them think that way. They might not think she could handle this, but she could.

Luke was not for her, even if she wished she could indulge. She had to be strong around him, keep him at a distance and remember why she was here.

She wasn't here to fall in love. That wasn't in the cards for her.

She was here to be a doctor. She was here to run the most prestigious private clinic in northwest Montana.

This job was her chance, because, even though everything about her medical career had been handed to her, according to her father she was a damn good doctor.

She was a damn good surgeon.

Are you sure about that?

They pulled up to the resort and Luke parked his snowmobile away from the main entrance. When the engine was off, Sarah clambered off the snowmobile, her legs shaking from the ride.

"That was my first and last snowmobile ride, I think," she said, trying to make light of the situation. She handed Luke back the helmet. "Thanks for being prepared."

"No problem. Now, no going back out onto the trails until that bear has been subdued."

"I hope you don't have to kill it."

Luke frowned. "I hope the bear returns to its den, but I doubt it. The game warden is combing the mountains, as well."

"Thanks again for coming to get me. I hope I didn't ruin your day."

"You didn't ruin it, but you put a serious dent in my plans." He winked at her.

"You're an idiot."

Luke was going to say something more, but they were interrupted when a front-desk person came running out of the side door.

"Thank goodness I found you both," she said. "There's an emergency up in Suite 501."

"What's wrong?" Sarah asked.

"A guest has gone into labor."

Luke's eyes widened. "Well, that's something I've never dealt with."

"Really?"

"Not many pregnant soldiers on the front line."

"Well, perhaps I can teach you something." Sarah turned to the front-desk woman. "Get her comfortable, call the air ambulance and tell them we'll be there in ten minutes."

The woman nodded and disappeared back inside.

"You've seriously delivered a baby before?" Luke asked with a hint of admiration in his voice.

"I'm a surgeon and part of the training was a rotation on the obstetrical rounds. I can do this."

"I'm sure you can. Not sure I can."

She grinned. "After today you will. Come on."

Luke nodded and they headed inside.

Sarah didn't want to tell him that she was nervous, too. She hadn't delivered that many babies, but right now she didn't have a choice. She couldn't be nervous. There was a job to do.

There were two lives to save.

CHAPTER FIVE

"COME ON, ONE more push," Sarah urged. "You can do it."

It had been a long time since she'd delivered a baby. She had been nervous for a moment, hoping she'd remember how.

As a trauma surgeon she didn't see many births. When a pregnant woman came into the ER Sarah would look at them briefly before an OB/GYN was called, but the moment she'd checked on the mother at the hotel everything she'd learned had come back to her.

Which was a good thing. This patient needed her.

Luke was behind the mother, holding her up, helping her. The air ambulance had arrived, but by the time they arrived there was no way they could move the mother. The baby was on the way out and moving the mother would put the baby at risk.

"You're doing great," Luke reassured the woman.

Sarah smiled up at him, but he wasn't looking at her. Instead he was focused on helping their patient and it warmed her heart. He could've stood back because he admitted that he didn't know anything about childbirth, but instead he threw himself into the work.

He was gentle. Kind.

For a man that was referred to around the hotel as a lone wolf, keeping people at bay, disappearing into his cabin up in the woods, Luke had a large amount of tenderness to him. It made her chest tighten just a little bit.

There was something about a rough, tough exterior and a gentle hand. It made him endearing.

The mother let out a loud yell and Sarah gently helped the baby girl into the world. Sarah rubbed the baby's back and soon the newborn was crying lustily.

"Good job," Sarah encouraged.

The mom laid back and Luke came over to help her. He was grinning ear to ear as he handed her sterile scissors.

"Good job, Doctor," he whispered in her ear. It sent a tingle down her spine.

She didn't say anything as she cut the umbilical cord and then wrapped the baby up in a blanket and handed her to Luke so he could give her to the mother.

"Congratulations, Mom," Luke said as he carefully transferred the baby to her mother's arms. He glanced down at the tiny girl as he did so, those blue eyes twinkling as he gently cradled her. So little in his big hands. It made Sarah's heart skip a beat.

Having a family had never been on her radar. Maybe because she'd had such a lonely childhood, even with a sister. They were raised by nannies in the old archaic "children should be seen and not heard" style.

How could she even contemplate raising a family when she didn't even know how one was supposed to function?

So she'd never entertained the idea, but in this moment, watching the joy on the mother's face, she yearned for something more.

"She's beautiful," Luke said.

The mother cried tears of joy and exhaustion as she took the small bundle from Luke. It was this moment that Sarah had always enjoyed when she'd been a resident and worked the obstetrical round. The moment of pure joy and elation. The moment when mother and child met. It could warm even the coldest hearts.

And watching Luke hold that small child melted hers completely.

What was it about him?

Most of the time he drove her completely around the bend, but there were times like this, when he was dealing with patients, that made her soften toward him. She wanted to get to know him and she never wanted to get to know anyone. What was it about him?

He's a mystery.

And maybe that was why she was so drawn to him. He was a challenge and she'd never backed down from a challenge before.

You need to back down from this one.

Sarah tore her gaze away from Luke and turned back to the patient. The paramedics stood at the ready. Even though the birth had been simple, mother and baby still had to be taken to the nearest hospital to be checked out.

Once she was finished the paramedics stepped in and started to get ready to transfer the patients. Her job was done. She cleaned up the mess and put it in a trash bag that she would take down to her medical-waste receptacle in her clinic.

Now you're picking up trash? Sarah, you weren't raised to do that.

You can't be an obstetrician. I didn't pay for your medical schooling so you can do obstetrics.

She hated the way her parents' voices were always in her head, trying to control her. For a long time she'd managed to tune them out, right up until she'd discovered what her father had done.

Now they were constantly there, questioning her every move.

Sarah would've liked to have been an OB/GYN surgeon, but her father didn't think it was dignified enough. Of course, he hadn't been too pleased when she gave up training to be a cardio-thoracic surgeon under Dr. Eli Draven, but Sarah preferred general surgery. She preferred trauma surgery.

Most people thought that general and trauma surgery was boring, but it wasn't. It was exciting. She got to work on so much with general surgery, and as a trauma surgeon she saw everything, but still she'd kind of missed her chance on working with mothers and babies.

Even though she'd always stressed that she didn't want to get married, that she wanted to focus on her career, there had always been a part of her that wanted the family she hadn't had as a child.

Sarah had grown up in wealth and privilege. She'd wanted for nothing except love and admiration from her parents. Maybe even to spend some time with them.

Watching this mother dote on her new baby made her wonder if her own mother had ever looked at her that way before, and seeing Luke smile so tenderly at them made her yearn.

In this moment she longed for something more.

She just didn't think that was possible.

Not in the near future anyway. Probably never.

Luke came over and peeled off his gloves and threw them in the bag, interrupting her train of thought.

"Good job, Dr. Ledet."

She chuckled. "I really didn't do much. The mother did all the work."

He smiled at her. "Still, you did a good job nonetheless. I would've been totally lost."

"What about your brother? He's the town doctor, doesn't he deliver babies?"

"He does, but he lives in town. That's at least a twenty-minute drive in this weather. He wouldn't have made it in time."

"No," she agreed. "That baby was coming quickly."

They moved out of the way as the paramedics passed them.

"Thank you, Doctors," the mother said, grinning ear to ear.

"Congratulations," Sarah said. "Everything will be okay."

Sarah watched as they wheeled her patient and the baby out of the suite. It had been so wonderful being a part of that moment, watching a family being formed. Being part of their love. She was sad to watch them go.

She sighed. "Well, that was certainly exciting."

"It was, but I don't understand it."

"What don't you understand?"

"I don't understand why a woman so close to delivering decided to come up here on a ski trip," Luke said as he moved away from her.

"I think it was a family trip. Perhaps she would've been left home alone. I think it was a good thing she was here."

He nodded. "Yeah. You're probably right."

Sarah knotted the trash bag and glanced around the suite. "I feel bad for Housekeeping, but honestly I think that mattress is no good anymore."

"That's the first birth I've attended. I mean, besides my own."

"You've never attended one in medical school?"

He shook his head. "I did most of my training in the army. My residency was in Germany at a hospital there. So not only do I speak fluent French, I speak fluent German, too."

"You're a man of many trades, Dr. Ralston."

"I have a lot of secrets." Then he grinned and winked at her in a way that made her heart skip a beat. She had to get out of the room. She had to put some distance between them.

"I'm sure you do, but I have to take this to the clinic." She held up the garbage bag.

"When are you going to show me your paintings?"

The question caught her off guard. Any time anything had ever gotten too personal between them, he'd disappeared into the woods. So when he asked about her paintings, it shocked her.

No one had ever asked to see her paintings before. And she never told anyone about them. If he hadn't caught her taking photographs, she wouldn't have told him. Most people thought her art and pursuing it was silly.

Again, another dream her parents quashed really fast. *They're called starving artists for a reason, Sarah.*

Her mother hadn't wanted her to be an artist, and yet her mother had supported the local arts scene in New York City. Bought paintings, attended galas and gallery openings. Then again, that was what women like her mother did. It was *the* thing to do in her parents' circles.

"You want to see my paintings?"

"Sure. You said you take pictures and then do paintings. I'm interested. I've never met a doctor who painted landscapes or drew or anything for that matter."

Sarah chuckled. "It's good for the hands. Especially surgeon hands. Keeps them strong."

"So, when do I get to see them?"

"I don't know. When do I get to see the house you built?" Then the blood drained away from her face when she realized what she'd just done. This was not keeping him at a distance. This was inviting him in.

"How about tonight?" he asked, surprising her.

"Tonight?"

"You have plans tonight?"

"No."

He nodded then, those blue eyes twinkling with something she wasn't sure of, but it made her heart beat a bit faster.

"Okay, then, so you'll come to my place tonight. I'll see some of your paintings and you can see my handiwork."

"Okay." Sarah looked away and hoped that she wasn't blushing. "I better get this to medical waste."

"I'll pick you up at seven."

She nodded and didn't look back at him. She couldn't, because if she did then he would see how he was affecting her.

Damn him.

And then she cursed herself a bit, wondering what the heck she'd just gotten herself into.

* * *

What have I done?

Luke had repeatedly asked himself that since he'd invited Sarah over to his house. He didn't have anyone at his house. Ever.

Only Carson and that was rare. Usually when Luke got together with Carson he went to Carson's place.

It was larger.

Luke went for the understated. An open-concept cabin. Carson referred to it as a shack, as if Luke were some kind of prospector up in Alaska on a gold claim.

Everything in the cabin he'd made. Well, the furniture anyway. So what if he preferred to live off the grid a bit? He wasn't totally off the grid. He had electricity and running water. No, he didn't have a phone or cable, but he had a radio if he ever got into trouble or if someone wanted to reach him.

There wasn't any cell phone reception where his cabin was and he still hadn't quite figured out why. Probably all the pine trees around it.

Christine had hated this cabin when he'd planned it. Even though it did have creature comforts like a sauna out back and a nice bathroom. Everything was too "rough" for her.

When he picked Sarah up at the hotel, he was actually hoping that she would make up an excuse and cop out, but she didn't. She was waiting for him at the front in her coat with a black portfolio slung over her shoulder.

He had no choice but to live up to his end of the bargain and take her to his home. The truck ride over was tense, because he didn't know what to say to her. All he could think about on the journey was how he was going to get out of this situation. A situation that was his fault. He only had himself to blame.

When he'd told Carson what he'd done, he'd thought his brother had witnessed a miracle healing the way his mouth had dropped open.

"You don't date. You said so yourself and you repeatedly made fun of me when I got together with Esme."

"It's not a date. She's a coworker."

Carson had grinned, smugly. "You keep telling yourself that, my friend. You're not fooling me."

Luke had decided he didn't need Carson's advice, called his brother a few choice names and left. Carson was certainly making him eat crow and maybe he deserved it just a bit, because he'd certainly given Carson a run for his money when Esme had started coming around more often.

Still, that was a completely different situation.

Carson was in love with Esme.

Luke wasn't interested in Sarah. Not in that way.

Liar.

This was a dangerous situation. They were in his cabin, in the woods and they were alone. That wasn't a good combo. His self-control was going to be tested tonight, because any time he was around her it was tested.

All he wanted to do was kiss those pink lips, to run his hands through her blond hair and hold her in his arms, to feel her body pressed against his.

Don't think about her like that. She's not yours. She can't be yours. That's not what you want.

Only the more he tried to convince himself of that the harder it was for him to believe it.

"Wow, so this is it?" Sarah asked as he parked his truck in front of his cabin.

"Yes, this is my shack, as my brother calls it."

"Well, at least it'll be warm. I can see you left the home fires burning."

"Yes, I have electricity, but my house is heated by my wood stove. I live a bit off the grid, as much as I can. I like to rough it."

"Do you grow your own food, too?" She was teasing him.

"No, I don't really have a green thumb. I forage mostly. Our dinner tonight will be moss and various pine needles."

She laughed. "Well, can we go inside? I'd like to see this old shack you built."

"Ha-ha." They climbed out of the truck and he opened the door for her. She stepped in first and stood in the small mudroom of his cabin. She was silent and he found himself starting to sweat, waiting for her approval.

Probably because the last time he'd shown a woman his place it had been Christine and she'd hated it and then it had been only the schematics and blueprints.

You expect me to live here?

You wanted a house when I was done with my tours. I'm building this for us.

Don't think about her.

She wasn't going to intrude into his thoughts. Not tonight.

"Well?" he asked, trying not to seem too anxious. "What do you think?"

"It's beautiful. I'm pretty impressed that you built this place." She took off her coat and hung it on the hooks that he had in the entranceway and then kicked off her boots and stepped on the thick Berber area rug that he had in the living-cum-bedroom area of his home. "The furniture seems to match the house perfectly."

"It should, I made it."

She cocked her eyebrows. "You made the furniture, too?"

He nodded. "Everything. Even the mattress."

Why did I say that?

Pink stained her cheeks when he said mattress, but she wouldn't look in the direction of the king-size bed that he'd built in the far corner. Seeing how he affected her made his own blood heat. Since she'd dropped into his arms in her office a couple weeks back, there had been countless times that he'd pictured her naked in his bed, her legs wrapped around his waist.

What he wouldn't give to peel that pale pink boat-neck sweater and those tight blue jeans from her body, to run his hands over her soft skin.

Get a grip on yourself.

He cleared his throat and ran his hand through his hair nervously.

"Yeah, I made the mattress out of feathers I'd collected over time. It used to be a straw tick, but that was quite uncomfortable."

"This isn't *Little House on the Prairie*, Pa."

He laughed with her and it defused the tension. He headed into the kitchen. "Would you like a glass of wine?"

"Did you press the grapes yourself?" she teased, setting her portfolio down on his coffee table.

"No. I do go to the grocery store from time to time. I'm not Davy Crockett."

"Could've fooled me." There was a twinkle in her eyes and she leaned over his counter. "I didn't expect dinner or drinks. I thought you were showing me your handiwork and I was going to show you some of mine."

He shrugged. "I rarely have dinner guests. I'm a bit of a Grinch around these parts."

"So I've heard."

"Who did you hear that from?" he asked.

"I went into town on my first week. Met a woman with these two twins and they mentioned how cantankerous you were. I had to agree with them at the time."

Luke groaned. "The Johnstone twins. Yes, they're not fond of me and I'm not too fond of them."

"Why? They looked like innocent enough children."

Luke snorted. "They delight in spooking my horse."

"You have a horse?"

He nodded. "I board her in a stable close to town in the winter. In the summer I have a pad out back that I keep her in. She can't handle the deep snow up here in the winter. She is getting on in years, sadly."

"You have hidden depths, Dr. Ralston."

You have no idea.

Only he didn't say that out loud. Instead he pulled down two wineglasses from where they were hanging on the wall and set them down before her.

"I'm afraid I only have white, but I think white will do well with the salmon I'm making."

"Salmon?"

"I smoked it myself."

She grinned. "I should've known. White is fine."

He pulled the only bottle he had in his house and uncorked it, pouring it into her glass and then his. He wasn't much of a wine drinker, but Esme really liked wine and so he figured Sarah would, too, but she took a sip and made a face.

"What's wrong?" he asked. "Did it go bad?"

"No, it's fine. It's just… I'm not much of a wine drinker. I like beer instead."

Now it was his turn to be shocked. "Who has hidden depths?"

She laughed. "My mother would be horrified if she knew that I was telling a man this. I was brought up to be prim and proper. I was not brought up to be a roughneck."

"A what?" he asked.

"My mother is from a very proper British family. A roughneck is someone who works offshore in oil or gas. Tough, rugged, dirty. I was meant to be refined and graceful."

"You're a bit of a klutz. I don't think you're all that graceful. I have seen you face-first in a snowdrift."

She laughed again and it warmed his heart to hear it. She had an infectious laugh and he couldn't remember the last time he'd felt so at ease around a woman before. Usually he was hiding behind his wall, but not at this moment. He was exposed and he didn't like that one bit.

What was she doing to him?

Sarah didn't know what she was expecting when Luke brought her out to his cabin. She must've been thinking more of a barren shack. Even though his home was rustic, it wasn't barren. It was cozy. It was homey.

It was the kind of place people from the city rented when they went on ski trips. The only difference was it would probably be larger. It was a little too small for most people, but she kind of liked it.

She was shocked that he made most of the furniture in the home, though she seriously doubted he made the leather L-shaped couch that was in the living room adorned with pillows and a polar fleece throw.

Then her gaze drifted off to the bed in the far corner of the open-concept cabin. It was a large wooden four-poster bed with a thick, down-and-feather-filled mattress. Well, according to him it was.

He made his own mattress?

She shook her head. Stop thinking about the bed.

He was in the kitchen checking on the salmon, his back to her. He'd handed her a beer a few moments ago and then gone about cooking the rest of dinner, leaving her to her own devices and the naughty thoughts that were running through her mind.

She sat down on the couch and tried to ignore the large bed, which felt like an elephant in the room at the moment.

Don't think about it. This is just dinner as friends.

Luke came out of the kitchen, holding a bottle of beer. "Just a little bit longer. Sorry about that."

She shrugged. "I didn't expect dinner tonight. It's a nice surprise."

"After all your hard work today, it was the least I could do."

"I just did my job."

"Yeah and you did a good job." Luke picked up her portfolio. "Do you mind if I look?"

"Go ahead. I am at your mercy." Blood rushed to her cheeks.

Luke grinned at her, that devious grin that made her insides turn to goo. "Well, let's see your artistic abilities."

Sarah's pulse thundered in her ears as he thumbed

through her very small portfolio. It was something she'd never shown anyone before. It was something she'd always felt she couldn't share with someone, but Luke had caught her in the act.

And she couldn't lie to him.

Or she didn't want to lie to him, but now she was regretting it because he wasn't saying much. What if he hated it? What if she sucked at it?

Who cares?

Only she did care. She cared if he hated it. What he thought mattered to her and that scared her.

"These are great. Where was this one done?" He held up a picture of the Black Hills. She'd spent some time around Mount Rushmore when she was a kid. That picture was something that she'd painted from memory, because that trip to Mount Rushmore with her parents was one of her last happy memories. They weren't this socialite family, they were just like everyone else. Except her father had rented a massive cabin on the outskirts of Keystone on this huge ranch that had horses and tennis courts, but still it was a happy time in her life.

"The Black Hills."

Luke glanced at it again. "South Dakota?"

She nodded. "Yes. Keystone, South Dakota."

"Yes, now I see it. I like South Dakota."

"You've been there?"

"Who hasn't? It's like Mecca for American families of our generation. Plus, it's not too far away for a family doctor to take his family for a summer vacation. My father was the only town physician in Crater Lake for a long time, so any vacation had to be taken in a drivable radius to home. Where did your family vacation, other than Mount Rushmore?"

"Jamaica, Brazil...India."

He raised an eyebrow. "Have you been around the world?"

"Pretty much." She took a swig of her beer. "My last job, teaching at different hospitals, took me to a lot of places, too. That's why I was in Missoula that day."

"Teaching?"

She nodded. "I worked with a surgeon who was developing a new technique in robotic trauma surgery. It was a good job."

"Why did you give it up?"

Her stomach twisted as she thought about those last moments. About when she'd found out that the job she'd been working on so hard hadn't really been something she'd earned.

It still made her angry.

"You look tense."

"I don't like to talk about the past too much." She set her beer down on the table. "Maybe I should head back to the hotel. I'm not that hungry."

"You're staying. I'm sorry, I won't pry." He set the portfolio down on the table. "Besides, I think it's done."

She watched as he walked into the kitchen. Why did he have to pry into her history? He didn't share his.

What was she doing here?

You're lonely.

She should just leave. It would be better if she left, only she couldn't.

She was a bit of a masochist.

"Have a seat at the table and I'll bring you dinner."

Sarah picked up her beer and headed over to the dining-room table, sitting down at the end. "Don't tell me you made this too?"

"Yep. I told you. I made most of the furniture here." He came out of the kitchen with two plates and set down in front of her a perfectly cooked filet of salmon, asparagus and new potatoes. It smelled delicious. "For a long time since I returned from the army, I didn't practice medicine and all I wanted to do was build stuff for my home."

"Why?" she asked.

He frowned and she knew she was treading on that dangerous ground. That moment when he would clam up. "I needed time."

"I get that."

He shrugged, but he didn't say anything else and an awkward silence fell between them. She wished that he would open up and share with her, but then again she wasn't exactly sharing much with him either.

So they were at a standstill.

And maybe that was for the best.

After dinner, she helped him clean up, though he insisted that wasn't necessary. Then they returned to the couch in his living room, where he continued to look at her paintings and drawings. As he was skimming through he found one that absolutely captivated him. It was a self-portrait she'd done and by the date on the bottom it was a few years ago. It took his breath away. The details in the drawing. It was just a pencil sketch, but there was so much life to it.

The kissable lips, heart-shaped face, nose that turned up again, thinly arched brows and beautiful eyes that captured him. In the portrait her hair hung loose over bare shoulders, like wisps. Usually she wore it back in a braid and tonight it was done up in a bun. He resisted the urge to undo that bun and let her hair cascade down all over her shoulders. So he could kiss and hold that woman in the picture. It was as if the drawing showed a hidden part of her.

The true Sarah.

And he longed to know the true Sarah, which scared him.

"Which one are you looking at so intently?"

Luke quickly flicked the page. "Uh, this one. The horse on the plains. It's beautiful."

She smiled. "You can have it if you want."

"Thanks."

The horse one was good. It actually reminded him of his own horse, who he hadn't seen in a couple of days, but he'd rather keep the pencil-drawn self-portrait she'd done.

Why torture yourself?

"You said you have a horse?"

"Yeah. I do."

"What's its name?"

"Her name is Adele."

"That's an interesting choice."

"Well, I didn't really choose it. When I bought her that was her name. I didn't see a point in changing it."

"I love horseback riding." Sarah sighed. "I miss it."

"You know how to horseback ride?"

She nodded. "Regular lessons. One thing I didn't mind my parents pressuring me into."

"Your parents have a large impact on your life?" he asked.

She frowned and then shrugged. "What parents don't?"

"True," Luke agreed, but there was something more

to what she'd said about her parents. He wanted to press her further, but decided against it.

He didn't mind this friendly chatter or when they worked so well together when faced with a medical emergency. Anything else was risky and he didn't want her to find a way in. He set down his glass.

"You know, I haven't seen her in a long time. I've been so busy. I should go check on her. Would you like to come?"

Her eyes lit up, as if he were offering her a thousand dollars.

"Really?"

He nodded. "Really."

"I would love that."

"Grab your coat." He handed her back the portfolio. "After I check on her I'll take you back to the hotel."

It was a short drive to the stable where he kept Adele. The owner of the stable was used to Luke keeping odd hours and didn't mind that Luke was here to visit his horse at eleven in the evening.

As they got out of the car a brilliant set of northern lights erupted across the sky, because the cloud cover that had been hovering over Crater Lake the past few days had dissipated.

"Oh, my God!" Sarah said, a cloud of breath escaping past her lips. "Look at that."

"Pretty spectacular, isn't it?"

"I've never seen one. Too much light pollution."

"I can imagine that. Cities are so ugly."

She shook her head. "New York isn't ugly. The lights are beautiful. Especially around the holidays like Christmas and Valentine's Day. They light up the Empire State

Building and then at Christmas there's this large tree at Rockefeller Square."

Luke wrinkled his nose. "Christmas sounds fine. Valentine's, why even bother? Besides, light pollution has nothing on this. Look straight up."

Sarah leaned back and he watched as her expression turned from amusement to awe. Now that the cloud cover was gone there were millions of stars splattered across the sky. As if Van Gogh's *Starry Night* were painted across the inky black sky.

"Amazing."

He smiled at her as he watched her stare up in amazement at the star-filled sky. He remembered so many times, after working on soldiers for countless hours, walking out of the OR and standing in the dark, staring up at the sky in Afghanistan and wishing for this.

The night sky was different.

And there was no aurora borealis.

Afghanistan's sky was beautiful, silent and cold at night, but nothing beat Montana, the mountains. Nothing beat home.

And in this moment, he wanted to take Sarah in his arms and kiss her. The urge was undeniable and he had to regain control before he did something he would regret.

Who said you'd regret it?

"Come on, I don't want you to catch your death out here. Adele won't like it too much if your teeth are chattering the whole time."

They walked into the stable and as soon as he did Adele stuck her head out of the stall, watching him.

"She knows you're here."

Luke grinned. "I know, but really she's just looking for treats."

"I don't know about that."

Luke's blood heated at her teasing tone, but he didn't acknowledge it; instead he cleared his throat and pulled out Adele's carrot treat.

"Hey, girl," he whispered against her muzzle. "How have they been treating you?"

"I'd love to paint her. She's beautiful."

"Come pet her. She doesn't mind. What she minds is people spooking her."

"Can you blame her?" Sarah asked and then she approached Adele slowly. Adele moved her head slightly, not used to the stranger who was about to touch her.

"It's okay, Adele. This is a friend. Another doctor."

Adele nickered and Sarah was able to stroke her muzzle.

"You're so beautiful, Adele," Sarah whispered.

Luke watched Sarah stroke and touch his horse, and his heart, which he'd thought was safely encased in ice, began to melt for her. She was like no other woman he'd ever met and his blood burned with the need to possess her. To have her for his own.

You can't have her.

"She's beautiful, Luke. So beautiful. I would love to ride her one day, if you'd let me."

Luke cleared his throat. "We'll see. I better get you back to your hotel. It's getting late."

"Sure." Sarah leaned forward and kissed Adele. "Good night, beauty."

And at that moment Luke knew he'd have to put

some serious distance between the two of them, or he was liable to carry her off and make love to her.

Right now.

CHAPTER SIX

"YOU'RE A SADIST—you know that, right?"

Luke just grinned at her, as he stood over her in the snow. Gone was the gentle soul of a man she'd seen last night in that horse stable, the gentle giant cradling that fragile infant. That man made her ache with need. She craved him like air, but this guy, torturing her with endless simulations, this guy she wanted to club upside the head.

He'd taken her outside to where the snow plows had been piling the snow from the parking lot. The large snowbank was littered with CPR dummies, half-buried. It was a simulation massacre.

Only he'd dubbed this as avalanche training.

"I thought we were going to do avalanche training inside?"

"How would that work?" he asked.

"We could pretend. Use our imagination."

"We were, until I found this snow pile. It's perfect."

"Great," she mumbled.

"You need to work harder to dig this man out."

Sarah rolled her eyes. "I'm just a hotel doctor. I'm not going to be the first line of defense called for this.

You are, your brother probably and every other first responder up here on this mountain."

"You'll be called, too. In situations like this, everyone with medical training will be called into action. That's how it works up in these remote communities. Are you saying that you're not going to come to an avalanche site because you're just a hotel doctor?"

Damn.

He was right. She wouldn't walk away from an emergency situation. She was a doctor and she was trained in trauma, just as he was.

"Fine." She kept digging away at the snow.

"Use your ice axe, too. Chip away at the hard stuff. Just don't hit the patient."

Sarah made a face at him and he just laughed.

"Do you think you can insert a chest tube in below-zero temps?"

"You're not serious, are you?"

"You said you worked in an ER. Haven't you inserted chest tubes before?"

"Of course," Sarah said. "But not in the bitter cold. Usually when I insert a chest tube it's in a trauma pod, sheltered and indoors."

Not negative eighty with a windchill.

"Ah, but sometimes there's no time to get the man down off the mountain and you have to do it in the field." Luke reached into his knapsack and pulled out a chest-tube kit. "Insert a chest tube. The patient's lungs are filling with blood—he needs a chest tube."

Sarah pulled off her mitts and fumbled with the chest-tube tray. She hadn't realized how cold her fingers actually were, but then she remembered that they'd been out here for an hour already while he went through avalanche drills with her.

The mitts were warm, but, after a while digging in the snow, their protective lining couldn't keep out the bitter cold forever. She cursed under her breath, as she prepared the chest tube and inserted it perfectly the first time.

She had always been pretty good at it.

"Good job," Luke remarked. "Now put on your gloves and keep digging."

"I need a break."

"You don't get a break on the mountain."

"This isn't a mountain. It's the snow from the main parking lot and as you can see we're the current entertainment." She pointed to the window where staff and a few guests were watching them cavorting on top of the dirty snowbank, with mannequins strewn everywhere.

"It's mandatory training, but I suppose you can have a break. You were up late last night."

Sarah smiled and tried not to blush as she thought about it. She actually hadn't wanted the night to end, though it had been for the best. If it hadn't ended she might have done something foolish, like kiss him, and maybe that one foolish kiss would have led to something more.

So it was good that the night had ended when it had.

Still, she couldn't remember when she'd had such a good time. "Yes, thanks for the fantastic dinner and the conversation. I enjoyed it."

"Me, too," he said, but then the small smile that he had for her quickly disappeared and he got up, to walk slowly down the side of the snowbank.

For a while after their awkward conversation it was

pretty quiet, but then he started asking about her art and her photographs, then the tension melted away. Still, at the mention of last night the atmosphere changed and put distance between them. Maybe he was regretting last night. She certainly hoped not.

He was the closest thing she had to a friend in Crater Lake. Loneliness had never bothered her before, but that was probably because she'd been busier as a surgeon. There were guests at the hotel, but not many as the grand opening was only a couple of weeks away on Valentine's Day and, even then, guests weren't always getting sick.

So far, since her arrival in Crater Lake, she'd treated about eight sunburns, three cases of some gastroenteritis, a bear mauling and a birth of a baby. And because she wasn't as busy as she was in her previous job, she had a lot more free time. A lot more time to remind her that she was alone.

Of course, she didn't really think that if she followed her mother and sister in their footsteps that she would feel any different. Her society friends weren't really friends at all.

None of them had called her since she'd decided to cut ties with New York and move to Montana. Actually, they'd been quite horrified when she'd told them she'd given up the prestigious job and was moving to Crater Lake.

Who cares if your father pulled strings? My father did, too. It doesn't matter.

It matters to me, Nikki. My father doesn't think I can do anything. He's thinks I'm this baby. He thinks I'm helpless. I need to do this on my own.

Thinking about that last conversation with her so-called best friend made her blood pressure rise. It made her angry. It made her remember that she wasn't sure if anything in her life was her own. She wasn't sure if she'd earned anything.

It was humiliating.

Don't think about it. Don't give them the time of day.

"Do you have avalanches here every year?" she asked, hoping that the conversation could turn in another direction and distract her. It would keep her mind off her parents, her so-called friends and Luke.

"Pretty much."

"To this extent?"

Luke shook his head. "No, thankfully we haven't had a major disaster like this in a long, long time, but being in a mountainous region there are always avalanches. Always. That's why we have avalanche zones."

"How do you determine what an avalanche zone is?"

Luke clambered back up the snowbank to stand beside her. He pointed toward the mountain. "You see that part of the mountain? You see how it's on a forty-five-degree angle? It's considered an avalanche zone. In fact we had a landslide on that slope last year."

"The landslide that almost killed Shane Draven?"

He nodded. "Yes, Dr. Petersen, my brother and I extracted him and got him down."

"All-hands-on-deck type of situation, then?"

He nodded. "You got it."

"So only steep slopes are considered dangerous."

"No, gradual slopes are at risk, too. And shady slopes can pose a threat."

"Why?" she asked. "Wouldn't the snow harden there as opposed to being in the sun?"

"No, the sun actually hardens the snow better. It

melts it and then at night ice forms and seals the snow-cap better. Shady slopes don't have that chance—it's just powder."

Sarah shuddered. "I hope we never have a bad avalanche, then. I wouldn't know what to do."

"As long as you're aware of the avalanche zones, you'll be fine, but that's why I'm training you. So you know what to do in an emergency. You can get seriously hurt. I broke my leg during an avalanche last winter. Avalanches are a mighty force. You need to learn how to survive." Luke moved behind her and she was very aware that he was close to her. He touched her arms and, even through all those thick layers, it was electric the way he affected her.

"What're you doing?" she asked, her voice hitching because he was touching her.

He leaned over her shoulder, his hot breath fanning the exposed skin of her neck. "I'm teaching you how to survive if you're ever caught in one. This is Special Forces training now."

"Oh," she said. "How can you fight fast-moving snow?"

"Swim." Then he took her arms and moved them gently in a breaststroke. "If you're ever caught in fast-moving snow, drop your gear because it will weigh you down, open your arms wide and swim to the side of the snow pack. Even if you can't make it across, the movement will help keep your head above the snow so you can breathe."

"Swim through snow?" Sarah smiled. "I've never heard of that before. And what happens if I'm covered with snow?"

"Bring your arms and hands to the front of your face

and wiggle back and forth. It will create an air pocket and you'll be able to breathe until help arrives."

"Have you ever been trapped in an avalanche?"

"No, never trapped and never been standing at the edge of an active one. The avalanche I was injured in was because I was rescuing someone. I jumped from a helicopter and landed the wrong way, losing my footing. I've never been trapped, thank God, and I hope I never am."

"I hope so, too." Sarah looked up at him, but his face was unreadable because his sunglasses were covering his eyes, protecting them from snow blindness.

"Thanks." He cleared his throat and moved away from her. "We should get back to freeing these victims."

"Good, 'cause I have big plans this afternoon." She was teasing, but his brow furrowed.

"What kind of plans?"

"I'm going to Crater Lake. I haven't been in town since I first arrived. I have the rest of the day off and I thought I would explore."

"I don't go to town this time of year," Luke remarked.

"Why not?"

"Valentine's Day is coming." He shuddered. "The town is going a little bit crazy about it because of the hotel's grand opening that day. There's going to be a big gala or ball or something."

"I know. Silas Draven is insisting all his employees go, but it sounds kind of fun."

Luke grunted.

"You're not a fan of Valentine's Day?"

"Nope. It's pointless."

"Love is pointless?" she asked.

"No, not pointless just…there's no need to celebrate Valentine's Day with such vigor."

"Why do you hate it so much?" she asked.

He just grunted again, but avoided her question and she wondered why Luke thought love was pointless. She didn't know many guys who actually liked Valentine's Day, but Luke was acting a bit like a Grinch about it.

Why should you care?

And really she shouldn't. When did she ever give two hoots about Valentine's Day before? Usually she was in the hospital, doing surgery and stealing candy from the nurses' station as she went from OR to OR.

She'd never had a Valentine before. Still, the idea of a town getting all decked out and celebrating it sounded as if it could be fun.

"I think it will be fun to see what the town is doing," she said, trying to change the subject before Luke shut down on her again and didn't say anything else.

"Well, have fun. I have to take a group of surveyors out on a trail for some training."

"More surveyors?"

Luke nodded as he headed down the snowbank to their next patient. "I guess some more people are trying to cash in on Silas Draven's bright idea to turn Crater Lake into the next Whitefish."

"I thought you worked exclusively for Silas Draven?" she asked.

He grinned. "No, I'm a free agent. Now come on, get down here so we can save this patient and then we can call it quits for the day."

Sarah groaned but climbed down the snow pile toward him, because she was tired of being in the snow. She was cold and, really, what was the point?

Luke was a closed book.

And that was all there was to it.

Luke had lost his mind. Well, he had for a brief moment there when he'd stepped behind Sarah and touched her. He didn't know what he'd been thinking about at that moment. Clearly, he was suffering from the cold.

He'd shown other people how to swim out of fast-moving snow and he did that without touching them. He just told them to open their arms wide and mimic swimming, but with Sarah he'd reached out and guided her arms.

And he had no idea why he'd felt the need to do that.

Probably because he liked to torture himself?

Or maybe it was because he couldn't resist her. When he was around her, he wasn't himself. He didn't guard his walls as carefully as he used to. She made him weak. As if she was his Achilles' heel or something.

Yet, like a masochist he kept going back to her. Kept reaching out to her.

She'll hurt you just like Christine did.

He'd done so much for Christine when they were newly married. She'd known he was going to serve in the army, but she hadn't cared. She hadn't wanted to accompany him to Germany, but their marriage had survived. And it had survived his first tour of duty, too.

It was only when she'd demanded he end his career, that he return home to start a family with his wife, that he'd learned she didn't want him.

She didn't want to be his wife.

She'd rather be Anthony's wife, because he'd always been there for her. Unlike him.

I gave up my commission in the army for you.

It was too late for me then, Luke. It was just too late. You could've come to Germany with me.

You never asked if I wanted to go to Germany. You just said we were moving there and, no, I didn't want to go live in Germany. I didn't want to stay here in Crater Lake either, but it was better than Germany. Of course, my dreams don't matter to you at all. Why couldn't you just open a practice with your father? What was wrong with that? Why couldn't you bend your plans for me or at least ask me if I shared them?

You want me to practice with my father and Carson. Fine. I will.

It's too late, Luke. You were selfish. My desires and wishes never mattered. I'm sorry, but I can't be with you anymore.

This was why he couldn't be near anyone. Why he thought love was pointless. For him anyway. What was the point of falling in love when it could be taken away in an instant?

Carson found love again.

He shook that thought away. That was a different situation. Carson never married Danielle. Carson was never betrayed as Luke was.

There was no room in his heart anymore. He couldn't let there be.

"So what's wrong with this patient?" Sarah used air quotes.

Luke groaned. "Why are you using air quotes? This is a serious situation."

Sarah laughed behind her hand and he couldn't help but smile.

Darn her.

Why was it so easy to be around her?

"Okay, so what is wrong with the patient?"

"Do you know how to perform a surgical cricothyrotomy?"

"Yes. I have done one before, but not when the patient is buried in a snowdrift."

"Peel off your mitts, because you're about to do one on this mannequin. It's better to perfect it here in this simulation rather than on someone who is actually buried under snow." He tossed her a cricothyrotomy kit. "I'll time you."

"Do you want me to go through the steps as I'm doing it?" she asked as she pulled off her mitts.

"If you want."

She peeled back the cover on the kit and began to work. "Damn, my fingers are already going numb. This is going to be more difficult than I thought."

"Which is why we're practicing out here."

Sarah nodded. "Cricothyroid membrane detected and trachea grasped. Making incision."

Luke squatted down and watched her. "You're doing good."

She cursed under her breath. "My fingers are already numb."

"I know, but you can do it."

"Okay, making incision."

Luke watched as she made a beautiful incision in the skin. "Now expose the membrane with the handle of the scalpel."

"Got it." She set the scalpel down and finished the rest of the surgical cricothyrotomy. As she was suturing she cursed again. "My fingers are frozen."

"I know, but that's what happens."

Once it was finished, he handed her the mitts, which she hurriedly put on.

"You did a good job." Luke moved away from her quickly. "Well, I have to get ready and take those surveyors up the mountain. I'll see you later."

"Okay. Thanks." She scurried down off the snow pile and headed back inside. He didn't mind that. It was for the best, because she was stirring up things inside him that weren't welcome. Things that he'd thought were buried deep down.

He admired her. He had fun with her and he was highly attracted to her.

He wanted her and that was not good.

That was unacceptable.

CHAPTER SEVEN

AFTER THE TRAINING SESSION, Sarah had a shower and changed her clothes before heading into town. Her hands were still a little bit numb from performing that surgical cricothyrotomy out on the snow pile.

When she got to town she couldn't help but smile to see all the decorations going up. Hearts on the lampposts. Hearts in store windows. It was a small-town feel, like something straight from the movies, and it made her smile, even though she'd never felt so alone.

That was the thing about small towns. Everyone knew everyone. Or at least it seemed that way. Sarah was a stranger. All she knew was Luke and a couple people up at the hotel, but were they really her friends?

None of them were here with her. Really, she had no friends and it had never really bothered her before. She'd spent so many years distancing herself from her parents' world, she'd put up a wall to keep out everyone.

It hadn't bothered her until now. Even then she didn't know what she wanted. She wasn't sure that she could bring down those walls that were safe.

That were comfortable.

Sarah headed into the coffee shop that was on the corner of the main street. She was still shivering from the cold. When she entered the coffee shop, a few people stopped their conversation and looked in her direction, but only briefly. Being new in town generated some interest, but not enough for someone to come up and talk to her. And Sarah wasn't the kind to go up and start up a conversation with a stranger either.

If they were in a hospital or her clinic, then it would be no problem. She'd be able to talk to them quite easily.

Here, not a chance.

She made her way to the counter and sat down. It was like something out of the fifties. The coffee shop was a mishmash of retro and bohemian, but as long as they served good coffee she didn't care too much.

"What'll you have?" the girl behind the counter asked.

"A large black coffee with a shot of espresso, please."

"Will do." The girl moved away and Sarah undid her jacket and glanced around at all the people chatting. She envied them a bit.

"You're the new doctor in town, aren't you?"

Sarah turned to see a short, blonde woman slip into the seat next to her. It shocked her. In Manhattan this would've never happened. People she encountered in coffee shops there were always in a rush or kept to themselves, just as she did.

"I am," Sarah said. "I'm Dr. Ledet."

"I know." She grinned, her blue eyes twinkling. "I'm Dr. Esme Petersen."

"You're the cardio-thoracic surgeon."

Esme nodded. "I am. Luke mentioned that there was a new doctor up at the hotel. He also mentioned that you briefly worked with Dr. Eli Draven."

"I did. Do you know Dr. Draven?"

Esme nodded. "He trained me."

"I'm impressed. Dr. Draven is a world-class surgeon. Wait, Dr. Petersen, weren't you the one who inserted that chest tube into Shane Draven last summer?"

"I was," Esme said. "How did you know about that?"

"I was the surgeon in Missoula that operated on him."

Esme frowned slightly. "I thought you were from New York?"

"I was training some surgeons on a new technique when I was asked to help with incoming."

"What will you have, Dr. Petersen?" the girl asked as she set down Sarah's coffee in front of her.

"Cappuccino, please, Mary. Thanks."

"Sure thing." Mary walked away again.

"How are you enjoying Crater Lake?" Esme asked.

"It's been great." Sarah took a sip of her coffee. "It's quiet, though."

"Oh, no," Esme said. "You didn't just say that, did you?"

"What?"

"Quiet. I thought you were a trauma surgeon?" Esme said teasingly.

Sarah laughed. "How do you know so much about me?"

"It's a small town and you're new and shiny." Esme winked. "I was new and shiny last summer. I remember clearly."

Mary set down the cappuccino in front of Esme and disappeared again. Sarah could see that a heart was made in the foam.

"Aww, that's sweet," Sarah remarked.

Esme made a face. "I don't like Valentine's Day."

"What? I thought a heart surgeon would love Valentine's Day."

Esme took a swizzle stick and stabbed at the foam heart. "You'd think that, right?"

Sarah laughed. "You're the second person I've met in this town that hates Valentine's Day."

"Really? Who is the other person? Perhaps I should befriend them."

"Dr. Luke Ralston."

Esme laughed. "Luke? Oh, yeah, I forgot. He's such a grouch. I'm surprised he's talking to you, though."

"Why is that?"

"Well, he had a serious hate on for the surgeon who argued with him in Missoula."

Sarah started to laugh. "Yes. We didn't exactly get off on the right foot and I think I've been a thorn in his side."

"That doesn't surprise me. Although, it could work both ways. I think he might be a thorn in your side, too. He is in mine."

"Is he?"

"I'm dating Luke's brother, Carson. So, yeah, he's a bit of a pain in my butt."

"Has he ever dragged you out in the woods and forced you to train for emergency situations in minus-forty weather?" Sarah asked.

"Oh, he made you do that? What a jerk."

They both laughed at that. It was nice to chat with someone. It was nice to talk to someone and feel as if it wasn't superficial. She'd never had an easy chat with another woman before and certainly not another surgeon. She was used to being one of many sharks in a shark pond.

Once the coffee was done, Esme insisted on paying for both and they walked back out into the cold together and stood on the street.

"Thanks for having coffee with me. I was feeling a bit isolated up there," Sarah said.

Esme nodded and wound her knitted infinity scarf around, making a pretty knot in it. "I get it. I was once the new kid in town. Some people around here don't really like change. A few resent the resort community up there and the fact that there are a couple more that will be built, but most are coming around to the idea. It brings more business."

"How do you feel about a fourth doctor in town?" Sarah asked. "Is your practice suffering or is the other Dr. Ralston's?"

"No. It's steady. I get a lot of people from the outlying towns as I'm the closest cardio doctor. Were you worried?"

"Yeah, I didn't want to see an old family practice collapse."

"It won't." Esme reached out and squeezed her arm. "We should have coffee again or maybe even dinner. Carson's not a bad cook. Maybe we can even convince Luke to come down off that mountain."

Blood heated her cheeks and Sarah shook her head. "I seriously doubt that. He's up there now gallivanting around with surveyors."

Esme smiled. "Well, we'd still like to have you over sometime. Have a good day. Watch out for falling hearts."

"What?"

Esme pointed to the lamppost. "They tend to fall in a

strong wind. It happened at Christmas. A Santa landed butt-first on a woman. It wasn't pretty."

Sarah nodded. "Thanks."

Esme walked down Main Street toward the clinic. Sarah glanced up at the glittery, tinsel hearts that were hanging off the lampposts. It made her smile. She jammed her hands in her pockets and headed back to her truck, but as she was walking back to the parking lot there was a rumble. A deep hollow sound followed by a large crack, like thunder, and then a roar like a jet plane was flying overhead. Sarah spun around and watched in horror as a cloud of snow spiraled up into the sky and moved like a wave down the side of the mountain.

It was an avalanche. She could hear screams from other residents of the town as the avalanche wiped away everything in its path.

It was close to home. It was large and it made Sarah's heart stop in her throat.

At least it was on the peak opposite the hotel. The peak was a remote site that could potentially be another hotel.

Then it hit her. That was the Lakeview trail that she'd been on only a couple of days ago. It was the trail that Luke was planning to take a group of surveyors up to.

Luke.

He was up there somewhere on that mountain and could be trapped.

Esme came rushing back up behind her. "Oh, my God. We have to get up that mountain."

"I drove the hotel's truck down."

Esme nodded. "Come help me grab supplies. Carson is already on his way from our place, but we need to get up there and see if anyone's been injured. Do you know where Luke is?"

"He was up there." Sarah pointed at the peak. "He was with surveyors."

Esme cursed under her breath. "I'm sure he's fine. He knows the danger signs. He wouldn't take them somewhere unsafe. Come on."

Sarah nodded, but she felt numb.

As if this weren't happening.

They just did a practice run of an avalanche emergency and now one had actually happened? She'd thought that Crater Lake would be a little bit more laidback, but a bear mauling, a birth and now an avalanche? This place was just as busy as any city.

And last summer there was a landslide?

She'd thought living in the mountains would be peaceful, but she was beginning to realize just how isolated and dangerous it could be and she prayed that Luke had had the sense to see that taking the surveyors up on the Lakeview trail was dangerous and that he'd got out of the way of the avalanche.

"Luke, you're okay?"

Luke turned around to see his brother approaching the hotel. He was out of breath, as if he'd been running.

"I'm fine," Luke said.

Carson nodded and gave him a hug. "When I heard that crack I feared the worst. I knew you were going out on the trails today."

Luke nodded. "I saw the break in the cap before I set out. So I kept the surveyors at bay. I really thought, though, for a while that it wouldn't go and that they would be ticked off at me for wasting their time."

"Was anyone else on the mountain?" Carson asked.

"No. I shut the trails down to everyone else until that bear was caught. The game warden hadn't given me the okay to reopen them since the bear was subdued. We've had some mild temperatures at night and I knew we were due for an avalanche. I'm glad it was contained somewhat, though I'm still waiting to see how far it reached. There are some remote cabins in the way. I'm hoping it didn't get as far as Nestor's place."

Carson nodded. "Me, too. I'm glad you're okay."

Luke was going to say something further when he saw the resort truck driven by Sarah pull up and in the passenger side he saw Esme.

Great. Just great.

"Who's that with Esme?"

"Dr. Ledet," Luke mumbled.

Carson grinned. "No wonder I haven't seen you for a while. I thought you were spending too much time up at the hotel."

"What's that supposed to mean?" Luke asked, glaring at his brother.

Carson nodded in Sarah's direction. "I've seen her. I'm not blind. Isn't that similar to what you said to me in the summer when Esme came to town?"

"Ha-ha. Your witty humor amuses me."

Carson laughed out loud. "This explains a lot."

"It explains nothing," Luke snapped. "And you better remember that. I do have a large hank of rope in my truck. I still know how to set snares that entangle animals bigger than you."

"Dad said you weren't allowed to snare me anymore, remember?"

"No. I don't." Luke turned his back on his brother,

giving Carson the hint he was done with this conversation and not to push him further. He looked back as Carson headed toward the truck to greet Esme and tell her that no one was hurt. Esme looked relieved and Carson kissed her.

Darn him.

Just for a moment Luke was jealous that his brother had that. Then he saw Sarah with a knapsack walking through the snow toward him and he smiled. She had a knapsack with her. She was learning and it made his heart melt, just a bit.

Don't let her in.

"I thought you were in town?" Luke asked gruffly as she set her bag down on the roof of Carson's truck.

"I was and then an avalanche hit. Was anyone hurt?"

"No. You are safe from performing any surgical cricothyrotomies for the moment."

She smiled. "That's great news. It looked so large I thought for sure someone was going to end up injured or worse."

"That actually wasn't too big. That was a medium."

Her eyes widened. "You're joking, right?"

"I don't joke."

"Right. I forgot. You're Mr. Serious all the time."

Luke grinned. "How did you know to bring up Dr. Petersen? I didn't know you knew each other."

"I didn't know her until today. We had coffee together."

Luke's stomach twisted. *Crap.* "What did you two talk about?"

"Wouldn't you like to know?" Her smile stretched from ear to ear.

Oh, Lord.

"Dr. Ralston?"

Luke turned to see one of the rangers coming toward him. "What's wrong, Officer Kyc?"

"The avalanche's zone has extended past Nestor's place. You're the most trained individual to go out and get him. If he was ten years younger and not suffering from cancer he'd be fine up there on his own, but…"

Luke nodded. "I'll get my gear together and go get him."

"Thanks, Dr. Ralston."

"Who's Nestor?" Sarah asked.

"He's a hermit. He likes to keep to himself. He really lives off the grid, taught me everything I know about surviving on the mountain. As much as the army did, but he's getting on in age and I'm not going to leave him up there to die."

"I'll go with you."

"Are you crazy?"

Sarah glared at him. "He might be injured. How are you going to get him down yourself?"

She had a point.

Carson wasn't equipped at the moment to go with him to get Nestor. It would take him over half an hour to get back home and change. There wasn't time. Luke wanted to get to Nestor before nightfall.

"Fine. Hurry up and get changed."

Sarah nodded and headed into the hotel. Luke scrubbed a hand over his face. What was he getting into?

She's just going to help me. Nestor needs help.

That was all there was to it. They were doing their job. That was it. They would go up and get Nestor and bring him back down to the hotel until they could clear a safe path for him to get to and from town. Luke had been giving him heck since the snow started to fly that he should move to town because of his cancer treatments, but Nestor wouldn't leave the mountain.

And really he couldn't blame him.

The mountain might be a harsh, cold and hard mistress, but she stood the test of time. She was more reliable than a heart.

CHAPTER EIGHT

THE SNOWSHOE WALK up to Nestor's cabin was brutal. Sarah knew it was going to be a long haul, but she really didn't have any idea until they were trudging through the snow, roped together for protection. Just in case one of them was swept away.

It terrified her, but she wouldn't back down.

She could do this. She was doing this.

At least Luke didn't treat her as if she were incapable of helping. In fact, he was the first person in a long time who actually appreciated her help. Instead of doing stuff for her, he taught her how. He pushed her to her limits. Made her work and feel things that she'd thought were buried deep inside her.

She hadn't thought that he would let her, to be honest. She knew that he was wary about letting her accompany him, she could see that plainly on his face, but one thing she'd learned about Luke Ralston was he wasn't an idiot.

Sarah knew, just as much as he did, that it would be faster for her to get suited up and assist him than it would for his brother, Carson. She knew that she would be traversing into dangerous territory, but a life was at stake.

She wasn't going to pass up on that. That wasn't the kind of doctor she was.

So without complaint she'd strapped on the heavy rucksack laden with supplies, strapped on the snowshoes and had let Carson tie a rope between Luke and her. It was a lifeline, just in case she slipped and fell. Or just in case the snowcap decided it would crack again and sweep them away.

When she finally saw the cabin in a small clearing she let out an inward sigh of relief at the sight of it and she quickened her pace to keep up with Luke.

Luke stopped in a small copse of trees and set down his rucksack, but he didn't make a move to untie it.

"Why are we stopping?" Sarah asked, though secretly she was glad. She was in pretty good shape, but she wasn't used to the strenuous pace that Luke had kept, or to how much of a sweat she'd worked up under all her winter gear.

"We need a break. Just five minutes to catch our breath and have some water. You okay with that?"

"Perfectly." Sarah dropped her backpack next to Luke's and pulled out her canteen, taking a big swig of water.

"I'm impressed you brought a backpack," he said.

"Of course. I wouldn't have heard the end of it if I hadn't."

He chuckled. "This is true."

"So, if this Nestor guy is a hermit how do you know him? Don't hermits usually keep to themselves?"

"*Hermit* is probably the wrong word. Nestor just likes to live off the land. He's a pioneer man."

"And how do you know him?"

"He taught me everything I know about survival. I

could make up a brilliant story about how he saved my life, or something, but really it was just because my father and he were friends. I always took a real interest in what he had to say. He's like a second father to me. Since my dad moved away and my brother, Carson, started dating Dr. Petersen I've been hanging around Nestor quite a bit." Luke smiled. "He's the only one who ever believed in me when I went to the army."

"Your father didn't approve?"

Luke snorted. "Not really. He wanted me to go to the same medical school as my brother and then to train in the same hospital. My father wanted Carson and I to be partners, but that's not what I wanted. I never wanted that." Luke frowned. "Anyway, Nestor was the only one who told me to follow my dreams."

Sarah was a bit taken aback. It was the first time Luke had ever really talked, opening up warmly about someone else. She'd thought he kept everyone out. That he was cold and closed-off. But underneath that hard surface there was something more about him.

Something warm and loving.

"Is he the one who taught you how to build a log cabin?"

Luke grinned. "He is. He helped me quite a bit. He would like me to live more off the grid, but I do like some modern conveniences."

"Are you sure about that, Pa?" Sarah teased. "You did make all your furniture."

"Yeah, but I like electricity and running water too much." Luke stood up. "We'd better get going. Night falls fast, and we don't want to be trying to bring Nestor down off the mountain in the dark."

Sarah nodded. "Okay."

They packed their canteens back in their bags and headed out on their journey again. Now she understood why Luke was so concerned about getting up there to see if Nestor was okay. It wasn't just the first responder training in him. Luke *cared* about Nestor.

He was worried, and she couldn't even begin to imagine what he must be feeling.

Can't you?

Then she remembered how panicked she'd been when the avalanche had first hit and she'd thought Luke was up there in its path. That was probably nothing compared to worrying about someone who meant something to you.

Luke means something to you, though, doesn't he?

Sarah shook that thought away. There was no time to think about things like that. She had to stay focused on the task at hand. She wouldn't be the one to slow Luke down from getting to his friend in an emergency situation.

When they were at the house, they dropped their knapsacks, undid the rope and took off their snowshoes, propping them inside the lean-to.

"If you think I'm rustic, Nestor is worse," Luke said, kicking the snow off his boots. Then he pounded on the door. "Nestor, it's Ralston. There's been an avalanche."

There was no response.

Luke knocked again. "Nestor, open up."

"It's awfully dark in there and there's no smoke coming from the chimney," Sarah said.

Luke grinned. "I'm impressed you noticed that. Most people from the city don't think about a chimney or smoke from a fire. I'm going to check in the back window."

Sarah nodded while Luke put his snowshoes back on and walked to the back of the house. Sarah stood there waiting. The only sound was her breaths. There was no wind howling in the natural wind break where Nestor's cabin was nestled. There were no birds, no rustling of evergreen needles. It was deadly calm, like right before a storm.

It was a nice spot, but as she glanced through the forest she could see a wall of snow from where the avalanche had barely missed his cabin. It was at least six feet high, with broken and snapped trees everywhere.

She shuddered. It was eerie. Something was not right. She didn't know what, but she could feel it in her bones that something was wrong.

"He's gone," Luke said as he came back into the lean-to.

"You mean he's dead?"

"No, I mean there was a note that he got down before the avalanche hit. He left for Missoula two days ago for his chemo treatment."

"For a hermit who lives off the grid on the side of the mountain I'm surprised he's undertaking chemo."

Luke chuckled. "Well, that might be my doing and his son's, too. Greg came up here last summer and gave his father a stern talking-to. He tried to convince him to move to Missoula with him permanently, but he refused. They struck this bargain. Well, the rangers will be glad to hear that he's not in harm's way. Though I wish he'd checked in with them or me at least."

"So we can head back to the hotel?"

He nodded. "Yep. Sorry, I know you're a bit bushed. Though I'm glad you came, and I'm glad you came prepared and were able to keep up with me. I know I move faster on snowshoes than you're used to."

"It's no problem. I had a good teacher."

Luke's easygoing smile disappeared. "Yes…well, I'm glad you came. Had he been injured, two sets of medically trained hands would have been better than one. Especially when both sets are trained in trauma."

She had obviously made him uncomfortable, which had not been her intention. She'd meant every word she'd said about him being a good teacher. A month ago she wouldn't have had a clue what to do.

She shrugged. "It's no big deal. I'm just glad he's not injured and we don't have to drag him back down."

"Me, too. Let's go before it gets too dark."

Sarah nodded and put on her snowshoes and slung on her knapsack. Luke led the way out of the lean-to and retied the rope between them. That was when she noticed that it was getting dark. Fast. The clouds were low, thick and full of snow. She might not be native to Montana, but, after living in New York and now here, she could recognize snow clouds.

"Do you think a storm is coming?" she asked when they were through the trees back out into the clearing, following the same path they'd taken before.

Luke stopped and looked around. "Yeah, I think so, but we'll beat it."

"You sure?"

"Positive, but we…" He trailed off as he looked up the slope. She looked where he was looking and saw a crack, spreading across a huge chunk of snow.

Oh, my God.

The horror dawned on her fast, because they were right in its path.

"Throw your pack and kick off your snowshoes. Now!" Luke shouted.

Sarah's pulse thundered in her ears and she heaved her knapsack as far as she could, before kicking off her snowshoes. She sank into the deep snow as a loud crack thundered across the slope. The rumbling struck dread in her, right down to her very core, as she tried to run back to the cabin. If the cabin was buried, at least it would be some kind of shelter. Nestor had been smart and built it into the slope, but running through the snow toward salvation was like trying to move through deep sand. It was heavy and it felt as if her limbs weighed a hundred pounds.

"Remember to swim, Sarah. Swim!"

Luke was close to her. All Sarah wanted to do was cling to him, but survival instincts kicked in and as that wave of snow hit she used her arms to swim, fighting the current of snow that tried to drive her down the mountain. Her body screamed in agony as she swam, the rope between Luke and her taut. She didn't even know if he was still there.

All she had to do was keep swimming. She had to keep her head above the snow. She had to breathe.

There was a yank on her arm and she was pulled out of the torrent of snow and fell on top of Luke, who was gasping for breath. One arm tightened around her as the snow roared and thundered past them.

She buried her face in his chest and tried not to cry. She just clung to him. He was her lifeline in this moment. When the roar stopped, only then did she lift her head up and see that their path was cut off and the snow swirling around them was a storm just getting started.

She didn't know how long they had been fighting

the avalanche. It felt like hours the way her body ached. Snow had crept through every crack of her snowsuit.

"You okay?" Luke asked. There was a deep cut to his forehead, by his hairline. It was bleeding profusely.

"I'm fine," she whispered and then she got off him and stood up, her legs weak and her head spinning. "You're bleeding."

"It's a scalp laceration. I'm okay. We need to get to shelter." Luke got up and winced. "At least we have Nestor's place."

Sarah saw that they had been pushed farther down quite a bit, but at least Nestor's cabin had only been partially buried. The lean-to was uncovered and they had access to the door. It was a way inside.

"Come on," Luke said. "We'll get inside and start a fire. Once the storm dies down, they'll send for help."

Sarah nodded and then she spied the backpacks a few feet down at the edge of the pile. "Look, the backpacks made it."

"Good. The snowshoes didn't. I'll break the path. You follow."

Sarah stayed close behind Luke as he broke a path down to the backpacks. Her legs were like jelly, but the storm was getting worse and they had to seek shelter. Once they retrieved their backpacks they headed up to Nestor's cabin.

Luke managed to force the door and they were out of the wind. It was cold in the cabin, but Sarah didn't care. At least they were safe in here. It was shelter.

"Can you tape some gauze to my lac?" Luke asked.

"You'll need more than a dressing. You'll need stitches."

"I know, but first you'll need some boiling water to

clean it out and sterilize and to do that I need to start a fire. It's hard to operate with blood dripping in my eye."

"Sure." Sarah pulled out the first-aid kit and did a quick patchwork on Luke's laceration. Then she helped him bring in a lot of wood. While he started the fire in the fireplace, she grabbed a large pot and filled it with snow from outside the lean-to so they could boil it. Nestor had an old-fashioned water pump, but it was frozen.

It didn't take Luke long to get a fire started, which began to heat up the small cabin in no time. Sarah pulled out their sleeping bags from the bottom of their knapsacks.

"Zip them together," Luke said, wincing slightly.

"What?" she asked.

"Body heat in the night. Nestor only has one small bunk over there. We won't both fit and he's shorter than I am. I know I won't fit on that bunk."

Sarah nodded and zipped the bags together. "I should really take a look at that laceration. Get it cleaned and stitched up. The blood is soaking through the gauze."

Luke agreed, his face pale as he sat down in front of the fire. Sarah found an oil lamp and lit it so she could see a little bit better. She carefully peeled off the bandage and inspected the wound and his head.

"I don't feel a fracture."

"I know," he said. "It's just a laceration. I'm fine."

Sarah glared at him. "Don't play brave with me. It's a deep lac. I'm the one with the needle. I'm sorry I don't have any anesthetic. I do have some morphine for after, though."

He shook his head. "It's okay. I'm not playing brave. I've been stitched up before like this. Just do it."

"Okay. At least it won't need a lot of stitches."

He didn't say much, just looked off into the distance over her shoulder as she got ready to suture. There were a few winces, but mostly he didn't make a peep as she threw four stitches into his forehead, disinfected and then bandaged up the wound. She threw the bloody gauze into the fire and then used the antibacterial foam to clean her hands.

Luke got up and started rummaging around in Nestor's cupboards.

"What're you looking for?" she asked.

"Something to numb the pain," he said.

"I have morphine."

"Ah ha!" Luke pulled out a bottle of amber liquid. "Whiskey. Much better than morphine."

She laughed. "Much better, but won't Nestor be angry that we're rifling through his cupboards?"

"Nah, he'll know this is an emergency. I'll replace everything we have to use."

Sarah began to shiver again. "I think my socks are wet."

"Mine, too. We have to get out of these damp, cold clothes and into the sleeping bag to preserve body heat."

What?

Only she couldn't say that out loud, because her mouth dropped open and she felt a bit dumbstruck at the moment.

Luke moved past her and started to strip off his outer gear and then took off his flannel shirt, exposing his chest and back. Sarah didn't need a fire at that moment, because she realized that he was expecting her to climb naked into a double sleeping bag with him.

"I can't get naked."

He glanced around, hanging up his clothes. The only thing on him was his trousers and she couldn't help but notice how incredibly ripped and tanned Luke was under all those flannel shirts he wore. Her body was very aware that she was going to see all of him in a matter of moments and that he would see her.

She'd never undressed in front of a man before.

The last time she made love to a man, she didn't undress in front of him. It was done in dignity with the lights out and, even then, she really couldn't remember much about that encounter because, like the rest of her past romantic life, it hadn't been overly memorable.

Who says you're going to have sex?

The cabin was heating up and it wasn't just the fire.

"What's wrong? Why can't you get undressed?"

She crossed her arms. "I don't get naked in front of strange men."

"I'm not a stranger. Besides, if you don't you'll most likely get hypothermia. Okay, I'll close my eyes until you get into the sleeping bag. I swear to you, nothing untoward will happen."

"What about the extra clothes in the knapsack?" she asked. "You told me to always pack extra clothes."

"They'll be too cold and we've been exposed outside too long. This is the fastest way to get our temperature back up. Besides, we're doctors. It's not like we haven't seen naked bodies before."

Dammit.

He had a point. The only difference was, she hadn't seen him naked before and vice versa. There was a difference between seeing a patient for an exam and seeing a man you were highly attracted to, naked.

"Okay." She began to peel off her clothes and hung

them near the fire so they could dry and just as she did that Luke peeled off his pants and her breath caught in her throat at the sight of his very muscular, well-defined backside.

She tried not to look, because she didn't want him to see the blush that she knew was slowly creeping up her neck into her cheeks.

This was going to be a very long night.

CHAPTER NINE

LUKE WAS TRYING very hard to ignore the fact that in a few moments he was going to be inches away from Sarah and that she was going to be naked. He'd fantasized about having her naked in his bed before, but this was not how he'd pictured it.

When he glanced over at her, her pale cheeks were flaming red and she was looking away. He felt bad for her, so he walked across the room to Nestor's bed and wrapped a blanket around his waist. Then grabbed another quilt and walked back over to her.

"I'm respectable."

She opened her eyes and he held out the blanket. "Where did you get these?"

"Nestor's bed. Besides, the extra blankets will help keep us warm."

She nodded. "Thanks."

He moved away from her and tried not to look at her as he climbed into the sleeping bag. He poured himself a shot of whiskey and swigged it down quickly, trying to numb the pain of his throbbing head and also to try and distract himself from the fact that Sarah was undressing a few feet away from him.

How many times had he thought about this? Too

many times. His pulse was racing, his blood had heated and he was fighting to control his yearning for her.

The only trouble was being in Sarah's presence did that to him.

When he was in her presence he lost all control.

He wished he could just take her in his arms and make love to her like he desperately wanted to.

Don't think about it.

Only he couldn't help it and he stifled a groan.

"You okay?" she asked as she wrapped the blanket around her and then climbed into the sleeping bag beside him.

"My head hurts, just a bit." He didn't want to admit to her that the groan he'd been trying to get under control had nothing to do with the injury to his head.

"Well, that's to be expected. I can get the morphine."

"Stop pushing drugs on me." He winked at her and she laughed, but she still seemed nervous.

She's not the only one.

"Fine. Have another shot of whiskey, then."

"I will," Luke said and he poured her a cup, handing it to her. "First you. It'll warm you up."

"Thanks." She took a sip. "That does help."

He nodded. "I told you it would. You did really good out there today."

"You taught me well." She took another sip of whiskey. "You told me to swim and I did, but that..."

"I know. When that avalanche hit us and I started to swim, it was powerful. More powerful than any current I've swam in, in water. Being in that avalanche was like nothing I've ever felt before. I'm glad we weren't swept away down the side of the mountain. It was a minor one."

"That was minor? I thought you'd experienced an avalanche before?"

"I've seen them, I've helped those injured, but never have I experienced almost being swept away by one."

"At least we weren't trapped." Sarah shivered; he could hear her teeth chattering. So he moved closer, wrapping his arm around her. His blood pounding between his ears, because he was touching her.

You're just keeping her warm. That's all.

Her breath hitched in her throat the moment he pulled her close. Her skin was so soft, the flowery scent of her silken, blond hair surrounding him and he wanted to pull it out of the braid she'd put it in and run his fingers through it.

"No, we weren't trapped. That's a good thing." Only right now in this cabin they were trapped by the storm. Being here with her, with nothing between them, was more dangerous to him than being trapped in that snowstorm.

He was nervous, but he couldn't pull himself away.

You're just warming her, he told himself again.

"That feels good," she whispered.

"What does?" he asked.

"Your arm around me." Then she moved in closer to him and touched his face. Her fingers lightly brushing over his skin, which made him feel as if he were on fire. Her lips so close to his. Then her fingers touched his lips and he closed his eyes, trying to regain control of his senses, but before he could maintain that control, before he could stop what was happening her lips pressed against his in a feather-light kiss. He tried not to cup her face and drag her tight against his body, as he wanted to. He'd forgotten what a woman's kiss felt like.

He'd forgotten what passion tasted like. It had been far too long and he was caught off guard by it. It rocked him to his very core and he didn't want it to end. He wanted more.

Oh, God.

Luke needed to put an end to this before he got carried away and forgot himself. Before he forgot why he distanced himself from women, about why he distanced himself from her.

"Why did you do that?" he asked.

"I wanted to. I've wanted to for some time." Her blue eyes sparkled in the dim flickering light thrown from the fire. "I want to kiss you again, Luke."

"I don't think that's wise," he said, though his body screamed yes, yes, yes.

"I don't think it's particularly wise either," she whispered, but then her hands ran through his hair and she was kissing him urgently.

He should push her away, but the moment she sighed and melted against him he was a lost man.

He was completely lost to her.

Luke undid the braid in her hair and gently ran his fingers through it. It was as soft as he'd imagined. Like silk. It fanned over her bare shoulder and he couldn't help but brush it away. Ever since he'd first met her, he'd dreamed of touching her skin, her hair, and now he was.

He'd forgotten what it was like.

Christine had hurt him so bad with her betrayal and he'd buried these feelings deep inside. He didn't ever want to feel like that again, but in this moment he was reveling in being with Sarah and he was worried that if he indulged then he wouldn't ever be able to stop.

That he'd want more.

And he couldn't have more.

He wouldn't put his heart at risk again. When Christine left him, he'd promised himself he wouldn't let another woman affect him like that. Love just brought pain.

Who said anything about love?

He moved away. He couldn't do this even though he desperately wanted to.

"What's wrong?" Sarah asked.

"I don't know if we should be doing this."

"Doing what?" she asked.

"Kissing."

"I think we should be." Sarah touched his face again and then kissed him. "I don't think we should stop."

"Sarah, I can't promise you anything."

She smiled at him. "I'm not asking for promises. I just want you. Here and now."

"I want you, too. I can't help myself, but I do."

And it was true. When it came to Sarah, he couldn't help himself.

Sarah wasn't sure what made her reach out and kiss Luke. It wasn't the whiskey, that was for certain. She could hold her drink better than most. No, she was sure it was due to the fact that moments ago she'd almost died.

Working in the ER Sarah had seen countless people face death, sometimes because of the simplest reasons, like a reaction to a medication or food and sometimes because of something more complicated that damaged their body. She'd wrestled with death in the OR, saving patients while she operated on them and, though they could never remember that moment when they came so close to losing the battle because they'd been under general anesthesia, she always wondered what it might be like.

Did they feel anything?

Did they see their life flash before their eyes, even in a dreamless sleep?

Did they understand how close they came and how hard they fought, how hard she fought for them? Overcoming death for her patients was a high. The lives she saved meant more to her than all the money her parents had.

It was why she did what she did.

So when her moment came it was surreal. When the snow came roaring down the hill toward her, there was a clarity.

Live or die.

And she chose life. She fought hard. She swam and when she came through it, it hit her how many chances she'd passed on. Not when it came to her career, but her life. She'd been fighting her whole life to prove to her parents she was her own person, to the point that she didn't know when to stop fighting. Maybe life didn't always have to be such a fight? Maybe she hadn't really been living her life, because she was so busy trying to show everyone that she was capable of doing things on her own that life was passing her by. She wasn't even sure anymore.

When she thought she had been living her own life, she hadn't. Her father had made that painfully clear. She'd spent so long building up walls that now she wanted Luke on the other side with her.

She wanted to live her life. Take chances, take risks, because even though that avalanche had been the most terrifying thing she'd ever experienced, surviving after the fact was equally scary.

Right now, in this moment with Luke, she just wanted to feel. She chose this and she wanted it.

Really she shouldn't but she couldn't fight it anymore. She wanted Luke as she'd never wanted another man before. It was something fierce. Primal, even. It scared her and thrilled her.

She wanted to feel again.

"Sarah, I'll ask again. Are you sure?"

"I'm sure."

Luke rolled over, pressing her against the floor and laying kisses against her lips, her neck and lower. He brushed his knuckles down the side of her face and kissed where her pulse raced under her skin.

"You make me feel," he whispered. Then he leaned down and brushed another kiss against her lips, light and then urgent. His body was pressed against hers. It made her feel right and she loosened the extra blanket he'd given her so they could be skin to skin. She opened her legs to let him settle between her thighs. Sarah arched her hips. She wanted him.

She craved him.

"I have to stop," Luke moaned.

"Why?"

"I don't have protection. One thing I didn't pack for."

Sarah grinned. "It's okay. I'm on birth control and I'm clean."

"So am I. Are you sure you want to, though?"

"Yes. I want to. The question is do you want me?" She bucked her hips and he groaned.

"Oh, I want you."

"How much?"

Luke kissed her again, his tongue pushing past her lips, entwining with hers, showing her just how much he wanted her.

"I want you so much." He ran his hands over her body, his hands hot, branding her skin as he touched her.

"I've tried hard to resist you," Sarah whispered against his neck. "You drive me crazy."

He grinned. "I want you, too, Sarah."

Luke's lips captured hers in a kiss, silencing any more words between them. Sarah pulled him closer and wrapped her legs against his waist. His hands slipped down her sides.

"So beautiful," he murmured.

His hand slid between them and he began to stroke her. Sarah bit her lip to stop from crying out. She wanted so much more. She wanted Luke inside her. She wanted him to take her and make her feel again.

Sarah wanted Luke to remind her of who she was, because she couldn't remember. She just wanted to forget it all and get lost in this one moment with him.

"I love having you under me," Luke whispered against her neck. "I want to be inside you."

"I want you, too."

He pushed her down, covering her body with his and thrusting into her. Sarah cried out then. She couldn't help herself. Being joined with him was overwhelming, but it was what she wanted. It was what she needed.

"You feel so good," he moaned. "Damn."

She moved her hips, urging him to move, but he wouldn't. He just held her still, buried deep inside her.

"You're evil," she gasped.

"I know."

Luke moved slowly at first, taking his time, and it drove her crazy. She wanted him hard and fast. She wanted to feel him moving inside her. She urged him to go faster until he lost all control and was thrusting against her hard and fast. Then she could feel her body succumbing to the sweet release she was searching for. Pleasure overtook her and she cried out again, digging her nails into his back, making him hiss in pain, but it didn't stop him. He kept going until his own release came a moment later.

He rolled away onto his back and she curled up on his chest, just listening to his heart race. It was soothing and reassuring. She'd always liked the sound of the heart. It meant life. Then tears started to roll down her face.

"Sarah, are you okay?"

She sat up, trying to brush the tears away. "I'm fine."

"Do you regret what happened?"

"No," she said quickly. "No. I wanted that to happen. What happened here tonight was a long time coming. It's just…we could've died today."

He smiled softly. "But we didn't."

"I know. You know, it was in that moment on the slope that I couldn't recall if the life I've been living has been my own."

Luke's brow furrowed. "How do you mean?"

"Everything I've accomplished is because my father has had a hand in it."

"What?"

"You want to know why I came here? I came here because my father got my last job for me. Just like every other job. So I came here, without his help. I'm tired of being labelled as his helpless daughter."

Luke nodded. "Stepping out of a parent's shadow can be hard. And you're far from helpless."

Sarah sighed. "I'm not sure if I know myself anymore."

"I understand that."

She frowned. "Do you? You're living out your dream here."

Luke shrugged. "I love the mountains, but it wasn't my dream to be a lone wolf. I was married before."

"You were?"

He nodded. "She left me for my best friend while I was overseas."

"No wonder you have trust issues."

"Yeah. I suppose I do."

Luke turned from her, withdrawing from her once more. But for a moment she had seen a little piece of himself that he kept hidden from the world.

Sarah had been absolutely shocked to learn that he'd been married before. He just didn't seem the type to settle down with a wife, and she couldn't help but wonder what he'd been like before he'd become this walled-off man.

And no wonder, when his wife had left him for his best friend. Two people he'd trusted completely had betrayed him.

It explained so much, but Sarah had a feeling there was more to it than that. There was something else he wasn't saying.

"It's hard to trust when you trust no one."

Luke turned back around. "What?"

"At least you have a family to turn to. I don't. I can't rely on my parents."

"Why?"

"They were never around."

"I'm sorry."

Sarah shrugged. "My mother preferred the company of her friends over her children and my dad was too involved with his businesses. Money drives him."

"Must've been a lonely childhood."

She nodded. The words, though the truth, stung. Her whole life had been lonely up until now. She had just never realized it.

How could she trust a man who guarded his heart so? He'd never open up fully. His ex-wife had hurt him terribly, and in the short time Sarah had known him she'd learned that he didn't give people a second chance.

He was stubborn that way.

Which was a shame.

"It was. I sometimes felt invisible," she said. She hadn't intended to say that thought out loud, but she had.

He moved toward her and touched her face briefly "I get not knowing who you are anymore. I get it, but I want you to know. I see you."

She wanted to believe him. She really did, but she didn't think anyone could see her, especially when she couldn't even see herself. So long she'd been under her family's thumb, she didn't even know it. How could she believe him, when she couldn't even believe in herself?

"You don't believe me," Luke said.

"What?"

"Your expression. I can read you like a book."

She glared at him. "Thanks."

"It's something I've learned to do as an army medic."

"Why did you leave the army?"

His demeanor changed almost instantly. "What?"

"What made you change your mind about the army?"

"I thought I had a wife waiting for me."

"I'm sorry."

Luke shrugged and then unzipped his side of the sleeping bag. "Are you hungry?"

"Sure." She watched him as he dug in his knapsack for his dry pair of pants and slipped them on. "Hey, I thought you said we shouldn't wear our extra clothes?"

He grinned. "That was when we were still damp and cold. I bet you're warm now."

She blushed and then grabbed her knapsack, pulling out the dry set of clothes and pulling on the pants, shirt and socks. There was a definite draught on the floor. She got up and padded toward the window. It was dark, but that was about all she knew. She couldn't see a thing. All she could hear was the howling from the wind.

"Still storming?" Luke asked as he pulled down some cans from Nestor's cupboard and set them down on the counter.

"It looks that way. How long do you think it will last?"

Luke shrugged. "I don't know. Probably not that long. Usually when a bad blizzard is about to whip up, they warn us. The only warning I heard for today was a squall."

"I think that's more than a squall out there."

Luke nodded. "Nestor has beans. I hope you don't mind."

"Yes. I totally mind." She walked over to him. "I don't think those hearts will survive."

"What?" he asked as she rifled through drawers.

"I was in town and they were decorating for Valentine's Day."

Luke snorted. "Of course. They're probably going overboard, too, because of the big party that's going to happen on Valentine's Day at the hotel. Just the idea of the town covered in all that paraphernalia makes me a bit queasy."

"Well, the resident party planners have been working around the clock since I arrived in Crater Lake. I think it's going to be a big party."

Luke snorted again. "Pointless."

"Why?"

"Darn it, do you think Nestor could keep things in a logical spot?" Luke cursed again and bent down to rummage under the counter.

Sarah rolled her eyes. There was no getting through to him. At least not about this or why he left the army. His ex-wife really did a number on him and she felt bad that he'd been hurt. He'd been betrayed by the woman he loved and she'd been betrayed by her parents in a way.

Though really it wasn't the same thing.

They were both damaged souls and she hadn't made any promise to him, just as he had never made any to her. She didn't regret what had happened between them here tonight. She was glad it had happened.

Even if it could never happen again, because she couldn't let it happen again. Luke was her friend and she wouldn't hurt him the way his ex-wife had hurt him and she doubted very much Luke would even let her in if she tried.

His heart was guarded, just as much as she had her own walls of protection up. At least he'd let her in just briefly, even for a moment.

It was better they remained friends. Just friends and coworkers. That was all they could be, but that made her sad and for one brief moment she wished for something more.

CHAPTER TEN

AFTER THEY HAD something to eat they curled up together by the fire to spend the night and even though Luke wanted something to happen again, he wouldn't allow it. If it were warmer in Nestor's cabin he would've had her sleep on Nestor's bunk and he would've stayed on the floor.

Sarah fell asleep almost instantly after they had something to eat, but Luke couldn't sleep. Which ticked him off. If the storm subsided they were going to have to hike out of here. He knew that Nestor had snow-shoes and skis in the lean-to, but in order to hike back down to the resort he would need his energy and that required sleep.

Especially after the strenuous activity that they'd engaged in a couple hours ago.

Don't think about it.

He didn't want to let Sarah in and risk his heart. The trouble was, she was already digging her way in there. He couldn't fall in love again. It was too much of a risk.

And living up on a mountain tracking bears and rescuing stranded people isn't?

What if Sarah decided to head back to New York?

What if she wanted him to give up his life here and when he couldn't she'd leave him?

He wouldn't be hurt again. He wouldn't put his heart in that kind of danger again. It wasn't worth it. It was pointless.

Luke cursed under his breath and slowly climbed out of the sleeping bag, making sure that he didn't disturb Sarah. He wandered over to the window and peered outside. The snowstorm was beginning to subside. He could see black instead of just a wall of white.

He glanced back over at her, sleeping so peacefully, her blond hair fanned out around her head, and he desperately wanted to go back and join her. If he'd been in a different place.

If he'd never married Christine.

When Christine had left it hurt, but it also relieved him because he was beginning to see that they weren't meant for each other.

It was a clean break.

Still, it hurt. The betrayal stung.

Trust was not something he gave easily or freely.

So yeah, risking his life on the mountain was not playing it safe, but the only one who was affected by the choices he made was him. There was no wife to think about. No kids. He was free.

Really?

He sighed. Yeah, he was free, but the cost of his freedom was loneliness. He hadn't realized how lonely he had been until Sarah ended up in Crater Lake. When he'd started working with her, he'd been dreading it at first, because all he'd remembered was the surgeon from the summer. The one who'd rankled him and had fire in her eyes.

This Sarah was different from that surgeon from the summer.

She still was a spitfire, but something had changed in her.

The fire was diminished. He shouldn't really care why, but he did. And he discovered that he looked forward to all their training sessions. Although, she didn't know that those sessions weren't Silas Draven's idea, but his.

At first he was supposed to show her a bit of emergency first aid and tell her about some of the common injuries that could occur on the mountain, especially injuries that would happen to guests, but, after taking her out that first time and seeing how she threw herself into everything she did, he wanted to show her more.

And he soon found that he liked spending the time with her. Which was bad, because the more time he spent with her, the more his walls came down and he didn't like that.

Those walls were there for a reason. Those walls protected him.

Those walls would protect her.

He didn't want to stop being a first responder. He didn't want to stop doing what he was doing, because it mattered and because of that he wouldn't leave a widow or children behind. A life of solitude was the only answer.

It was the only way. That way no one got hurt.

I need to put some distance between us.

As soon as they were back at the resort, Luke was going to sever ties with Sarah for a while. She'd move on and find someone else. He had no doubt. She was beautiful, kind, funny. Of course, thinking about someone else kissing her made him angry.

She can't be yours.

And he had to keep reminding himself of that fact. The squalling stopped, almost as suddenly as it had started, which was good. He just hoped another system wasn't about to start up again. He didn't want to eat all of Nestor's rations.

Just as he was about to turn away, he saw lights coming up off the trail. Several lights and he realized they were snowmobiles.

"Sarah, wake up!" he shouted.

She bolted upright. "What's wrong?"

"Our rescue team has arrived."

She was confused. "What?"

"The squall ended and there's a pack of snowmobiles headed this way."

She got up and ran over to the window. "Oh, thank goodness. At least we don't have to hike down the mountain tomorrow. I'll start packing up."

Luke nodded and then grabbed his dry flannel shirt, quickly pulling it on as well as his socks and boots. If he didn't know any better, his brother or Esme would be on one of those snowmobiles and he wasn't going to have them catch him half-naked in a cabin with Sarah. He wasn't going to be subjected to their constant questioning for the next few weeks.

As soon as his boots were on there was a knock at the door.

"Luke?"

It was Carson. Luke opened the door and his brother let out a sigh of relief and pulled him into a bear hug.

"You're freezing and I just got warm. Get in here."

The rescue team shuffled into the small entrance way of Nestor's cabin. Carson and two other first responders had come up the mountain.

"We were about to call off the search," Carson said. "Then I saw smoke coming from Nestor's cabin. We found out about twenty minutes after you and Sarah left that Nestor was in Missoula with his family getting chemotherapy. And then the avalanche. I'm glad you're okay. I'm glad you're both okay."

"Yeah, we learned he was gone when we got here. We were heading back when the avalanche struck, but we got out of it."

"We swam," Sarah said.

Carson and the first responders looked at her in shock. "You swam? You mean you were hit by the avalanche?"

"Yeah, but it was minor. Then the squall hit, so we got back to Nestor's and broke in. I owe him some provisions and some firewood."

"I don't think he'll mind," Carson said. "We should get back down the mountain before another squall hits. Last check on radar was another one was brewing to the northwest of here."

Luke nodded. "We'll pack our things and get our gear on."

Carson and the other two men stepped outside into the lean-to.

Sarah was shoving the last of her things into her knapsack. The zipped-together bags were undone and the blankets had been folded and put back on Nestor's bed. It was as if what had happened between them had been swept away.

It's for the best.

"I'll be glad to get back to my own bed. Maybe even a hot shower," she remarked as she zipped up her coat.

"Yeah. Me, too." Which was a lie. Even though he knew it was for the best this was happening, deep down he secretly wished he could spend the night with her, but he shook that thought away as he finished packing his things and putting out the fire.

Sarah was already outside, by the time the fire had been extinguished and the oil lamp turned off. The cabin was so dark and lonely. The small window panes illuminated by the headlights from the snowmobiles.

He wished they could stay, just for a bit longer, but this was better.

Luke was getting the distance he needed from her.

And if he did that, he would have a chance for his walls to rebuild.

Yeah. Right.

It was the fastest ride she'd ever been on. One of the re-sponders, named Lee, had said that there was another squall brewing and they were trying to beat it back to the resort.

Sarah didn't care at that moment. All she wanted to do was get back to her bed, electricity and a hot shower. She didn't want to be stuck in another squall, in a shack and eating beans. Although, the company was fine.

She didn't mind that in the least.

Luke was on the snowmobile with his brother and Sarah wished that he were driving one of the machines and that she were riding with him.

Something had changed up there and she didn't know what it was, other than he was more closed off than before. He barely looked her in the eye and it frightened her.

Who cares? You both were consenting adults and didn't make any promises.

Only, when it was all over with, she found herself craving more. She wanted him again, but that was not possible. If she took up with Luke, her mother would be somewhat happy that she'd found a doctor to settle down with, but then her father would say to her again that she couldn't handle the job in Crater Lake on her own.

You try too hard, pumpkin. You don't need to try so hard.

She hated when her father talked down to her like that. As if she were still four years old. She was the baby and therefore couldn't make it on her own.

As much as she wanted to be with Luke, maybe a little distance was a good thing. Besides, he wasn't telling her something. There was some hurt still buried there. How could she trust him if he couldn't trust her?

He didn't seem to take much stock in love. As was evident by his hatred for Valentine's Day and intimacy.

She didn't understand why he felt this way, other than his failed marriage, but there had to be something more to it than that. How could someone have so much hate for an emotion that also brought joy? Yeah, love did hurt, but in the end wasn't it worth it?

Of course, she wouldn't know anything about love.

She'd never been in it. She'd had crushes or relationships, but love? That was something she'd never experienced. It was scary and messy. She just didn't have time for it.

Why not?

She shook that thought from her head as the snowmobiles slowed down and came to a stop in front of the hotel. Sarah's legs were shaking, but she held her ground and walked toward the entranceway.

There were still people milling around from earlier, but she didn't linger. She just wanted to get back to her room and forget about what had happened between Luke and her.

"Sarah!"

She turned and Luke was headed toward her.

Just say good-night. Turn around and walk away.

Only she couldn't. She was so weak.

"Yeah?" she asked.

"Thank you for stitching up my head."

She nodded. "You should get that checked out later by Carson. Try not to get it wet. You probably know the drill when it comes to stitches."

He smiled. "I do, but thanks."

Turn around. Walk away.

"Will I see you tomorrow?"

You fool.

"Probably not. I have to get back up to Nestor's place and restock some stuff. I actually might rest for a couple of days."

"Of course. Take it easy and thanks for saving my life up there."

"I didn't save your life. You saved your own."

"If you hadn't shown me, I wouldn't have known what to do."

"If I hadn't shown you, you would've never been allowed to come up there with me," Luke said, and she realized his tone had changed. "You shouldn't have been up there with me."

"What are you talking about?" Sarah asked, confused. She'd thought he was happy that she'd gone up the mountain with him. He'd said so. What had changed? Why did he look so guilt-ridden?

Luke grabbed her by the arms, giving her a little shake. "You could've died in that avalanche."

"You could've, too."

He shook his head. "You could've died and it would've been my fault. I couldn't have borne that."

"I wanted to go with you."

Luke pushed her away and cursed under his breath. But she wasn't going to let him run away so she stood in front of him, blocking his path.

"I wanted to go with you," she stated again. "You said you were glad I was up there. You were glad to have the extra set of medically trained hands. You didn't force me up that mountain. It was my choice. Just like you couldn't have forced me down the mountain. You wanted me up there and I wanted to be there."

"What I wanted doesn't matter. It doesn't matter when it comes to your life. I won't be responsible for that."

And before she could say anything else to him he turned and walked away. She wanted to go after him, but she recognized that look.

He was going to retreat back up into the mountains. When he was ready, she'd see him again, but only when she was ready.

Right now, she wasn't ready to see him for a long time.

CHAPTER ELEVEN

SARAH HADN'T SEEN Luke in the week since they had spent the night together up in the cabin caught between a snowstorm and an avalanche. She'd been expecting it. Any time she got too close to Luke, he hid in the forest for a while.

It was the same with her.

Only she hid in her clinic.

She didn't regret what had happened between them. She'd wanted it. And she'd meant what she'd said about not promising anything to him. It had been only about the moment that night.

Only now she missed him and she wished they'd promised each other that it wouldn't be weird after. That they could still be friends. And she wished he didn't feel so guilty about putting her into a dangerous situation. It had been her choice. He had nothing to feel guilty about, but there had been no telling him that.

She'd gotten so used to him being around, his absence made her heart ache. Loneliness had never bothered her before, until now.

Though she didn't have much time to dwell on it. The hotel was busier than ever. As Valentine's Day and its grand opening approached more and more guests were coming to Crater Lake. Including a lot of wealthy A-listers. The population of Crater Lake went from just under six hundred people to more than a thousand overnight.

And it wasn't just Silas Draven's hotel that was selling out.

All the guest accommodations in town were full. Even privately owned rental cabins, which had never been rented during the winter season before, were full. Crater Lake was turning into a winter hotspot.

Sarah had been go, go, go since she came down off the mountain. Her clinic was busy with superficial stuff, stomach bugs and someone requesting a bikini wax and Botox, which she didn't do and promptly sent them to the on-site spa. She hadn't a moment to think for herself. So when she finally did get a break she headed to town to grab a cup of coffee and some peace and quiet.

As she walked down the street she spotted Esme in a stationery store and headed in to visit her. Esme was standing beside a large rack of Valentine's Day cards, mumbling to herself and frowning.

"You look like you're going to be sick," Sarah teased, coming up behind her.

"Oh, hey!" Esme laughed then. "I might. Did I mention that I hate Valentine's Day?"

"Yes. You mentioned something about that the first time we met. If you hate it so much, then why are you standing here in a shop that's overflowing with abomination?"

"Because my boyfriend likes Valentine's Day." She wrinkled her nose. "So I thought I would be nice and get him a card that I can shove in his face when he forces me to go to that Valentine's ball gala thing next week and makes me dress up like a princess or something very fluffy."

Sarah chuckled. "Not really romantic to shove something in someone's face and dressing up can be fun."

Esme grinned. "It depends on the dressing up, though."

"I don't know you well enough to talk about that." And they both laughed.

"He knows how much I hate it. He bought tickets just to annoy me." Esme pulled out a card. "This one is perfect. What do you think?"

The card in question had a large chimpanzee on it, making a kiss face. There was also faux fur glued to the outside. It was tacky and hideous, but Esme seemed so pleased with her find.

"That's an interesting choice. What does it say?"

"It says 'It's no monkey business, because I'm bananas for you.'" Esme grinned. "Yes, this is the one."

"That's a terrible card," Sarah said between chuckles. "It makes me cringe. Besides, that's clearly a chimpanzee and not a monkey, so really it's false advertising."

"Which is why it's so perfect. So, how are things with you?" Esme winked and Sarah groaned inwardly. What had she learned? Did Luke say anything and if so what did he say?

Just play it cool. Pretend as if nothing happened.

"I'm good."

"Good, huh? I hear your clinic has been busy."

"It has. More and more guests are arriving every day. A lot of big names."

Esme's expression hardened. "Hollywood A-listers?"

"Yeah, why?"

Esme sighed. "I used to run in that crowd before I came here. It's not my favorite crowd. You know I was engaged to Dr. Draven's son."

"No. I didn't. Wait, you were engaged to Shane Draven? When?"

"A couple of years ago. I ended it and I fell out of grace with that group of people. I don't miss it at all."

Sarah nodded. She didn't miss the glitterati of Manhattan or the so-called friends she'd made in the circles of society her parents traveled in, because once you weren't in that circle anymore you became a ghost. Just a memory that was briefly touched upon during lulls in conversation.

"I couldn't agree more." Sarah picked up a card with a red heart. One thing she did miss about this time of year was when they would light up the Empire State Building with pink or red, sometimes even a heart.

"Have you seen the other Dr. Ralston lately?" Esme asked.

"Luke?"

"Yeah." There was a twinkle in her eye.

"Why?"

"No reason. I didn't mean to put you on the defensive. Carson told me what happened up there."

Sarah groaned. "Oh, he did?"

"Yeah. I can't even begin to imagine being caught in an avalanche. You were so lucky that you weren't swept away. Why, Glacier National Park had several avalanche-related deaths last year. It's scary. I never really thought about snow as a threat."

"You wouldn't—you come from California."

"I'm actually from Ohio originally. I have a respect for winter, but never seen an avalanche. Heck, until last summer I'd never really seen a landslide and apparently there's a dormant volcano around here."

Sarah laughed. "Guess we really did move to a danger zone."

Esme shrugged. "It's beautiful here, though. I love my life here. I wouldn't change it for anything."

Sarah nodded. "Well, I better head back to the hotel. I only had a small break and I'm sure there's another group of people wanting me to laser off their hair or inject them with silicone or something."

"I hope you're kidding?"

"I wish I was. Why they come to me instead of heading to the spa I can't understand."

She missed being a surgeon. She loved living in Crater Lake and the opportunity to work in Silas Draven's hotel was fantastic, but she missed the ER. For the first time in a long time, she actually missed the hustle and bustle of the ER.

She hadn't thought that she would when she'd first left active trauma surgery, when she'd taken on that job and started touring the country and training doctors. Despite what her father had done, she'd really enjoyed the travel and connections she'd made working with some of the finest surgeons in the world.

Returning back to the ER as a trauma surgeon had seemed like a step back, but now she realized that really this job was a step back. The only thing that really excited her was working with Luke. The bear mauling, the birth, even operating on Shane Draven last summer, all of those instances when she was called in to help in an emergency situation were when she felt like herself.

When she felt free.

And she missed it; she just hadn't realized how much she had until now. She'd leave, but she had a contract to fulfill and she wouldn't back down. She finished things she started. On the other hand she didn't want to leave Crater Lake.

She didn't want to leave Luke.

"Well," Sarah said. "It was nice to see you again, but I have to head back."

Esme nodded and then reached out and squeezed her arm. "It was nice talking with you, too. Will I see you at the Valentine's ball?"

"Yes. I have to go. Silas Draven's orders. I would skip it since I have no one to go with and I'll probably be too busy the next day dealing with hangovers. It would be nice to get the extra sleep."

They both laughed at that. Sarah waved goodbye and headed back in the cold. If she could only remain in Crater Lake, but as an independent doctor, then she wouldn't mind that too much, but how many doctors did a small town need?

If she wanted to return to surgery, she'd have to leave Crater Lake.

It was as simple as that, but she might be persuaded to stay if Luke wanted her to. Even though that was very unlikely.

Luke was not ready for love and she doubted he would ever be.

She couldn't put her career on hold on the off chance Luke might want her. That was no way to live a life, so, as much as she hated the thought, once her year was up at Crater Lake she was going to find a hospital and go back to her first love of trauma surgery.

Even if it meant breaking her own heart in the process.

Then she thought of that painting he loved. The watercolor she'd done of the horse on the plains. She'd told him to take it, but he hadn't. Maybe she could give that to him as a peace offering.

If they couldn't be anything else, she wanted them to be friends. When she got back to the hotel she grabbed the painting and scrawled *For Adele* on the back before slipping it into an envelope.

Then she headed back to her clinic.

When she arrived she was surprised to find Luke pacing outside her office. The sight of him made her pulse quicken and she could recall every kiss of his lips on her skin, the weight of his body on her and the warmth. It had been over a week since she'd seen him, but looking at him now it felt as if it were just yesterday and that moment in the cabin came flooding back to her.

She both hated and loved the effect he had on her, but she was glad he was here. She'd missed him.

The only telltale sign that time had passed was that he'd had the stitches removed, but the gash had healed nicely, only leaving a small red mark barely visible at his hairline.

"Luke, what a surprise." And she held out the envelope ready to give it to him, but he didn't look at her.

"Where were you?" he snapped.

"In town. It was my morning off."

"I thought you would be here." He was clearly agitated.

"I'm here now. What're you so worked up about?"

Luke didn't say anything; he opened her clinic door, which she'd thought was locked, and dragged her inside, shutting the door behind them and locking it.

"What is up with you?" She tried to touch his laceration. "Do you want me to check your head?"

He grabbed her hand by the wrist and stopped her, shocking her, and then he let go of her hand, but didn't offer up an apology.

"It's not me," he said. "It's Nestor."

"Nestor?" She understood why he was so upset.

He's like a second father to me.

"Where is he? I'll see him right away."

Luke nodded and took her to one of the exam rooms, where Nestor was lying on a bed, pale and barely moving, cocooned in blankets. You could see the effects of chemotherapy. His face was gaunt, yellowish and there wasn't a hair on his face or head.

"What happened?" Sarah asked, setting the envelope down on the counter.

"I found him in a snowbank when I went up to cut some more wood for him. I don't know how long he's been out there. It's hypothermia—I think it's moderate. I knew I had to get him here. I would have administered warm IV fluids, but the cabinet is locked."

Sarah didn't question the fact he'd broken into her clinic and tried to break into her medicine cabinet. He was trying to save his friend's life. There was no time for arguments as she tossed Luke the key from her pocket.

"Not lactated Ringer's. With the chemo I don't know

how well his liver is functioning and if he has hypothermia his liver might not be able to metabolize the lactate."

"I know," Luke called over his shoulder.

Sarah pulled out her stethoscope and the moment she touched him, he was cold, but, as she was taught in medical school, the patient was not dead until he was warm and dead. His temperature when she took it was twenty seven. Which was another reason she didn't want lactated Ringer's solution. He was too cold. He was heading toward profound hypothermia.

She tried to listen to the heart, but couldn't hear anything.

"Asystole!" Sarah shouted, then she felt the carotid artery; there was a faint thready pulse. "No, there's a pulse."

The heart was moving, but barely.

Luke came running back with bags of warmed IV fluid. "There's a pulse?"

"It's weak, so no CPR. Let's get the warm bolus into him."

Luke set up the IV and she grabbed warmers. Right now the most important thing was to heat his core; limbs could wait. The best way though to warm up a body that was this cold was cardiopulmonary bypass, but she was not equipped to do that here. Esme might be in town, but Nestor was here and they couldn't move him.

They could lose him if they took him out.

Hopefully the warmed IV would help, but given the state of Nestor's body, which had been ravaged by the chemotherapy, he didn't have much of a shot.

"Come on, Nestor," Luke whispered to the old man.

"Come on. You're not going to go out like this. You said you wanted to go out riding a bear like a horse off the side of a cliff. This is not the way to go."

Sarah's heart broke as she watched Luke gingerly touch the old man's face. She knew Nestor was important to Luke, because Nestor had taught him how to survive in the mountains. It pained Sarah to see Luke like this, but there was not a lot she could do here with severe hypothermia.

Watching Luke beg his friend to keep fighting brought tears to her eyes. Here, in this moment, Luke was so raw, so real.

This was the genuine Luke Ralston. Not the lone wolf everyone else saw. This tender, concerned Luke, begging the man he admired so much to hang on, was the man she longed to know.

The man who could feel.

The man who could teach her how to feel.

As she watched the two of them she knew that she didn't have that kind of parent-child relationship with her parents and probably never would.

It made her sad to watch Luke suffer so much. She didn't have the heart to tell him that Nestor might not make it. Though she probably didn't have to tell him that. He probably already knew.

"Did you call the air ambulance?" Sarah asked.

"I did, but we have to warm him up before we can get him out to meet the ambulance."

She nodded, but didn't say anything.

When a patient's core temperatures were below thirty, they required to be rewarmed internally through cardiopulmonary bypass, gastric lavage and other means. Ways that Sarah couldn't provide for him in this private clinic.

Usually people that severe were taken straight to the hospital where aggressive rewarming could start instantly. All they could do with what she had was blankets, heaters and the IV. She took Nestor's temperature again, but it was dropping fast.

She knew what was going to happen next. His heart would stop completely and if they rewarmed him too fast, his heart could collapse, but she couldn't use CPR to keep the brain alive until after he was asystole.

"What's his temperature?"

Sarah sighed. "Twenty-five. Luke, the lowest someone has come back from such a severe hypothermia is thirteen point seven."

"He'll make it."

She listened for cardiac activity, but there was none that she could make out. She felt for the carotid artery and the pulse was gone. He wasn't warm enough to start CPR, but she had no choice.

"Starting CPR. Get the AED."

Luke nodded as she began CPR.

Come on, Nestor. Don't die here. Don't die on me.

Luke got the AED ready and Sarah stopped CPR while Luke shocked Nestor. There was no response. Sarah continued with the CPR and they alternated.

"Nestor, come on," Luke urged.

When she looked at the clock, she could see that they'd been doing CPR for far too long. The ambulance had still not arrived.

"Take his temperature," Sarah said as she continued CPR.

"Dammit, it's fourteen."

Come on, Nestor.

"I can't pronounce him but…"

"Don't say it," Luke begged. "Don't. People survive hypothermia all the time. Cancer kills, but hypothermia can be cured."

Sarah sighed, and continued, but there wasn't much hope. Luke turned his back on the scene. His fists clenched as she worked on. He obviously couldn't stand to watch his friend slip away.

She didn't have any hope…and then Nestor's heart came back under her hand and he groaned, before coughing.

"Oh, my God," she whispered.

Nestor opened one eye, groaned, and passed out again. But the point was, he was alive.

"What?" Luke asked, then leaned over. His eyes widened in shock. "You got him back?"

Sarah had never brought back a person with such severe hypothermia, with a body already so weakened by chemo, from the brink of death. Tears of joy stung her eyes and she laughed out loud because she couldn't contain herself.

Luke smiled at her briefly before turning back to his friend.

She was so relieved. She hadn't wanted to be the one responsible for not saving Nestor's life. She hadn't wanted to hurt Luke like that, and she hadn't wanted him to be reminded of Nestor's death every time he saw her.

She didn't want Luke to remember her like that.

"You brought him back," Luke said, stunned. "I've never seen that."

"I've never done it in this situation before. And especially not outside a hospital."

"I can't believe you did it."

Nestor was still unconscious, but he was stable, and when she took a temperature again it was rising. He had a good shot at making it now.

The paramedics came then and took over, Sarah gave an update about Nestor's temperature and how long he'd been down. They were going to take Nestor to the hospital and continue to warm him up, but Nestor wasn't out of the woods yet. Chemo took its toll. As did Nestor's age.

She followed the paramedics down out of her clinic and made sure Nestor was in the air ambulance and on his way.

Luke stood beside her, his expression unreadable and his gaze trained on the ambulance as it disappeared from view and on to the nearest hospital. There they could work on him. They walked back up to the clinic to clean up the mess.

Luke cursed under his breath as he picked up Nestor's hat, which had fallen on the floor of the exam room. His eyes were wild, but he wasn't about to cry. It was rage she saw there.

That brief moment of tenderness and joy after she'd saved Nestor's life had faded away. Luke's walls had gone back up again. Like armor.

She wanted to tell him that he didn't need to guard himself in front of her.

He could be himself.

How can he be himself when you can't be yourself?

Sarah touched Luke's arm. "I'm so sorry that happened to him. I wonder what caused him to collapse in the snow."

He shrugged it off. "People don't die from hypothermia and he won't either."

"They do, Luke. You don't know how long he was in the snow for. Or how he even got there. He's alive, but with chemo…his body's been through a trauma."

He scrubbed a hand over his face. "What I meant was that people don't die of hypothermia on my watch. They don't. No man gets left behind. Every life gets saved. Nestor has fought cancer, he can fight this."

"Is that what you would tell yourself in the army?"

His gaze was positively flinty. "What?"

"Why did you leave the army, Luke? It's clear to me you're so passionate about it, why would you leave it?"

Luke snorted and tried to push past her. "I don't have time for this."

"Of course you don't. You never do."

"What's that supposed to mean?"

Sarah shook her head. "It means you'll disappear off into the forest, like you always do, and when you're done sulking you'll come back and pretend like nothing happened. I can't deal with that kind of hot and cold, Luke. I won't deal with that."

"How do you expect me to act, Sarah? A friend of mine almost died. Never leave a man behind, that's the way I've always lived and yet…" He trailed off and then shook his head. "I'm done. I can't deal with this. This is why I keep to myself. This is pointless."

He turned and started to walk away.

"It is. You're a coward, Luke."

He spun around. "I'm the coward? How do you figure that?"

"You're a coward because you won't let anyone in. You won't let anyone help you. I'm sorry you were burned before by people you care about. I'm sorry that you've lost people important to you, but you can't run away from your fears. You have to face them."

"Is that a fact?" He crossed his arms. "And what do you think you're doing here?"

Honestly, she didn't know. She didn't know why she was bothering with him. He clearly didn't want her involved in his life. She should know better.

She was better off alone. Then she only had to answer to herself for her own actions and mistakes. Maybe Luke had it right.

"Working and trying to save lives."

"I mean why are you in Crater Lake? You gave up a prominent job because you were afraid you weren't good enough. You were afraid that everyone would think you were just riding on Daddy's coattails. You ran away from your talent. You're just as much a coward as I am."

"You're a jerk." She threw the envelope at him. "This was for you, because I thought we were friends. Clearly, I was wrong."

Luke touched his face where the envelope had hit him, snickered and then walked away from her. His words had stung, as if he'd cut her open with a scalpel, but then the truth did hurt. It hurt all the more that it came from him.

Someone she'd thought she could trust enough to tell

her darkest fear to. She'd never told anyone else that she'd given up the job because her father had gotten it for her. That was her shame to bear. She'd thought Luke would understand, but she was wrong.

Then again, she was wrong about a lot of other things.

This was no different.

CHAPTER TWELVE

"LUKE, I KNOW you're in there. I can see you."

Luke looked over at the window to see his brother peering through. He'd thought that if he retreated to Nestor's cabin, to clean up a bit and close it up until Nestor could come and claim it, it would help get his mind off the fact that he'd probably broken the heart of the woman he loved.

When he'd said those things to Sarah, the moment they'd slipped from his lips he'd realized what a mistake he'd made. That this time, he'd hurt someone he cared about, but she would move on. Like Christine had and he would be the only one with a broken heart.

It served him right.

Sarah hadn't made any promises the night they made love. That was what he'd thought he wanted; that was what he always wanted. He didn't want any commitments. He didn't want anyone to love, but the problem was she'd gotten underneath his skin.

When she was working so hard to save Nestor's life, when she thought it was completely hopeless, she still fought and she was doing it for him. And she'd brought him back. He knew that. Sarah did the best she could with what she had. She could've turned him away, but she hadn't. She wasn't that kind of person and he admired her for it, but Sarah was not meant to be his.

She deserved so much more. He'd hurt her, dragged her into dangerous situations and he demanded so much of her.

Sarah was better off without him.

He didn't deserve love.

Luke didn't know anything about love. He hadn't been able to keep Christine happy when they were married. He'd chosen his career over her. She hadn't wanted to live in Germany. She hadn't wanted to live in a cabin in the woods, yet he'd been selfish and tried to have it his way.

No wonder Christine had left him.

How could he have love, deserve love, if he couldn't change or bend, too? It was too hard, too painful. The problem was, Sarah had somehow snuck in and captured his heart. He didn't know how, but she had.

Of course, that was all ruined now.

He'd taken that piece of her, the one she'd shared with him, and thrown it back in her face. He'd used it to hurt her. To drive her away. So, no, he didn't deserve love. She'd given him that horse painting, as well. Another piece of her she'd shared with him that he'd tossed back at her like garbage.

He hated himself for it.

He'd made his bed and he was going to lie in it.

Of course, coming back to Nestor's cabin was a huge mistake. Not only because it made him emotional, thinking about the friend he'd almost lost, but also because it reminded him of being in her arms. When she kissed him, when she opened herself up to him. The night they became one. That night he was lost to her because she entrusted him with a piece of her.

Now he'd shattered her heart.

Her words might have stung him, but he'd deserved it because the unseen wound he'd inflicted on her was a thousand times worse.

He'd seen her once in town. He'd wanted to tell her that Nestor had pulled through, that they had managed to warm him with lavage, but she hadn't looked at him. She hadn't said anything to him. She had been silent, which was odd for her. Since they first met she'd always been frank about what she thought about him.

The cold shoulder had been too much for him to bear. Even though he'd deserved it. So he'd retreated back to the mountains, under the guise that he was cleaning up Nestor's cabin for the family, but really he just wanted to be alone and mend the broken heart he'd caused himself because he let Sarah in and then pushed her away.

You don't know if she loved you back.

Which was true, but it didn't make the pain better and was pointless now, because he'd completely ruined it. Then he glanced at the painting on the mantel where he'd placed it when he came up here. The horse that looked like Adele. Something she'd painted herself; he could see her slender, graceful hand in each delicate brush stroke. Detailed and precise, as a brilliant surgeon should be. It was a piece of her and just knowing that hurt all the more.

"Luke, it's cold out here. Let me in." Carson's shouting from outside interrupted his train of thought.

Luke groaned and got up to open the door. Carson burst past him and stomped his feet at the door.

"What're you doing here, Carson?"

"Looking for you. After Nestor's accident, you disappeared."

Luke shrugged. "I came up here to clean it up. Nestor's son Greg won't be back up here until spring, possibly summer. I wanted to make sure nothing would go bad. I wanted to make sure everything was squared away. Nestor's lucky to be alive. He'll be in the hospital for a while."

Carson nodded. "Right."

"What's that supposed to mean?"

"Exactly what you think it means."

Luke cursed. "I don't have time for this."

"Why? Because you're so busy up here moping?"

Luke glared at Carson, but his little brother was holding his ground and looking quite smug about it.

"What are you grinning about?"

"I'm thinking back to a conversation we had this summer. Do you remember that particular conversation?"

"No."

Which was a lie. Luke vaguely remembered it. He remembered his brother coming to get him in Missoula, struggling with the fact that he was in love with Esme and was scared of getting a broken heart. Scared of possibly walking away from a family practice, because Carson had put it on himself to carry on the family legacy in Crater Lake.

Luke had told him, in a nutshell, to snap out of it and live.

And now the jerk was throwing it back in his face. Typical.

"I believe you said to me, and I quote, 'Forgive yourself. And for once follow your heart. Do what you want to do. Live.' Wasn't that the line you fed me?"

"It sounds vaguely familiar."

"You're an idiot. You also told me, 'She'll walk away, she's going to walk away and you know who I'm talking about,' and now it applies to you."

"Do you have an eidetic memory or something?"

"No. I just stored those particular lines away for future blackmail and use."

Luke rolled his eyes. "I said those words to you because you deserved Esme. She loved you and you love her."

"Sarah loves you and you're an idiot if you think any different."

Luke shook his head. "You don't know what you're talking about."

"And I'll say it again, you're an idiot."

"I don't deserve love. I blew my first marriage because I was too selfish. And this time around I shut her out because I didn't want to get hurt. It was selfish. I threw it away. For me, love is pointless."

Carson sighed. "Luke, you gave up the army for her. That doesn't sound like someone who is selfish."

"I should've given it up earlier."

"Why? Christine knew your passion for the army before you were married to her. She was just as selfish as you. You gave up the army for her, you tried for her. She ruined it. She found happiness, why can't you? You deserve happiness."

"No. I don't. Maybe it was all me. I can't take the risk again. I don't want to take the risk again. It's better that she leaves. It's better she walks."

Carson took him by the shoulders and shook him. "I love you, but you're an idiot."

"So you've said."

"I'll say it again, like you said it to me. Forgive yourself. Take a chance and live. You love her. You may not admit it, but I can see it as plain as day."

Luke walked away from his brother and sat down on the edge of Nestor's bunk, running his hands through his hair. His hand brushing over the tender scar from the laceration Sarah had stitched up.

That was one of the scariest moments of his life, when he saw that avalanche raging down the side of the mountain toward them and saw the look of horror on her face. All he could do was tell her to do what he'd taught her. In that moment he didn't care much about his life. Only hers, because he couldn't bear it if he lost her.

Yet, he had lost her.

He'd driven her away.

Carson was right. He was an idiot.

"You've realized what a moron you are now." Carson was grinning ear to ear.

"I thought I was an idiot?"

Carson shrugged. "Both, I think."

Luke laughed. "Yeah, you're right."

"I know what happened between you and Christine was bad and the fact that she ran off with Anthony sucks. It does, but you said so yourself, you wanted different things. I think you and Sarah want the same things."

"And what would that be?"

"She's a trauma surgeon and so are you. You're a great first responder, Luke, but you have to get off the mountain and become a surgeon again. Don't you remember what it was like in the OR? I know you loved it. I remember the emails. You were born to be a surgeon. You are a surgeon, you just stopped practicing."

"I don't think she wants to be a surgeon anymore. She left that life behind her."

"She thinks she has. She's a surgeon. Just go live. Do you think that soldier who died would want you mourning his death for the rest of your life? No. Go live your life, Luke."

The words sank in slowly.

He'd been blaming himself so long for his heartache that he didn't realize he'd given up the thing he'd loved the most and that was surgery. He was so busy trying to rescue everyone that he didn't see that he was the one who needed rescuing. He was going to make it up to Sarah. He was going to win her back, even if he didn't know how exactly or if he ever would, but he was going to try.

He couldn't live without her. Of that he was certain.

Luke got up and clapped Carson on the back. "Thanks."

"No problem. I just hope she forgives you." Carson winked. "Now, are you coming down off this mountain? Tomorrow is Valentine's Day. I think that's a perfect time to make up."

"I don't have tickets to that dance," Luke said.

Carson reached in his pocket. "You can have mine. Esme and I aren't going to that dance. I suspect tomorrow we'll have more important things to celebrate."

Luke cocked an eyebrow. "Like what?"

"I'm proposing to Esme tonight. She has no idea."

He grinned. "It's Friday the thirteenth. You know that, right?"

Carson chuckled. "I know, but she really hates Valentine's Day. I mean really hates it. I found a card with a chimp on it."

Luke shook his head. "Would you get out of here? I'll come down off the mountain in time for tomorrow."

"Good." Carson punched him on the shoulder. "Good luck."

"You, too. It's about time you did that, by the way."

"What?"

"Propose to Esme."

Carson snorted. "Look who's talking."

Sarah's heart hurt. It had been a few days since she'd last seen Luke in town briefly. It had looked as if he'd wanted to talk to her, but he'd turned away. He'd looked pale and emotionless. Several times she'd talked herself out of going over to him and comforting him, because really what good would it do?

He would just push her away.

You need to fight harder.

She let out another sigh, because she was all out of fight. How could she fight for the man she was in love with when she couldn't even stand up to her parents? Luke had been right, she should've stayed in that job she'd thought she earned and proven to them she was more than a name.

Even though she'd saved Nestor's life, she'd done so much good here and she wanted more.

She missed the OR.

She missed the chaos of a busy emergency room, the beauty of an OR being prepped by scrub nurses, the feel of the water on her arms as she scrubbed in and the calm she felt as she waited for the patient to go under and the magic of saving a life.

Being around Luke reminded her of that.

How long had she just been walking through the paces of life and not living it?

A long time.

With Luke, she mattered and working with him made her realize she was a damn good surgeon in her own right. As soon as her yearlong contract was up, she was going to find an ER job again. Even if it meant she wasn't running the ER, she still wanted to be where she belonged. She'd known the moment she'd picked up her first scalpel that she didn't belong in her parents' penthouse on the Upper West Side.

Just as she didn't belong in a clinic treating minor injuries.

She belonged down on the front lines and on the surgical floor.

Just as she and Luke belonged together, even if he didn't think they did. She'd never fallen in love before, but, with him, she fell hard and the answer was simple. He brought out the best in her. He made her work harder than she'd ever worked before.

Around him, she felt like herself and she hadn't felt like herself in a very long time. She was so busy distancing herself from her parents, trying to step out of their shadows to prove that she didn't need them, that she didn't realize she'd blocked out everyone.

Including herself.

"Excuse me, are you still open? I know it's four o'clock on Friday and your clinic states you're only open until four, but I'm hoping you can see me."

Sarah looked up from her chart and saw a middle-aged woman, guarding her side, standing in the doorway. She seemed vaguely familiar, but perhaps she'd treated her earlier.

"Of course. Come in."

The woman looked relieved and followed Sarah into an exam room.

"Why don't you have a seat, Ms…?"

"It's Mrs. Vargas, but I can't sit, I'm afraid. I fell while I was skiing and I'm terrified I broke a rib."

Sarah smiled. "It must've been a nasty fall."

"It was. I've never skied before, but my husband insisted we come here for a romantic Valentine's weekend, when really I should be back in Great Falls and working."

"What do you do, Mrs. Vargas?"

"I'm the head of a board of directors for a hospital. We've scouted an area just outside of Crater Lake to build a small hospital that deals mostly with trauma. There's a serious lag around here. Missoula and Great Falls sees most of the trauma, but those locations are too far away to do any help."

"So you're going to build a hospital that only deals with trauma?"

She nodded and then winced. "I'm sorry for boring you, but I thought you might be interested in that seeing how you're a doctor and everything."

"You're not boring me. I totally agree this area is seriously lacking in a trauma center. I can only do so much here."

"Well, I know there's a cardiac surgeon in town and we've offered her use of our operating rooms. It's just a matter of finding a trauma surgeon for next year."

"Well, Mrs. Vargas, you don't have a broken rib."

"Are you sure?"

Sarah nodded. "Positive. If you had a fracture in your ribs you wouldn't be talking to me so easily. You're guarding, but I suspect you've given yourself a nasty bruise. Inhale deeply for me."

Mrs. Vargas did that.

"Did it hurt or was it hard to do?"

"No."

"I'll prescribe you some painkillers, but rest now and put some ice on it."

Mrs. Vargas nodded as she filled out the prescription and handed it to her. Mrs. Vargas stared at it. "Ledet? Are you related to Vin Ledet from New York?"

Sarah groaned inwardly. "Yes. He's my father. Do you know him?"

"No, I just remember someone telling me that Vin Ledet's daughter was a brilliant trauma surgeon. They said you saved their life last summer. Who was it? Oh, yes, Shane Draven. His uncle owns this hotel."

"I really can't say brilliant, but I was that trauma surgeon. I did work on Shane, but he came to me in stable condition thanks to both Dr. Ralstons and Dr. Petersen, who tended to him in the field. I just happened to be a locum surgeon in Missoula, throwing in a hand during a busy stint."

"Well, you're not blowing your own horn. Shane Draven spoke very highly of your skills." Mrs. Vargas pulled out a business card. "If you're interested in returning to an ER and running it as chief of surgery, please do call me."

Chief?

"I think you'd want someone more experienced?"

"The way Shane talks about you I'd say you're experienced enough. I did do a quick background check on you, before realizing you were here. Everyone speaks highly of you as a surgeon."

Sarah blushed. "Thank you, Mrs. Vargas."

"Will I see you tomorrow at the Valentine's Day dance? I would like to introduce you to some members of the board."

"*I* will be at the dance. Silas Draven wants all his staff there, but I don't want to see *you* at that dance. Are we clear?"

Mrs. Vargas winked. "Very well. Please do think about my offer. I would love to have a surgeon of your caliber in charge of this project."

Sarah walked Mrs. Vargas out and when she'd left, Sarah stared at the card for a long time. The offer came because of Shane Draven, not her father. Mrs. Vargas was aware of who her father was, but it was her own merit that preceded her. Not her father pulling strings.

She would take the job to stay in Crater Lake. She loved it here.

She was making friends here.

She was finding her place in this world, when for so long she'd felt as if she was drifting.

Here she wasn't Vin Ledet's daughter. Here she was a surgeon, a doctor. She'd found herself and she'd been foolish not to look sooner. She'd been so busy trying to show her parents who she wasn't that she couldn't show them who she was.

She didn't have to prove anything to them, because there was nothing to prove. Their opinion of her was never going to change and, for the first time in a long time, she was okay with that.

Chief of surgery sounded like a dream job. And she could stay in Crater Lake.

What's keeping you in Crater Lake?

And that realization made her sad.

Luke had made it clear how he felt about love. He thought it was pointless and he'd shut her out. She didn't want to remain in a town where he was.

She loved him too much and it was clear that he didn't return those feelings. So the best thing to do after her contract was up was make a clean break, for both of them.

Even though a clean break was the last thing she wanted, because all she wanted was to be his. To be by his side and in his arms.

She was in love with him and she doubted that feeling would disappear anytime soon, but Luke loved Crater Lake. This was his home. It wasn't her home, even if she wanted it to be. So she'd leave.

Because she loved him so much, she'd leave and let him get on with his life without her. She could find roots in another town, even though she loved Crater Lake.

And she would find another job and of that she had no doubt now.

CHAPTER THIRTEEN

A MONTH AGO you couldn't have paid him enough to be at a gala like this. All the people, the drinking, the noise and decorations were enough to set him on edge. Luke didn't really like being around people who pretended to be nice. Who were putting on a show.

He avoided social situations like this for a reason.

So, no, he wouldn't be at an event like this, not for all the money in the world, but for Sarah he'd walk through fire. For her he'd do anything. She deserved it all and if she let him, if she forgave him, he would spend every waking moment making it up to her.

Since Christine left him he'd always stated his only mistress was the mountain, but the mountain was cold. So cold his heart had been frozen.

Until Sarah came.

Now all he wanted was her and he was going to do everything and anything to get her back.

She was across the room now and he caught glimpses of her through all the people. She was so close, but so far away. To get to her, it would be like walking through fire for him.

He waited until she was alone and not talking with

Silas Draven. He didn't want anyone to interrupt this moment.

Carson and Esme had helped him get ready, since the only suit he owned was from when he was eighteen and married to Christine. So that was unacceptable, coupled with the fact it no longer fit him.

So he wore Carson's suit. It was designer and, even though he felt completely awkward in it, Esme had swooned over him. He knew then it was good. That he would fit in for her. He'd even shaved his beard off.

Now he stood on the other side of the gala, remaining in the shadows at the edge of the dance floor watching her. She took his breath away. She was wearing a bloodred, sparkling evening gown that was a halter, so he got to admire her creamy white shoulders, but the seller for him was her white-blond hair was pulled to one side, but down. So it just brushed the top of her shoulder. Just like in that self-portrait she'd done. The one he loved the most.

Of course, when he was presented with the real thing, the drawing paled in comparison. Sarah was beautiful. She was radiant and he noticed other men admiring her, which ticked him off, but no one else approached her. So he didn't have to inflict any bodily harm on would-be suitors.

She looked unhappy standing off to the side and he knew that was his fault. Something he aimed to fix in a moment, because right now he just enjoyed the sight of her. He enjoyed drinking it in. He didn't want to disrupt the magic she was weaving.

He didn't deserve her, but he would work hard to rectify that for the rest of his life. If she would only let him, and he hoped she would. He pulled at his tie and headed toward her.

Luke had faced many dangerous situations in his life. Things that would scare others, but here, in this moment, crossing a dance floor to beg forgiveness and put his fragile heart on the line for the woman he loved was the scariest thing he'd ever done. But for her, he would do anything.

Sarah didn't want to be at this dance. Mostly because everyone who was at this gala was with someone and she was standing off to the side of the dance floor in her red evening gown, like a wallflower. It was like junior high all over again.

Still, it was a great success. She could see this Valentine's Gala becoming a yearly event for the hotel.

Valentine's never really bothered her, but right now watching all the happy couples dance, kiss and enjoy themselves made her envious.

She should just leave.

Silas Draven had introduced her to all his important guests and then she'd discreetly snuck away, wandering along the edge of the dance floor as the band played endless romantic songs. She was hoping that Esme would be here tonight, so at least maybe she could talk to someone she knew, but Esme hadn't shown up and Sarah hoped that it wasn't because of that goofy chimpanzee card she'd picked out.

The thought of that card made her laugh to herself. A waiter walked by with a tray full of champagne flutes. Sarah took one and as she glanced back across the dance floor her breath caught in her throat at the sight of a man in a well-tailored tuxedo walking across the floor toward her.

And it wasn't just any man. It was Luke and he was clean shaven.

Oh, my God.

Her knees buckled. Those intense blue eyes fixed on her as if he were going to devour her whole and devour her in a good way. A way that made her blood heat with need, with a craving she'd been trying to suppress since he'd walked away from her and broken her heart.

His beard was gone and she could clearly see those delectable lips, which had kissed every inch of her, turning up in a mischievous smile. He stopped in front of her and pulled on the cuff of his jacket, adjusting what looked like cuff links. His brown curls were tamed in a debonair coif, he had a tie on and it didn't look like a clip-on. He rolled his neck and pulled at the tie again. He must be so uncomfortable.

Good.

Even his boots were gone, replaced by dress shoes.

He spun around. "How do I look?"

So good. Only she didn't say that thought out loud. "Fine."

He cocked any eyebrow. "Just fine?"

No, she wasn't going to be drawn in by his cute banter. She wasn't going to let herself be drawn in by him again. She couldn't.

"I… What're you doing here?"

"I've come to the gala. Am I not dressed appropriately?"

"You're dressed fine. I told you that."

It's more than fine.

In fact she was having a hard time controlling herself from throwing the champagne flute aside, hiking up her long skirt and jumping in his arms, but she controlled herself. She was angry at him.

"Can I have this dance?" He held out his hand, his blue eyes twinkling.

Say no. Say no.

"Okay." She took his hand and he led her out on the dance floor, spinning her around gracefully before pulling her back up against him. "I didn't know you could dance."

"I have hidden depths."

"I'm aware of those hidden depths," she said sarcastically. "I don't know why I'm dancing with you."

"Because you're a forgiving sort of person."

"Am I?"

"I think so."

"I hope you're right. I don't feel so forgiving right now."

"I loved my painting. I put it on the wall," he said changing the subject.

Her heart skipped a beat. "You did?"

Don't fall for it.

Only she couldn't help it when it came to Luke Ralston. She was so weak when it came to him.

He nodded. "Thank you for that. It's beautiful, but that wasn't my favorite the night you showed me your drawings."

"It wasn't?"

"No, it was the self-portrait you'd done." Then he reached out and ran his hands gently through her hair and brushed her shoulder. "It was the pencil drawing with your hair down, your shoulders bare. That's the drawing I loved."

Her pulse thundered in her ears. That was a drawing she'd always hated. One she'd never got right. At least she didn't think so. Maybe because she couldn't truly see herself through her own eyes. She was her own worst judge. But looking into Luke's eyes at this moment, in his arms, she could see what he saw, even if only for a brief moment, and it almost made her cry.

"Why didn't you tell me?"

"I didn't want you to know at the time."

She blushed. "I'm surprised you're here. I thought you didn't like Valentine's Day. It's the one thing you and Esme have in common."

"Me, too, to be honest." He chuckled. "Actually, Esme may be warming up to Valentine's Day, or at least Friday the thirteenth."

"Why?"

"Carson proposed last night and Esme accepted."

Sarah smiled. "Oh, how wonderful. I'm happy for her. I'm surprised they're not here celebrating."

"Well, they wanted me to come here."

She blushed again, her heart racing. "So what're you doing here?"

"I've come to beg for forgiveness."

Her heart skipped a beat. "What?"

"I've been an idiot. I thought love was pointless, but only for me."

"Only for you?"

He nodded. "My first wife left me because I was selfish. I was so focused on what I wanted that I didn't let her have a say. I wanted to be in the army and serve my country as a surgeon, I wanted to train at the army hospital in Germany and nothing was going to stop me. Not even the woman I loved, or thought I loved at the time. Actually, I'm surprised she didn't leave me sooner."

"I understand that kind of drive. You loved serving your country, so why did you leave it?"

"Because I left for her, but by then it was too late. I gave up my commission, but it wasn't enough. So I turned to the mountain. Being alone meant I could live my life the way I wanted. I never wanted to feel that pain or be responsible for inflicting that kind of pain on someone. I thought it was easier to shut people out. To be alone, and then you came along."

Tears stung her eyes. "Oh, Luke. Things aren't so black-and-white."

"I know that now. When you walked into that OR last summer, I knew there was something about you. I knew that you would break through, even if I didn't want to admit it. I love you, Sarah. I'll go wherever you need me to go. If you need to be a surgeon in New York again, I'll go there. I just can't lose you. I need you. I'll change my life, give up everything to be with you."

Her knees went weak and she wasn't sure she'd heard him correctly. No one had ever offered to give up everything to make her happy.

Everyone expected pieces of her, for her to conform, but Luke was offering all of himself to her and she was overwhelmed by it.

She knew there were tears running down her face but there was no stopping them.

"For so long I've been fighting to prove to the world I'm not someone they think I am, I didn't know who I really was, but with you I found who I was again. I shut everyone out. Even me. I shut myself out. I was convinced I didn't need love. That I didn't want love…

that I could make it through this life on my own. I was wrong. I love you, Luke. I love you so much it hurts. You see me."

He pulled her tight against him, cupping her face, and then kissed her. His kiss gentle at first, before it deepened. She melted into that kiss, wrapping her arms around his neck, not caring who saw her kissing him. Her whole world had righted itself. She was where she wanted to be. She was who she wanted to be.

She had found out who she was thanks to this man.

When the kiss ended she laid her head against his shoulder, moving with him as they swayed gently on the dance floor. She didn't want to let him go. She'd missed him. She'd missed this Luke Ralston. A man she'd only met in brief glimpses. A man who had been surrounded by high walls.

A man she desperately wanted to love.

"So am I forgiven?" he teased.

"Yes. Though I should've made you work harder."

"Yes. You should've."

"Now you tell me." She glanced up at him and kissed him again. "Thank you for coming here tonight. This is the best apology ever."

"So, where should we move to?" Luke asked. "There's no surgical jobs in Crater Lake sadly."

"There will be next year when my contract is up here at the hotel."

"What?" He was clearly confused. "There's no hospital in Crater Lake. They talked once last year about building one, but nothing ever came of it."

"Not yet. A trauma and surgical center is going up outside of town. A board of directors from a large hospital in Great Falls realized there was a shortfall up in this area for one."

Luke grinned. "You want to stay in Crater Lake?"

"Of course. It's home now. You're my home." And it was true. She'd found a home. She'd found what she was looking for. She'd found herself in him.

Luke kissed her again. "And you're mine. I love you, Sarah."

Sarah kissed him back. "Happy Valentine's Day, Dr. Ralston."

EPILOGUE

Valentine's Day, a year later

SARAH WALKED SWIFTLY through the halls of the new trauma center. Her ER was running smoothly. Her board was in good working order, which made her slightly apprehensive. She'd learned early on as a trauma resident that a smoothly run ER and good board would mean that a huge trauma was due any second to muck it all up.

They'd only been open a month, but already there had been several large traumas, a couple of emergency births and an avalanche. Thankfully no bear mauling.

Sarah shuddered recalling that moment.

The man had pulled through, but required several plastic surgeries.

She'd seen several bears in the summer when Luke was working on building onto his cabin. Their cabin. And a bear had crashed Esme and Carson's wedding that summer, but thankfully none of the encounters had been violent.

Once she'd got the trauma center open, her father had come to tour the facility and he'd donated money to the pro bono fund, which had shocked her, but what was the most shocking moment was when he told her he was proud of her. That she had done well for herself.

And she had.

She was happier than she could ever remember.

Now, if only her boards would stay quiet tonight.

"Dr. Ledet, can you come to OR Four? There's a problem."

Sarah saw a very pregnant Esme running toward her. Esme operated on her cardio patients at the trauma center, but Sarah wondered when she was going to give it up because soon she'd be giving birth.

"You shouldn't be running," Sarah said. "You're due in, like, three weeks. Why are you even working now?"

"It's only an angio," Esme said, as if an angio were nothing. Which was odd for her.

Sarah glanced up at the board and then back to her. "You said there was a problem. If it's only a simple angio, then what's the problem?"

Esme bit her lip. "Oh, I'm not in OR Four. I'm in Three. That board is wrong. I finished my angio, but I was passing OR Four and they were having a problem."

Speak of a quiet board, get swift retribution.

"Okay, let's go." Sarah jogged behind Esme. They put on their surgical caps and then scrubbed. "So what's wrong again?"

"It was a mauling," Esme said. "It's pretty bad."

"Oh, no. Are you serious? Why do tourists insist on disturbing a bear during its hibernation cycle?" She walked into the OR, her hands up and waiting to get gloved when she saw Luke, gowned and standing in the OR alone.

"Bears don't hibernate, Sarah. Have I not taught you anything?"

Sarah glanced back, but Esme had disappeared. "What's going on here? I thought there was a mauling."

"No, no mauling, but I wanted to get you here fast, without arousing your suspicions."

"Well, now I'm suspicious. You're supposed to be in Missoula visiting Nestor. What's going on?"

"Nothing is going on."

"Is Nestor okay?" Sarah asked.

"He's fine. I swear. He hates city living, but you know that."

Sarah sighed in relief. She was glad to hear the older man was okay. She'd grown fond of him and went with Luke to visit him every month.

"So what's going on?" She asked.

"Well, picture this room full of rose petals." Luke grinned. "Only I know it's not."

"Which is good because if it was I would have a panic attack thinking about having to sterilize this OR again top to bottom. Do you know how many patients are allergic to scents?"

Luke crossed his arms. "Really? Don't you have any scope of imagination?"

"No, not on a night when the ER is quiet and my board *was* running smoothly."

Luke moved to stand in front of her. "Well, I was trying to be romantic, but I realize now it's kind of hard to be romantic when we're both wearing surgical masks standing in an OR."

"Yeah, why are we here?"

"Because it was in OR like this that I first met you. You told me to get out of your OR."

"And I'm telling you that now, too." She laughed nervously and then it hit her when she spied Esme in the scrub room, crying. "Oh, my God."

Luke got down on one knee and pulled out a ring. "Don't worry, it's been sterilized. It won't contaminate this surgical field."

"Oh, my God," she said again in disbelief.

"Sarah, I can't live without you. You brought me back from the dead. You taught me to love again, to feel again and I want you to be my wife. Marry me."

She began to cry, soaking the paper surgical mask. "Yes. I'll marry you. Yes!"

Luke slipped the ring on her finger. "Good. Nestor will be thrilled I finally found the nerve to ask you."

Sarah laughed. "Remind me to kiss him next time I see him."

"Kiss him?" Luke asked then ripped off his mask. "Sorry, but you're going to have to sterilize this OR again. I need to kiss my fiancée properly."

Sarah removed her mask and let him kiss her. It wasn't the exact OR where they'd first met, but it was an OR where they worked together constantly, together saving lives, but most of all it was a place where they'd saved each other.

And being in his arms was right where she needed to be.

"There's something else I need to tell you," Sarah said. "It's important."

Luke groaned, but grinned. "You want to move back to New York."

"No. Look, it's…"

A tap on the glass interrupted their conversation and she turned around to see Esme in the scrub room looking quite distressed.

"What's up with her?" Luke asked.

Esme hit the intercom. "Um, I think we need to sterilize that room right now. My water just broke."

Sarah chuckled as Esme was pointing frantically at her belly. "I believe that we're about to be an aunt and uncle. Even though technically I'm not an aunt until we actually get married."

Luke's eyes widened as the reality of what she was telling him sank in. "What?"

"I would go find Carson and bring him here. Esme has gone into labor."

Luke shook his head. "Only her baby would be born on Valentine's Day. I'll get Carson."

"And I'll get Esme comfortable." She kissed him again. "Be careful."

"You, too. I have a feeling she's going to fight back when that pain starts to hit."

Sarah went to Esme and helped her stand, because she was bent over the scrub sink, holding the side as pains rocked through her.

"Sorry, I thought I had more time," Esme panted.

"You can't control it."

Esme cursed under her breath. "It figures, though— my kid had to come on Valentine's Day."

Sarah laughed. "I know, but let's get you to a birthing room and wait for Carson to come."

Sarah walked Esme down the hall and tried not to think about the fact that in nine months she might be walking down this very same hall, with Esme holding her up, and she couldn't help but wonder what Luke was going to think when she told him, because that was something they'd never talked about in their year together.

She'd been going to tell him but then Esme had gone into labor.

Right now their conversation would have to wait, but pretty soon she wouldn't be able to hide it any longer.

"Come on, one more push." Carson was behind Esme, holding her shoulders, and Luke was pacing by the door.

"Stop pacing," Esme shouted over her shoulder. "It's annoying me."

"Sorry," Luke mumbled.

"Come on, Esme. Ignore him and give me one more push."

Esme used some choice curse words that were directed at Carson, but she gave it that one last push and soon Sarah was catching Carson and Esme's baby girl in her hands. The baby didn't even need a back rub; she began to cry lustily.

"It's a girl," Sarah announced. Esme began to cry and Carson kissed her. "Carson, you want to come cut the cord?"

Carson moved toward her and Sarah tied off the cord and handed Carson the sterile scissors. He cut the cord and then took his daughter gently in his arms, bringing her to Esme, who waited for her with open arms.

"If this doesn't change your mind about Valentine's Day, Esme, I don't know what will," Carson teased as he kissed Esme's sweaty brow again.

Sarah's heart swelled with happiness.

She wasn't used to this kind of love, this kind of family, but she had it all here and as she glanced up at Luke she could see the wonder in his eyes as he looked down at his little niece with love.

A nurse that was on duty took the newborn to weigh

her, rub ointment in her eyes and give her a vitamin K shot. Luke did the APGAR on his niece with Carson watching over his daughter and Sarah helped Esme.

Once everything was done, the newest, swaddled, seven-pound-five-ounce member of the Ralston family was handed to Esme again.

"What're you going to name her?" Sarah asked as she gently touched the baby's head.

"Not Valentine," Esme said quickly, glaring at Luke and Carson respectively.

Sarah laughed. "Well, we'll leave you alone for a bit, but really you've come through that beautifully. You can go home in the morning if her vitals remain stable."

Carson nodded. "Thanks, Sarah."

"No problem." She washed her hands and then walked out of one of the two birthing rooms they had in Crater Lake.

"That was amazing," Luke said. "You never cease to amaze me."

"What do you think they'll name her?"

Luke laughed. "My brother's so head over heels for her and the baby, he'll agree to call her anything that Esme wants. And really that's the way it should be."

"Really?" Sarah asked. "So you wouldn't object if I called our baby something like Asterix or Cantaloupe or some other fashionable name when it comes this fall?"

Luke paused. "What?"

"I was trying to tell you, but Esme interrupted us. I'm pregnant." She waited with bated breath for his reaction, but she didn't have to wait long. Before she had a chance to tease him with other names she was in his arms and he was kissing her.

"Truly?"

She nodded. "Truly. Though I'm terrified I don't have the best example in parents. What if I end up like them?"

"Highly doubtful." He wrapped his arms around her. "You'll be a great mother."

"And you'll be a great father."

"I love you, Sarah." He kissed her again and she melted in his arms. "You're my life, I would do anything for you, but I'm not naming our baby Cantaloupe."

Sarah laughed. "I love you, too."

And as she kissed him again she realized that she'd found her place. She'd found herself and she was right where she needed to be, in Luke's arms.

* * * * *

MR. DANGEROUSLY
SEXY

STEFANIE LONDON

To my fellow Blaze Babes, it's been a blast.

1

ADDISON COBALT'S FATHER had made a living out of taking down bad guys, so she knew the world had an ugly underbelly. But knowing it and experiencing it were two different things. She smoothed her hands over the printed email that sat on her desk. Hateful words stared up at her.

"I don't understand what's going on here," she said, furrowing her brow.

Rhys Glover, the IT manager for Cobalt & Dane Security, pursed his lips. "He's threatening you."

"Yes, I got that from the 'I'm going to kill you' section of this email. But I don't know who could have sent it or *why*. I don't have any enemies."

"Clearly, you do."

Raking a lacquered red nail down the neat rows of twelve-point print, she searched for a clue as to the identity of the anonymous email sender. "You'd think that if he was going to threaten my life, he could at least introduce himself first."

Rhys narrowed his dark eyes. "You don't seem to be taking this very seriously, Addi."

One of Rhys's staff members had come across the email

that morning when she'd been combing through the spam filter on an unrelated assignment. She'd brought it directly to Rhys. The message had never made it to Addison's email address because of its excessive profanity.

"I'm not sure how anyone could take an email seriously from someone who calls themselves 'your worst nightmare.' I mean, how clichéd is that?" She rolled her eyes. "Thanks for bringing this to me, but it's probably a hoax. Just some guy who hates women and wants to get his jollies by sending a nasty email. I'm not too worried—"

"I think we should involve Logan."

Addison bristled. "He has bigger things to worry about than some misogynistic idiot."

Truth was, she didn't want Logan getting involved. She tried to keep anything remotely personal as far away from him as possible. Their relationship was strictly business, and it had to stay that way. It was bad enough that she had to accept that everyone viewed *him* as the boss despite their being equal partners, and she'd rather stab herself in the eye with her own stiletto before admitting she needed his help.

Besides, there was the issue of her top secret plans to start her own business separate from Cobalt & Dane. Having Logan stick his nose into her personal life wasn't something that she could allow at the moment.

"The safety and well-being of everyone in this company *is* his responsibility." Rhys ran a hand over his cropped dark hair.

"*Our* responsibility," she corrected. "Since my name is on the wall here, his responsibilities are also mine."

"You know what I mean. This is Logan's bread and butter, not yours."

Like she needed the reminder. "That might be true, but I'm still your boss."

"Are you telling me not to say anything to him?" Rhys shook his head. "I'm not comfortable—"

"That's exactly what I'm saying." She scanned the email again. "Whoever this person is, they haven't made a move. This email was sent two days ago and I haven't had any strange phone calls or anyone stopping me in the street. It's a load of crap."

"The things he says are pretty specific."

"Precisely my point. If he were planning to execute any of this, why wouldn't he keep his mouth shut instead of leaving a happy little trail of evidence like some kind of deranged version of *Hansel and Gretel*?" She shrugged. "Now, security might not be my 'bread and butter,' but that seems a little odd to me."

Rhys made a noncommittal noise. "Better safe than sorry."

"I *am* safe. My apartment is totally secure, as are the offices here. I appreciate the concern, Rhys, but I'm fine."

Addison drummed her nails against the surface of the desk. She wouldn't admit it to Rhys—or anyone—but the email *had* shaken her a little. It was so angry. So vitriolic.

But if there was one thing she knew for certain, it was that people were much braver in front of a computer screen than they were in real life. Addison was an active participant in several women-in-business groups. She'd seen firsthand the kind of crap people posted online, but she'd bet her last dollar bill that none of them would have the guts to say those things to her face. So she didn't put much stock in this email.

And she certainly wouldn't subject herself to asking Logan freaking Dane for help.

"You're not worried?"

She shook her head. "This is just some weak little person sitting high and mighty behind his keyboard trying to get his thrills by scaring a woman who dares to be in a position of power. I'm not falling for it."

"I still think we should tell Logan."

"Rhys, I promise if anything else seems out of the ordinary I'll bring it up with him." She folded the email in two and tucked it into her organizer. "But we've got the leadership retreat starting on Monday and I have a ton of stuff to do in preparation. *And* I want Logan's eye on the prize with this strategy stuff. He'll do anything to get out of it. Don't give him the distraction."

"I *really* don't feel comfortable sitting on this," Rhys said.

"I don't care." Addison stood and made a shooing motion with her hands. "Now, get out of here and don't stay late. You should be spending the weekend with that lovely woman of yours. If she stops sending brownies into the office, the staff will have my hide."

"Fine." Rhys pushed up from the chair on the other side of her desk and went to leave. "But promise me you'll let one of us know the second you see anything odd. Okay?"

"Cross my heart and hope to die," she replied, making a cross over her chest with her finger. "Now get out of here."

She smiled to herself as Rhys left. Her IT manager was a great guy, if a little too uptight in her opinion. But once he was gone, a feeling of unease developed in her chest. Surveying her office, she tried to shake it off.

It's nerves about the retreat, that's all.

The Cobalt & Dane management team would be spending three days in Addison's cottage in upstate New York assessing their progress against the business strategy they'd developed six months ago. It was also an excuse to get the team together to socialize, which they were often too busy to do. But despite their crazy workload, the team was small and tight-knit. Addison's father had always cultivated a close bond with his team back when he first started the company. She'd made it her mission to keep that legacy alive.

Except now she wanted to leave her father's company and strike out on her own. Completely on her own… well, except for taking a few key staff members with her.

It wasn't just that Logan was viewed as the boss over her, but in a company that dealt with security she was out of her element with the subject matter. The thing was, Addison took care of *everything* that wasn't security. That included finances, human resources, payroll, training, business development, internal communications, etc. The list went on and on. At times her lack of security knowledge worked to her advantage because she was unbiased and could offer a fresh perspective that hadn't been colored by bad assignments.

But despite her valuable input and the fact that she was the one who kept the lights on by ensuring the company paid its bills and its employees, she was still seen as the number two. That wasn't going to change; she'd never be top dog here.

Worse still, she'd never command the respect her father did. And for a girl who was competitive to the bone…that hurt.

Shaking off the negative thoughts, she brought her

attention back to the task at hand—preparing for the retreat. It had become her tradition to head up to the cottage the weekend before so that everything was ready to
go for the Monday morning welcome session.

Her body relaxed in anticipation. A weekend alone at
the cottage sounded like absolute bliss. She had a new
book, a few bottles of her favorite wine and a swimsuit
already packed. All she had to do was finish up at the
office and then she could start the slow trudge out of
Manhattan.

Scanning her list of things to bring from the office,
she found the last item unchecked: the binder with all
the notes from the last retreat, which sat neatly on the
top shelf of her bookcase.

There were few things as precarious as trying to navigate a step stool in Louboutins, but Addison wasn't about
to let OH&S get in the way of her love for a good pair
of high heels. She climbed to the top of the stool, her
fingers reaching for the thick binder. Of course, the one
thing she needed was on the highest shelf. Wasn't that
always the way?

"You know, I'm not sure I ever believed in heaven," a
deep voice said. "But my dad always told me I'd find the
answer to my questions if I looked up to God."

Logan Dane leaned against the door frame to his
partner's office, a smirk tugging at his lips. Any chance
to throw Addison off guard was not to be missed. Although truth be told, a chance to torture himself with the
vision of her amazing legs was not to be missed, either.

"I've got good aim, Logan. Don't make me throw
something at you."

Instead of coming down, she leaned farther forward,

causing her fitted pencil skirt to ride higher up the backs of her legs. His breath caught in his throat when a sliver of lace revealed that her stockings stopped midthigh. Sweet mother of all things holy.

Between the tight skirt, the black lace and the candy-red soles on her shoes, it was a picture fit for a dirty dream.

Yeah, 'cause the thing you need right now is another image of Addison to avoid fantasizing over. Don't you have enough guilt on your shoulders already?

"I'd like to see you try," he said.

She retrieved a binder and climbed down, making a show of smoothing out the wrinkles on her skirt. Her red nails matched the underside of her heels.

"Did you want something, Logan? Or are you just here to ogle my legs?"

He cleared his throat. "I wasn't—"

"Sure you weren't."

Busted. "I can't help it. You've got some damn fine pins."

Shaking her head, she bent down and picked up her bag from the floor. This time he kept his eyes away from her ass. Willpower, when he had it, was a wonderful thing.

"You all ready for the retreat on Monday?" she asked, ignoring his comment. "We've got an early start."

"Don't worry, I'll be on time."

"No, be early." She gathered up her organizer and slid it into her bag. "I'll need help setting up for the first session."

"Yes, ma'am. Anything else you want me to do, Miss Bossy Boots?" He walked into her office and placed his palms on her desk. "As if it isn't bad enough you'll be talking numbers at me all through the retreat."

"Just arrive in one piece." Her eyes flickered over him, sending a trail of heat straight from his chest to his groin. "I'm not sure what your weekend plans are, but I don't want you rolling up hungover and with lipstick on your collar."

He'd done that *once*, and she'd never let him live it down, though he absolutely deserved the censure. He hadn't been subtle when he'd started dating his ex. But he'd put a stop to that soon after—no more women, no more fooling around. Still, Addison had kept her distance ever since.

"I wouldn't let the staff see me in that state." He pressed his hand to his chest. "You know that."

"Oh right, to them you've got to be the Big Bad Wolf." She continued packing her bag without looking up, her long golden hair slipping over her shoulder to conceal her expression. "Lucky me, getting to see the real you."

He detected the slightest waver in her voice, undercutting the otherwise frosty tone. The show with his ex had been partly for Addison's benefit, though it was hard to keep reminding himself he'd done the right thing by them both. Knowing that he'd hurt her so badly made him feel like a bastard.

"You're one of the lucky few, Addi."

"I count my blessings," she said drily. "Anyway, I'm heading off early. Got to make a head start down to the cottage before this traffic gets insane."

"You sure you don't want a weekend guest?"

"Absolutely positively one hundred percent sure." A smile twitched on her lips, and his heartbeat kicked up a notch. "I'm going to sit in the hot tub until my hands turn to prunes. I'm going to drink wine and do yoga and be totally peaceful. No one is going to ruin that for me, especially not you."

"Message received."

Despite his best effort to keep his mind on the business retreat, a thought skittered through his brain like a pebble skipping over a pond. Was she the bikini type, or would she wear something more sophisticated in the hot tub? Black or white? Or something colorful?

Would it have one of those string tie-ups that could be easily loosened with a single—

"I *said* is there anything else you need before I go?" She hoisted her bag over one shoulder and picked up a box of supplies with *retreat* neatly printed on the side in black marker.

"Nope, I just came in here to wind you up."

She shook her head. "Now that's the first honest thing you've said to me all day."

"I said you had great pins," he corrected as he held the door for her. "I stand by that."

She muttered something under her breath as she walked past him, but he caught a rueful smile on her lips.

They had an odd relationship. But he'd take their strange mix of teasing and power struggles over not having her around any day. Addison was one of the few people who meant something to him.

Just remember that next time you get tempted to take a closer look at those pins, Dane. She's off-limits. One slip does not make it okay to go back for seconds.

Her tinkling laughter carried through the open-plan office as she stopped to say goodbye to her team. One of the young guys in accounts took the box from her hands and could barely keep his tongue in his mouth as he escorted her to the elevators. Logan's fists clenched instinctively.

Sure, he knew she was off-limits, but that didn't mean he could stand the thought of someone else touching her. Having her. He was all too familiar with how good she felt, how her body reacted to the barest touch. She was sensitive in the best way possible, and he'd given in to her all too easily once.

"Never again," he muttered under his breath, turning away from the sight of her and the young staff member before he said something he would regret. "She's not yours."

A few minutes later, Logan was knee-deep in work. Running Cobalt & Dane kept him busy, and Friday afternoons were no exception. Besides, Addison would have the team on a tight leash during the retreat next week, which meant he needed to be on top of things before finishing up for the weekend. He'd never quite understood the necessity of taking time off to discuss boring stuff like financials and recruiting strategy—surely that was a job for all those bean counters he'd hired at Addison's request.

A knock at his office door pulled him out of his thoughts.

"Logan?" Rhys leaned in, a wary expression on his face. "You got a second?"

"Sure." Logan motioned for him to enter. "What's going on?"

"I'm concerned about an email we received. I took it to Addison and she asked me not to bother you because of the retreat next week, but…"

Logan frowned. "But?"

"Here." Rhys slid a piece of paper across the table. "I think we need to be worried about this."

Logan scanned the email, his fingers gripping the paper tighter and tighter as he read until it crumpled under the pressure. His instinct was to lash out, to curse Addison and Rhys for not bringing this to him right away. But this was his fault. He knew why Addison didn't want him involved—and it wasn't because of the retreat. It was because he'd put distance between them and now she was teaching him a lesson.

"Have there been any other emails like this?" he asked, smoothing the paper down flat on his desk.

"Not that we've seen. I've put a flag on this email address so I'll know if he tries to contact anyone in the company from this point on." Rhys bobbed his head. "Addison isn't worried about this guy, but I don't think we can ignore him."

"You should have come to me first." Logan raked a hand through his hair.

The vile words glared up at him from the paper, the threats waving at him like giant red flags. How could Addison have thought this was nothing?

Because she'd rather prove herself to be independent than come to you for help.

"It's addressed to her, Logan. What would she have done if I took it you first?" He threw his hands up in the air. "I get that you two have this weird tug-of-war thing going on, but I'm sick of walking on eggshells around you two instead of doing my job."

"If you see anything else like this come in, you come to me. Got it?" He banged his fist down on the desk. "I don't care if the email says 'top fucking secret, for Addison's eyes only' in big bold letters."

Rhys sighed. "Fine. But you'll have to back me up when she flips out."

"If she's alive and well enough to be shouting, then I'm happy."

He'd promised Addison's father—the man who'd been his boss and his mentor—that he would always look out for her. That he would keep her safe from this crazy, screwed-up world they lived in. Only once had he broken that vow. One night two years ago, when his willpower had failed him and he'd given in to the desire he'd managed to keep at bay for almost a decade.

"I've got my team looking into the sender's details," Rhys said. "But I'm not sure how much we'll be able to turn up from a webmail account. People don't usually use their real details, especially if they're planning to send emails like this."

"Just find out whatever you can."

Rhys nodded. "You know she's going to be all by herself this weekend, right?"

"No, she's not." Logan folded the printed email up small enough to fit in his pocket. "Addison is going to have a guest at the cottage, whether she likes it or not."

2

ADDISON ROLLED HER shoulders as she settled in for the last leg of her journey. After driving for more than three hours, her muscles were desperate for a stretch, and she wanted something to eat that wasn't birdseed masquerading as an energy bar. Thankfully, it wouldn't be long until she reached her father's cottage on Cayuga Lake. Then she could reheat the lasagna she'd prepared last night and crack open a bottle of wine. Her stomach grumbled at the thought of a hot meal.

"Just a little farther," she said to her reflection in the rearview mirror. As if in response, her phone vibrated. "Again, Logan?"

He'd been calling every half hour or so since she'd made it through Newark. Despite ignoring him because her phone's hands-free unit wasn't hooked up, it had become clear he had a bee in his bonnet. That was Logan in a nutshell: dogged persistence.

Addison pulled over at a gas station and killed the engine so she could answer the phone. "Okay, crazy person. What's going on?"

"Where are you?"

She pushed the door open and got out of the car. The air was balmy with summer warmth and she took the opportunity to get the blood flowing through her limbs. "I'm on my way to the cottage."

"No, I mean specifically." There was an urgency in his voice that made the hairs on her arms stand on end.

She told him the name of the gas station as she walked through its doors. Bright, harsh lighting made her squint and she was hit with a chilly blast of air-conditioning. If Logan was going to hold her up, she may as well grab a drink.

"What's going on?" she asked as she opened the door to the refrigerator, stilling at the bellowing sound of a semi's horn on the other end of the line. "Are you on the road?"

Silence.

"Logan Matthew Dane, you better tell me what the hell is going on right now." She grabbed a Diet Coke and marched to the cashier. The man behind the counter eyed her warily as she handed the money over to him with what must have been a murderous look in her eyes. "If you intend on ruining my relaxing weekend I swear to God—"

"I saw the email."

She groaned. "Then tell Rhys he's fired. I mean it, turn around right now and go fire him."

"That might be difficult."

Addison wedged the phone between her ear and her shoulder so she could open her drink. "Why would that be difficult?"

"I'm already on the interstate."

Goddammit. "You're coming to the cottage?"

She walked out of the gas station, shaking her head.

If Logan showed up tonight she would send him straight back home. Or at the very least, to the nearest town. Spending the weekend alone with Logan Dane was *not* in her plans.

"I'll be there shortly," he said. "And don't take it out on Rhys. He did the right thing."

"So the right thing is not listening to his boss when she gives him a *direct* order?" She leaned against her car and tipped her drink up to her lips. "I know for damn sure you wouldn't let anyone pull that shit on you."

Another car had driven into the gas station, and the guy gave Addison a sleazy once-over as he filled the tank of his red truck. Grimacing, she turned away.

"That's beside the point. In this case, we need to take precautions." Logan sighed. "I realize this isn't what you had planned for the weekend. But the cottage is huge. You won't even know I'm there. Unless of course you think my presence is too strong for you to ignore…"

"Your *ego* is too strong for me to ignore."

"Ahh, come on. I'm looking out for you, Addi. I promised your dad—"

"I remember what you promised him. But you're all overreacting. There is no threat. That email was sent days ago, and if Rhys hadn't found it we'd be none the wiser." She screwed the cap back onto her drink. "And *I* would be about to enjoy a peaceful weekend without having you around to bug me."

"I won't apologize for being careful when it comes to your well-being."

She wanted to ask why he thought her well-being was his business. Or his responsibility. But she already knew the answer to that. Two years ago, during her father's final hospital visit—the cancer eating away at his frail body—he'd passed the baton for her protection over to Logan. It was bad enough that he'd chosen Logan to fill his shoes as the head of Cobalt & Dane, but he hadn't even trusted her to take care of herself.

"Don't go into the cottage until I get there," he added. "Wait in your car and keep the doors locked. I'm not far behind you."

Gritting her teeth, she ended the call and slid into the driver's seat. This weekend was going to be a freaking nightmare.

On the bright side, at least now she could count on Logan being at the retreat on time. A wicked smile curved on her lips. If he wanted to play protector all weekend, then she'd give him something productive to do. He hated spreadsheets with a passion, so she'd hand him some of the biannual forecasts to read. *That* should keep him busy.

She turned the engine over and flicked on her headlights. The sun had dropped significantly since she'd arrived at the gas station. It would be pitch-black soon, and the cottage would be dark. Secluded.

What if Logan and Rhys were right? A shiver raced the length of her spine.

"There's no stalker, just like there's no bogeyman," she reminded herself. "There's no zombies, no killer llamas, no Freddy Krueger and no…whatever the hell that thing was in *Donnie Darko*."

But the words didn't comfort her. A tiny seed of fear had been planted by the email, and now it was flourishing under Logan's paranoia. She tapped the lock button and with a *click*, all four doors secured her inside. Shaking her head, she cursed herself for letting Logan get to her.

As she pulled onto the empty road leading toward the cottage, her lights swept across the horizon. Tall trees rushed past her windows in a blur of deep green. Growing up, the cottage had been her happy place—a haven where she'd spent time with her father and did all the things his busy schedule ordinarily excluded. Like fishing, inspecting butterflies and making homemade pizza.

Lights flashed in her rearview mirror as a car drove up behind her, pulling her out of her memories. The high beams shone in her eyes, blurring her vision.

"Inconsiderate moron," she grumbled under her breath as she adjusted the mirror to redirect the glare.

The car behind her was close. Too close. Like one sneeze away from a rear-ender close.

"What the hell?" Addison glanced at her speedometer and confirmed that she was indeed driving at the limit. "Give a girl some space, would you? Jerk."

With one lane of traffic in each direction, she couldn't pull over to let the impatient person pass. But no cars appeared to be coming the other way, so why didn't they simply overtake her? She pressed the accelerator down to put some space between them, but the other driver ate up the distance in seconds. The vehicle looked high, maybe a truck of some kind. But the lights were so blindingly bright that she couldn't make out any specific details like color or model.

"Go around," she said, motioning with her hand for the driver to pass her.

She reached for her phone and hit redial on Logan's number. If he wasn't too far behind—as he'd said—then maybe he could get the plate number.

"Miss me already?" Logan's voice sounded far away on her phone's tiny speakers.

"Have you passed the gas station yet? There's this idiot tailgating me and I'm hoping you can get his plates." She pressed harder on the accelerator and glanced anxiously as the needle on the speedometer climbed higher. "He's making me nervous."

"I should be caught up to you soon, but I haven't passed the gas station yet. Drive carefully, okay?"

At that moment the truck pulled out beside her. "All good, looks like he's going to overtake me. About freaking time." She sighed. "No need to—"

A loud *crunch* cut her off and her car swerved violently. The gut-wrenching sound of metal on metal filled her ears and she had to yank the steering wheel to right the car. Her head snapped to the side in time to see the other vehicle coming back for seconds. She screamed. But it didn't make a lick of difference. Seconds later, her Audi hit dirt on the side of the road.

"Logan!" she cried out.

Another sickening *crunch* boomed and the car shook with impact. Then her headlights bounced around in front of her and she was flying over the gravel.

"ADDISON!" LOGAN YELLED through his phone, but the sound of squealing tires drowned him out. Her frightened scream cut into him. "Hang in there, Addi! I'm right behind you."

Except he wasn't. The road was dark and long and he wasn't exactly sure how much distance was between them.

"Logan, please—" Addison's terrified voice was cut short when the call died.

"Fuck!" he roared and planted his foot down on the accelerator.

The sides of the road weren't well illuminated and he *still* hadn't found the gas station. This was the usual route she took to the cottage—they'd driven it many times together. He was sure of it. But what if she'd gone another way tonight? What if she'd tried to find a short-cut or avoid the toll roads?

What if, what if, what if...

If something happened to her... God help him. He'd tear down every building in the state until he figured out who'd done this to her.

His car shot through the darkness, well over the limit. It didn't matter; nothing mattered except finding her. He eased off the gas as he rounded a corner.

"Come on, come on, come on," he chanted.

His eyes scanned the next stretch of road. Then a faint glow grew in the distance. Signs displaying the price per gallon appeared as he approached and he checked the name. Yes, this was it. The gas station she'd mentioned earlier. She shouldn't be too much farther along this road.

Pushing his car as hard as it would go, he reached for the glove compartment and flipped it open. His SIG P226 sat where he'd placed it earlier, the last resort he hoped never to need. But if anyone had brought harm to Addison, he wouldn't hesitate to use it.

The gas station whizzed past and darkness stretched out before him. Flicking on his high beams, he scanned the side of the road on both sides. Nothing.

"Come on, dammit." He slammed the steering wheel with the heel of his hand, tension tightening the muscles in his shoulders and arms. Making him ache. The blood drained from his knuckles, leaving them white.

His headlights brushed over the empty road and the

trees. At a curve ahead, a glint of something red caught his attention. The dot grew bigger. A truck.

Easing off the accelerator, his eyes scanned the area and sure enough, a trail of skid marks exited the road not too far up. He frantically searched for Addison's silver Audi, his heart in his mouth.

Her sporty little car wouldn't have been able to stand up to this much bigger vehicle. What if she'd…?

"Stop that right fucking now," he said to himself as he pulled over to the side of the road, a few feet behind the truck.

Freaking out wouldn't help anyone. If there was one thing he'd learned in his years of dealing with dangerous situations, it was that you had to stay cool, calm and collected. In control. No matter what horrors you might see.

He forced down the wash of dark worries and killed the engine. His fingers wrapped around his gun. The cold, hard steel of his SIG reassured him, helped him to slip into work mode. He knew the grip, knew the weight, knew how it would behave. And he let the familiarity soothe him.

Taking a deep breath, he flipped the safety off.

The night air was still around him when he stepped out of his car, as though the weather sensed that something was about to go down. Not even a breeze whispered past. Moving quietly, he peered farther down the side of the road. That's when he saw Addison's car.

The silver Audi was covered in brutal scratches. The metal of the back door had been pushed in. Her taillight was shattered. Thankfully, it appeared that she hadn't hit any of the trees that peppered the area. But the light from the road didn't extend far down the dip, and he couldn't see if she was in the car.

Moving quickly but soundlessly, he came around the red truck and checked the driver's seat. Empty. He wasn't about to stop and take notes, but a quick glance at the front of the car confirmed this person was driving on New York plates.

Logan scooted down the steep grass-covered ditch beside the road, balancing himself with his free hand. Something moved at the side of Addison's car. A man was trying to open the driver's side door.

He had two choices. Go in quietly and hope to sneak up on the guy, risking that the creep might get to Addison first. Or scare the shit out of him now and make sure he kept his grubby hands to himself. Logan couldn't see Addison, but it appeared as though she'd locked the door per his instruction.

Good girl, Addi. I'm coming for you, just hang in there.

All of a sudden a loud snapping sound cut through the night. *Shit!* A branch crunched beneath his feet and the guy froze next to Addison's door.

"Back away from the car," Logan said calmly, the gun pointed straight forward. His voice carried across the clearing.

"I was just trying to help her, man." The guy popped his hands up by his head and took a step back.

His face was covered by a hood, and despite the balmy weather, he had on long sleeves, gloves and jeans.

"You normally wear gloves in the summer?" Logan advanced, moving quicker now that he didn't need to keep quiet.

The other man continued walking backward, heading toward the edge of the trees. He was going to run; Logan could feel it in his bones. But he still couldn't tell if Addison was okay, and time wouldn't allow him to have it both ways. He could check on her *or* he could go after the guy. Blindly shooting at a man wasn't an option, even if Logan was positive that this guy was aiming to do *anything* but help her.

"Hold up," he called out. "That's far enough."

The guy slowed down for a second, but his twitchy movements told Logan he wouldn't stay put long. The car was close, but the damn darkness hid what was inside. If Addison was hurt, he needed to get to her. Now.

Then the guy turned and took off like a shot. Logan swore under his breath and broke into a sprint. Tall grass whipped past his legs, his shoes catching over a dip in the ground and tripping him up. Blood rushed in his ears, his heart pounding with adrenaline. All he could see was the back of the guy's hoodie as he disappeared into the trees.

Logan skidded to a stop at the side of the Audi, his gun still pointing ahead. But the area was dark and he'd have no hope of catching the guy now. Leaning down to the passenger side window, he found Addison inside. Her tearstained face looked up at him, relief seeping into her features.

He'd found her. And now he wouldn't be letting her out of his sight.

3

ADDISON'S HANDS TREMBLED so much that she struggled to open the door. The whole crazy event had happened in a blur. After the truck rammed her, the Audi had skidded off the road and hurtled down a small hill. Luckily, her brakes were in fine working order and she'd avoided crashing into the trees.

But being trapped in the car while some crazy person tried to wrench the door open was easily the most terrifying thing she'd ever experienced. He'd been hunting around for something to break the glass when Logan had showed up.

What if that lunatic had been able to get inside? How would you have defended yourself then?

The warm summer air filtered into the car as Addison finally got the door open. Then Logan's hands were on her, helping her stand. He wrapped his arms around her so she could stay upright on her shaking legs. She melted against him, needing something solid and real to keep her from falling into a heap.

"Are you okay?" His hand brushed the hair from her forehead—but the gesture wasn't tender. He was checking for injuries. His thumb snagged a sore spot and she winced.

"I don't think anything is broken," she said. "But I bumped my head."

He checked her over as best he could in the dark. Her cheek throbbed and she was pretty sure there would be bruising on her chest from the seat belt. But she was in one piece, which was a whole lot better than what would have happened if her attacker had gotten inside her car.

"I should take you to the hospital," Logan said, continuing to inspect her.

"No, I'm okay."

"Are you sure? I'll have to keep an eye on you in case there are signs of concussion." He scanned her face. "If anything feels off, you have to tell me, okay?"

"Okay." Her eyes darted to the dark patch of forest in front of her.

"He's gone, Addi."

That's when she noticed the gun in his hand. "You didn't shoot him?"

"I'm not going to open fire on the side of the road." He looked down at her, less analytical this time. His rich brown eyes searched her face. "Not unless I need to. You know the rule."

"Guns are the last resort," she repeated her father's words and pressed her hand to her head. Squeezing her eyes shut against the throbbing, her heart rate slowed. "But the bastard got away."

"I wasn't going to risk leaving you by yourself in the car in case you were hurt." He pulled her to his chest and rested his chin on top of her head. "You come first, remember?"

Her stomach pitched. This was how he'd held her before all her boundaries turned to shit two years ago. That simple movement of tucking her head against the crook of his neck, cradling her like she was the most precious thing in the whole world, had obliterated her. Her hand came to his chest, her fingers curling into his soft cotton T-shirt.

For a moment they stood there, silent and unmoving. His hand cupped the back of her head, his warmth seeping into her. The furious beating of his heart vibrated under her fingertips. From the outside no one would know that he was worried—he hadn't broken a sweat, hadn't lost his cool. But she could feel his fear. His care.

"What the hell do we do now?" she asked, pushing away from him and bracing her hand against the damaged car. She couldn't deal with Logan being kind to her, not knowing that soon she'd be leaving him. Distance was important right now. "I hit something pretty hard on the way down. I have no idea if I can drive this thing."

Logan crouched and checked under the car. "It's possible you've bent the axle. Let's leave it here and I'll call a tow truck when we get to the cottage."

They grabbed her things and walked up to where Logan's car sat on the side of the road. The red truck was still there, so he took a photo of the plate and tried the doors. Locked. Nothing helpful could be seen through the windows.

An hour later they were settled at the cottage. Logan had called a tow company for Addison's car and had reported the incident to the police. Tomorrow they'd head to the local station and make a statement in person. But chances were, whoever had chased Addison off the road would go back to collect his vehicle. Logan couldn't leave Addison alone at the cottage, however. And potentially putting her in harm's way by taking her back to the scene wasn't an option, either. So the pictures of the vehicle would have to do.

"He'll probably clean it out and then dump it somewhere," Logan said as they sat at the dining table eating her lasagna. He was in full-on work mode now. "It'll turn up, but if he's smart there won't be much for the police to go on."

"You really think it's the guy who wrote me the email?" She poured them both another glass of wine, concentrating so that her hand didn't shake.

"It would be a hell of a coincidence if it wasn't. I mean, road rage happens, but if you say you didn't do anything to antagonize the guy—"

"I didn't."

"Then why would some stranger run you off the road for no reason?" He shook his head, his brow furrowed. "No, it has to be him."

"But how would he know that I was coming out to the cottage? That I'd be on that road?"

"How would he know your email address? He might be following you. He might have hacked into your laptop. It could be a number of things." Logan forked a piece of lasagna into his mouth. "In any case, we'll figure it out. No need to worry, we're in this together."

"I'm not worried," she lied.

Maybe it was stupid, but she didn't want Logan to suspect how much the incident had shaken her. Sometimes she wished she'd gone into the security side of the business like she'd wanted to—then she'd be better prepared for these kinds of incidents. Instead, she'd studied business because she had a natural talent for numbers and her father had said that's what the company needed from her. What *he* needed from her. And she never could say no to him.

Still, she wondered if he'd only said that as another way of trying to protect her. In reality, all it had done was leave her without the respect of her staff.

She shoved the thoughts aside. The last thing she needed was to crumble now and prove to Logan that she couldn't handle this situation.

"You have every right to be worried, Addi." He looked up from his meal. "Most people would be in pieces after what you went through tonight."

"I'm *not* most people. I've heard all of Dad's stories and all of yours. I can deal with this."

His eyes softened and a ghost of a smile passed over his full lips. "I am well aware of that."

"I don't want you to think that you need to be my bodyguard or anything." She pushed her food around on her plate for a moment before abandoning it and reaching for her wine. "I'll be okay."

He looked like he was about to argue, but instead he rubbed the back of his neck. Whenever Logan was trying to figure something out, he kneaded that particular spot. It was the tell that'd allowed her to kick his butt in poker for years. For some reason, it made her belly flip watching his strong hands work at the muscle like that.

Her mind wouldn't let her forget how it felt to have those hands on her. Caressing her. Holding her. Dragging her into position. He was the perfect blend of rough and smooth—hard and soft—and he walked the line between them with delicious ease.

"I made a promise and I intend to keep it." He leaned back in his chair, his eyes smoothing over her. Filling her with liquid heat.

"What if I don't want you hanging around and being my shadow?" Or worse, what if she *did* want it?

"Worried it might upset the guys you date?" He raised a brow. "I can be discreet."

It would have pleased her to no end to tell him that guys were lining up at her door, but the truth was far lonelier than that. Most of the men she met were terrified of Logan—he was like an overprotective big brother. Except he happened to be a crack shot and had a military background to boot.

When she started dating someone, he'd make a point to "drop in" and introduce himself to the guy. Not once had he outright told someone to stay away from her, but then again her dates didn't usually stick around long enough for her to find out if Logan would take that next step.

"I'll believe that when I see it," she said drily.

"What? You won't even know I'm there."

"Are you going to sit in the corner and watch while I take a guy to bed?" It was clear from the way his jaw twitched that her words had made their mark. "What? You moved on after we slept together, so why shouldn't I?"

"I told you I regretted what happened." His voice was tight. Brittle.

"It's too late for regrets." She carved off a small piece of lasagna and forked it into her mouth. It tasted of nothing. "And you're not my father, Logan. You don't get to vet my dates."

"I know that."

"And you can't keep watch over me twenty-four/seven."

He folded his arms over his chest, the muscles curving outward. Defined and honed to perfection. "I will be until we figure out who's after you."

He wore a fitted black T-shirt—his uniform—and damn, it looked so good her mouth watered. Ugh, why couldn't she be attracted to normal men who didn't have hero complexes?

But as much as she was loath to admit it, he made her feel safer than anyone else on the face of the earth.

"You can't have it both ways."

"What's that supposed to mean?" His eyes flashed. "I'm trying to do the right thing."

"By chasing off any chance I have of finding a decent man? Anyone who gets close to me is treated like a potential terrorist. Then they quickly decide I'm not worth the trouble."

Frustration bubbled up within her; the argument was well-worn between them. Normally she was able to tell Logan to go to hell and get on with her day. But not now, not after he'd been proven right. Not after she'd almost been…

The reality of her situation suddenly crashed over her like a wave. Someone had run her off the road; they'd tried to get her out of her car. She'd been trapped like an animal in a cage of her own making, defenseless. Vulnerable.

If he hadn't shown up, God only knew what might have happened to her.

"You *are* worth the trouble, Addi." He raked a hand through his longish hair. "Fuck, I'm sorry that I'm such a thorn in your side. But I can't *not* take care of you…"

For a moment she studied him. It was easy to see why women went crazy over Logan—the overlong, light brown hair, heavy brows and strong jaw made him look dangerous. Powerful. His hands were rough and calloused; his muscles were rock solid. There wasn't anything polished about him. Not even running a successful company for two years had smoothed his sharp edges.

There was a rawness to him, a brutal honesty, and an unfiltered, unbridled passion for what he believed in.

"I guess I could assign one of my guys to look out for you. One of them might be a little less…" A crease formed between his brows. "Intense."

"You wouldn't trust someone else to do what you think is your job," she said, shaking her head. "That's the problem. You're trying to take responsibility for me when I'm telling you that I'm a grown woman. I want to live my life."

"But you never know what kind of shit people are hiding. All I'm saying is that you need to do some due diligence, especially now." He paused. "You're too trusting."

She gulped the remainder of her wine, feeling a slight sense of relief as the alcohol wore down her nervous energy. "You've got to be kidding me. After the way you treated me, I don't trust *anyone*."

He stood suddenly, pushing the dining chair back so hard it almost toppled over. "I said I was sorry, Addison. Christ, what more can I do? I crossed a line, I realized my mistake, and I made a promise that it would never happen again."

And by "crossed a line" of course he meant that he'd given her the greatest night in her very sheltered existence. The moment Logan had walked into her father's office as a damaged, angry twenty-two-year-old, she'd been in love. Her sixteen-year-old self had fallen hard and fast.

But Logan had been Mr. Morals when it came to her—except for that one night. But then he'd moved on so quickly that she'd gotten whiplash from it.

"We had sex, Logan. You make it sound like you forced me." She pushed her food away, her stomach twisting itself into knots. "I *wanted* it. God, how I wanted it—"

"STOP." HE HELD up a hand like she was some misbehaving toddler and instantly regretted it.

But hearing her talk about how she'd wanted him was more than he could take. It was more than his resolve could take. Walking out of Addison's apartment the morning after they'd been together had been the hardest thing he'd ever done. Ignoring her hurt had damn near killed him. But it had been the right thing to do. Because he'd promised her father he would care for her.

Not fuck her.

Fire flashed in her dark eyes. "Am I that hideous that you can't even stand being reminded of what we did?"

Hideous? "You're out of your mind if you think I wasn't right there with you."

"Then why did you run out of there like a bat out of hell the next morning?" Her hands twisted in her lap.

The red lacquer on her nails glinted in the light. It was the only remaining sign of the hyperpolished image she presented at the office. She must have changed for the drive—gone were the sexy heels and stockings, gone were the pearl earrings and the tight skirt. Instead, she wore a pair of soft jeans that hugged her small hips and long legs. A loose white T-shirt revealed a hint of a pink bra beneath.

Addison had a thing for lingerie, and now so did he.

Before her, he'd been happy to have a girl as she'd been made—without a stitch of clothing. But Addison had taught him to appreciate lace and silk and those damn fiddly clasps that held her stockings up. All in one night, she'd changed him. Changed what he liked, what he craved.

What he wanted for his future.

"It was a mistake," he said, swallowing hard against the lump in his throat.

It was the best mistake he'd ever made.

"Why?" she demanded. "We were two consenting adults. We used protection and we didn't do it in public. Our having sex hardly threw the world off its axis."

Except it did—his world, anyway. "You're like family to me—"

"Oh, spare me." She pushed up from her chair. "We're not related, thank God."

What the hell was he supposed to say? That he walked away because he was terrified of screwing things up? Or that something might happen to her and that he'd flip out and lose his grip on reality? Again.

Or that when he was with her he couldn't seem to control himself and that scared the hell out of him?

"The reason I walked away had *nothing* to do with my attraction to you." He rolled his shoulders back and tried to dispel the tension in his limbs. "That wasn't a factor."

"So you *were* attracted to me?"

He cleared his throat. "Of course I was."

"It wasn't a pity fuck? You know, because of…" She blinked and straightened her shoulders. "Because Dad had just died."

He gritted his teeth and tried to keep his voice at an appropriate volume. "No."

"Are you still attracted to me?" She stepped forward.

It was too much: her messy blond hair, the wine on her lips. The hungry look in her eyes.

"I'm not answering that."

She stepped closer again and now he could smell the faint remains of perfume on her skin. Chanel No. 5. He'd bought her a bottle for her birthday. Damn expensive crap that smelled like old ladies in the bottle but transformed into heaven on her skin.

"Why not?"

"Because that's not why I'm here."

"Right, I forgot. You're playing bodyguard." She rolled her eyes. "You know I always did have a thing for role-playing."

Tension snapped in the air between them and she seemed about to say more, but she simply shook her head and turned back to the table. Plates clattered as she cleared up their abandoned meal.

"One day you'll push me away hard enough that I won't come back," she said quietly.

"What's that supposed to mean?" His stomach knotted as a sense of foreboding fell over him.

"I'm just saying that it won't always be like this. Change happens and I might not always be around."

Change. A dirty fucking word as far as he was concerned. Change always meant pain; it always meant loss. And loss meant destruction.

"I don't want things to change."

"We don't always get what we want, now do we?" she said, not looking at him. "Anyway, you'll need to make up the bed in one of the spare rooms. I was going to do that over the weekend. You remember where the sheets are?"

"Yeah."

"I'll see you in the morning."

He'd been dismissed, apparently. By trying to do the right thing, he'd screwed up again. It seemed to be his lot in life.

"Probably for the best," he muttered to himself.

He wasn't cut out to care about people, because loss was inevitable and it turned him into a wild beast. Losing his mother had ended his military career, losing Daniel had sent him straight into Addison's arms, and if he lost her...who the hell knew what he'd do.

But that didn't mean he didn't want her. Far from it. He just knew that he couldn't act on his desires.

4

LOGAN SET HIMSELF up on the couch with his laptop and a cup of decaf. He was far too wired to sleep, and his vantage point allowed him to watch the thin beam of light from under Addison's bedroom door. Every so often a shadow flickered, telling him she was unpacking and setting up her room.

Being run off the road wasn't enough to deter her from organizing every little thing the way she liked it.

He smiled to himself. She'd always been that way—needing to have everything just so. Teenage Addison had been a straight-A student with neat-freak tendencies. She used to visit her dad at the office after school and would happily spend hours reorganizing his filing system and making sure the staff kitchen was clean and tidy. Logan had always pretended not to notice her, of course.

Daniel had once told him that Addison developed her organizational habits after her mother died. A sense of order in her physical environment had helped her sift through the pain and confusion in her head, apparently. Her father had encouraged her to take those skills and turn them into a fruitful career, which she had. Addison was the reason Cobalt & Dane had been able to grow as a company. Without her, they'd still be a couple of scruffy guys too focused on the security side of things to get the rent paid.

He envied her ability to turn her loss into something useful. His pain never seemed to cause anything but pure destruction.

Sighing, he raked a hand through his hair and stared at the laptop screen. Going through his emails might help him relax. Daniel had set up an extensive security system when he'd first bought the cottage, so the chance of anything happening without Logan's knowledge was slim.

Eventually the light under Addison's door disappeared, but that didn't stop Logan's gaze from wandering there every few minutes. This weekend would be torture. Bittersweet torture.

"Lucky you're a natural-born masochist," Logan muttered to himself.

After an hour of trying—and failing—to get any work done, he snapped his laptop shut in frustration. If he wasn't going to be productive then he'd go to bed and attempt to sleep. A few hours of shut-eye might help his concentration.

"Yeah, 'cause sleep is the problem," he grumbled as he walked past Addison's door to the linen cupboard.

It was packed with clean sheets, towels and blankets and smelled musty in a way that brought a rush of memories to him. He'd come to this cottage often, spending Thanksgiving weekend with Daniel and Addison since his own father had made it clear he wasn't welcome with the shiny new family he'd acquired. Those long weekends had been filled with fishing, eating and letting Addison beat him at poker until she got good enough that she whipped his ass all on her own.

His fingertips brushed a piece of floral fabric sandwiched between two plain blue sheets. The flowers had faces, but the pattern had faded over the years. Time, the cruel mistress that it was, had robbed them of their smiles.

A noise caused Logan to turn. He tiptoed to Addison's door and pressed his ear to the wood. The muffled sobbing caused pain to wrench in his chest. He touched his palm to the door and sucked in a breath. What the hell was he supposed to do in this situation?

If Addison was in danger, he wouldn't hesitate to act, because protecting her came second nature to him. But a tearful Addison was totally outside his experience. The only other time he'd seen her cry was at her father's funeral…and look how that'd turned out.

He should walk away. Let her cry it out and emerge in the morning with her mask intact. Isn't that what she'd want?

Walk away, you useless son of a bitch. Be a deserter. Isn't that what you do best?

Logan gritted his teeth and eased the handle down on her bedroom door. The room was dark, with only a thin shaft of moonlight illuminating the bed. The cool bluish light showed the outline of her sleeping form. The curve of her hip and the gentle dip at her waist. The soft gleam of her blond hair.

"Addi?" He let the door shut behind him.

She was crying, more softly now. As his eyes adjusted to the dark, he could make out the tremble in her curled-up form. She was facing away from him, her body so small and vulnerable in the center of the large bed.

"Addi? Are you okay?"

She muttered something under her breath and then sighed, but he couldn't make out the words. For years he'd teased her about the way she talked in her sleep—he'd witnessed it on the few occasions when she'd fallen asleep on his couch after having an argument with her dad. Sometimes it was a soft jumble of syllables and other times it was full sentences. Often the words had no meaning.

"Logan," she sighed.

He tiptoed over to her bed and knelt on the mattress with one knee. Both her eyes were shut and her cheeks were damp with tears. The wet skin seemed to shimmer in the bright moonlight. But she slept on.

And dreamed about him, apparently.

He brushed his knuckles along her arm, his breath sticking in his throat when she shivered at his touch. Her body was covered by a white sheet, but a spaghetti-thin strap of black silk curved over her shoulder and a hint of lace peeked out from the top of the sheet.

Sweet mother of—

"Logan?" She shifted on the bed, her voice groggy.

"It's just me, Addi. I heard you crying." He brushed the hair away from her face.

"I was sleeping."

"I didn't mean to wake you. I came in to check that you were okay." His heart thudded in his chest so hard it felt like the organ was trying to punch its way out of his rib cage.

"Oh?" She touched her fingers to her cheek. "I must have been dreaming."

"I'll let you sleep." He pulled away, but she rolled and reached out for him. The movement caused the sheet to slip farther down, revealing a black silk camisole gleaming under the moonlight. The glossy fabric looked almost wet.

"Stay for a minute," she said sleepily.

Maybe *he* was the one dreaming. Addison never asked him to stay with her for anything, not these days. The car accident must have shaken her worse than she'd let on.

"Lie with me. Just until I fall back to sleep." She tugged him to her and he lowered himself onto the bed. "I had trouble drifting off before."

Propping himself up on one elbow, he rubbed his hand up and down her arm. Her skin was clammy. Damp.

"Hmm." She mumbled under her breath and turned so she was facing the wall again. "That's nice."

He tried to pull the sheet back up, but she swatted him away with a protest about being hot. Little did she know it was more for him than it was for her. The sight of her bare skin against the black silk was jacking up his pulse. Not to mention he was fighting off the beginnings of a rock-hard erection.

All you have to do is get her to drift off, then you can back away. Tomorrow, you'll pretend you never came in here.

He kept a few inches between them as he lay down beside her, but she wriggled until her back lined his chest, the curve of her ass cradled perfectly in his lap. A jolt of arousal shot through him, but he held his breath and forced down the excitement. It was like trying to swallow a pill without water.

"What if you hadn't followed me tonight?" she whispered groggily. "What would have happened if...if..."

A tremor ran through her body and he wrapped his

arm around her, hugging her to his chest. "I'll find this guy and take him down, I swear."

"I want to take care of myself."

He held his tongue. There was no point arguing with her now—he knew how she felt about being independent. About wanting to prove that she could handle things on her own. Of course, he disagreed. She wasn't weak, far from it. In fact, Addison was the strongest person he knew. But she didn't have his training, his experience.

Daniel had sheltered her from the ugly aspects of their world, and to the best of his ability, Logan would continue that. He could never lose her, never let anything happen to her. Because without her...well, he didn't even want to think about a world where she wasn't part of his life.

"I want to take care of you, for once." Her whispered voice prickled at his resolve; it picked apart his defenses.

His brain scrambled to find the right thing to say, but that had never been his forte. Some guys had a knack for words; they knew how to seduce and influence and placate. But Logan was only good with his hands.

"Shhh." He brushed her hair back, smoothing his fingertips over her temple with each stroke. "You need to sleep now."

For a moment he thought she'd drifted off; her breathing became soft and her body seemed to melt against his. He'd been holding himself in check but the slight shift of her body, the gentlest brush of her ass against his lap, yanked open the floodgates. His cock leaped from half-mast to full attention and a groan stuck in his throat.

As he was about to extricate himself from her bed, she moved again. This time he realized it was on purpose, and knowing that made him even harder. His brain screamed at him to go, but she felt so damn good in his arms. Soft yet firm, silky smooth. So tempting.

"Logan," she breathed, rolling her head back against his chest. Her hand slipped between them and she felt for his cock. His whole body was about to go up in flames.

Yeah, flames. Because you're going straight to hell.

"Addi, we shouldn't—"

"Shh." Her fingers danced along the length of his fly. He strained painfully against the confines of his jeans, the zipper barely keeping him in. "I can feel how much you want it."

"It's not about my wants," he gritted out. How could he be so weak to end up in this position again?

"Is it about what *I* want?" Her hand moved away from his cock and he thought he might be off the hook. But she captured his wrist and pulled his hand down until he cupped her between the legs.

Heat radiated through the sheet. Even with the material stopping him from fully exploring her, he could feel how ready she was. She kept her hand over his as she circled her hips into his touch.

"Dammit, Addi." He moaned into her hair. It was all he could do not to rip the sheet from her body and plunge his fingers into her sweet, hot sex. "This isn't right. Last time was…"

"Sex, Logan. It was sex." She huffed. "I'm not some delicate flower, you know."

She pushed the sheet down, exposing the full glory of the silk camisole as it hugged her incredible body. When she pushed up to straddle him, her breasts bounced, unconfined. He remembered how she'd felt under his tongue, the way her rosy little nipples had stiffened when he'd kissed them. The way her back had bowed when he'd sucked on them. The way her skin had tasted sweet and earthy and unique.

"I can read you like a book." She pressed down, tilting her hips back and forth so that she rubbed her sex along the hard length of him. The sensation was too good; he forced his eyes shut and his fingers dug into her hips. "You want me."

If he wasn't careful that gentle rocking of her hips was going to make him come in his pants. But he couldn't seem to push her away. She was right—he wanted her. He wanted her more than the air in his lungs.

Always had, always would…against his better judgment, anyway.

"If you don't stop that, I'm not going to be able to walk away."

A wicked smile curved on her full lips. "I doubt you'd be able to walk anywhere right now."

ADDISON SWIRLED HER hips in a figure eight, feeling the rasp of Logan's jeans against her sensitive skin. Hovering over him—knowing he was fully at her mercy—was a power trip. In every other aspect of their lives he was in charge; he was one step ahead.

She might not be able to have control in the boardroom, but in the bedroom…this could be her domain. *This* was where she could gain control back, where she could have the upper hand.

You sure it's nothing to do with the fact that you could have died tonight? That you could have lost him for good?

Fear wrapped its hands around her throat but she shoved the troubling thoughts away. Now was not the time for weakness. She leaned forward, hinging at her hips and giving him an eyeful of her breasts. Obviously she hadn't packed the camisole for him, since she was supposed to be spending the weekend alone. She simply loved the feel of silk on her skin.

But she liked the feel of his hands on her even more.

"Keep pushing me, Addi. I dare you." His face was hard-set, the angle of his jaw sharp in the near darkness.

"I'm not afraid of you," she whispered, bending forward so that her lips brushed his ear. "Everyone thinks you're the Big Bad Wolf but I know you're just a teddy bear."

His big hands slid along her thighs, catching the hem of the camisole and pushing it up. "Is that so?"

"Mmm-hmm."

His hands inched higher. "You're making one terrible mistake right now."

"What's that?"

His thumb brushed the sensitive skin of her sex. "Thinking you're in charge just because you're on top."

Before she could retort, he felt for her clit with his thumb. Pleasure rocketed through her the second he made contact and she fell back, bracing herself on her hands. It was shameless how she thrust her hips toward him, determined to get as much friction as possible. The slow, sensual seduction was over.

That exactly was what Logan was like in bed. To the point. He didn't mess around. Rather, he went straight in for the kill.

"Oh God." Her head lolled. "You're too damn good at that."

"Tell me how good," he urged her on, his voice shredded and rough. "If I'm going to hell I want to know you've enjoyed the ride."

A low chuckle came from her throat. "And you still say you're in charge?"

He grunted and grabbed her hips, yanking her forward and pushing himself down on the mattress at the same time until her body hovered over his face. Was he going to…?

He latched his mouth onto her sex and his tongue lapped at her with a focus that made her whole body quake. Tremors racked her, but his hands held her down over him. She pitched forward and planted one hand on the wall behind the bed to stop herself from falling over.

"Logan!" His name dissolved on her tongue as orgasm swept through her. Her muscles clenched and released as pleasure poured through her veins. Obliterating her. Turning her to mush.

As the tremors subsided, he guided her back down to the bed. She curled into him, her hands seeking out the warmth of his chest and the vibrations of his heart.

"Score one, Team Dane," he said as he wrapped his arms around her.

"Screw you."

He chuckled against her hair. "Is that a request?"

"It's an order."

The ridge outlined by his jeans told her that he was at bursting point. That meant she'd have to take it slow, tease him for as long as she could before giving in. Prove to him that he wasn't in charge here. This was *her* domain.

She drew his zipper down, the sound cutting through the quiet. Thankfully he hadn't worn a belt today, so all she had to do was pop the button at his waist. His cock strained forward, peeking out the top of his boxer briefs.

"Who's in charge now?" She drew him out slowly,

reveling in the way he tried to conceal his moan by clamping his teeth together. The twitch in his jaw gave him away entirely.

"You know I am, Addison."

"I don't think so." Wrapping her fingers around him, she moved her fist up and down his length, giving his tip a light squeeze with every stroke. "You're at my mercy now."

His hips bucked as she increased her pace. A string of curse words flew out of his lips as she bent forward and ran her tongue over the swollen head of him. The taste of him flooded her with memories. That night... that sweaty, passionate, dirty night.

"Say it," she said, blowing cool air over his heated skin.

"No." He ground the word out, but he was already fishing around in his pants. He found his wallet and flipped it open.

"I won't let you finish until you do." Her strokes slowed and she watched him, her whole body alight with energy.

"You started this," he said, pulling out a foil packet and tearing it open. "I'm going to finish it...and then I'm going to finish you again."

Pushing her hands out of the way, he rolled the condom down his length. That simple action had never excited her with other men—it was the business part of sex. No glove, no love, right? But watching Logan handle himself intoxicated her. Arousal hung over her like a heavy cloud; it fogged her mind, and she didn't protest when he reached for her hips again, dragging her into place and seating himself deep inside her.

Being filled by him was a pleasure of the most exquisite variety. He fit perfectly inside her, as if he'd been designed for her.

"No arguments?" he asked with a sly smile.

"I'm still on top." She planted her hands on his chest as he thrust up into her.

"We can fix that."

In a second, he'd flipped her onto her back and had pinned her hands above her head. His hot breath whispered over her skin as he kissed her neck, sucking and biting until she writhed beneath him.

Damn him. He knew exactly what to do.

"Don't fight it, baby. I'm better when I'm in charge."

When his mouth came down on her hers, she was lost. The insistent press of his tongue, the stubble on his jaw and the faint taste of herself on his lips was enough to send her over the edge again. She pressed her face against his neck and chanted his name over and over as her body shook.

"That's it, tell me." He pumped into her faster. "Tell me."

"It's you, Logan. It's you."

He thrust into her once more and roared as he found his release. Cradling her in his arms, he rolled them onto their sides and threw one thigh over her. Claiming her.

Reminding her that tomorrow she'd need to regain her distance if she had any hope of protecting her heart....

5

ADDISON'S EYES SNAPPED open at the sound of a bird chirping outside her window. The blare of horns and wail of sirens that usually greeted her in the morning were suspiciously absent. She pushed herself up and blew the hair out of her eyes to see that she wasn't in her sleek and stylish Manhattan apartment.

Of course, she was at the cottage.

The events of last night came rushing over her like an avalanche. The long drive, the car accident, fighting with Logan…making up with Logan.

"Ugh." She ground the heels of her palms into her eyes.

There would be no escaping Logan this weekend, not if she might be in danger. A delicious shiver rippled through Addison's body. Everything ached in that way that could be achieved only by orgasms and hot, spontaneous sex. It had been too long since she'd felt this good, *far* too long.

The empty space in the bed was cool and fairly unrumpled, which meant he hadn't stayed long. Not that she was surprised. When it came to the morning-after dash, Logan made Usain Bolt look slow.

A dark thought tugged at the corner of her mind. Last time she *had* been taken by surprise, because she'd been stupid enough to think that he might want to stick around. That he might feel something real for her. But less than a week later, she'd turned up at his apartment to find another woman answering his front door.

That's not going to happen this time. You know the score, and you've got plans to make it on your own. Sex doesn't change that.

And having sex with Logan was fine so long as it suited her needs: pleasure for her body, but not for her heart. She didn't regret seducing him last night, not even a little bit. Being in his arms—distracting herself from the night's events—was exactly what she'd needed. But that was *all* she needed from him.

Addison threw on her bathing suit and then layered a floaty cotton dress over the top. This weekend was going to be all about rest and relaxation, regardless of whether or not Logan wanted to participate. No one was going to get her down—not him, not the guy who'd run her off the road. No one.

Logan paced the length of the deck out on the back of the cottage. The morning sun was light and buttery yellow. Soft, beautiful. Like Addison.

Christ, you're comparing her to the morning sun now? Get a fucking grip.

He raked a hand through his hair and stared across the land that stretched out in front of him. It was so peaceful here, so serene. But all he could feel was how isolated they were. How no one would hear or see them.

They could do anything and the world would be none the wiser.

Having that level of freedom wasn't a good thing for a man like Logan. He needed to know someone was watching, keeping tabs. In the office, he had guys like Rhys and Owen and Aiden to keep him in check. *His* team, his men. They didn't realize it, but they kept him in line. Simply by giving him their loyalty, he was bound to do right by them as Daniel had done for him. But out here, anything was possible.

And that scared the shit out of him.

"Morning," Addison said as she came up next to him. Her hair flowed loosely around her shoulders, her legs and feet bare under her summer dress.

He wasn't sure how he should greet her. With a kiss, or would that be too familiar? A hug, perhaps. But that could be too brotherly.

This is exactly why you shouldn't have overstepped. You got all caught up in the passion of the moment and then things got weird.

He had too much to lose by getting entangled with Addison—it wasn't just that he'd be dishonoring the memory of the man who'd mentored him. The company was his whole life, and he needed Addison by his side to take care of all the things he was clueless about: finances, health and safety, and all that other administrative crap that made his eyes turn square. Sure, there were other people who could do her job, but none who would do it as well as her. None that he trusted.

She was Cobalt and he was Dane. Without one of those elements, Cobalt & Dane didn't exist. Which meant he couldn't risk any type of personal relationship with her. Especially given his track record for screwing things up.

"Fancy a coffee?" she asked, eyeing him with unconcealed curiosity. "I've just put the pot on."

"You're speaking my language."

He followed her back into the house and closed the door behind him, flicking the lock. A good security system wasn't worth crap if you didn't make use of it.

Addison swanned around the kitchen, humming to herself. She didn't seem adversely affected by last night…though he wasn't sure what he'd been expecting. They hadn't made any rules or set any boundaries.

"So, uh…about last night," he said, sliding onto a stool at the edge of the kitchen's island counter.

"Yeah?" Addison raised a brow as she placed two mugs next to the coffeepot.

"Should we…talk?" He drummed his fingers on the countertop. "Or something?"

"I'd like to know what the 'or something' is before I say yes," she teased. Steam curled up from the mugs as she poured their drinks.

"You get what I mean."

"It's just sex, Logan. It was consensual. We used protection." She shrugged. "What more should we discuss?"

"I don't know. I just figured that's what women normally like to do afterward."

She laughed. "The women you date might like to talk afterward, but I'm fine."

Truth be told, he'd never tried to initiate a conversation after sex before, so he had *no* idea what women wanted.

"I don't expect anything from you," she said, placing his coffee in front of him. "If that's what you're worried about. It wasn't anything more than blowing off steam."

"Right."

"I'm not going to ask you for any commitment. Whether we do it again or not…" She shrugged. "It's no-strings in my mind."

He wasn't sure how he felt about her assessment—was it possible to be both relieved and disappointed at the same time? Her silky skin was still freshly imprinted on his memory. His palms tingled with the urge to touch her again, but they had business to take care of. And forty-eight more hours until the rest of their team showed up.

"We should head down to the police station and make our report today," he said, blowing at the curl of steam winding up from his coffee. "What do you remember about the guy?"

Her eyes dropped, long pale lashes obscuring her rich brown eyes for a moment. "Not much. It was dark and it all happened so quickly."

"What was he wearing?"

Logan remembered, of course. He'd cataloged that information away the second he'd spotted the guy. But starting with a simpler and more obvious detail was a technique often used to unlock memories. Memories could be followed like bread crumbs until something useful was found.

"His face was hard to see—he had a hood covering it." She sucked on her lower lip, her eyes fixated on something in the distance. "He had gloves on, too."

"Did you see his face at all? Were there any marks or tattoos?"

She shook her head. "He was white, but beyond that…"

"Did he say anything to you?"

Addison raised the mug to her lips, her hand trembling. "He said 'let me in, you fucking bitch' but I don't know what that's going to tell us."

"He didn't ask you anything? Did he call you by name?"

"No. So I'm not sure what the police will be able to do." The doubt in her tone belied the neutral expression on her face. He suspected she didn't want to seem scared, but after last night they were well beyond pretending how she felt.

Still, he knew Addison. She had to feel in control at all times. This situation must be eating her up inside because it was something she couldn't dictate.

"They'll chase down the vehicle and ask around some of the local businesses to see if anyone spotted him. That kind of thing. It might not yield any leads, but we have to try."

She nodded. "Okay."

"You didn't notice anything suspicious when you stopped at the gas station, did you? Was anyone following you?"

"No, I don't think so." She scrunched up her nose as she tried to remember. "Actually, there was this one guy who leered at me, but I don't know if you'd call that suspicious."

Men staring at Addison was hardly something he'd find unusual, either, but he'd come to realize in his line of work that even the smallest piece of information was worth looking at. "Did he say anything to you?"

"No, at least not that I heard. I was on the phone to you so I turned away."

"What kind of a car was he driving?"

"A truck." Her brow creased suddenly. "It might have been a red truck. I can't quite remember but…"

"But?"

"I think it was red." Her skin had become pale, wan. Her coffee sat untouched on the island countertop. "Maybe he was watching me for longer than I realized."

"But you didn't notice anyone following you on the road."

"It's a straight road, Logan. Everyone's going in the same direction and I didn't notice anything until he got too close."

"It's okay, Addi. We'll tell the police about the guy at the gas station and they should be able to get a hold of the security cameras. Then we'll know if it was the same person."

She nodded, but her eyes didn't meet his.

A few hours later—after they'd been to the local police station and reported the incident to Addison's insurance company—Logan logged into his work email. Since it was the weekend, nothing much had come through, but Rhys had checked in to confirm that he was still welcome at the retreat. Logan chuckled to himself. His IT manager was a rule-follower to a tee.

"I think you owe Rhys an apology," he said, glancing up from his screen.

Addison sat on the couch with her long legs stretched out, the edge of her sundress tantalizingly brushing the tops of her thighs. "We're incentivizing staff disobedience now, are we? I thought you of all people would understand the consequences of not following orders no matter how someone personally feels about the situation."

"That's a low blow."

Her defenses had to be up if she was using his past to make her point. Not that he could blame her entirely;

she'd had a rough day. The officer at the local station hadn't seemed too interested in her report—then he'd asked a few pointed questions about her driving history, which had gotten Addison's back up. Luckily, Logan had been able to stop her from storming out of the station. Still, he wasn't holding his breath for anything useful to come from the report.

"I'm just saying that Rhys wouldn't have gone against something *you* told him to do." She tucked a strand of blond hair behind her ears. "I would simply like the same level of respect."

"The staff *do* respect you. But I train them to follow their instincts. Security staff are useless if they ignore what their guts tell them. Luckily, I didn't fire him as you asked," he joked, but she flashed him an irritated look. "He was worried about you, that's all. It wasn't meant to be a sign of disrespect."

Her red nails clicked on the keys of her laptop as she typed. He'd grown to enjoy the sound as he often heard it coming from her office late in the evenings when they were the only two people left.

"What are you working on?"

"Just preparations for Monday. You know, what I'd planned to do before you gate-crashed my weekend." She didn't turn away from her screen, but the corner of her lip twitched.

"Glad to hear I'm always welcome."

THE NEXT FEW days dragged for Logan, which wasn't unusual. The retreat always made him restless because he hated to be away from the action. His hands would twitch with the need to do something, while all of

Addison's reports and numbers made his head spin. And made his mind go numb.

But this time his restlessness had more to do with the barely tempered chemistry he shared with Addison. No amount of work would fade the memory of his hands on her skin or the feeling of her warmth wrapped around him. Of the taste of her on his tongue. All he wanted to do was kick out his team and have her to himself.

"You look tense, boss." His employee and longtime friend, Aiden Odell, dropped down onto the bench next to him.

The retreat's work portion was over and now the team was relaxing, having a few beers and catching up on personal stuff. But watching Owen flirt with Addison had been enough to make him want to throw something, so he'd gone outside to cool off. It wasn't Owen's fault. Apart from the fact that he was a notorious ladies' man, he had no idea that there was anything at all between Logan and Addison. No one did.

"Just ready to get back to the office. You know numbers aren't my thing."

"You'd be lost without Addison, then." Aiden grinned and swigged his beer. "Hopefully she continues to put up with your shit."

Addison's words echoed in his ears: *Change happens and I might not always be around.*

On Friday night he'd assumed she was talking about her own mortality, but what if she meant that she might want to leave Cobalt & Dane?

"I'm not *that* bad," he said, as if trying to convince himself.

"Man, I'm the only one who's known you long enough

to be able to call you on your crap. Let's be honest. You're difficult as hell."

Logan grunted. "I have high expectations, so what? If people want to work for someone soft, they know where the door is."

"All I'm saying is, this isn't the military. Not everything is life-and-death."

That was the problem, though. People became complacent with their security and then bad things happened. Addison hadn't perceived her email to be a threat and it had gotten her run off the road. If it hadn't been for Rhys, she would have a lot bigger problems right now than a totaled car.

On her request, he'd kept the accident quiet from the rest of their team. But that didn't change what'd happened. Still, what if she *was* thinking of leaving him and their company?

"It's okay to lighten up occasionally, you know, let down that luscious hair of yours." Aiden cracked up when Logan shot him a nasty look.

"Says the guy who should be in a shampoo commercial."

"The ladies love it." Aiden raked a hand through his messy dark curls. "Well, one lady loves it."

"Speaking of crazy hair, how is Quinn?"

Aiden lost his joker smile and he twisted the near-empty beer bottle between his hands. "I'm going to ask her to marry me."

The news hit Logan like a punch to the sternum. "Why the hell would you do that?"

"Because I'm not stupid enough to hide my feelings from her." He shrugged. "She's it for me, Logan. I'm tapping out of the single life."

"I don't even know what to say."

Aiden chuckled and drained the rest of his beer. "How about 'congratulations,' like a normal person would say?"

Logan's eyes were fixed on the distance. Green land spread out for miles around them, the sun growing heavy in the distance. Sometimes he wondered what it would be like to pack up and leave the city behind. It was all too easy to imagine sitting here, drink in hand, with Addison curled up beside him. Her head resting on his shoulder.

You're not allowed to want that. Cobalt & Dane is your life, your purpose. You owe Daniel all that and more.

"I'll congratulate you when she says yes," Logan said with a smirk that belied the confusing swirl of thoughts in his head. "People turn down proposals all the time."

Even a playful swipe couldn't remove the smile from Aiden's face. "Thanks for the vote of confidence."

For a moment Logan envied his friend. But that life wasn't for him. Logan wouldn't be a husband or a dad. He couldn't, not when he was well aware how cruel the world could be. When he knew that grief could crush a man's dreams. Aiden hadn't experienced those things in his life—sure, he'd lost part of his hearing while working for the FBI. But he had a family who loved him, a woman who made him grin like an idiot. Fate hadn't stolen anything from him yet, so he didn't understand how devastating it was to lose someone you cared about.

That's why Logan needed to keep a firm hand on his life, stay in control. Minimize variables and change.

"Is something going on or are you just practicing your resting bitch face?" Aiden nudged him on the shoulder.

"Nah, I'm just ready to head home." He pushed up

from the bench and drained his beer in one long gulp. "I imagine you're ready to get back to your future wife."

"Don't say anything, all right? I want to keep it on the down low."

"Man, the day you catch me talking about weddings will be the day you're obligated as my best friend to shoot me in the head."

"Duly noted."

They abandoned the late-afternoon sun in favor of the cottage's cool, airy kitchen. Addison was sitting on the island bench, her feet swinging back and forth as she chatted with Owen. The heels of her shoes knocked against the wood.

"Probably about time that we get this show on the road," Logan said, tossing his empty beer bottle into the recycling bin.

"Owen's offered to drive me home," Addison said, her cool gaze revealing nothing. Her long blond hair had come out of her ponytail and she wore the hair elastic around her wrist just like she'd done as a teenager. "He said he was heading back to the office to grab something anyway."

Logan's primal instincts roared at him. He had to stop himself from telling Owen to back the fuck away, because that was *exactly* what Addison had complained about the night they arrived at the cottage. And really, he couldn't claim that he didn't trust Owen. The guy was one of his best consultants, a hard worker with far more intelligence than his joker tendencies implied.

"I appreciate it." She smiled and touched Owen's shoulder, all the while keeping her eyes on Logan. "I can't believe the car decided to break down all the way out here. *So* inconvenient."

"It's no problem." Owen patted her hand.

Logan's jaw twitched and he drew a breath.

It's just a lift. And you don't *have the right to tell her who to ride with. Besides, it's not like Owen would make a move.*

Or would he? An image of them flashed into Logan's mind, Owen's hand sliding up Addison's bare leg and catching the hem of her dress, pushing the fabric up. No fucking way.

He cleared his throat. "Actually, Addi, I was hoping we could go through one of those reports before we left. But I don't want to hold the whole team back."

Aiden raised a brow and looked at him like he'd lost his marbles.

"Which report?" she asked with a frown.

Crap. If only he could remember any of the damn spreadsheets that she'd made him look through the last couple of days. "The uhh...cost benchmarking analysis...report."

She cocked her head, her glossy lips pursed. "I'm not sure which one you mean."

Damn her, she wasn't going to let him off the hook that easily. "The one with the...competitor analysis."

"That was just a draft. Surely we don't need to get into that right now. I'll have Renee schedule a time for us to catch up tomorrow."

By this stage the rest of the team had slunk away, sensing the mounting tension between him and Addison. They were known to argue on occasion—each of them as stubborn and fiery as the other. If only his team understood what fueled the fire.

"You're always complaining that I never take any interest in this sort of stuff and now you're saying it can wait?" Guilt streaked through him when her shoulders relaxed and a sheepish smile tugged at her lips.

"You're right, I'm glad you're taking an interest in my stuff for once. I'll tell Owen not to wait."

Could he be any more of a bastard? Not likely.

He watched as she headed over to Owen, her body language so much more relaxed than when she stood with him. The tension had eased out of her lips and she smiled readily. Maybe it would be better if she ended up with someone like Owen, someone who would make her laugh. Someone who would make her life easier.

"If you want to grab a drink later tonight, let me know." Aiden slung his carryall over one shoulder. "That's if you're not too busy going over this report that doesn't exist."

It was Aiden's way of asking if everything was okay. "I won't interrupt your time with Quinn. She'll have my hide if I drag you out after you just got home."

"True. But the offer still stands." Aiden slapped him on the back and then waved to the team.

As the rest of the team filtered out, Addison bade them all individual goodbyes. She was amazing with their employees—firm and yet caring, a true leader who was able to inspire and educate. The problem was that only her own team was as passionate about the numbers side of things. The bean counters and HR folks— or the "fun police" as he'd called them on a number of occasions.

As Owen left, Addison squeezed his arm. They looked good together with their matching blond hair and wide smiles. His gut wrenched. The thought of Addison being with anyone else made him want to hurl.

"So," she said, picking up her laptop from the couch. "You wanted to go over the competitor analysis?"

She padded over to him, barefoot. Her heels lay in a heap by the door and her blue floral dress swished around her knees. The fabric clung to her curves, outlining her breasts and hips in a way that was subtle and yet insanely sexy. He wanted to tear her clothes off with his teeth.

Think of a question about the report.

"Uh, yeah." He rubbed at the back of his neck. "So, what was your overall conclusion about our competitive position?"

She rattled off her answer but he immediately zoned out. Right now, his brain was clogged with too many questions. Who was after Addison and why? What did she *really* expect from him? And what the hell had she meant by her statement that things would change?

"Logan?" Addison waved a hand in front of his face. "I asked if that all made sense."

"Uh yeah, that's great." He nodded and her expression darkened by the second. "So what did you mean before when you said things would change and that you might not always be around?"

"I thought we were supposed to be talking about the report." She planted a hand on her hip. "That's why you asked me to stay back."

"And we just discussed it. Now I want to discuss this."

"It was nothing," she said, turning away from him. She slipped on her shoes and concentrated on the fiddly little straps. "Just a throwaway comment."

"You don't do throwaway comments, Addi. I know that for damn sure."

She was hiding something from him. The more he

thought about what she'd said, the more he suspected that it wasn't simply a product of the accident. Something deeper was going on.

"I was frustrated and tired and...scared." For a second all her confidence and bravado slipped away, and she looked totally vulnerable. "It's a true statement, sure. Things always change—but I didn't mean anything by it."

"You sure about that?"

"I am." She nodded. "Now you can answer a question for me. Why did you really ask me to stay back? Because it sure as hell wasn't for me to repeat the exact same thing I told you earlier today."

"Yeah, about that..." He rubbed his neck again. There was no sense in lying to her now—she'd see right through him. "I wanted to be the one to take you home."

"Logan Matthew Dane, you..." she spluttered. "Are unbelievable."

"I would have thought me doing that was very believable."

She huffed and snapped her laptop shut. "You're also *totally* unapologetic, and I don't know which is worse. What the hell would be wrong with Owen giving me a lift?"

"It's my job."

"To be my taxi driver?" She shook her head and stormed over to where her packed bags sat in a neat pile. As she bent over to stash her laptop away, he caught a flash of blue lace.

God help him. "No, to check your apartment out and make sure it's secure."

"Since when were you going to check my apartment out?"

"Well, obviously I would do that. You've had a threat on your life, Addi. We need to check everything."

"And Owen couldn't have done that? You're always telling me how he's your best consultant and we certainly pay him accordingly. Yet he's not up to the task of checking a few locks all of a sudden?"

Well, damn. What was he supposed to say to that without validating every complaint she'd voiced the other night?

"You didn't want anyone else to know what happened. And besides, I want to do it myself."

Yeah, great. That'll go down like a lead balloon.

She shook her head. "Don't feed me this crap about you wanting to do a security check yourself. I'm fully aware of what you're worried about, and, frankly, it's a little insulting. Even if he was bold enough to make a move, I wouldn't have let him."

Had he been that transparent? He must be losing his touch.

"Do you think I would sleep with you and then jump straight into bed with him?" she continued, her eyes flashing. "Out of the two of us, I'm not the one with *that* track record."

It wasn't possible for him to regret the past any more than he did right now. He'd treated her badly. Reprehensibly.

"Let me drive you home and I'll quickly check out the apartment. Then I'll be out of your hair." He picked up her bags and carried them out to the car.

He might be pushy and overprotective, but he was still her partner. Her friend. And he wasn't going to risk her safety until they knew more about who'd targeted her... and what she meant about things changing.

6

ADDISON SPENT THE duration of the ride home stewing in silence. Her life was a mess. A big, hot, crazy mess. How could she have been so stupid as to let something slip about her not always being around?

She was usually better at controlling her emotions. Now that Logan had gotten a whiff of her secret, he wouldn't let it go. He was a dog with a bone whenever he thought she was hiding something.

Logan was getting into her head and that was *not* a place he should be. They'd been at the cottage for five days and still she couldn't evict the memories of the night they'd had sex from her mind. The memories swirled, gathering steam and distracting her in quiet moments. Like in the dark when she'd lain still, trying desperately to fall asleep.

An aching hunger had gnawed at her, urging her to slip out of her room and into his bed. If it wasn't for the fact that her team was in the cottage with her, she might have.

But Logan was bad news. Bad news for her head and bad news for her heart. What had happened with Owen was a case in point. It was as if his need for control flared up the second there was a whiff of competition. It was a drug for him—he *had* to win. The whole thing was laughable. Owen was a flirt, sure. And gorgeous to boot. But he wasn't interested in her like that; they were friends. Nothing more.

"Are you going to give me the silent treatment the whole way home?" Logan asked.

They'd made it to Manhattan as the sun set. The city was a glittering disco ball around them, and Addison instantly felt safer. There were no deserted roads, and the sheer volume of people comforted her. It was home. She pressed her palm to the passenger window as they wove through the streets.

"I'll take that silence as a yes," he grumbled. "Hate me all you want, that's fine. But I'm still going to be here."

She turned to him, ready to retort, but she didn't have the energy. It was hard to stay mad at someone like Logan. You might not always agree with his behavior—and she certainly didn't—but he lived by a code. So at least he was *consistently* annoying.

The street lights flickered over his profile, etching shadows along his face. They carved out his cheekbones, the harsh angle of his jaw and his straight, perfect nose. Stubble darkened his skin and she had to fight the urge to reach out and touch it.

"You're always here. Like a grumpy shadow." She folded her arms across her chest and snuggled further down into the seat. "Like an antisocial guardian angel."

"Whatever works," he said drily. "Are you going to give me a hard time about checking out your apartment?"

"No." Her lips curved into a sly smile. "Because you're going to order me dinner as well."

"Am I?"

"It's part of the security service. The 'protection and pizza' package."

There was a lull in conversation as they got closer to her place. By the time they'd parked the car and entered her building, Addison was feeling more tired than annoyed. All she wanted was to curl up in bed and bury herself beneath the covers, pretending that she had her life under control.

The night security guard sat behind the concierge desk and Addison waved as they walked past. The man tipped his head in greeting.

"So what exactly are you going to look for upstairs?" she asked as they arrived at the elevators.

"I'll make sure no one has tampered with the locks. It might be worth taking a quick look at your computer as well. I'll have to check in with Rhys, but I've been thinking that if this guy tried to email you at work, he might have tried your personal email, too."

Shit. Her inbox had plenty of evidence that she was planning to move away from Cobalt & Dane, including a conversation with a real estate agent about a potential office space. How on earth was she going to be able to hide that from him?

After what she'd let slip earlier, she'd have to tread carefully. Logan had a nose for secrets.

"Is that necessary tonight?" She feigned a yawn. "The retreat really took the wind out of me. I just want to go to bed."

"I thought you wanted pizza?"

The elevator arrived and he motioned for her to enter ahead of him. A woman with a huge stroller took up most of the space and Addison squeezed herself into the corner to make room for Logan. With his big shoulders and her luggage, there was little room to breathe. As the elevator whooshed upward, she tried not to let herself be intoxicated by his scent. He never wore aftershave, yet he always managed to smell like wood and fresh air.

The elevator stopped and Logan moved to let the mother out. He brushed against Addison, his hand skimming the bare skin of her thigh. Goose bumps rippled across her body, and suddenly she was very much awake. She still wanted to be curled up in bed, but sleep was the last thing on her mind.

"Was that a yes or no on the pizza?" he asked as the doors slid shut, leaving them alone.

"Yes. I'm suddenly quite hungry." Seems she *hadn't* gotten him out of her system.

The air crackled like a fire, heaving with tension. She ran her palms down her dress, trying to slow the beating of her heart. But his magnetic energy was affecting her. Deeply.

"Are you hungry?" she asked.

His eyes were blackened. "Like you would not believe."

She hadn't realized they'd drifted closer to each other until the *ping* of the elevator broke them apart. He juggled the bags and walked into the hallway ahead of her. There was a tightness to his shoulders, a rigidity to his movement. It was clear Logan was also still fighting the attraction between them.

"Addison!" A voice interrupted them as they reached her door. Addison turned to see Mrs. Hollings from down the hall hurrying over. "Wait a second."

Addison stifled a groan. She didn't want to deal with

this right now. The old lady was sweet, but a total busy-body. "Yes, Mrs. Hollings?"

"I'm sorry to interrupt your…" Her birdlike eyes darted to Logan. "Date?"

"You remember Logan Dane, my business partner? He used to work for my father." She forced a smile. "What can we do for you?"

"I wanted to talk to you about something." Mrs. Hollings patted her coiffed silver hair while openly admiring Logan, who looked irritated by the whole thing.

"Go on."

"There was a man asking after you a few days ago. I thought he might have been a suitor calling on you."

Addison frowned. "What was he doing?"

"He was knocking on your door." Mrs. Hollings smiled. "Only he was knocking on the wrong door. He thought you were in the Lims' apartment. But I set him straight."

She looked so proud that Addison didn't have the heart to burst her bubble. "Did he happen to leave a message or a name?"

"No, dear. I asked him if he wanted to because I figured you would be interested. He was very attractive." She tittered.

"What did he look like?" Logan asked, his voice sharp as a gunshot in the quiet hall.

Mrs. Hollings blinked, taken aback by Logan's dark expression. "Oh, well, it was a few days ago…umm. He was tall, dark hair. Very uhhh…" Her hands fluttered at her chest. "Strong-looking."

"Thank you, Mrs. Hollings. I'll be sure to keep an eye out for him." She touched the older woman's shoulder and smiled warmly, trying to ease the worried expression on her face. "I appreciate you looking out for me."

"Oh, of course. Of course." She shuffled back down to her apartment with a wave.

"I hope she realizes she's put you in danger by divulging your address," Logan fumed. "Who does that?"

"She didn't know any better, Logan. Calm down." Addison shoved her key into the lock and opened her front door. "She thought it was a 'suitor' coming to sweep me off my feet."

Logan muttered something under his breath as he shut the door behind them. The apartment was clean and organized, exactly as she'd left it. But she wasn't greeted by the same sense of relief that she usually was upon returning home. Instead, anxious butterflies flittered around in her stomach.

"Is it possible that someone from work came by to drop something off?" she asked without holding much hope. "A tall guy with dark hair could be anyone."

Logan shook his head. "It's not anyone."

"Do you think it's him?" Her heart hammered in her rib cage. When she shut her eyes, she could see him. Well, not him exactly, but the shadowed face that had peered through the window of her car. His voice echoed in her head.

Let me in, you fucking bitch.

Logan's arms were around her and he tucked her head under his chin. "If it is…we can't take any chances. He knows your address."

"I honestly don't understand why this guy is after me."

She'd lived a fairly quiet life, and her role in Cobalt & Dane was strictly on the business side of things. Accounts, payroll, HR. Nothing to anger a dangerous person, at least not that she knew of.

"I don't know, either." His hand brushed the hair from her face. "Why don't you stay at my place tonight?"

"That's not a long-term solution."

"True, but it's late. You're tired. I sure as hell won't sleep if you're here by yourself."

Her cheek rested against the soft cotton of his shirt, the warmth from his skin seeping into her. She pressed a hand to his chest. "What about tomorrow?"

"We'll check the place out more thoroughly then. I'll talk to the building manager and we'll have a look at the security footage. I'll also call the officer who took your statement a few days ago. Hopefully he'll give me access to the gas station footage." He paused. "You'll need to stay with me for a few days, until we have a better handle on this situation."

"Is that a good idea?"

"It's a better idea than you staying here."

Neither of them mentioned the third option of a hotel room. They were in the biggest city in the country; accommodation would not be hard to come by. But the truth was Addison had been well and truly shaken up—as much as she tried not to let it show. If anyone could take care of her security, it was Logan.

So long as you don't mistake his concern over your safety for his caring about you intimately. You are not *changing your plans.*

"I can set you up in my spare room. There's space in the closet for you to hang your things and you'll have free rein of the place."

Addison wasn't sure if Logan was being gentlemanly by assuming she wouldn't want to be in his bed, or if he was drawing a line in the sand. And she wasn't sure which scenario she preferred.

"Sure." She nodded. "I'll go and pack my things."

At least if they camped out at his apartment she'd have a better chance of keeping her business plans a secret.

THE FOLLOWING DAY Logan sat in his office at the Cobalt & Dane headquarters, wondering what the hell the universe was trying to do to him. He'd spent the night tossing and turning. He'd swung from opposite ends of the emotional spectrum. Battling a desperate desire to sneak into Addison's room and reenact their sexy night together. To beating himself up for thinking about such things when he should be occupied with solving the mystery behind her stalker.

Luckily, he had something to keep his mind busy today. The building manager for Addison's apartment complex was an old friend of her father's. When Addison had moved into the place four years ago, Daniel had made it his business to ensure his little girl was well protected in her new home. Therefore, upon hearing the news that someone was targeting her, the manager had granted Logan immediate access to the security footage for her floor.

Unfortunately, the recording hadn't given him much to work with. A guy in a dark coat and a baseball cap had entered the building by tailgating another resident. Since the concierge appeared to be on patrol at the time of the incident, the man had made it straight up to Addison's floor without anyone vetting him. Logan made a mental note to talk to the building manager about that flaw. The man on the camera had then stopped at the door next to Addison's apartment, though it was difficult to tell what he was doing. Trying to pick the lock, perhaps? The footage also showed Addison's neighbor talking to the man and pointing toward Addison's door.

Logan gritted his teeth. The crazy old bat had no idea what she'd done. What kind of danger she had put Addison in. But as always, Addison had seen the good in a person whereas he'd seen the bad.

A knock interrupted his thoughts. Rhys stood in the doorway of his office. "We got another email."

Logan waved him in. "Close the door behind you. We don't need anyone else to hear about this."

The door shut with a soft *snick* and Rhys took a seat on the other side of the desk. His shoulders were bunched beneath a neat white shirt, and a groove appeared between his eyes. "Shouldn't we involve Addison in these conversations?"

"Just give me the update."

Rhys looked as though he was about to argue but instead he sighed. "The email is from the same address as last time," he said. "It contains more threats, but there was also an attachment. Apparently it's supposed to contain some 'scandalous' pictures of Addison."

Logan's fingers bit into the edge of the desk chair. "Say what?"

"The email sender claims to have nude photos of her. But the attachment looks to be an .exe file, which tells me it's probably a Trojan virus. More than likely, there are no pictures. He's saying whatever he thinks will get her to open the file."

"Why would he want her to open a virus?"

"These types of viruses are designed to grant unauthorized access to a device—in this case, Addison's computer. From there he'd be able to see her emails, watch her browse the internet. He could also skim information like credit card numbers and banking passwords. If she's using the office phone he might even be able to listen to her calls because of the VoIP connection."

Logan's blood ran cold. So this guy wasn't a garden-variety stalker…he was a hacker as well. "But he hasn't gotten access yet?"

"No, I don't believe so." Rhys shook his head. "My team ran an additional scan just in case, and there doesn't appear to be spyware or viruses on her computer or on the network."

"At least one thing has gone right," Logan muttered. "What can you tell me about this guy so far?"

"Not a lot. He's using a generic email address from an online provider. They keep their user information locked up tighter than Fort Knox, so unless we get law enforcement involved we don't have much chance of finding out who this guy is via the email information alone."

"And the chances of the police caring about some faceless person sending a virus is pretty damn slim unless we can connect it to the guy who ran Addison off the road."

Rhys's brows shot up. "Someone ran her off the road? I *thought* the story about her car breaking down seemed odd."

Shit. So much for keeping Addison's secret. "Don't you dare breathe a word of it to anyone. Anyway, all I care about now is what we're going to do next."

"We'll set up a dummy device that's configured to look like Addison's computer. I have an old laptop that will do the trick. Then we open the file in this email and give the hacker access."

"So we can monitor him?"

"Exactly. I can set the dummy up to have access to the internet, but keep it separate from our corporate files. He'll be behind the company firewall, but we'll control his access. We can put the laptop in the DMZ—"

"I don't need the tech talk, Rhys. Just tell me what happens when we give him access."

"We watch him. See what information he's looking for, then do a trace route and follow the bread crumbs. That way we should be able to locate his IP address and use that to find his computer." Rhys flattened his lips into a harsh line. "Then we hunt him down."

"Do it." Logan ran a hand through his hair and tried to stop his mind from racing. "And keep it quiet."

"What about Addison?" Rhys asked, his eyes wary.

"Don't you worry about her. I'll handle it."

The last thing he wanted was for Addison to be any more upset than she was already. He'd bring up the email once Rhys's plan was in place. At least that way she'd know they were doing something to catch this guy.

In the meantime, he wasn't letting her out of his sight.

7

ADDISON JUMPED WHEN her phone rang unexpectedly and shocked her out of her groggy state. Trying to sleep in Logan's spare bed had proved futile last night. Clearly, he didn't believe in investing in a good mattress. The thing had been about as comfortable as a concrete slab. Plus, Logan had padded around his apartment until all hours of the night, his footsteps trampling on any chance she had of slumber.

Part of her had hoped he'd sneak into her room like he had at the cottage. But the other part of her—the part that had gotten a gold star for solidarity—had willed him away. Her life was suddenly far more complicated than she wanted it to be, and the last thing she needed was Logan freaking Dane shaking up her plans.

The more she thought about starting her own company, the more she was certain it was the right move. When her father had convinced her to study business, he'd promised her a seat at the head of the company. A voice. Influence.

But what she'd been too naive to realize at the time was that someone without security expertise would always be a step behind. That her work would only be talked about if something went wrong. Really, it was a behind-the-scenes job—and she *wasn't* a behind-the-scenes kind of person.

Running her own consulting company would give her the best of both words—a way to use the skills she'd honed working for her father *and* an opportunity to sit at the head of the boardroom table. To be taken seriously.

Her phone continued to ring, but Addison couldn't muster up the energy to answer it. Eventually the call diverted to her assistant's phone, and she could hear Renee's perky greeting through the closed door.

Addison checked her email again, as she had done every five minutes for the previous eight hours. It was stupid to think she'd get a nasty message in her inbox, considering the last one had gotten caught in the filter. And Rhys hadn't come to her with any updates. But still, something wasn't right. She could feel it down in her bones.

"Addi?" Renee's voice came through the intercom on her desk phone. "I know you're busy but I've got a gentleman calling from a real estate company. I'm not sure what it's about, exactly."

She snatched the phone from the cradle. "That's okay, put him through." A second later the phone clicked. "Hello?"

"Is this Addison Cobalt?"

"Yes, it is."

"I'm Richard James from Comrade Real Estate. We've been in contact regarding a potential office space in Park Slope?"

She bit down on her lip. The consultant must have gotten her work phone number from her email signature when she'd sent a query. How could she have forgotten to delete it? Stupid, stupid, stupid.

"Yes, Richard. Thanks for your call. I am so sorry to cut you short but I can't speak right now. Would it be okay if I called you back later?"

"Of course, not a problem at all." He read out his number and Addison jotted it straight into the notes section of her phone. After a promise to call him back after she'd left the office, she ended the call.

Crap. All the calls in the office were recorded. Given the nature of their work, they often needed to revisit phone calls between consultants and clients. She had to hope that her move would be all sewn up by the time anyone looked at the call log. The last thing she needed was Logan finding out her plans.

And what will you do if you leave Cobalt & Dane and the stalker comes after you again? How will you defend yourself?

She'd have to cross that bridge when and if she came to it. No one would get in the way of her plans, and she wasn't going to live her life being afraid of every shadow. Her father wouldn't have let some wack job kill his dreams, and neither would she.

Deep down she knew her father would have been proud of her decision to start her own business, even if he'd hated the thought of her being alone in the big bad world.

Addison glanced at the photo on her desk. It was an old one with three smiling faces—father, mother and daughter—taken a few short months before her twelfth birthday. A few short months before heart failure claimed her mother and turned Addison's life upside down. Her father had quit his job as a sergeant major in the army and started Cobalt & Dane with a few ex-military friends. Except it had been only Cobalt Security back then.

Before Logan had come along and taken her place as heir to the company, planting his name alongside her father's on all their letterhead and business cards. All because she'd let her father convince her to take the "safe" route.

Well, she couldn't change the past. But she *could* change the course of her future. Could and would.

As if by some form of magic, Logan appeared in her doorway. "Time to go."

"Go where?" She looked at her phone and realized it was almost seven. How long had she been sitting here staring at the photo?

"Home. Dinner. Wherever."

He was rakishly handsome today, much to her despair. A pair of black jeans and black boots made his legs look strong and lean, while a gray sweater with a short V-neck hugged the muscles in his chest and shoulders. His light brown hair curled around his ears, too long and yet totally perfect. It was the right length to hold on to, to thread between her fingers and pull. Hard.

"Who said I was ready to leave?" She turned back to her computer, needing to look away from him before she forgot that she was supposed to be putting distance between them right now.

"I did. We're going home."

Oh right, *home*. Also known as Logan's place and her temporary prison. "Do you have to be so damn bossy all the time?"

"It's part of my charm." He grinned and she had to bite back a laugh.

"You're totally shameless." She clicked out of her

email and stood, realizing that she was not going to be shaking her sexy shadow anytime soon. And after the week she'd had so far, he was probably the lesser of two evils. "Well, I'm going to need food."

"I've got us a reservation at Maria and Bruno's, that Italian place you said looked nice last week." Renee poked her head into the office and grinned. Her assistant was determined to set Logan and Addison up. If only she knew what they'd done over the weekend. "Logan said you might want to eat out, so I took the liberty."

"That's very…proactive of you."

Renee shrugged, mischief dancing all over her expression. "It's what I do."

Addison stood and smoothed her hands down the front of her black-and-gray shift dress, aware that Logan's eyes were following her every move. Last night, when she'd thrown a few days' worth of clothes into her suitcase, she'd picked this one because she knew how much he liked it.

Two black panels hugged her sides, curving over her hips and legs, making her look tall and slender. The neckline skimmed the boundaries of appropriateness for the office—showing a little cleavage, but not too much. Walking the line between professionalism and sexiness with elegant ease. But the things that made her feel best were the black silk panties she wore underneath. They'd cost more than the dress and were twice as heavenly.

You're a goddamn glutton for punishment, Addison Marie Cobalt. You must love playing with fire.

Perhaps. But her job required her to be confident and in control. And when everything was going to hell she could always rely on her clothes to make her feel powerful. Every little bit helped.

"Fine. Let's head off. Are we driving?"

"I thought we'd walk. It's only a block or two." His eyes lowered slowly, caressing her every curve, until he reached her feet. "Unless your heels are too high."

"Never."

They walked through the office, neither one saying much until they'd made it outside. The sun hadn't yet set, so the air was balmy and pleasant on Addison's bare arms.

"Sometimes I think you choose your outfits to torture me," he said as they walked toward the restaurant.

"Spoken like a true narcissist," she said, smirking. "Not everything is about you."

The street was still busy with office workers, suited men and women bustling in all directions around them. The traffic trudged past, steady but slow. Addison dodged a woman charging past in the opposite direction.

"I suppose your dumb boyfriends might fall for those quippy lines," he said. "But I know better than that."

Her lips curled into a smile but she wouldn't give him the satisfaction of admitting he was right.

"Keep convincing yourself of that."

"Look me in the eye and tell me I'm wrong." His hand snaked around her waist as he guided her out of the path of a couple coming in the other direction. "Tell me you don't think about me when you wriggle into those tight little dresses."

She resisted the urge to melt against him, but instead concentrated on putting one foot in front of the other. Her heels clicked against the pavement. "Is it wrong to want some appreciation?"

"Not if you own it."

"Fine. I like it when you look at me." She'd gotten

hooked on his attention from the moment he'd seen her not as a child, but as a woman. "So sue me."

"How about we have a drink before things get litigious?"

They pulled up in front of the restaurant and Addison cursed Renee under her breath. The restaurant screamed "date" with its intimate tables for two and gentle candle-lit atmosphere. She was hardly going to be able to concentrate on keeping carnal thoughts from her mind in this setting.

"After you." He held the door for her.

They were seated right away, at a table tucked into the back corner of the dining area. No doubt Renee had requested it. She made a mental note to give her assistant a few "guidelines" on booking an appropriate location for a work dinner. Because that's what this was—work.

Yeah right. And you think he *needs to stop bullshitting himself.*

"This seems…" Logan scanned the room. "Cozy."

"I did not suggest this to Renee as an option for dinner. I simply said the dessert menu looked good." She shook her head. "That's what I get."

Logan appeared unconvinced, but he didn't say anything further on the matter as the waiter arrived to take their orders.

"I've arranged to have Aiden help me at your place tomorrow," he said as the waiter left. "I trust him to keep the situation under wraps. We'll do a sweep of the apartment and change the locks. You can be there to supervise, if you like."

"You're inviting me to my own house," she said drily. "How considerate."

"It has to be done this way." Logan rolled his shoulders back and she tried not to stare as the soft sweater stretched across his pecs. "So, was that a yes or a no?"

"Yes, of course I want to be there."

If she was there, she'd be able protect her plans. She could convince Logan she was perfectly capable of handing her laptop over to Rhys by herself, which would give her time to dump the files onto a USB and wipe them off her computer.

Maybe you should come clean and tell him?

Sneaking around was hard work, but she knew what Logan would say. He'd try to convince her to stay, and she didn't want to be vulnerable to his influence the way she'd been to her father's all those years ago.

Her dad hadn't wanted her anywhere near the business at first, hoping to shield her from the dark side of his world. But doing her father proud by joining the family business was the only wish she'd had as young girl. Then precious Logan had come along and taken up residence by her father's side. She should have hated him for that. She'd *wanted* to hate him on some level.

But her brain and her heart never seemed to agree where Logan was concerned.

"You got serious all of a sudden," he commented, his eyes searching her face.

"I was thinking about Dad. I can't believe it's been two years."

"Sometimes I walk into your office hoping I'll see him behind that desk." Logan's voice was almost lost under the sound of conversation from the adjacent tables. "It's like I forget he's gone, just for a moment."

"And then it all comes rushing back, doesn't it?" She swallowed at the sudden lump in her throat.

"Yeah."

Logan hadn't talked much about his feelings over losing her father, but she knew he'd taken it as hard as she had. Over the years she'd gleaned bits and pieces about Logan's past; she'd learned that he'd lost his mother like she had. That he'd left the military and that he didn't get along with his father, but she wasn't exactly sure why. If she pressed him for more details, her questions were usually silenced with a glare sharp enough to cut bone.

"Sometimes you sound just like him," Logan said. "Especially when you jam the copier and swear at it as if it can hear you."

"He hated that damn machine." She smiled at the memory.

Her father had generally been cool, calm and collected…but not when it came to technology. A self-confessed Luddite, he'd eschewed the internet when it had first come along, had refused to get a smartphone and had a tendency to break things out of frustration when he couldn't figure out how to operate them.

"I was sure I'd turn up at the office one day to find that he'd taken a baseball bat to it." The candlelight caught Logan's dark eyes, the flame reflecting in their depths.

"I'm glad I managed to inherit such great qualities from him," she said with a laugh.

"You got plenty from him, Addi. Your fiery spirit, your ability to think on your feet. And your fierce loyalty, you definitely got that from him."

Fierce loyalty. Would he still think her loyal when she up and left?

"Got that snarky quick wit from him, too," Logan added.

For a moment he looked lost. Haunted. It was an expression she saw on his face occasionally—when his mind drifted to dark things that he never wanted to talk about. Now he looked so much like that lost twenty-something boy who'd turned up at her father's office with a chip on his shoulder and a permanent scowl. She'd realized later that he was scowling at himself, not at those around him.

"I know you think I'm a pushy bastard, but I won't ever stop trying to protect you." Logan gazed at her with an intensity that made her heartbeat kick up a notch. "I sat with your dad at the hospital, watched him fade away, and I *promised* him I would keep you safe. You were more precious to him than anything in the world."

She blinked back the tears prickling her eyes. God, she missed her father so much it hurt her to breathe. People kept telling her that time would heal all wounds, but she found that grief came in waves. Like an ocean of longing and pain lapping at her—sometimes gently and other times with the ferocity of a tsunami.

"I haven't kept many promises in my life, but I won't break that one. No matter how much you hate me for it."

"I don't hate you for it," she said. "I just want to live my own life."

The urge to open up to Logan, to unburden herself of the secret, tugged at her again. But it wasn't the right thing to do. She might trust him with her body and her safety, but she certainly didn't trust him with her dreams, or her heart.

LOGAN REACHED FOR the glass of scotch that the waiter had delivered. The single ice cube bobbed in the rich amber liquid, clinking against the glass as he raised it to his lips. The smoky warmth soothed him, quieted the demons.

He had no idea why he was getting into this with Addison now, but some part of him felt the need to connect with her on a deeper level than their usual to and fro.

She took a sip of her wine. "On the upside, no further contact from my stalker."

She tried to make light but Logan cringed inwardly. Keeping the second email to himself was the right decision, at least until they had a plan in place that would make Addison feel safer.

"Call me crazy, but some days I want to be the girl who falls in love with a guy at the grocery store and then grows old with kids running around her feet." She opened her mouth as if she was about to say something else, but then she snapped it shut as their food arrived at the table.

"Why do you think you'll find Mr. Perfect at the grocery store?" he asked as he tucked into his pasta.

Addison blew on the steam curling up from her dish, her glossy lips pursing in a way that made Logan shift in his seat. Those lips had been at the center of many a fantasy of his. They were perfect—full, ripe. Naturally pink.

"I don't know." She stuck her fork into the mound of spaghetti and twirled. "Isn't that the kind of thing you see in the movies? The girl is picking out the perfect orange and then she turns and bumps into the man of her dreams. It's sweet."

"It's fiction."

"And I can't indulge my imagination? It's better than reality."

"Reality isn't all bad." At least not the reality of their night together.

Damn, it'd been so good that he couldn't go three minutes without his mind drifting into fantasyland. If only he could take Addison to bed and stay there. Forget about his job, forget about his promises. Forget about everything but the silken feel of her skin under his palms.

"Reality is complicated." She sighed. "And I don't like complicated."

Which was exactly why they'd never work as a couple. He was the definition of complicated—fucked-up family, abandonment issues and a hero complex. Not exactly a rom-com catch.

Not exactly a catch by anyone's standards.

He cleared his throat. "Me either."

"Why do we make things hard on ourselves, Logan? And I mean the royal we, as in people in general." Her tongue darted out to capture the sauce clinging to the corner of her lip. "For example, we had sex and now both of us are dancing around it like it's some big bad thing."

Logan raised a brow. "We are?"

"Yes, we are. Tell me, did you consider coming into my room last night?"

He contemplated lying, but Addison was always good at seeing through his poker face. "Yes."

"But you didn't. Why not?"

Because I'm worried that I'll fuck things up and dishonor the promise I made to your father.

A strand of golden hair had escaped her updo. It fell against her cheek, catching the candlelight and looking like spun gold. Everything about her was so perfect, so angelic. It would be wrong to inflict his messed-up life on her.

"Well?"

He sighed. "I'm trying to preserve our relationship."

"And why would sex make that difficult? Are you

planning on using me and then shacking up with someone else…again?" Her lips were pressed into a flat line.

God, if ever there was an opportunity for him to take something back, that would be it. The shock of losing Daniel had driven a crack right through him. It'd formed a gaping hole so dark and so ugly that he'd filled it the only way he knew how. With drinking and sex and running away.

Only he'd run away emotionally, rather than physically. He'd pushed Addison away—horrified that she might finally see how vulnerable he was deep down—by finding someone else to share his bed. Someone he didn't care about.

This was why he would never deserve her. No matter how many times he atoned for his sins.

"No," he said. "I won't be repeating that mistake."

"Good." She sighed. "Look, I know you're attracted to me. I'm attracted to you…why are we dancing around it so much? It's not as if I'm expecting you to give me the white picket fence dream. I know that's not you."

"Because you deserve the guy at the grocery store. You deserve the happy ending."

"That can wait. Besides, we agreed that we wouldn't get emotionally involved. No expectations, remember?"

Under the table he felt something brush his leg. Her foot was tracing a line up the inside of his pants. Was she going to take it further? Right here?

"Right now I want a different kind of ending."

Holy shit. Logan almost knocked his drink over when her foot migrated into his lap, nudging his cock until it stirred. He was hard in an instant.

"Addison," he said, his eyes darting to the table next to him. The other diners appeared to be none the wiser of their little game. "If you keep that up I'm not going to be able to get out of this restaurant without poking someone's eye out."

She continued to rub him, and his cock swelled in response. "We can slip out the back."

His mind whirred. "Out the back?"

"Into the alley."

"It's not safe, and if it *is* safe that means they'll have cameras." He shook his head, trying to separate rational thought from the part of his brain that wanted the pleasure she was offering. "I'm not sharing you with anyone."

"Boring," she teased. "You're always so sensible."

"One of us has to be." She didn't know that he was balancing on a knife's edge. "I'm not going to risk you getting mugged with your skirt up around your waist, either."

"That would be quite a story." A smile quirked on her lips. "But I bet we don't make it home before you start tearing my clothes off."

"You think I'm that weak?"

"No. I think *I'm* that good at pushing your buttons."

"Those are fighting words." He reached under the table and captured her foot. The silk stockings that covered her legs were smooth in his palm. "You want to fight me, Addison?"

"Very much so." Her eyes were wide, dark. Excitement lit her cheeks.

He rubbed his thumb over her ankle, tracing the delicate bone in circles. "What's the wager?"

"Full control for the next three days. If I win, you'll fix up my apartment and then leave me to my business unless *I* ask for your protection." She folded her hands neatly on the table. "And you have to tell everyone at work that I'm a better boss than you are."

A smile twitched on his lips. "And if I win?"

"You can boss me around as much as you like. I'll do anything you want without complaint."

Her words rocketed through him, scorching him from the inside out. "Anything?"

"Whatever your wicked heart desires."

8

ADDISON'S THUDDING HEARTBEAT filled her ears as she waited for Logan to take the bait. His hands were on her foot, rubbing her calf, while she slowly stroked his cock.

She hadn't intended to seduce him in a restaurant full of strangers when the evening started, but something about the way he'd opened up…it had gotten to her. He might not be her "grocery store guy" like in the movies, but he cared about her on some level. That much she knew. And if she wasn't expecting a happily-ever-after from him then what was the harm in indulging in a long-held fantasy? Especially if she could use it to her advantage by getting him out of her apartment.

Even last night—torn as she'd been about the way he was behaving—she knew damn well that if he'd walked through her bedroom door she would have welcomed him with open arms. Her body craved him, and so long as she kept her heart locked up, that wasn't a problem. Addison was sick of being at the mercy of Logan's whims—he wanted her, then he pulled away. Hot, cold, hot, cold.

Like a goddamn Katy Perry song.

So it was time for her to take charge.

"No expectations?" he clarified.

"Only that I'll win."

"Doubtful. I hope you know it's dangerous to give full control to a guy like me," he said. "You never know what I'll do with it."

Ain't that the truth.

"I want to take a few more risks in my life," she replied. "I'm tired of being the good girl."

His eyes narrowed. "Fine."

"Fine?"

"I accept your dare."

"Good." She reached for her wine and then drained it in one long gulp. "I just need to use the restroom before we go."

When she returned, they abandoned their half-eaten meal and Logan threw some bills onto the table. A thrill ran through Addison's body as they wove through the now-crowded restaurant. Logan's hand landed possessively at her waist, his presence radiating behind her.

Nobody gave them a second glance, and that made her all the more excited. Like they shared a secret. A naughty secret.

Addison wasn't usually the instigator of such things. The two times she'd slept with Logan it had been spontaneous, driven by some deeper emotion that had fought its way out. With other men—the few there had been—she'd let them take the lead because she'd always been a little anxious, a little unsure. But with Logan she felt powerful and sexy and fierce.

She felt safe.

He would never harm her, not physically. Even if she gave him full control. He would never push her to do something she didn't want to do. Knowing that, she could make this bet. Though she was confident she'd win.

After all, if she could get him hard as stone with just her foot, then she could bring him to his knees when all her faculties were at her disposal.

"Are you curious about what I'll make you do when I win?" he asked as they stepped out into the balmy night air.

"I don't usually spend much time pondering the impossible, but I'll indulge you this once." She smiled. "What have you got planned? Some role play? Maybe you want me to dress up and wait on you hand and foot? Or maybe you want to tie me up and tickle me mercilessly?"

His jaw twitched.

"Or *maybe*," she said, linking her arm through his and leaning in close to his ear, "you want to bend me over your knee and spank me until my ass is good and pink."

She let her lips brush the sweet spot next to his ear. As much as the teasing was meant for him, the image of her folded over his lap—his hand swatting her—made her blood fizz.

For a moment she thought she had him—his eyes squeezed shut and he exhaled a long breath through his lips. He barely moved except for the slight bob of his Adam's apple.

But Logan Dane wouldn't go down on the first blow. Anticipation skittered through her.

"I was thinking I'd get you on your knees," he said, his composure back in place. His eyes were intense, shadowed. "To start."

"Yes?" she breathed.

"You see, my filing cabinets are quite low. So you'll

need to be kneeling so you can rearrange them properly."
He burst out laughing when she glared at him. "Oh come
on, Addi. You didn't think I'd bend that easily, did you?"

"You might be laughing now, but you're at risk of
breaking a zipper." They stopped at a corner, waiting for
the pedestrian sign to change. She leaned in, pretending
to peck him on the cheek, but instead she slipped her
hand down and felt for him.

Just as she'd suspected, hard as a rock.

"A lucky guess," he muttered.

"Luck has nothing to do with it."

The sky was dark now, affording them a little more
cover. They had a good four blocks before they reached
Logan's apartment, which should be ample time for her
to work him into a frenzy. She was high on the competition. High on the idea of getting him to bow to *her*
will for once.

The lights changed and they crossed the road. "So,
of *all* the things you could possibly get me to do, your
mind went to filing? That's sad."

He chuckled and the sound rippled through her. "I
had to think of something that would calm me down.
Paperwork seemed the best option."

"I bet I could make it interesting."

"You're already going to lose one bet tonight. I'd be
wary about taking on another."

"Okay, Mr. Smarty-Pants. If you're going to be like
that, I won't play nice anymore."

She reached into the pocket on the inside of her bag
where she'd cheekily stashed her panties after returning
from the restroom back at the restaurant. Initially, her
plan had been to surprise him closer to home on a quiet
little side street and let him feel his way to that discovery.

But he was playing hard to get.

Her fingertips brushed the expensive silk and she toyed with the little ribbon that held the sides together. As they rounded a corner, she pulled the panties out and stealthily tucked them into his hand.

"What the hell?" he said, looking at her and then dropping his eyes down to his hand. "Christ, Addison. Are these what I think they are?"

"If you think they're a pair of Agent Provocateur *ouvert* panties, then you're correct." The style was her favorite, with little cutouts and fiddly ribbons that made her feel like a million bucks. "Spoiler alert, I'm wearing the matching bra."

He stuffed the panties into his pocket but not before she saw him rub the silk between his fingers and his nostrils flared. His cool was slipping.

"I figured I'd save you the trouble of getting them off. They're delicate and I didn't want you to rip them." She slipped his hand over her shoulder and turned her face up to his. "Save your teeth for me."

He swore under his breath, his arm tightening around her. "You're going to be the death of me, Cobalt."

"At least you'll die happy, *Dane*."

"Die happy and go straight to hell. Sounds about right." He grinned at her with a rakish devil-may-care expression.

It wasn't often that he looked at her that way. Since he'd barreled into her life he'd been moody and dark, any joking or teasing undercut with a current of tension. Restraint.

"If everyone got sent to hell for having great sex, then I'd be happy to go there, too. It'd be quite the party."

"So it's *great sex*, huh?"

Heat crept into her cheeks, and she hid it by resting her head against his shoulder. "What would you call it?"

"Words aren't my thing."

They crossed another road and his apartment building loomed ahead. A quiet alley was a few feet off to their right, so she took his hand and pulled him toward the shadows. "Show me then."

The alley was little more than an exit for the underground parking of one of the apartment towers on the block. On the other side was a fence that sectioned off a children's playground. It was dark, but anyone looking closely would be able to see them.

She led Logan past the parking lot entrance and into the shadows. "It's just us now."

Heart hammering, she pulled him close and wedged herself between the hard muscle of his chest and the brick building. Her hands went to his pecs, sliding up until they curled around his jaw. Rough stubble scratched her palms and she tugged him closer. The moment his lips hit hers, she was lost. Obliterated.

His tongue pushed between her teeth and he pinned her against the wall. The hard jut of his cock sent her brain into meltdown. All she wanted was to feel him inside her.

"Addi," he moaned as he ground himself against her. He yanked her leg over his hip and slid his hand up over the band of her thigh-high stocking until he cupped her bare ass.

The cool night air caressed her naked skin. She'd never done anything so wicked as this, so brazen. But it felt good to step out of her shell, to take charge of her life. To throw caution to the wind.

Logan's hand skirted her hip, his fingertips tracing

a red-hot trail to her sex. Her whole body was alight. "God, you feel good."

A car came out of the parking lot then, its headlights brushing over the alley and narrowly missing them. For a moment everything was light and then they were dropped into shadows again. For some reason, the realization that they could be caught made Addison even more excited.

"Do you know exactly what I want to do to you right now?" Logan's breath was hot against her cheek as his fingers brushed her.

"What?"

"I want to feel you come against my hand." He circled her clit, gently at first. Lightly teasing. "I want those beautiful thighs to tremble."

Her head lolled back against the brick. "Yes."

She had him right where she wanted him. Victory would taste so sweet, but she wouldn't dare interrupt him. Orgasms first, gloating second.

"I want your whole body to shake with pleasure." His teeth scraped down her neck, his fingers increasing the pressure between her legs.

"Logan," she sighed.

Her tummy fluttered, pleasure flooding through her as her sex clenched. Voices floated down the alley as a couple walked past the parking lot. She clamped a hand over her mouth but Logan didn't slow down. The couple kept walking, none the wiser to what was going on a few feet away.

"You want to play games, Addi?" His voice was as rough as the bricks behind her. Hard. Edgy. "You know I love to win."

A smile curved on her lips. "Do you?"

He stroked her in soft circles, picking up the pace as her breath hitched. She was so close her heart hammered in her chest, but he held her on edge. Balancing her pleasure so that she hovered at the entrance to nirvana—release just out of reach.

"I do and I *am*. Which is why this is going to feel even better." He slid a finger inside her, all the while grinding the heel of his palm against her sensitive clit.

White light exploded behind her eyelids and she bit into her hand to keep from crying out. The world seemed to slide from beneath her feet and she was floating. Falling. Flying.

Her knees shook but he held her up, allowing her to loop her arms around his neck while she found her strength.

"I guess I can order you to carry me home now?" she said, her eyes fluttering open.

"Wrong." He pressed his lips to her forehead. "We're walking to my place now and then I'll be ready to claim my prize."

"You've already lost." She straightened and tugged her skirt down, fiddling with the bands of her stockings.

"No, I haven't. The bet was whether or not we'd make it home without me tearing your clothes off." He grinned. "And luckily for me you removed the one piece of clothing that I needed off."

Her mouth fell open, but her brain was too lust-addled to form a comeback.

"I would say the pleasure's all mine, but I don't think that's the case." He grabbed her hand and pulled her away from the wall. "Come on, time's a-wasting. I'm ready to start bossing you around."

IF SHE WANTED to start taking more risks, then it was better that she take them with him rather than with someone who might not have her best interests at heart. At least that's what Logan was telling himself. Because really, did bringing her to orgasm in a city alleyway count as looking out for her best interests?

"If I had known you were such a cheater I wouldn't have made the bet with you," she said, huffing as they walked onto the street.

The sound of her heels clicking against the pavement made his blood thrum. "Don't be mad at me. You were the one who didn't think the bet through."

"'Tearing someone's clothes off' is a figurative term." She narrowed her eyes at him. "I simply meant that you wouldn't be able to keep your hands off me."

"Then you should have said that. I'm a literal guy."

"You're something, all right," she muttered.

Bringing her pleasure made him feel as powerful as a god. At the same time, he swallowed down the burgeoning guilt as it climbed up his throat, threatening to strangle him if he wasn't careful. He wouldn't hurt Addison as he'd done before by running away the morning after.

He would need to process their situation, roll it over in his mind so that he could rationalize his behavior.

But he wouldn't inflict that kind of pain on her again.

And you believe tomorrow you'll both go on your merry ways as if nothing happened? You've been thinking about her constantly since the weekend. That won't change.

Maybe not. But nothing—with the exception of her putting on the brakes—would stop him from having her now. Not guilt, not the ghosts of his past. Not his own fucked-up issues.

He wanted her. And for the first time, he was going to let himself revel in having her.

They arrived at his building and he pulled his key card out of his wallet. "You know my prize kicks in the second I walk through those doors." He reached for her hand. "And I've been walking for four blocks with a very stiff cock because of you."

The annoyance slipped from her features, replaced by vulnerability and naked excitement that lit up her dark eyes. "Are you going to punish me?"

"You're going to enjoy it. So I'm not certain it can be classed as punishment."

"Well," she said, plucking the key card out of his hand, "we'd better get inside, then."

"Does this mean you're going to be a gracious loser?" he asked as they walked through the quiet foyer.

"Hardly."

The man behind the security desk gave them a brisk nod, but Logan didn't miss the way the other man's eyes lingered on Addison. Instinctively, he slipped an arm around her shoulder and pulled her close. He wasn't sure what the caveman-style display said about him—not likely anything positive.

So what else is new?

She stayed close to him as they rode the elevator up, her fingers interlaced with his and her thumb stroking the ridges of his knuckles. The sensation made his chest clench. They'd been here before.

When her father had died, they'd sat together outside the hospital room. Holding hands. Silent. She didn't cry—rather, she'd sat like a statue, shock freezing her body. He'd touched her in this same way, a gentle brush of his thumb over her knuckles. A small movement, private. Meant to comfort.

Then he'd blown it all to hell by treating her like shit.

"Addi?" He leaned his head against hers his mind scrambling for the right words to say.

"Yeah?"

The feeling was there, the desire to tell her that he was sorry. But the words clogged his throat. God, he sucked at the personal stuff.

He swallowed. "I hope you're prepared for an ass-swatting."

"I'm all yours for the next few days, so do with me what you will." A tremor ran through her. "Just don't hurt me too bad, okay?"

"Addi, my aim is to make you feel good."

I never mean to hurt you.

The elevator dinged and they walked down the corridor toward his apartment. "I want to make you feel good, too," she said quietly.

"You do, baby. No doubt about that."

He dug his key out, fumbling with it as he tried to open the door. What the hell was wrong with him? He was nervous all of a sudden. Anxious at the thought of what would happen once he got her inside his apartment. Desperate to get his hands on her again.

Finally, he got the door open. If Addison noticed his nerves she didn't say anything. But Logan could practically taste the excitement fizzing on his tongue. He held the door for her and she walked past, her hands trailing across his thighs. Skirting the bulge in his pants.

"You're such a tease," he said.

She lifted a delicate shoulder as she discarded her bag. "Where do you want me?"

"So it's like that, is it? Straight down to business."

"I figured you wouldn't want to waste time."

She stood in front of him, a few blond hairs escaping her neat updo. They were the only sign of their "detour" on the way home. The rest of her was polished and poised, as always. He stuck his hand into his pocket and pulled out the panties. When she'd given them to him before, he'd only felt the silk and ribbons.

But now, in the privacy of his apartment, he could take his time to appreciate them. The panties were black—a mixture of high-quality silk, bound with ribbons and a slight frill that would have curved around her ass. Strategic cutouts were designed to show as much as they concealed. Teasing without giving away the goods entirely.

"I can't wait to see what the rest of this set looks like." He closed the distance between them and her breath stuttered in the quiet.

"Can I show you?" Her hands went to the zipper that ran down the side of her body, but he stopped her.

"No. That's my job."

He drew the zipper down slowly, letting the dress gape open to reveal a hint of black silk at her bust. The stark contrast with her fair skin made his blood pulse hotter. She shrugged out of the dress and it pooled at her feet. Holding her hand, he helped her step out of the fabric.

Logan let out a long, low whistle of appreciation. "Christ, Addison."

Her lips twitched. "You like?"

His gaze swept over her, drinking in the bare skin and black finery. Sheer black stockings stopped midthigh, capped with thick bands of lace. The pencil-thin heels made her look even taller and leaner. And the bra—if you could even call it that—forced her breasts up and out, the creamy mounds all but spilling over the tiny, semisheer cups.

"'Like' doesn't even begin to describe it." He smoothed his palms up and down her waist, his hands flaring out over her naked hips. "Turn around."

She obeyed. Her ass was round and ripe as a peach, perfectly pale and unmarked.

Not for long.

"Put your hands on the couch." His voice didn't sound as though it belonged to him anymore; he was in a dream state. "Spread your legs."

She moved into position, bracing herself on the back of the couch. God, she looked so beautiful laid out like that. Blood rushed in his ears, his body primed and very ready for her.

"You've got me so wound up," he said. "I want to be inside you so bad I can barely see straight."

"Then do it." She gazed back at him over her shoulder. "I'm all yours."

He drew a fingertip down the length of her spine and she bit her bottom lip. Her strangled moan sent a surge of lust through him.

"Say it again," he growled.

Goose bumps rippled across her, peppering her perfect white skin. Her lips parted. "I'm all yours," she whispered.

If only that was true. For now, he would have to forget the past, forget his promises. Forget everything but how much he wanted her. And how good he was going to make her feel.

9

ADDISON SHIFTED IN her heels, the silence unnerving her. Why was Logan hesitating? Was he going to pull away and leave her hanging? Her stream of questions was cut short when a soft hand landed on her hip.

"I've got you for three days. Three whole fucking days, and I want to take full advantage." His lips pressed against her spine and he slowly kissed his way down it until he stopped above her backside. "What do you say if you want me to stop?"

"I won't," she breathed. "I won't want you to stop."

"What do you say, Addi? Pick a word." He stilled. "I'm not giving you anything until I hear it."

She wanted to squeeze her thighs together, anything to stop the throbbing. Anything to get some friction. "Paperwork," she said, grinning into the fabric of his couch. "That's my word."

Behind her, a deep, throaty laugh rumbled. "That *will* make me stop in my tracks."

Before she could come up with a retort, his hands were between her legs, smoothing up and down the inside of her thighs. Tracing her. Learning her. They brushed high, but not high enough. The throbbing intensified.

She shut her eyes and silently begged for him to take the next step. The buildup would bury her if she didn't get what she needed soon. But Logan was stringing things out, relishing his power over her. The sound of a zipper being drawn down ratcheted up her heartbeat. Something soft hit the floor. Yes, yes, *yes*.

His palm came down onto her ass with a sharp *crack*. "Oh!" The cry flew out of her mouth before she could stop it. After all that waiting, she hadn't been sure what to expect.

A gentle touch followed, his hand rubbing the stinging spot in circles. Soothing. Preparing. Warmth radiated through her, the sharp pain fading quickly. Another swat followed on the other cheek, and her body jolted.

"You're pink already," he said, his voice strained. "So pretty and pink."

Another hand came down. Addison's whole body hummed in response, delicious heat flaring in her like a struck match. *Smack, smack, smack!* Her sex ached for him; it clenched with each hit. His hands smoothed over her, helping to spread the tingling throughout her body.

"I can't wait anymore." His hands left her and a moment later she heard foil tearing.

Then he spun her around, picked her up and planted her on the back of the couch. When he finally pushed inside her it was sweet relief. She arched, tilting her hips to let him go as deep as possible. Pain flared as his fingers bit into her tender backside, holding her firm while he thrust into her.

"So tight." He pressed his face against her hair. "So soft."

Addison wrapped her legs around his waist and her arms around his neck, clinging to him like she was falling and he was the hand that could save her. In that moment he was the only thing tethering her to earth. The only thing she cared for.

"You make me crazy," he muttered as he brought his lips to hers. Peppering kisses all over her.

"You *are* crazy," she panted.

Her head lolled back, but he fisted his hand in her hair and yanked her face up, crushing his lips down to hers. His tongue drove its way into her mouth and she moaned into him. Every one of her senses was overloaded—from the warmth on her skin to the sound of his labored breath as he thrust into her. The scent of sweat and something uniquely him. The taste of scotch on his lips. She wanted to absorb it all.

"Only when I'm with you." He palmed her breast through her bra, rolling her nipple between his thumb and forefinger until she writhed in pleasure. "Always when I'm with you."

The words pushed her closer to the edge. In his arms she felt as though she mattered, as though they were equals. Her whole body clenched as he increased the pace, practically lifting her off the couch while he slammed into her.

"I'm so close." She ground the words out. "Please, Logan. Please."

Their bodies were mashed together, tight and hot. Slick with perspiration. He angled her back to increase the friction and a moment later she exploded with sweet release. Her muscles clamped down on him and he followed her over the edge, saying her name over and over like a prayer.

SOMETIME LATER, AFTER they'd showered and gotten lost in each other again, they sat on Logan's balcony. Addison had raided his freezer and found an unopened pint of Ben & Jerry's Cherry Garcia, which she'd claimed. She dug her spoon into the chunky dessert and popped some into her mouth.

"You never struck me as an ice cream guy," she said, licking the spoon clean. "Especially not chocolate cherry flavored."

"It's yours, remember?" He interlaced his fingers behind his head and stretched back. "We were working on a board presentation a few months ago. You said my cupboards made you sad."

"And you never opened it? Geez, ice cream doesn't last longer than a day or two in my freezer." She chuckled. "I guess some girls want to leave a toothbrush and I just want something sweet."

"You've always had a thing for sweets. Remember that time we went to Magnolia Bakery? You begged me to go because you'd heard the older girls at school talking about when they'd seen it on *Sex and the City*."

"And Dad wouldn't let me watch it. I was so mad at him." She sucked on her spoon. "But then you took me there and bought every little cake that I pointed at."

The memory made her smile. Gruff twentysomething Logan in his combat boots, shoulder-length hair and all-black outfit and a sheltered, seventeen-year-old Addison who still hadn't grown out of her pink phase. What a strange pair they'd made. Eventually she'd grown up and he'd mellowed out until they found a middle ground. But he'd looked out for her from the beginning, even if it was only to smooth over her teenage drama with her dad.

"I've never seen such a small person devour so much

cake in all my life. I think I blew half my paycheck on that trip."

"Worth it. That was some damn tasty cake."

Addison closed her eyes and let the cool breeze brush over her skin. The warm weather was gathering steam and soon the city would turn into an oppressive, sticky mess like it did every summer. They probably only had another week or two before it hit.

"We should get to bed," Logan said, looking down at his watch. "I want to get an early start tomorrow so we can knock off after lunch and check out your apartment."

"Can't I just sit here and pretend everything is normal?" Her eyes scanned the glittering skyline.

Sometimes Addison would sit on her own balcony and wonder about all the people scurrying through the city, small as ants, while she sat and watched from above. Who were they? What were they doing? Where were they going? It made her feel small, but in a good way. Like her issues were only a speck of dust.

"Everything will *be* normal, once we figure out who this guy is. But until then, we can't ignore reality." He stood and held a hand out to her. "Come on, I'll even let you pick which side of the bed you want."

"Is that your way of asking me to stay with you tonight?" She slipped her hand into his, relishing his strength as he hoisted her to her feet.

"I'm not asking, Addi. I'm telling. Remember our deal?" He motioned for her to walk ahead of him. "Now get that precious ass inside before I get the idea to spank you again."

THE NEXT MORNING Logan woke early. He wasn't used to sharing his bed, nor to being woken up in the middle of the night by wandering hands and muffled sleep-talking. But stroking Addison's hair until she'd calmed enough to fall into a deeper slumber had dislodged something in his chest. Almost as if a piece of the wall around his heart had broken away.

And what good will that piece do floating around in your chest? It'll carve you up.

He'd dressed quietly, taking only a moment to watch the goddess in his bed. Her blond hair had spilled over his navy sheets, and a pale hand hung over the edge of the mattress while she slept facedown on his pillow. She had taken up the whole bed, her limbs stretched out like a starfish.

They'd both grown up as only children, so sharing wasn't something that came naturally to either of them. But he liked that about her. She wasn't afraid to make her presence known; she didn't shrink into a corner or stand at the edge of a crowd.

Addison was nobody's wallflower.

Unable to bring himself to wake her, he slipped out. The fresh air would do him good before he started his workday, and he didn't know if Addi needed a coffee first thing. She'd made one at the cottage. Better, in his mind, to burn a few dollars on a drink she may not want than potentially face the wrath of an uncaffeinated woman.

He walked back from his favorite coffee spot with a latte for her and an Americano for him. The city was starting to wake. People filtered out of their homes onto the tree-lined street, dressed in suits and all manner of fashionable things. Despite growing up in such a cosmopolitan city, Logan had little time for fashion…unless it was related to Addison's lacy underthings.

A wave of lust washed over him. Last night he'd let

himself go in a way that was truly foreign. He'd been unable to hold back. Unable to rein in his passion and desire. The fact that she'd trusted him enough to hand him the keys to the kingdom unsettled him to his core. He didn't deserve it.

But now he'd tasted the forbidden fruit and he was hungry for more.

A woman exiting his building held the door for him and he nodded to her with a quick smile. He'd lived in this building for four years and he didn't have a relationship with a single one of his neighbors. He knew plenty *about* them, as any good security guy would from general observation. But that was how he lived his life—with a divide between him and the people around him.

He juggled the two coffees in one hand while he unlocked the door, almost walking smack into Addison. "Leaving without me?"

"Oh, I thought you'd already left." She shook her head, her hand fluttering up to the pearls sitting along the neckline of her sleek emerald-green dress.

He swallowed past the lump that sat like a boulder in his throat. *Of course* she'd assumed he would walk out without saying goodbye. "Here, I got you a coffee."

"Thanks." They stood awkwardly in the middle of his apartment, neither one ready to make the first move.

In the light of day, they were unsure where things stood. Did she want to continue with the bet? Or had she changed her mind now that the lust-frenzied moment was over? Should he mention it or let it go?

Grow some balls, will you? It's like you've never spoken to a woman before.

He cleared his throat. "You look very nice."

To his surprise, a hearty chuckle bubbled out of her.

"Logan." She pressed a hand to his chest. "We don't have to pretend that we're dating. So cut the crap with the niceties, okay?"

"Fine. Is our bet still on?" He sipped his drink, silently giving himself a point for the faint blush that fanned out over her cheeks.

"I don't renege on a bet, no matter how unscrupulous my competitor."

"Then take off your panties."

She sucked on the inside of her cheek for a moment before placing her coffee and purse down on the table and reaching under her dress. Her hips wriggled as she dragged a scrap of lace down her thighs. He wasn't even sure a piece of material so small counted as underwear.

"Where do you want them?" She held them up with one finger, her direct expression daring him to balk.

"I don't care where you leave them, so long as they don't come to the office with you. I want to spend all day knowing there's nothing but a breeze under that pretty dress of yours."

"Your wish is my command." She dropped the thong onto the floor right where she stood. "Shall we go?"

She picked up her coffee and purse, shooting him a smug expression as she walked past him to the front door. "That bulge might be a bit of a problem in the office."

He didn't give her the satisfaction of looking down to what he already could feel was a rock-hard erection. "My bulge, my problem."

"Whatever you say, *Master*."

They walked to work in relative silence, but they didn't bother to enter the building separately. It wasn't unusual for them to arrive around the same time, so none of the staff members looked at them strangely. But Logan felt a prickle of unease under his skin. His life had been upended by Addison and her games.

And he was adding gas to the fire by bringing the teasing out into broad daylight.

"Good morning, Logan." His assistant, Emily, smiled up at him as he walked past.

Logan nodded briskly. The games could wait. He would not let his employees see that anything was going on between him and Addison.

"Rhys was here a moment ago looking for you. He said it had something to do with what you talked about yesterday," she said, cocking her eyebrow. "Very cryptic. Your calendar is clear until nine thirty if you want to catch him before your one-on-one with Owen. Rhys said he would be at the café downstairs."

Logan didn't even bother to check his emails before he turned tail and headed back the way he'd come. If there was an update on Addison's stalker, he wanted to know about it immediately.

As Emily had said, he found Rhys in the back corner table in the Brunswick Café, a regular haunt for Cobalt & Dane's employees.

"I hear you wanted to see me," Logan said, taking the seat across from Rhys. "I'm hoping you've got news."

"I do." Rhys sipped on a tall black coffee. "It might not be exactly what you want to hear, but we have some progress."

"Talk me through it." Logan leaned back in his chair. "In English, if possible."

Rhys smiled. "All right, boss, I'll dumb it down for you."

Logan grunted. "Watch it."

"So, after our chat yesterday we created a fake pro-file and email account for Addison and loaded it onto the dummy device. Then we enabled the virus by opening the attachment in the email. I had Quinn monitor the ac-tivity overnight, and yes—" he held up a hand "—before you ask, I told Quinn to not to talk about it. Despite the fact that I completely disagree with you keeping Addi-son in the dark."

"I appreciate that."

Rhys shook his head, but didn't argue. "The bad news is that our stalker figured out pretty quickly that it was a dummy account. We didn't have time to create fake content and files to keep him hunting around."

"Okay, so what *did* you find out?"

"Well, he's smart enough to use a proxy server to hide his location. So he might not be a tech genius, but he knows enough to cover his tracks, to some extent. How-ever, we may have found something in the Trojan itself."

"Inside the virus?"

"Well, in the code. Quinn decompiled it so she could see if there was anything hidden inside that might point to the identity of either the hacker or, at the very least, to the person who wrote the code. Often these people will hide messages or signatures, kind of like how an artist might sign a painting."

"They're *not* artists," Logan said, his lip curling at thought of this guy plotting to harm Addison behind the safety of his computer screen.

"Well, they kind of are. Not all of this kind of code is bad. Sometimes it's used for penetration testing. We use a similar code to—"

Logan held up a hand. "Can we focus on the impor-tant stuff?"

"Right." Rhys nodded. "We found the name DaZetta1 in the code. I have no idea if this is our guy or just the person who made the Trojan, but it's something. I've got Quinn going through a few popular hacking forums to see if we can figure out who DaZetta1 is. As soon as I have more information, I'll let you know."

"Well done. I appreciate your work on this."

"Does this mean I'm back in the good books?" he asked drily.

A smile tugged at Logan's lips. Rhys had gotten himself in hot water a few months ago by sleeping with the employee of one of their clients. In some companies, it would have gotten him fired. But Logan knew loyalty when he saw it, and Rhys had the heart of a lion. Still, all Logan's employees were aware that if they crossed a line they'd be made to pay their penance.

And how are you paying your penance? What the hell would Daniel say if he knew what you'd done with Addison?

He swallowed his worries and pushed up from his chair. "Help me catch this fucker and then we'll talk."

10

ADDISON STOOD INSIDE the elevator, tapping her Louboutin heels impatiently while she watched the floor numbers count down. Her phone had rung twice during her last meeting and she knew it was the real estate agent calling about the office space.

With everything that'd happened last night, she'd forgotten to call the guy back. However, succumbing to a night of passion with Logan didn't mean her plans had changed. She *would* strike out on her own and she didn't want to do it working at her kitchen table or in a coffee shop. If people were going to take her seriously for once in her life, she needed to look the part. And that meant having a place of business.

Besides, she'd already decided to poach two of her staff members: one of her bright young recruits from the communications team and her HR manager. The three of them would make a fabulous team, and Addison couldn't do it all on her own. Hopefully they trusted her enough to make the leap from an established company to a start-up.

The elevator pinged as it arrived at the ground floor

and Addison quickly made her way through the foyer and out into the sunshine. The sun was high in the sky, the air starting to thicken with humidity. She found the missed call and dialed the number back.

"Hi, Richard, this is Addison. I'm sorry I didn't have the chance to call you back yesterday." She stood out of the way of the afternoon crowd, watching the city hustle and bustle right before her eyes.

"That's no problem at all," Richard said. "Is now a good time to talk?"

"Yes, absolutely."

Richard rattled off the details of the office space that was going to be available for viewing next week. Eight hundred square feet with one glass-walled office and room for a few desks in the main area. It shared a bathroom with one other business on the second floor. Close to the subway. Lots of natural light.

"It sounds perfect." Addison felt a flutter in her stomach. "It's exactly what I'm looking for."

"I can take you through it next Wednesday. The owner is in the process of clearing out his furniture as we speak."

"That's great." They arranged a time, and Addison put the meeting into her work calendar from her phone, being sure to mark it private so that Renee wouldn't be able to see it.

"What sort of business are you opening up?" Richard asked. "I have to double-check. The building owner is fairly conservative and has final say over all the tenants who move in, and I don't want anything to trip us up."

"It'll be a communications and corporate culture consulting company. We'll be helping small businesses manage their internal communications and staff development programs so they keep their best employees and attract the right candidates."

"Ah, okay." The *click-clack* of a computer keyboard sounded in the background. "I don't expect any issues with that."

"Perfect."

"The owner will also need to see your financials to make sure you can cover the first few months' rent. Do you have a statement you can send me?"

"I can get that information, but I'd prefer to look at the place before I hand any of my details over." She might not be a security expert, but she'd learned a thing or two, especially when it came to preventing identity theft and fraud.

"Sure, that's fine. I'll see you next week."

Addison ended the call and held her phone to her chest. This was really happening. Soon she'd be her own boss, a *real* boss. The idea of being totally independent thrilled her. Cobalt & Dane had been her whole working life to date, and while it would be hard to leave behind the company her father had started from nothing, she'd never feel like she'd be truly in charge of her own destiny until she did the same thing.

A breeze brushed along her legs, lifting the edge of her skirt. She suddenly remembered that she wasn't wearing any panties per Logan's order. Fisting the green fabric in one hand, she kept the dress pulled tight around her thighs. Guilt and excitement twisted in her stomach, wrapping around each other until she couldn't tell the two feelings apart.

Logan would be shocked to learn of her plans to leave. The company was everything to him, and he probably assumed it was everything to her, too. That shock could very well turn into anger when he found out that she planned on taking two staff members with her. He held loyalty in such high regard that he'd probably take the poaching personally.

It's not personal, it's business.

Leaving Cobalt & Dane was about her, not him. And she wouldn't be one of those women who feared chasing her dreams out of worry that people might not like her. If he took it as a personal attack, then that would be on him. She couldn't be held responsible for his feelings.

"What are you doing out here?" Logan's voice cut through the rush of traffic and people.

He walked toward her with Owen, the two men looking handsome as ever in their work outfits. They were quite the duo. Owen the ladies' man and Logan the heartbreaker.

No, he did not break your heart. He taught you a valuable lesson: that you shouldn't want relationships with men who have hero complexes.

"The office was getting a little stuffy," she replied, painting on a false smile. "I wanted some air."

"Good timing. We were coming back to collect you." Logan stopped in front of her, his closeness sending a thrill through her veins. "We're going to check out your apartment."

"Oh, goodie." Addison rolled her eyes.

"Don't argue." He leaned in closer. "Remember, you're mine for the next three days."

"How could I forget?" She tried to say it sarcastically but her body wasn't playing along. A warm flush spread up through her cheeks and she shifted on the spot.

"You're holding that dress pretty tight." He said with a glint in his eye. "Windy day?"

Part of her wanted to be annoyed at him for taking

advantage of his win. But if she'd come out victorious, she'd be using it against him all she could. They were two peas in a pod like that—competitive, fiercely so.

"Nothing I can't handle."

Owen raised a brow, barely stifling his smirk as he pretended not to notice the tension. It surprised her that Logan would flirt with her in front of Owen, but perhaps he was sending a message. Making sure his subordinate knew to keep his distance.

Ugh. She was no one's property.

"Owen, are you helping us out?" she asked, sending him a dazzling smile.

"You got it. We'll make sure your place is safe and sound." He raked a hand through his sandy hair.

"Excellent. I feel safer already."

She turned and walked back toward the building and Logan quickly caught up with her. "So you don't have a problem with Owen looking out for you, but when I do it I'm a monster?"

"More like a thorn in my side." Another breeze whooshed past and Addison kept her hands down by her sides, ready to hold her dress in place.

"What's the difference?"

"Owen would back off if I asked him to." She walked through the main doors to the Cobalt & Dane building. "You, on the other hand, are relentless and pushy."

"I happen to consider those two of my best qualities."

"And I'm sure one day you'll find a woman who appreciates an overbearing protector. But until that time, I'd appreciate some say in what goes on in my life."

THE WORDS HIT Logan square in the chest. Addison expected him to move on from her, to pursue other women as he'd done before. She assumed she wasn't the right woman for him. Or perhaps she thought they were incompatible on some basal level. And why should she think any differently? He'd said as much to her a few days ago and he'd given no indication that he'd changed his mind. But now, as he felt her slipping through his fingers, it made him want to hold on tighter…which was the very thing she was rallying against.

The thought bounced around in his head like a Ping-Pong ball. Of course he didn't want to lose her. She'd been part of his life since the moment she'd welcomed him into her home when his own family had abandoned him. She'd slipped her small teenage girl hand into his and dragged him through her front door. She'd squeezed an extra portion out of their meal for two and had given up her roast potatoes when he'd cleared his plate in record time. From day one, she'd made sure he knew he belonged.

But she was finally sick of his bullshit.

"I'll back off after my three days are up," he mumbled, raking a hand through his hair. "But right now, we need to check your apartment out."

"I know. And don't worry, I'm not going to ask you to change," she said. "I'm smart enough to realize you won't."

Owen caught up to them at the elevators and said something funny to Addison. The tinkling sound of her laugh was rattling around in Logan's head. He'd invited Owen along because he was trying to prove a point—that he wasn't threatened. That her safety came first.

But now he regretted that decision. They'd have to search through Addison's things to make sure that no one had managed to break in and bug her place. It felt wrong to have Owen do that, but if Logan changed his mind he'd have to face more questions—from both of them—that he wasn't ready to answer.

"I'm going to grab my things and I'll meet you out front in a few minutes, okay?" Addison didn't wait for a response and Logan watched the swish of her green dress as she walked away. Knowing there was nothing beneath the silk fabric was driving him insane.

"Is everything okay between you two?" Owen asked as they waited in the Cobalt & Dane reception area.

"Sure, why?"

Owen shrugged. "Sometimes I can't figure out if you want to kill each other or tear each other's clothes off."

In spite of himself, Logan let out a sharp laugh. "It's complicated."

"There's something more to this security issue, isn't there?"

Logan glanced around the space, making sure there were no prying eyes or sneaky ears in the immediate vicinity. "Yeah, there is. We didn't want to worry the team, but we have reason to believe that Addison has a stalker, and he's tampered with her apartment."

"Shit." Owen shook his head. "I'm happy to help out in any way I can."

"Good. The first thing you can do is keep that information to yourself."

"Done."

By the time they made it to Addison's apartment, she was jumpy as all hell. He tried to ease her nerves by joking around, but she was having none of it. The three of them rode the elevator up to her apartment in awkward silence. A crease had formed between her brows as she stared at the numbers climbing up on the small screen. No wonder Owen couldn't work out whether they wanted to kill each other or tear each other's clothes off—they had this crazy push and pull of attraction that made even Logan's head spin.

What was he supposed to do? This was a very real threat to her safety. Perhaps it was unwise to withhold the information about the second email from her. But he'd tell her about it once Rhys had more information. She was stressed enough as it was, and telling her that they'd found a hacker's pseudonym wouldn't put her mind at ease.

The elevator dinged and they filed out into the hallway. When Addison stopped at her front door, keys in hand, Logan spotted something on the floor.

"Wait," he said as he bent down to scoop it up. A white envelope had been partially slipped under the door. No name or any other identifying information was on the paper.

"Don't say you're going to start opening my mail, too?" Addison held her hand out.

"Of course not, but open it slowly. We don't know what's inside." He felt over the envelope before giving it up. There didn't appear to be anything inside except for paper.

She slipped her thumb under the seal and opened it. Blood rushed in Logan's ears as she pulled a single sheet of paper out. It could be anything—a notice from building management, a request from a neighbor. But his gut told him it was something far more sinister than that.

He resisted the urge to take the paper from her as her face paled. "What does it say?"

"An eye for an eye." Her voice was small, shaky. "It says that Dad took something from them and now they're going to take something from me."

"They?"

"There's no name or signature." She drew a breath and turned the note around so they could read it. Basic white paper, Times New Roman font. Nothing that could possibly tell them a goddamn thing about the sender.

"We'll figure this out," Owen said, placing a hand on her shoulder. "You've got the best security company in the world at your disposal."

"That's very reassuring." She tried to smile but it didn't quite reach her eyes.

"Come on, let's do the inspection." Logan nodded toward the door. "I'll talk to building management when we're done and check out the camera footage again."

Addison unlocked her front door and they entered her apartment. Sunlight streamed in from the windows that ran the length of the main room, the light bouncing off her pristine white furniture. It was hard to believe anything sinister would happen in a space that looked more like a magazine spread than a home.

"Owen, you examine the front door and see if the lock has been tampered with, while Addison and I start from the back rooms. We'll meet in the middle."

"Sure thing." Owen got to work and Logan motioned for Addison to follow him.

"What are we looking for?" Her hands knotted in front of her.

"Any signs of tampering with the locks on your doors or windows. It's unlikely anyone would be able to get in via the balcony, since we're quite high up. But I've seen stranger things. Then we'll check for monitoring or surveillance devices." He paused outside her bedroom door. "Rhys also gave me a program to install on your laptop which will run a scan for any viruses and give him access to monitor your device until we figure out what's going on."

"What do you mean he's going to monitor my personal computer?" Her eyes narrowed. "Didn't either of you think to consult me on this?"

"If this person tried to contact you through your work email—where there's likely to be some high-grade security—it stands to reason he might have tried your personal computer, too. We've talked about this."

"But I haven't received any strange emails on my personal computer."

"It's no big deal, Addi. We won't be reading your diary or anything."

She gritted her teeth. "You don't get it. How can you agree to these things on my behalf without consulting me first?"

"Because I'm doing my job, like I would with any other client."

"I am *not* your client." Her dark eyes flashed.

"The only reason you would be so pissed about this— especially after the note left on your doorstep—was if you were worried about us finding something on your computer." He leaned against the door frame at the entrance of her bedroom, the uneasy feeling returning. Addison treasured her independence, sure, but she also understood what evil they faced in the world. There was only one reason she'd be getting *this* upset about a routine computer scan. "What are you hiding?"

"Nothing." Her face was pale, drawn. "Is it so inconceivable that I want my private life kept private?"

In Logan's experience, the people who were overly concerned with privacy were the ones who had skeletons in their closets. "It's not inconceivable, but your privacy is the lesser concern right now."

"Fine. I'll fire the laptop up while you do whatever—" she waved her hand in the air "—you need to do. Then we can go to the store and buy a baby monitor so you can keep an eye on me overnight."

He sighed as she walked off, her heels loud in the quiet apartment. Something was up with Addison; the certainty of it dug deep in his gut. She'd always battled with her overprotective father for her independence—and then against him more recently. But this time there was a real and ongoing threat to her safety. And yet she refused to accept it, which combined with what she'd said at the cottage made him suspicious. She might not like the way he went about things, but he would get to the bottom of this mystery—both who was after her and what she was hiding.

11

ADDISON'S HEART AND head pounded in unison. If Rhys got access to her computer, all the documents she'd been working on—business plans, budget spreadsheets and research—would be at his fingertips. And if she knew anything for certain, it was that Rhys's loyalty lay with Logan.

She couldn't have either of them finding out her plans until she was ready to put them into action. Until everything was set up so they couldn't talk her out of it.

Addison found her laptop sitting on the pristine white coffee table. She dropped down onto the couch in preparation for damage control. The best she could do was hide the files and hope that they would simply monitor the computer rather than snoop around on it.

She made her planning folder invisible and dragged all the relevant emails from her inbox into a folder called "Online Shopping." No man would venture there, surely. It wasn't perfect, but it would have to do.

A few moments later, Logan reappeared. "Hey, is the laptop all booted up?"

"Yeah. It's all yours." She pushed it toward him and leaned back into the couch. "Will it take long?"

"No, it should only take a few minutes. Why? You got somewhere else to be?" He said it in a way that diverted her attention from all the security drama and funneled it into the dirty section of her imagination.

Why did he have to be so goddamn addictive? She couldn't seem to go an hour without thinking about how much she wanted him. Even with all his annoying habits.

"Maybe," she said cryptically.

"Have you forgotten our deal?" He'd plugged a USB into her laptop and was installing Rhys's program as though they weren't talking about a sex game within earshot of their employee.

"No, I have not."

"So you're reneging" He didn't look up.

"I don't renege"

"Good. Because we've got plans tonight."

She rolled her eyes. "Want to clue me in on what they might be?"

"We're going to find out what 'an eye for an eye' means."

"I know what it means."

"Not in this context. Unless you're keeping something from me?" He glanced up from the laptop. "Are you?"

"Of course not," she huffed. "Besides, you know everything about my life so I doubt something that big would have slipped past your eagle eyes."

"We'll talk about my eagle eyes later," Logan said under his breath as Owen approached them.

"I've checked out the door. There doesn't appear to be any tampering of the locks." Owen paused, his brow furrowed. "One of the neighbors came past. I talked to him but he hasn't seen anything unusual of late. He didn't know anything about a letter being dropped off, said most mail goes straight into the boxes downstairs."

"That's right." Addison nodded. "Which means this creep has been snooping around again."

"I called building management and asked them to keep an eye out for anyone trying to sneak past." Logan rubbed at the back of his neck. "There's someone at the concierge desk twenty-four/seven, right?"

"Yeah. If a strange man came past, the concierge should have stopped him." She drummed her fingers on her leg. "All guests are supposed to sign in but he did manage to slip past last time, so it could have happened again."

"Are there any people who don't have to sign in?"

"The guys who deliver takeout to the building. The concierge buzzes them in and they go straight up to the floor." She knew for a fact that they often breezed right through the foyer of the building without attracting much attention. It would be the perfect cover.

"Okay, good. That'll give us something to look for on the surveillance footage." Logan bobbed his head. "From my search, it doesn't seem as if the guy has done anything here other than the delivery of the note. So I think that and the security cameras should be our area of focus."

"What else can I do to help?" Owen asked. For the guy who was always laughing and joking, his face was uncharacteristically serious.

"Head back to the office and update Rhys, but keep it quiet. We're only telling those who need to know—no sense in worrying the troops."

Owen nodded. "Good call."

"My full focus is on figuring out what this guy wants and ensuring that Addison is kept out of harm's way," Logan said. "So I have to ask you to step up and take care of the day-to-day stuff, okay?"

"Consider it done." Owen raked a hand through his shaggy blond hair. "If there are any problems, I'll check in."

"Good. We'll touch base on Monday morning."

Addison stayed on the couch as Owen left. She'd kicked off her heels and tucked her feet up underneath her. Her life was feeling further and further out of her control by the minute.

"I don't understand what this guy wants," she said. "An eye for an eye? What did Dad do that was so bad?"

"He put the bad guys away for a living. Think about how many people might have been sent to jail because of evidence he gathered in the course of his career." He shrugged. "I know for a fact that he received threats on a few occasions."

He'd never told her that. Neither of them had. It was simply one more thing they'd shared that she hadn't. One more thing she wasn't allowed to be part of because she needed to be "protected." She swallowed against the bitter taste in her mouth.

"It comes with the territory, unfortunately," Logan continued. "You go up against dangerous people and they bite back."

"But why now? Dad's been gone for two years and he was out of the action for a good twelve months before that because of the cancer." A lump lodged itself in her throat, but she jammed the emotions down. He would want her to focus now, not grieve. "Why would someone come after me out of the blue for something my dad might have done more than three years ago? It doesn't make sense."

"There has to be something we're missing. A catalyst."

She rolled her eyes. "Obviously."

"You being so testy about everything doesn't help the situation." He frowned at her. "I know this is an imposition and I'm sure you'd love to kick my ass out of here—"

"I would."

"But that doesn't change the fact that there is someone after you who's most likely unhinged and who has already proved to be dangerous. Addi, I don't care if this makes you hate me. I've fucked up too many times in my life to let your annoyance get in the way of doing what's right." He sighed. "Your dad was the only thing that kept me from ending up in jail after my mom died. I don't take my promise to him lightly."

She tilted her head, intrigued in spite of her bad mood. He'd never talked much about how he came to work for her father. "Why do you think you would have ended up in jail?"

"I was on a bad path back then."

"After you left the army?"

"After I got kicked out, you mean."

It didn't surprise her; his stubbornness wouldn't suit military life. But he'd never admitted it before. "Why were you kicked out?"

"I went AWOL. When I found out my mom had died I just..." His Adam's apple bobbed. "I didn't know what to do. I couldn't handle being on base, I couldn't handle my commander screaming at me. I took off, like a coward."

"You were young." She reached out to him, her fingers curling over his hand. "That was enough for them to kick you out?"

"Yeah, because I was gone longer than forty days and the commander had it in for me from the start. That was all he needed to give me an administrative discharge. He could have disciplined me, but he said I had 'no viable future' with them. That I wasn't fit to be in the army." Logan's eyes were fixed on something in the distance, as though the answers to his personal turmoil were located high in the late-afternoon skyline. "He said that no good would come of a messed-up kid like me."

"That's awful." Her chest clenched as though her body were trying to absorb his pain. "Why did you take so long to go back?"

"I had only intended to stay for the funeral, but…" His face became marble-hard. "I found out my dad had already shacked up with another woman. His wife's body wasn't even in the ground yet and he was already fucking someone else. And he'd invited her into our home. They were there when I arrived."

Oh God. She couldn't even begin to imagine what that must have been like. Her own father had never even looked at another woman after her mom passed. He'd been as devoted to her as a widower as he'd been as a husband.

"I lost it, just about smashed every plate in the house. He's still with that same woman now, so you can see why I'm not too welcome at family gatherings." He shook his head and let out a bitter laugh. "A friend referred me to your dad, said he had a security gig and was looking for muscle. When I started working for him, it was the first time I felt like I might have a future after all."

There wasn't an ounce of emotion in his rigid expression, but Addison knew that was a sign of a storm raging inside him. He'd tempered himself over the years, learning to react internally first. To use his poker face as protection. To hide the anger and sadness that had been brewing in him for years.

But she knew where to look for the truth.

"He cared about you a lot," she said, moving closer to him on the couch and leaning her shoulder on his shoulder. "You were the son he never had. I was so jealous when you came along."

His head snapped in her direction, his dark eyes burning intently into hers. "Why on earth would you have been jealous of me? You were his pride and joy."

"Because you shared things with him that I couldn't. You talked shop, you chased the bad guys together, and I had to sit at home like some delicate little bubble girl." The catch her voice belied her calm tone. "You did all the things that I could never do. You had a place by his side because he *wanted* you there."

"Addi." The tension around his eyes softened. "He wanted you by his side. Why do you think he brought you into the business? He was so proud of you."

"Not enough to let me do the *real* work," she said bitterly. "I wanted so bad to be in the security side of things, but I let him talk me into business school. I thought it was because he valued my skills in those areas but I'm not so sure about that now."

"You believe he manipulated you?"

"It sounds so bad when you say it like that…but, yeah." She swallowed. On the surface she should have been mad at her father, but she couldn't bring herself to give in to resentment. He'd done what he could to raise her right—being a single father couldn't have been easy.

He'd had to play both mother and father to her, doing everything from helping her with her homework to braiding her hair to wading through the atrocities of puberty. And never once had he complained.

"Did you really want to work on the security stuff, or was it about being closer to him?" Logan asked.

The question stalled her. Logan was right; it wasn't that she was particularly passionate about security. It was something much deeper than that. "I wanted to be equal. I wanted to be *respected* instead of being the paperwork girl."

"You know, he told me once that you joining him at the company was the proudest moment of his life."

The words hit her like a freight train to the solar plexus. "What?"

"Remember that day we switched over the payroll system and we almost wiped out all the employee data?"

She groaned. "God, do I ever. I thought we were going to have to key it all in manually and that we'd miss the deadline to pay everyone that month."

"Your dad said to me that if it wasn't for you managing those areas of the business, that he would never have been able to expand the company the way he did. *You* were the reason we could grow, because you kept the lights on when things got bad. You made sure that our bills got paid, that we always had an office space, that we kept track of our money."

"Just doing my job." She tried to make light of his words, but the truth was she could barely breathe. Of course she knew her father loved her, but he was a tough man. One who'd never spoken his emotions aloud.

"No, Addi. You're the heart and soul of Cobalt & Dane. You're the only person who could fill your father's shoes and…" He raked a hand through his hair, suddenly looking like that boy she'd fallen for all those years ago. "Thanks for not walking out on me after what I did."

Guilt trickled like poison through her veins. Never once had he acknowledged that she'd stuck by him—in a business sense—even after the personal stuff had gotten messy, much less thanked her for it. Why did he have to start being a good guy now?

"My pleasure," she whispered.

ADDISON DIDN'T MAKE eye contact, her hands toying with the hem of her dress. He would have seen less confusion on her face if he'd announced aliens were about to land on the planet.

This is why you don't do the touchy-feely stuff. You can't even give her a compliment without fucking it up.

"Anyway." He paused to clear his throat. "We should probably go through some of the old case files."

"You think we'll find something there?"

"It's a place to start. The security footage is probably not going to give us any more than it did before, so we have to get creative. The note *has* to mean something."

"Why would he leave a note if it could possibly give us a clue as to his identity?"

"Maybe he's getting frustrated at his lack of progress. Or maybe he wants to toy with you. Guys who do these kinds of things can get cocky, thinking they hold all the power."

"Right." She nodded. "Well, let me get changed. I don't want to be digging through files in this dress."

She was still so close to him on the couch. So close that he wanted to bundle her up in his arms and keep her safe and warm and close to him, where she belonged.

She doesn't belong to you, idiot. You blew that chance.

He watched as she stood, her long, lean limbs so graceful in movement. Like a dancer. What he'd give to wake up to that body every morning. To that smile. To those loving hands and lips and eyes.

"Addi?" He reached for her hand.

"Yeah?"

"I swear on my mother's grave that we're going to find this guy. I will take personal pride in nailing him to a wall for you."

A smile quirked on her lips. "That's the most romantic thing anyone has ever said to me."

"I guess I'll have to try harder then."

Her rich brown eyes didn't reveal anything. She was too careful for that.

HALF AN HOUR later Logan and Addison walked into Cobalt & Dane's archive room. It was on a different floor from their main offices. The dusty little room was full of cardboard boxes and needed to be dragged into the current decade.

"Aren't you glad I forced everyone to come through and label all these boxes correctly?" Addison tossed a smug smile over her shoulder as they walked through the door. "At least now we'll know what we're looking at."

He was grateful for her system, but he wasn't about to admit it to her. "I bet you have dirty dreams about organizing things. Just you and some hot stud with a calculator."

She snorted. "And what do you dream about? Having a girl on her knees while she submits to you in every possible way? Oh, wait. That's probably true"

Damn right it was. The thought of getting Addison

down on her knees made his cock stir. He'd love to bind those delicate wrists and bend her over the rickety little table in here.

He cleared his throat. "You said it, not me. And don't be putting ideas in my head. We've got work to do."

When he'd seen the outfit Addison had changed into back at her apartment—her gorgeous body poured into a pair of tiny denim shorts and a tight white tank top—he'd wanted to throw her onto the couch. They'd acted like the conversation about their families, about their regrets, had never happened. Because that's what he did. Avoiding emotion was the only way to go, because a bleeding heart had never served him in life. He had to be careful around Addison because she had a way of making him open up like a tap.

"Where do we even start?" She threw her hands up in the air.

The room was lined with metal shelves containing box after box of files. Not all of them were case files, though, they had boxes of records to keep for tax purposes. Old employee files, training documents. The list went on.

Thanks to Addison, the different types of files had been sorted into areas and labeled. Case files were marked with a big red *C* in the top right-hand corner of the box, followed by the month and year the case was closed. Cases that hadn't been closed were marked with a *U* for unresolved.

"My guess is that we can leave the unresolved cases for now," Logan said, placing his laptop onto the table in the center of the room. "We've got the basic records in the case management system, so let's look for cases that resulted in a handoff to police and go from there."

She nodded. "That seems like a logical approach."

"I do come up with *some* good ideas," he teased as he pulled up their case management database.

It wasn't a fancy one like some of the bigger companies might use, but it allowed them to keep track of the important information for each case—like the date Cobalt & Dane was engaged, which consultants worked on the job, the initial request, the date the case was closed and a brief description of the outcome. Each case was assigned a type to indicate whether it was an ongoing or onetime service, and the outcomes were sorted to allow them to analyze how the company was most commonly being utilized. The entire system had been Addison's design, her knack for information and organization making their lives easier in situations like this.

"Okay, so we'll narrow the search to find only closed cases." He clicked the appropriate checkbox and Addison hovered over his shoulder. The end of her long ponytail tickled his shoulder and he tried not to be distracted by the scent of her perfume. "Let's cut the date off around the time your father stopped working. We'll keep it open from the very beginning, although I think some of the earlier cases don't have much information."

"No, Dad had the same approach to paperwork as you do."

He ignored the dig. "We'll look only at cases that resulted in a handoff to police." He stared at the screen warily, knowing how many cases would *still* show up in the search. "Let's filter it also by cases that were assigned to your dad."

"This seems like a lot of guesswork."

"There's a good deal of guesswork in what we do.

Besides, if this thing spits out ten thousand records, is that going to get us anywhere?"

"No," she admitted. "But filtering out the right records won't help us, either. It's like a wild-goose chase."

But sitting around worrying would also be futile. Logan was still waiting to hear from Rhys if he'd uncovered any further information on the person who'd created the Trojan. He made a mental note to call Rhys once Addison was distracted with the case files.

He clicked the search button on the computer system and the screen filled up with prospective cases for them to look at. "Okay, now we start searching. Let's work from the most current cases and go backward."

Addison stared forlornly at the boxes lining the walls. "This is going to take forever."

He read out the dates from the first few files and they pulled the corresponding boxes. Dust plumed as they tossed the lids onto the floor. Each box was filled with slim folders labeled with case numbers. The plan had always been to digitize the old files, since they'd now moved to a paperless system, but no one had gotten around to it.

"What exactly should I be looking for?" she asked.

For once, she was seeking out his advice. Small step though it might be, the fact that he could help her with something pleased him.

"The sheet on top of the file should have a summary of the case. Look for anything that references a conviction or punitive measure. Something bad enough that might cause a crooked guy to seek revenge."

"I hope we find the guy in these more recent files," she said. "We haven't been doing the summary sheets for all that long. Dad thought they were a waste of time when I first suggested them."

"Stubborn men can be resistant to change."

"You talking about yourself or about him?" She tiptoed her fingers through the files in the box until she found what she was looking for. "You seemed to think it was wasted effort as well, if my memory serves me correctly."

"Sounds like something I would say." He pulled a file from his own box and leafed through the information inside. Nothing.

"I still haven't managed to figure out if you're difficult on purpose or if it's just something that comes naturally." A smile quirked on her lips.

"Me, difficult? Never." He pulled another file. "Now, you on the other hand…"

"Only someone who has as strong a personality as I do would be able to put up with having *you* as a business partner. So really, our stubbornness makes us well matched. Two perfectly difficult peas in a pod."

"Whatever you say, Addi."

Her fingers tucked a loose strand of blond hair behind her ear as she leaned over the file box. Tension formed a crease between her brows. "We're going to figure this out, aren't we? I mean, you do these kinds of things all the time and you always find the bad guys, right?"

The tightness in her voice blew a hole in his chest. Strong as she was, even Addison could be worn down by the fear of someone watching. Waiting. Hoping for a moment to strike.

"Of course we will. Trust me, there's nothing I won't do to take care of you," he said. An odd feeling clutched at his chest, squeezing the air out of his lungs.

On any other case, he'd be cool as a cucumber. But this was different. He *had* to figure out who was after her, because his gut told him that the creep wouldn't stop at vague notes and computer viruses. He wanted to harm Addison, and Logan wouldn't let that happen.

12

A FEW HOURS later Addison leaned back against the shelves and rubbed at her foot, which had fallen asleep. The pile of cases requiring further review had grown as they'd worked, though far fewer ended in some kind of police involvement than Addison had initially surmised.

"This could be something," she said, tapping the open folder in her lap. "It's a case from five years ago. A maintenance manager in a co-op building was breaking into apartments while the tenants were on vacation."

"You'd be surprised how often that kind of thing happens," Logan said. "What was the outcome?"

"The notes say he ended up getting a felony conviction for aggravated robbery even though the defense argued that no one was in the apartment at the time of the burglary. I guess they must have had some proof he carried a weapon even if there was no intent to use it."

"A harsh sentence could certainly make for an enemy, especially if he feels like the charges were inflated."

Addison nodded. "But wouldn't he still be in jail if he got that kind of a conviction?"

"What's his name? We'll look him up." Logan pushed

up from the floor, taking a moment to stretch his arms above his head.

She tried not to look as his T-shirt revealed a sliver of taut skin at his belly. The cotton stretched across his chest, revealing the outline of muscles she knew felt like heaven under her palms. It would be wonderful to forget all about her stalker and her secret and indulge in a little pleasure.

When did her life get so damn complicated?

Addison forced her eyes back down to the file. "Uh, his name is Adrian Marco Vendetti. Born 1955, Brownsville, New York."

Logan leaned over the small square table where his laptop sat and typed the name into a search engine. A few moments later he let out a surprised *hmm*.

"He's dead."

Addison blinked and rose to join him. "Huh?"

"He was killed during a prison riot, it seems. According to this article, Vendetti's son is suing the state for wrongful death." Logan paused while Addison leaned over him to see the article. "Vendetti had been denied a transfer after a fight with the guy who ended up killing him."

"Brutal."

He scrolled further down the page. "His son is the one pursuing the legal action." He cocked his head. "Michael Zetta. Why does that name sound familiar?"

"No idea." Addison shook her head. "It doesn't sound familiar to me."

At that moment her stomach grumbled loud enough to startle them both. Logan chuckled. "I guess we should take a dinner break."

She glanced down at her watch. It was 9:00 p.m.

"Why don't we call it a night? We'll take the files back to my place and keep working on them over the weekend."

"Is that your way of saying you'd like me to hang around?" He closed the laptop and turned to her.

"I've accepted the inevitable. You're not going anywhere, so I may as well embrace it." For some reason the words comforted rather than stifled her.

In the past week, Logan had been by her side more than ever. They'd rekindled the spark that had drawn them to each other over the years, the spark that she'd thought had been extinguished when she'd turned up at his door to find him with another woman.

Just because he cares about you doesn't mean he knows how to treat you right. Don't get attached. Don't be vulnerable again unless you're prepared to get hurt.

"Well, it's not a glowing invitation, but I'll take it." He offered her a roguish grin. "You're a hard woman to please, Addison Cobalt."

"Yeah, right," she scoffed. "You're insufferable. I'm sure other guys wouldn't find me hard to please."

"And you think another guy could rev you up the way I do?" He folded his arms across his chest, the muscles bulging under the cotton of his T-shirt. Clearly, her words had hit their mark. "Would another guy have been able to convince you to go to work without panties? I bet you didn't even put them back on when you got changed."

Heat flared through her, pooling in her cheeks. And between her legs. "What makes you say that?"

"Because you like the thrill of being bossed around."

Oh, how she wanted to slap the smug expression off his face with one of the case files. "Bullshit."

Hate it as she might, there was no denying the denim shorts did brush deliciously against her bare sex. She ached for him. Against her will, her body craved his like a drug. And he was right; the power play between them only served to build excitement in her until it felt as if a tornado were blowing through her body. No other man had ever come close to making her feel the way he did.

Don't let him suck you in.

"Prove it," he challenged. "Take your shorts off now and show me you put your panties back on."

"No way." Her eyes darted around the room. "There are cameras in here."

"Cameras that *we* own." He shrugged. "That's the best thing about being the boss—no one can punish you. We can do whatever we like."

"This is…ridiculous."

Dammit, why did he have to be so right about her? He knew her better than anyone, and right now he was totally using it to his advantage.

"What's ridiculous is you maintaining this charade." His smile morphed from amused to wolfish. His dark eyes practically glittered with excitement. "I'm in your head, Addi. And you love it."

He took a step toward her and she immediately backed up. "You've got an inflated sense of your abilities, Dane."

"Oh I'm *Dane* now, am I? What's the matter, baby? Too afraid to say my name in case your shorts melt right off your body?"

"You're *so* full of it." She rolled her eyes, but as her back hit the shelves she realized she was in trouble. "So goddamn full of it."

"I think the lady doth protest too much." He stalked over to her, his hands landing on her waist. His thumbs brushed the waistband of her shorts, pushing up her tank top. "It's okay. I'm more than happy to conduct an independent investigation."

He lowered to his knees in front of her, his warm breath tickling her bare skin. A ripple of awareness shot through her, like he'd found a secret *on* switch to her entire nervous system. Everything was heightened—the sensitivity of her skin, the feel of his palms running over her hips. He electrified her. Burned her from the inside out.

But that was the thing about flames—the warmth was great until you got too close.

"Let's see what you've been hiding under here." He toyed with the button on her shorts for a moment before popping it loose. "Are you as immune to me as you say?"

The moment he grabbed the zipper and dragged it down, the fight left Addison's body. He had her. Cornered. Trapped.

Totally and utterly at his mercy.

"Just as I thought." He dragged the denim shorts down her thighs until they pooled around her ankles. "You're a good girl at heart, Addi. Good at following orders. Good at giving me what I want."

"Screw you," she bit out, ready to push him away.

But the moment his lips pressed against her sex, she was lost. His tongue pushed between her folds, seeking out her clit. Not a moment was wasted. "Oh, you will. You'll be so ready to screw me that I won't even have time to get you back to your apartment. You're already so wet for me."

A cry caught in her throat as he sucked at her. He extracted one foot from the shorts tangled around her ankles and threw her leg over his shoulder, and she melted. His fingers dug into her ass, supporting her. Holding her steady while he feasted. It was the kind of reckless abandon that she never allowed herself in life. The kind that came with an inherent sense of risk.

But it didn't matter now. Nothing mattered except the orgasm that welled deep inside her.

"I can feel you shaking," he murmured against her. "It's so good, Addi. So fucking good."

"No kidding," she gasped, her hands threading through his hair as a tremor ripped through her. "Oh, Logan."

"That's it, Addi. Let it all out."

Her head lolled back against the case files as she struggled to stay upright. Waves of pleasure lapped at her. Her hips rolled in time with the sensation, her body seeming to move of its own accord.

"I'm close," she gasped.

"Not yet." He pulled away, ignoring her cry of protest. "I want to be inside you when you come."

Fishing the wallet out of his pants, he located one of the condoms he kept stashed there. In seconds, he'd stripped his pants and sheathed himself. His body seemed to vibrate.

"Come here." She reached for him and they landed hard against the shelving unit.

"God, Addi." He tugged her leg over his hip, guiding his cock to her entrance with his hand. "I need you so bad."

"I need you, too." She gasped as he pushed inside her.

The feeling of him breaching her tight sex was near divine. His warm skin and greedy hands overwhelmed her senses as he thrust into her. Hard. Desperate. This wouldn't be delicate. It wouldn't be sweet or even sensual. Whenever they came together, there was a rawness that undid her.

"Take me," she gasped.

He hoisted her up and she wrapped both legs around him, her thighs squeezing his waist. The metal shelving unit groaned as they writhed. She reached up with one hand and wrapped her fingers around the edge of a shelf, trying to find leverage to meet his thrusts.

"You ruin me." He buried his face into the crook of her neck. "This feels too fucking good."

His hands were all over her, as though he had to touch every inch of her in order to survive. Her body trembled as she lost herself. Eyes clamped shut, she let the feeling take her over. Lights danced behind her lids and she was vaguely aware of his name falling from her lips.

As she tried to push the post-orgasm fog from her mind, she felt his strong hands lower her to the ground. Being in his arms shouldn't have felt like the best place in the world. Being at his mercy shouldn't have felt like everything she'd ever wanted.

But it did. And now she was at risk of giving herself completely over to him.

As ADDISON'S BREATH SLOWED, she stirred against Logan's chest. How long they'd been standing there wrapped up in each other, he had no idea. But he wasn't about to move until she was ready. Truth be told, he would have stood in that same position until he lost all sensation in his arms just to have her curled up against him.

"I'm starving," she mumbled, her face rubbing against the base of his neck. "Need pizza now."

They grabbed the files and swung past their regular pizza joint on the way back to his apartment. It struck him how at ease he was with Addison—how well he knew her favorite pizza toppings, the jokes that would make her laugh, that she was superstitious about not stepping on a crack in the street.

She'd pulled away from him in the last two years and he'd studiously ignored how much he missed her. How his life had a giant gaping hole in it.

And now, even though she'd come back to him, there was a sense of panic that wouldn't budge. A foreboding hanging over his head like a thundercloud. He was at risk of losing her again, but he didn't know why.

"I regret the way we ended things last time," he blurted out.

They walked into his apartment and Addison raised a brow as she put their dinner onto the coffee table. "What?"

"Last time." He cleared his throat as he lowered the box of files to the floor. "After we, you know…"

Someone take me out to a pasture and shoot me. It'll be less painful.

"Since when are you the blushing wallflower?" She laughed, but her eyes avoided his. It was easy to see that hurt still lay there. She hadn't forgotten what he'd done.

"It was a dick thing to do."

She shrugged. "You don't owe me anything."

"I owe you my respect." He raked a hand through his hair, grappling for the right thing to say. If only he could better express himself. Unfortunately, years of keeping his distance from others made it hard for him to open up. "And, uh, jumping into bed with someone else right away wasn't very respectful."

"Why did you do it?" She folded her arms across her chest, creating a shield between them.

Why, indeed? Because he was stupid to epic proportions.

"I was terrified of losing someone else." First his mother, then his father, then Daniel...he seemed to lose people quicker than he could build relationships.

"So you made sure you *would* lose me. That doesn't make a whole lot of sense."

"No, it doesn't. But I guess my screwed-up brain figured that I couldn't technically lose you if I didn't have you in the first place." It sounded even dumber aloud than it had in his head. "And I felt like I'd pissed on your father's memory by being with you in that way."

"You think he'd prefer for you to treat me like a piece of trash?" Her voice trembled. "I'm not disposable, Logan."

This wasn't going the way he wanted it to. It was clear Addison still didn't trust him, and why should she?

"I'm sorry." She held up a hand, her mask clicking back into place. "I shouldn't have said that. It was out of line."

He swallowed. "I deserve it."

"No, you don't. You're only human and so am I." She sucked in a deep breath. "I have high expectations and sometimes that makes me go a little crazy. We weren't in a relationship, so I had no claim on you."

This was the out he'd hoped for all those months ago. The acknowledgment that technically he hadn't done the wrong thing. But technicalities were worth shit and *nothing* would make him feel better about hurting her.

"Still, I shouldn't have rubbed it in your face like that."

"True, but the past is the past. Right?" She smiled brightly. Fake. "Let's not talk about this ever again and I promise I'll try to forget it happened."

It should have been what he wanted, but her suggestion turned like sour milk in his stomach. He didn't want her to forget. He wanted her to remember his hands tangling in her hair, his teeth marking her skin. He wanted her to be consumed by the memories of the fire they'd made together, just as he was.

He wanted her to be his.

"Sure." He shook his head, the thoughts bouncing like Ping-Pong balls against the inside of his skull.

What do you mean you want her to be yours? So you can inflict your fucked-up issues on her? No way, no how. Not ever.

"We should eat," she said, opening up the pizza box to grab a slice. "You don't want to see me when I'm hangry."

"Nothing you could possibly do would scare me. I've seen a lot, trust me." He dropped down beside her and patted her knee as if nothing was wrong.

But his feelings for Addison had deepened. They'd gone from an insistent whisper to a roar that had the force of a buffalo stampede. How much longer would he be able to pretend that casual sex would satisfy him? Fulfill him?

But you can't give her what she deserves.

Couldn't he? For Addison, maybe he could be the upstanding guy who communicated and compromised and trusted. For her, maybe he could change. If she didn't leave him first.

13

BY THE TIME Monday rolled around, Logan and Addison had barely left his apartment. Between the white-hot sex and the old case files, she'd been unable to concentrate on anything else. On any*one* else.

They'd cooked dinner together last night and let it burn in the saucepan while they lost themselves in pleasure on the dining table.

"You'd better hope I can get that horrible burned smell out of this place," she said as she turned the coffee machine on. "You're such a distraction."

"Me?" He pressed a hand to his chest in mock outrage. "You were the one who decided it would be a good idea to cook naked."

A sly smile lifted at the corner of her lips. "I had an apron on."

"Yes, and that glorious ass of yours was hanging out. What was I supposed to do?" He growled the question into her ear as he pressed her against the kitchen counter. His hands were everywhere—cupping her face, kneading her backside, parting her thighs so he could stroke her still-needy sex.

"You're like a drug. You know that, right?" She sank her teeth down into her lip as he rubbed his stubble-coated jaw along her neck. "Potent. Intoxicating. Addictive."

"Addictive?" He nipped at her. "And here I was thinking it was time to up the dosage."

Her head lolled back. "I don't know how much more I can take."

Like any good drug, Logan made her forget the potential side effects. The risks. She'd sink into his pleasure-filled fog without a worry about her heart. Without a worry about what would happen when reality came crashing down on them. He'd get bored, find another woman. Leave her in pieces.

He said he regrets what happened. Maybe he won't *hurt you again.*

Still, there was the slight matter of her plans to start her own business. Even if Logan had dealt with his commitment issues, Addison still needed to be her own boss. To do something that made her feel worthwhile. How could she indulge in fantasies about living happily ever after when she was planning to break away from him?

"You're a lot hardier than you think," he said. "You've taken a lot of knocks over the years and you're still here, still fighting."

"I am, aren't I?" She turned her face to his and captured his lips with her own.

A tremor ran through her as he slid his tongue along hers. God, he tasted so good. Earthy. Male. Like sex and sin and home all rolled into one.

His hands snaked up her back, crushing her to him. He was hard again, ready. Always ready.

"Logan," she groaned. "We have to go to work."

"Do we?" A wicked grin pulled at his lips. "Why don't we play hooky?"

"We can't."

"I'll give you a permission slip." His teeth scraped down her neck and he filled his palm with her breast. "Valid for one day of mind-blowing sex and as many orgasms as you can handle."

"But what about the case files?"

He stilled and she could practically hear the cogs turning in his brain. "You're right."

Over the weekend, it'd been easy to pretend that her stalker was nothing but a figment of her imagination. She and Logan had created their own perfect bubble, impenetrable to the outside world. Complete with locked doors and her own personal bodyguard. With him, she was safe and secure. Wanted.

But that could all be blown apart when she came clean about her plans.

"I'll keep my hands to myself." He released her and she was suddenly cold and empty without his touch. "For now."

"It's only eight hours." She stifled a smile. "You can last that long without me."

"I went two whole years without you because I was an idiot." His thumb brushed her cheekbone. "I don't want to do that again."

The words sucked the air from her lungs. And judging by his own wide-eyed expression, it wasn't a planned speech.

See, maybe he has *changed. Maybe this is real.*

"I, uh…shower." He shoved his hands into his pockets and turned toward the bathroom.

"That wasn't a real sentence but I'll let you get away with it this time," she teased, trying to play it cool.

But her heart thumped, her blood raced, and the most magical feeling danced along her veins. Gripping the edge of the kitchen counter, she sifted through the facts.

For all the times she'd cursed his name and wiped away tears he'd caused, it hadn't made her want him any less. It hadn't made her want *them* any less. The truth burned bright and furious inside her. She cared about him.

But she wouldn't start a relationship with secrets between them. Tonight, she'd tell him about her plans and hope that he understood why she had to leave Cobalt & Dane. What striking out on her own meant to her.

LOGAN HAD NEEDED a hell of a cold shower to get the thoughts of Addison's naked body out of his mind. That woman had him tangled up worse than a pair of Apple earbuds. Nothing diminished his growing feelings for her—not staying away, not trying to get her out of his system, not confronting his emotions. Nada.

Screw your head back on. The stalker is priority number one. Nothing can happen until you deal with that, because if anything happens to her...

He couldn't even think about what might come next. It was as if his brain simply powered down at the possibility of her being harmed. That meant he needed to regroup and refocus. Everything else could wait.

"Logan?" Emily poked her head into his office. "I've got Rhys and Quinn here to see you."

"Send them in."

His employees entered the room looking like some

funny remake of *The Odd Couple*. Everyone in the office knew they were a tight-knit team but Logan was always struck by how different they were. Rhys was tall, serious and straight as an arrow. He wore a collared shirt and wool suit pants every day. Quinn, on the other hand, was quirky and alternative. Today she had on slashed jeans, a *Legend of Zelda* T-shirt and combat boots. Her highlighter-pink hair hung in a long braid over one shoulder.

"We've got an update on Addison's, uh…" Rhys trailed off.

"Psychotic email acquaintance?" Quinn offered.

"Yes, yes." Logan rolled his hand around. "Go on."

"I'd tasked Quinn with identifying the creator of the Trojan," Rhys said, motioning for Quinn to share what she'd found.

"Right. So, the virus turned out to be a keylogger Trojan. It's a piece of software designed to record keystrokes." Quinn drummed her fingers on her knee as she spoke. "They're mostly used to capture sensitive data like passwords, banking and credit card details, and key identity information such as birth dates, Social Security numbers, et cetera."

Logan frowned. "So he's looking for something specific?"

"I believe so. Using a keylogger means he wants to capture information that's not generally stored in a file or email account. Banking information is definitely the most common target."

"It shouldn't surprise me that this is about money, but why the threatening email?" Logan asked. "If he wanted to access her bank account details why risk the attention? The only reason the email didn't make it to Addison the first time is because of the profanity tripping the filter."

"You're right, if it's about money there's no need for that. Makes me think in this case there's something personal going on," Rhys said. "Quinn was able to trace the name we found in the code to a hacking forum. Turns out DaZetta has been quite busy."

The connection clicked. DaZetta. Michael Zetta. Son of the man Daniel Cobalt had put in jail. The man who'd *died* in jail.

That couldn't be a coincidence.

"I believe he lives in New York." Quinn slid a piece of paper across Logan's desk. "I couldn't confirm his real name, only that the email he used to sign up for his forum account was registered here. I also found an account on Facebook that used the same name and IP address. The address is listed as belonging to a coffee shop in Midtown called Café Mid."

"So we don't have an actual address for him?" Logan asked.

Quinn shook her head. "I'm afraid not. But if he does his business there, then we might be able to hunt him out. There's a chance I could try to get something onto his computer so we can track him, but it's not exactly legal."

"Let's do it the old-fashioned way. Besides, I have an idea how we can figure out his whereabouts."

Logan took a few minutes to fill Rhys and Quinn in on the case he'd come across, which had a link to the name DaZetta. The more he talked it through, the more he was certain Michael Zetta was their guy.

"So what do we do next?" Rhys asked.

"Let's see if we can find a link between DaZetta and Michael Zetta. Anything that ties the two identities together or provides a link to the court case that's going on at the moment." Logan riffled through his files and pulled out the one marked "Vendetti." "The father and son have different surnames, which could possibly mean there is a mother out there who we might be able to press for information, depending on how her relationship with Vendetti ended."

"No mother worth her salt would turn on her son," Quinn said. "Why would this be any different?"

"It's all in how you spin the facts. We might be able to get her to provide information if she feels it will get her son out of hot water," Logan said. "I'll leave it to you two computer whizzes to gather all the technical information, and then if we need to chat with the mother, I'll take care of it. In the meantime, we keep eyes on Addison constantly as well as on the café."

"We should get Addison up to speed." Rhys folded his hands in his lap. "This concerns her directly. She needs to be involved."

Logan nodded. "Agreed. Now that we have more information and an action plan, it's the right time."

Rhys made a face that said he thought the right time had passed. But he didn't comment further.

"Should we call her in?" Quinn asked.

"No." Logan pushed up from his chair. "Leave Addison to me."

ADDISON CRADLED A large coffee cup in her hands while she waited for a reaction from the woman sitting across from her. Penny, her HR manager extraordinaire, sat wide-eyed, processing the information she'd received.

"I never thought you would leave this company," Penny said, sipping her coffee. "Frankly, I'm a bit shocked. I mean, your father was a legend here."

"It's true." Addison nodded, trying to stifle the sharp

pain in her chest that still struck anytime she thought of her dad. "But the one thing I learned from him was that it's possible to build something from scratch. I want that satisfaction, Penny. I want to know what it means to create something yourself and watch it grow. Besides, I'm *positive* this business will be successful. You see how the security guys here couldn't organize paperwork to save themselves."

"It's true." The redhead nodded, a wry smile on her lips. "Owen submitted the files for one of the new hires and forgot to ask the guy to sign his contract. I swear, they have selective attention to detail. If it's for an assignment, they're on point. If it's for HR stuff…" She shook her head.

"I really want you to come with me. I've said from day one you're the best HR person we've ever hired. I need smart, forward-thinking people like you." She sucked in a breath and set her coffee cup down. "I realize this is a bit of a risk for you, but I've planned everything out. This won't be one of those companies that fails because the owner had no idea how to manage the details."

"I don't doubt you at all, Addison. Especially not in that area." Penny paused, her bottom lip drawn between her teeth. There was something more that she wasn't saying.

"Spit it out."

"Have you told Logan? I mean, this company is important to both of you, and I don't want to leave with any bad blood."

Addison raised a brow. "What do you mean?"

"Can I speak frankly?"

"Of course."

"I want to know that you're not trying to poach me to spite him."

Addison blinked. "Excuse me?"

"It's obvious there's something between you two. Everyone can see it, plain as day. Chemistry like that can't be hidden. But I'd hate to think you were only interested in me because it would hurt him." She pressed her lips together. "I just… Please don't take this the wrong way, Addison. I respect you, but I don't want to be caught in the crosshairs."

"It's not like that." She shook her head. "I appreciate your concern, Penn. And Logan doesn't know, but I'm going to tell him soon. I *do* love this company and I want it to succeed with him at the helm. But this whole security business was always Dad and Logan's thing. I never leaned the ropes. And as much as I sometimes hate to admit it, Logan is the better person to run this business because of that. I guess the reason I want to strike out on my own is because I want my skills to be front and center."

"Working in HR, I totally get that. We do always seem to play second fiddle to something more exciting, don't we?"

"Exactly."

Penny tilted her head. "Well, I'd be lying if I said I wasn't tempted. I love working with you."

"The feeling is mutual. But I understand it's a big decision. You don't have to make it now. But I'm meeting with the real estate agent this week about an office space, so things are definitely moving."

"Got it. I won't take too long." Penny stood and picked up her coffee cup. "Thanks for thinking of me."

"You're most welcome."

As Penny exited the coffee shop she walked past Logan. Even from a distance, Addison could see the blush spread across her cheeks. All the girls had a crush on him, even if they were a little scared of his tough managerial persona. But Addison knew the real him; he was a teddy bear underneath it all. A stubborn, pushy one, but a teddy bear nonetheless.

Penny pointed in Addison's direction and when Logan looked over at her it was as if a bolt of lightning shot through her body. What that man could do with a single glance...

"How's my favorite bossy boots?" he said as he sauntered over.

Damn, he looked as tasty as a slice of cherry pie. Fitted dark jeans, black boots and a black-and-white-checked shirt rolled up at the sleeves made him look slick yet relaxed. Addison wondered how hard she'd have to tear at the fabric to make the buttons fly off his shirt.

Get a grip. Fabulous sex will commence in T minus five hours.

"I'm trying to work myself up to tackle the OH&S reports upstairs," she said. "So far, not even coffee is helping."

"Have you got a second to chat?"

"For you," she said, motioning for him to take a seat, "always."

"Maybe we could go for a walk. The coffee might be more effective if you're moving around."

"Unlikely, but it's worth a try." She bundled up her purse and drink and followed him out of the café.

They walked into the sunshine and the hustle and bustle of the Manhattan workday. Addison breathed in the sensory overload—the blare of horns, the scent of pretzels, the warm blast of summer air on her skin. This place was hot and messy. It was noisy and chaotic. But something about that gave her comfort, like the craziness was her blanket. Her shelter. Manhattan was brazen and up-front; what you saw was most certainly what you got.

It reminded her a lot of Logan.

"What did you want to chat about?" she asked, casually linking her arm through his and not caring if anyone from the office might see them. If Penny was right, the cat was not only out of the bag, it had already taken off down the street.

"It's about the guy who's been trying to contact you."

For some reason, the way he said it settled uneasily in her stomach. "Go on."

"We've gained some information on who he might be and I suspect there's a link to one of the cases we looked at on Friday night."

"Oh, well that's good. I guess." She stared ahead as they walked. "Something to go on is a positive thing, right?"

"Yes, it is."

"How did you figure out the connection?"

Logan cleared his throat. "Well, we received another email from him and it contained a virus that we were able to trace. Rhys and Quinn managed to figure out who created the virus and that's when we found the link to one of the old cases."

"I don't remember receiving any more emails. Or did it get caught in the filter again?"

"We'd flagged the email so it wouldn't come to you, just in case it contained any malicious software like this one did." He paused for a moment. "We couldn't risk you accidentally clicking on anything that might put our systems at risk."

With each step she took, Addison's uneasy feeling grew. He was choosing his words carefully, dancing around the truth. He was keeping something from her. "When did the email come in?" She removed her hand from his arm, pausing to look up at him.

"Last week."

She sucked in a breath. "And you thought it would be a good idea *not* to tell me about it until now?"

"I wanted to have a few things in place before I mentioned it."

This was it. The reason she and Logan would never work, because no matter how many times she asked him to view her as an equal, he didn't. Her stomach sank, but she shoved the feeling of sadness to one side. She would not give Logan more opportunities to see her hurting.

"Did it not occur to you that it would be a good idea to inform the person being stalked that her worst nightmare had tried to contact her again? You know, so I could take some precautionary measures?" Sarcasm dripped from her tongue.

"I was with you almost every moment since then."

The words stung as if he'd slapped her across the face. "And here I was thinking you were using the whole 'Mr. Protector' thing to get in my pants."

"Oh, come on."

"Come on what? Is it so fucking hard to understand that I want you to treat me as your partner?" She threw her free hand up into the air, her voice climbing an octave. "Hell, I'd settle for me being treated as well as a client at this point. You keep *them* in the loop, but not your own business partner. Not your own…"

Frustration choked the rest of her words. Were they lovers? Friends with benefits? A future in the making?

Right now it felt like they were strangers.

"Addi, please. Everything I do is in your best interest."

"You do *not* get to decide what is and isn't in my best interest." She jabbed him square in the chest with her pointer finger. "I'm sick of you treating me like some delicate piece of crystal. I won't break at the slightest bump, and the fact that you don't see that is…"

Her chest heaved under her blouse. Everything suddenly felt too tight, her clothes, the air, Logan's presence. She drew in a deep breath, willing her body to calm the hell down. Having a panic attack now would discredit her.

"It's insulting, Logan. I thought you knew me better than that."

"This is exactly *why* I have to look after you. You put your pride before everything else. You're so busy trying to prove your independence that you put yourself at risk."

"Oh, explain to me how I've done that?" People walking past stared at them while they argued, but she didn't give a damn.

"You didn't want us to check your apartment out. I had to argue with you to let us put a simple thing on your computer to make sure he didn't get at you another way. Fuck, Addi. I care about you. Don't you see that?" He raked a hand through his hair. "It's more than that, I—"

"Stop." She held up her hand. "I don't even want to hear what kind of manipulative shit you're going to say next."

His eyes flashed and the muscle worked in his jaw like he was grinding his teeth. "You think I'm manipulative?"

No, she didn't. Not really. But dammit she wanted to

hurt him now; she wanted to make him understand that the way he treated her was wrong. But there wasn't much point. He wouldn't change.

"I'm leaving, Logan." The fight receded within her as quickly as it had bubbled up.

Being angry was an exercise in futility, so she had to pull away. As much as she wanted to be with Logan—and this weekend had certainly planted those seeds of hope—she refused to be treated like a child.

The blood drained from his face, his dark eyes becoming even stormier. "What do you mean you're leaving?"

"I'm leaving Cobalt & Dane to start my own business."

14

ALL POSSIBLE REACTIONS collided within Logan. He wanted to scream, put his fist to a wall. Run. Most of all he wanted to run.

You promised you wouldn't do that again because you're not a goddamn coward anymore.

But the instinct was there, clawing at him. Building up his walls brick by brick. Isolating his heart.

"Don't do this," he said, the weight of his guilt crashing down and suffocating him. He couldn't be the reason she wanted to leave her own company, and if he was…then he'd failed. "Let's take a moment to think about this."

"It's not a rash decision, Logan." Her dark eyes glittered and everything in her demeanor screamed at him to back off, from the crossed arms to the hunched shoulders to the drawn expression. "I've thought it through."

You've done this to her. Again.

"I'm sorry I didn't tell you about the email, but leaving isn't the answer." He tried to reach out to her but she flinched from his hand.

The greatest thing he'd feared was that she would

leave him—like everyone else. Now it was happening before they'd even started, before they'd even had the opportunity to see what they could become. After the incredible weekend they'd spent together, he knew one thing only: that Addison was the most important thing in his life.

Truth was, he'd always known that. Maybe that's was why he was crazy about protecting her, because without Addison he was lost. Incomplete. She was his family, his partner.

His love.

It should have shocked him, but it didn't. The feelings had been there for a decade, whether he'd acknowledged them or not.

"Logan, it's not about the email." She pressed her fingertips to her temple. The sunlight caught the small, clear stone dangling from her ear as she shook her head. "It's been in the works for a while."

For a moment, he thought his chest had been split in two. "How long is *a while*?"

"A few months. More." Her eyes swept over the street, not focusing on anything in particular. Looking anywhere but him. "I don't want to do this anymore. I don't want to be living in your shadow for the rest of my life."

"You don't live in anyone's shadow." His mind spun, desperate for a Band-Aid. Desperate for some way to wind back the past so he could un-fuck this situation. "We can fix—"

"No, we can't. I thought it might work between us, but I was clearly deluding myself." Her eyes glimmered. "I care about you, you know that. But this—" she waved her hand between them "—I'm not doing this anymore.

I'm going out *on my own* and if you have even an ounce of respect for me, you'll let me go."

She'd drawn a line between them and he was screwed either way. If he tried to stop her now, it would prove that he didn't see her as an equal. That he couldn't put her needs before his own. But letting her go would be torture. The company wouldn't be the same without her.

He wouldn't be the same without her.

"I'm walking away now and I don't want you to follow me." She hitched her purse higher up on her shoulder.

"We should still have surveillance on you," he said, swallowing against the lump in his throat. "I'll assign someone else to you."

"I'd appreciate that." She squared her shoulders. It looked as though she might say something else, but instead she turned back toward their office and marched down the street.

Logan shut his eyes for a moment, fighting the urge to race after her. Acting on his emotions had brought him nothing but a world of pain. So, for once, he was going to let his head lead and if that meant he needed to watch her disappear, then so be it.

He pulled his cell from his pocket and dialed Owen's number. "Hey, I need you to take care of something. Find Addi and stick by her all day, okay? I'll fill you in later."

He was going to fix this. No matter what it took, no matter what he had to sacrifice. He would make sure Addison knew what she meant to him.

ADDISON BOUNCED FROM one foot to the other, unsure of what to do. What to say. She'd been home for an hour with Owen. But it wasn't like hanging out with Logan, where she could fully relax. Owen was still her employee.

Sure, he was a friend, but right now she wanted to be alone with her thoughts. Alone to wallow in her misery.

"I can wait outside if you'd prefer," Owen said from where he sat on her couch.

Compared to Logan he was all light—a white shirt, breezy surfer-blond hair and pale denim jeans that matched his eyes. He was funny, slightly irreverent, always at ease. Relaxed and calm.

Here's the problem: you compare everyone to Logan. And still, even though he screws up at every turn, you think no other man could ever come close to him. Your comparison system is broken.

"No, it's fine. I don't want you scaring the neighbors."

"*Moi*? Please." He grinned and she could practically see the light reflecting off his perfect teeth. "I'm as harmless as a puppy."

She snorted. "I'm sure you'd like people to believe that."

"It's true. Logan scares everyone enough that I don't need to play the tough guy." He patted the couch beside him. "Why don't we sit and chat? You standing in the kitchen pretending to be busy is kind of weird. I know you're not doing anything."

A laugh bubbled up her throat. "No, I'm not." She opened the fridge and relished the cool blast of air on her skin. "Want a beer?"

"Sorry, doll. I'm on the job. Wouldn't want to disappoint my boss."

Addison grabbed a drink for herself and twisted off the cap. "I'm sure Logan wouldn't mind."

"Firstly, yes he would. He'd kick my ass from here to Canada. Secondly, I was talking about you, Ms. Boss Lady."

She brought the beer bottle up to her lips and tipped her head back. Getting drunk could be the answer—it'd sure helped her last time she'd had issues with Logan. She could drink until she fell down and decided to sleep on the floor.

Yeah, real mature. Dad would be so proud.

"You don't take orders from me," she muttered as she made her way to the couch.

Owen cocked his head. "Sure I do. Nothing better than being bossed around by a gorgeous woman."

"Don't make me spank you."

"Oh, I won't. Not that I wouldn't like to see those little chicken limbs trying to do some damage, mind you." A wicked smile curved on his lips. "But I've known Logan long enough to fear his wrath."

"He doesn't own me." She drew on her beer again, willing the frothy liquid to work its soothing magic.

"No, he doesn't. But cares about you a lot, Addi."

"He's got a funny way of showing it." She plonked her beer bottle down onto the coffee table with an aggressive *clink*. "He keeps secrets, he lies, he pushes me away the second anything starts to feel real." She ticked the items off on her fingers. "And yet he thinks that I should be totally honest with him at all times. It's a two-way street."

Addison clamped her mouth shut when she realized that her voice had shot up to an octave high enough to call the neighborhood dogs to her front door. This wasn't Owen's problem, and she shouldn't be dumping it all on him because he happened to be the unlucky sucker assigned to keep watch over her.

"I'm sorry," she began, but Owen silenced her by holding up his hand.

"It's fine." He squeezed her shoulder. "Logan's a difficult person sometimes. I wouldn't have been able to put up with his control-freak ways over the years if it wasn't for the fact that he's one of the good guys. Everything he does is with the best intentions."

"Intentions don't count for shit if your actions don't stack up," she said with a frown. "If he got out of his own head a little more often, it might be easier to understand him."

"Fair." Owen nodded. "I'm not trying to say he's perfect, because let's be real, he's far from it. But I am saying that you matter to him more than you could possibly understand."

She stared straight ahead, fighting the urge to believe Owen. To let the anger leach out of her body. She couldn't stop being angry, because then she might let herself fall for Logan—harder and faster than ever. Now was not a good time to have her heart broken. Again.

"He'd do anything for you," Owen added.

"Anything except let me live my life."

"Did you know that when your father died, he phoned every florist in the city to find that wreath of yellow roses for the funeral?"

Addison snapped her head toward Owen. "I thought Emily organized that."

"Nope. He remembered that your dad bought you yellow roses every time you argued as a way of saying sorry. And even though there was a rose shortage around the time of the funeral, Logan wouldn't rest until he got that goddamn wreath. He said your dad would have wanted to say sorry for leaving."

Emotion rushed up the back of her throat and she had to choke down a sob. Tears pricked her eyes and she blinked furiously. "No, I didn't know that."

"And when you decided that caffeine was bad for you, Logan made sure we stocked decaf coffee in the kitchen as well as the regular stuff."

"I'd forgotten about that." Against her will, a smile crept across her lips. "I didn't last long on decaf. That stuff is terrible."

"He told me about a year ago that he screwed things up with you after your dad's funeral."

"He told you that?" She reached for her beer and sipped.

"Yeah, he got wasted one night after work. I think the stress of running the company without your dad had finally caught up to him and he went HAM. I got a call from the bartender to come pick him up because he couldn't even stand. Puked his guts up on the side of the street and everything."

"That's unlike him."

"Totally. He was slurring his words something crazy, said he loved you and that he'd ruined everything."

"He said he loved me?" A lump lodged in her throat.

"Sure did, told me a good hundred times before I managed to get him home. I don't think he even remembers me coming to get him that night." Owen chuckled. "But seriously, Addi. I know he isn't always great at expressing himself with words, but he's got the feeling where it counts."

"That's very sage of you, Owen. I had no idea you were such a softy."

"Don't let it get around, okay?" He winked. "I've got a reputation to uphold."

She threw her arm around his shoulder for a brotherly hug. "You sure do."

"So you're going to cut him some slack?"

"I honestly don't know what to do. I feel like every time I get close to him the walls go up and I'm left standing in the cold." Addison rested her head on Owen's shoulder.

Early-evening light filtered into the apartment, catching the sleek glass bowl on her coffee table. Her apartment was like her—carefully presented, stylish. A little impersonal. Guarded.

You think you don't push Logan away, too? You're as scared and self-protecting as he is.

"I want to be in a relationship where I'm equal with my partner—not held up on some untouchable pedestal, but not seen as weak and unable to take care of myself, either." She rubbed her temples with her fingers, trying to ease the tension there. Logan always seemed to get her tied up in knots...even after she'd decided to walk away.

You're hooked on him and walking away won't change that. He makes you feel too good to forget about him.

"And you believe Logan views you as weak?" Owen asked.

"Sometimes. He's confusing as hell. On one hand, I'm this untouchable, perfect thing, and yet on the other he wants to make all my decisions for me." She shook her head. "I've tried talking to him, but he's so stubborn. I can't be someone else's puppet."

"You'll *never* be someone else's puppet, Addi. You're too smart for that."

"I don't think he means to do it, but I went through the same stuff with Dad. Goddamn overprotective men." She huffed. "I want some space from that...just for a while. I need a little room to breathe before I figure out how to tackle Logan."

"Then you won't hear another peep out of me unless

you want to talk about it." Owen made a motion of zipping his mouth closed and throwing away the key.

"You're going to make some girl very happy one day," she said, finishing off her beer. "I'm certain of it."

"Nah." He shook his head, untamed blond hair falling about his eyes. "I don't do relationships. Too messy."

"You're telling me," she muttered, looking out the window as the sun dipped. "I've seen horror movies with less gore."

THE FOLLOWING MORNING, Addison woke with a start. Her sleep had been restless and filled with disturbing dreams. It was as if all the dark thoughts she'd shoved to the corners of her mind had slunk out in the dead of night. Ready to haunt. Ready to terrorize.

She pushed back sweat-dampened hair from her face and let out a long breath. Owen's words were still swirling in her head. Everything he'd said about Logan simmered in her mind, waiting for her to make a decision. The yellow roses had popped up in her dreams, the image of the buttery petals as vivid and real as if she'd been thrown back into the past. Her hand twitched, preparing to reach out and touch the flowers that had comforted her so much on the day she said her final goodbye. Even the memory of how they'd smelled—sweetly reassuring—was in the forefront of her thoughts.

He'd done that. He'd known her well enough to find the one thing that would give her peace on a day where pain was to be irrevocably tattooed onto her heart.

Regret coiled in her stomach like a snake. She'd blown up at him yesterday, perhaps more than was necessary. Sure, he'd done the wrong thing by keeping her out of the loop, but Owen was right. He might not be perfect, but so much of what he did was for her. Maybe they could find a balance between protection and independence.

Addison would always live her own life, be her own person, and if Logan truly did care for her then they would make it work. She could be independent and in love at the same time, without compromising her values.

In love.

The words made butterflies flutter their wings low in her belly. Wasn't love supposed to be sunshine and rainbows rather than passionate arguments? Wasn't love supposed to be easy?

No. Her parents had been very much in love, but they'd argued over much the same things as her and Logan. Safety. Security. Fear. But her parents had loved with a ferocity and wholeheartedness that she'd inherited. That kind of love wasn't easy; it wasn't soft and gentle.

It was rough, jagged. It sat just under the skin.

Was she really in love with Logan? Her fingertips traced the embroidered flowers on her bedspread. Yellow roses.

Yes.

Her body sang with relief at the realization. "I do," she whispered to herself in the quiet of the early morning. "I love him."

But she still had to deal with the issue of her plans. Her business. Love didn't mean giving up on her dreams; she could only hope that Logan would support her to go out on her own, trusting that she would come back to him and be his partner in another way. In a more significant way.

15

"WHERE ARE WE at with Michael Zetta?" Logan leaned back in his desk chair and arranged a mask of calm over his face.

If he'd learned one thing in his life, it was not to let his fear show. But he'd spent the night twisting and turning in his bed, until he'd woken up in a tangle of bedsheets with a pounding in his skull that was loud enough to wake the dead.

He hadn't gone near Addison in two days, not since their fight, and it was killing him.

You would *be near her now if you'd done the right thing and told her what was going on. You've dug this hole; time to bury yourself in it.*

"We weren't able to get eyes on Zetta at the coffee shop," Aiden said, holding his hand up as Logan prepared to bark at him. "But we were able to find out where he worked after tracking him down on LinkedIn. He's employed as an accountant at a small firm in the Financial District."

"Seems odd, then, that he'd be doing his hacking at

a coffee place in Midtown," Rhys commented. "It's not exactly around the corner."

"Could be closer to where he lives?" Aiden shrugged. "Or maybe that's exactly why he chose it, because he wouldn't be recognized there."

"So we've got eyes on him around his work," Logan clarified, eager to keep the conversation on track. "What did we come up with?"

"Not a lot," Aiden admitted, raking a hand through his dark unruly hair. "He seems to lead a pretty normal life. Gets up, goes to work, goes to the gym and comes home. We haven't seen him go into the coffee shop since we started tailing him on Monday."

"It's only been a few days, so we can't count on that to mean anything." Logan drummed his fingers on his knee, his mind trying to fit the pieces of the puzzle together. "Have we got any further information from the tech side?"

"Quinn managed to track down some old posts under the DaZetta username and it turns out he's fairly new to this whole hacking thing," Rhys said. "He had help building the Trojan virus that he sent to Addison. But there's not much else to go on. Her personal computer has come up clean, so we're assuming he doesn't have her other email address."

"I wonder if we could approach him and put the pressure on," Aiden suggested. "He works for an accounting firm. I doubt they'd take too kindly to one of their employees doing some illegal hacking on the side."

"It's worth a try. But it means we'll have to show our hand," Logan said. "Unless you think you can get something more from this virus, Rhys?"

"Unfortunately, no." Rhys shook his head. "I can

only get whatever he gives us at this point, and I'm still confident that he's figured out we're watching since the dummy device won't be sending him any data. Quinn is digging around online to see what else she can find out about him, but it seems he's keeping a fairly low profile. He hasn't posted much on the forum since before the virus came through."

Logan looked over his case notes. "How did things go with the truck that ran Addison off the road?"

"No go," Aiden said. "I checked in with one of my old buddies who's now at the DMV, and we couldn't find any red trucks registered to Michael Zetta. The plate number you gave me is currently unregistered."

"Of course it is." Logan rolled his eyes and pushed up from his chair. "And we didn't get much from the security cameras at the gas station, or from Addison's building security footage. Just a male with dark hair, nothing we didn't already have. Well, if we have someone watching him then let's give it a little longer before we approach Zetta. I want to be sure this is our guy, especially since we haven't got much to tie him to the virus other than a surname, which isn't enough. When we nail him, I want it to stick."

He left his team to keep working and went in search of coffee. Detouring past Addison's office, he noticed she wasn't there and stopped to chat to Renee. Addison's assistant sat behind her desk, which was covered in photos of her adorable twin girls.

"Hi, Logan, what can I do for you?" She smiled brightly as she paused from her lightning-speed typing.

"Where's Addi?" He didn't mean to bark the question out so forcefully, but his nerves were on edge since their fight. Cringing, he tried to smooth his voice out. "I mean, what time do you think she'll be back at her desk?"

"She's sitting in on the finance team meeting at the moment," Renee replied, swiveling toward the second screen on her desk where Addison's calendar sat. "Looks like she'll be in there for at least another half hour. But between you and me, they *always* go over. I think Jeff enjoys hearing the sound of his own voice." She tapped a perfectly manicured finger to her chin. "So I'd give it forty-five to be sure. Would you like me to send her over when she's done?"

"Thanks, Renee, that would be great." He hovered on the spot. "Uh, how is she today?"

Renee raised a brow. "How is she?"

"Yeah, as in…" He cleared his throat. "Mentally."

"Uh, fine, I guess. She looked a little tired this morning but she seemed okay."

"Tired, right." He bobbed his head. Had she been up all night?

An image flitted across his brain—a taunting flash of Addison and Owen together. He gritted his teeth and shoved the thought aside. No, that's not what it would be. She wouldn't jump straight into another man's arms.

Yeah, that's more your move, remember?

"Thanks, Renee."

He headed back to his office and tried to shake the restlessness from his limbs. A feeling of dread plagued him. And that intuition—like an impossible-to-reach itch under the skin—wouldn't let him go.

Something bad is going to happen.

No, it wouldn't. He had to stay on his game, and that meant not letting the dark worries distract him. Addison would be fine. *They* would be fine.

They.

God, how could he have been so stupid? It was a miracle that Addison was still talking to him after everything he'd done. He wouldn't waste that gift. Sure, he couldn't promise that he'd never piss her off in the future by doing what he felt was right, but that wasn't the point, was it? He should have kept her in the loop; he should have talked to her.

Communication. His family had never been good at it.

He hadn't even known his mother was ill until she died. All that time she'd lain there in the hospital, battling complications from her diabetes, he'd been none the wiser. His father had said that he'd wanted to protect Logan from the pain of seeing his mother suffer. But it hadn't done any good. Secrets didn't help anyone.

His mother had been alone—a cheating husband and absent son leaving her to die all by herself, surrounded by beeping machines and strangers in white coats. Pain coursed through him. If only his father had manned up and told him what was going on...

He didn't want to be like his father, which meant he needed to tell Addison how he felt. He needed to promise her that he was ready to be the man she deserved. Honest, open. Trusting.

ADDISON FOUND HERSELF staring off into space while the company's finance director, Jeff, droned on. Normally, she'd be totally engaged in the team meeting. But today her mind was elsewhere.

"Don't you agree, Addison?" Jeff asked from the head of the boardroom table. The rest of the team turned toward her, awaiting her response.

A clock ticked in the silence. The meeting should have ended twenty minutes ago.

"Of course, but, Jeff, I'm afraid I need to run. I've got another meeting that I'm late for." She stood and grabbed her phone, tripping on her chair in her haste to get out of the stuffy room. "Great job, everyone."

Curious eyes stared at her from all around, and she pasted a bright smile on her face before darting out of the room. So what if they all thought she was crazy? No one would say anything to her directly. One of the perks of being the boss, as Logan would say.

Logan. Her tummy flipped as her mind conjured an image of him, but before she could delve too far into the confusing swirl of thoughts in her head, her phone rang.

"Addison Cobalt speaking," she said, pressing the phone to her ear.

"It's Richard James, Comrade Real Estate. I'm calling to confirm our appointment this afternoon." He paused. "I have another buyer who's asking about the property, so I wanted to make sure you're still interested."

"I am," she said resolutely. "I'm leaving the office now."

"Excellent. I'll see you soon."

This was it, the first step in her spreading her wings. If she had the place all lined up before she spoke to Logan, he might take her seriously and not try to convince her to stay at Cobalt & Dane. She could even take him there and explain what it meant to her. She could *show* him how important it was.

Excitement bubbled up in her stomach.

"Addison." Renee waved to catch her attention. "Logan was looking for you earlier. I said I'd ask you to stop by his office when you were done."

"I can't. I've got to run out for an hour or so." Addison sailed past Renee's desk to grab her purse. "Was it urgent?"

"He didn't say." Her assistant cocked her head as she peered at her computer. "Where are you headed?"

Since she'd revealed her secret to the most important person in her life, she wouldn't have to keep her big plans in the shadows for much longer.

Smiling, she straightened her shoulders. "I'm meeting with Richard James from Comrade Real Estate. It's personal…kind of."

"Do you need me to call a car?"

"No, it's okay. I'll grab a cab." She waved over her shoulder as she sailed out of the office, high on the possibilities that lay ahead of her. "I'll be back by three."

By the time Addison made it out of the building and into a cab, her whole body buzzed. It wasn't butterflies in her tummy any longer, but great winged beasts. Dragons, maybe. Something fierce, like her. She stifled a grin, thinking about how proud her father would be. He'd always raised her to be hardworking and creative.

The cab crawled through the city at whatever was slower than a snail's pace. Each block felt like ten, each red light another hurdle to jump. She toyed with her phone, resisting the urge to call Logan. The discussion they needed to have wasn't one that should happen over the phone. They should be face-to-face when she told him that she wanted him. Not for a night or two, but forever.

Hold your horses, Cobalt. Let's tackle one thing at a time—deal with this office space and then think about what to say to Logan.

The cab made it to the bridge and Addison watched

the water rise up to the side. It was a perfect New York summer day—with blistering sunshine and sticky heat. Some people hated it, but she lived for summer. Lived for the freedom that came with tossing all her layers into a cupboard and locking them up for another six months.

She wondered if her new office would have a view, if she'd be able to make it feel cozy and homey.

"We're almost there," the cabbie said as they headed in the direction of Prospect Park.

A guy in a suit stood with a folder on the corner of the street. He waved at the cab as if he recognized her. Funny, since they hadn't met in person. But there were no other cabs around, so she shrugged the thought off.

After paying the fare, she stepped out into the street. "Richard?"

"You must be Addison," he said. She expected him to stick his hand out but he kept a slight distance from her, instead raking his hand through dark hair. "The property is on the other side of the street. We'll need to walk through here."

He gestured to a small lane between two buildings. Unease settled in Addison's stomach, but she looked up at the bright sky and big leafy green trees. It was probably nerves and the weight of her decision settling in.

"Lead the way," she said.

Her heels clicked noisily against the pavement as they walked, echoing down the quiet street. This section of the neighborhood seemed to be peaceful and pretty, exactly what she was searching for. She might even give up her Manhattan apartment for a place closer by—perhaps a cute brownstone. She wondered what Logan would prefer, and then stopped herself.

One step at a time...

The lane became darker as they walked into the shadow of the building next to them. No one appeared to be coming or going.

"Are you sure this is the right way?" Addison asked. She gazed down to a fence at the end of the lane. "It looks like it's closed off."

At that moment Richard turned to her sharply, and she realized he had something in his hand. Fabric. But before she could register what was going on, he had his hand up to her mouth.

Then she faded to nothingness.

16

LOGAN CAME OUT of his office around four to see where Addison had gotten to. It wasn't like her to avoid a meeting, even if she *was* pissed at him. The Addi he knew wouldn't shrink in the face of conflict. He strolled to her office and found Rhys and Quinn chatting with Renee outside.

"She's not back yet," Renee said before he'd even had a chance to open his mouth. Her hair was falling out of its bun and she looked the very definition of frazzled. "I know everyone wants a piece of her time, but I can't magically make her appear."

Logan frowned. "Did she have an appointment somewhere?"

"Yes, but it wasn't in her calendar. Apparently she had a meeting with a real estate company. Comrade Real Estate, I think she said." Renee sighed. "Sorry if I seem snappy, but she promised she'd be back before three, and now I'm trying to rearrange all her afternoon meetings. She won't answer her phone, either."

That didn't sound like Addison at all.

"Can we call Comrade Real Estate?" Quinn suggested. "Maybe her phone died."

Logan nodded. "Yeah, let's do that."

Why would she be meeting with a real estate company? Perhaps after what'd happened she no longer felt safe in her apartment.

"I made a note of the person she was meeting," Renee said. "Richard James. I'll look up the company website and find a phone number."

That prickling unease returned, burrowing under Logan's skin. He tried to dismiss it; Addison was her own person, so she could meet with whomever she wanted about whatever she wanted.

So why did he feel like something was on the verge of going horribly wrong?

"Oh, here we go." Renee picked up her desk phone and dialed the number listed on the Comrade Real Estate website. After a few minutes her eyebrows crinkled. "It's disconnected."

Logan leaned over Renee's shoulder to examine the website. "Is it my imagination or is this the most generic-looking real estate website I've ever seen?"

"You're right." Quinn wrinkled her nose.

After a few clicks around the site they'd learned nothing new about Comrade Real Estate. There were a few headshots of the agents with general bios, but the only number listed was the disconnected one.

"I feel like I've seen this guy before," Quinn said, pointing at Richard James's photo. "He looks so familiar."

Renee dragged the image into a search bar and the man's face popped up several times with different expressions. "It's a stock photo. I recognize him because we used his photo on one of our line management guides."

Rhys shook his head. "Why would they have a stock photo on their website?"

"Check the other images." A sinking feeling settled like a stone in the pit of Logan's stomach.

Sure enough, the other two images also appeared to have been sourced from the same stock image site.

"This doesn't smell good, boss," Quinn said to Rhys with a shake of her head. "Something's not right."

"Okay, let's not panic." Logan held up his hands and drew a long breath so he didn't Hulk-smash a hand through the wall. "Quinn, you check the website out further and see if there's anything else funky about it. Rhys, try tracking Addi's cell phone. And find Aiden and tell him to locate Michael Zetta. Renee, call Addison every few minutes until she picks up."

Everyone went their separate ways. Logan stalked into his office, barely able to suppress the rising fear that churned like foamy black waves in his stomach. As calm as he might appear on the outside, on the inside he was a mess.

Addison was in danger and it was because of him. Because he'd kept her out of the loop. Because he hadn't listened to what she wanted.

He slammed his fist onto his desk and relished the pain as it ricocheted up his arm. "Fucking dammit!"

"Is everything okay?" Emily poked her head into his office, her young face creased with concern. She mustn't have run into Renee yet.

"Addison's missing." He ground the words out, the admission carving pain into his chest. "We're trying to find her."

"Missing?" Emily bit her lip. "How do you know that?"

"She's gone off to meet someone from what appears to be a fake company, and she's not answering her phone." He tried to compose himself, but quieting the noise in his head seemed impossible.

If he lost her now…

"I'm sure she's fine," Emily said. "Maybe she wanted some time to herself. She might have gone shopping."

That showed how little Emily knew about Addison. She put her work before *everything*, which was why he was still reeling from her news that she wanted to strike out on her own.

Before he could respond, his desk phone rang. The screen flashed up "Rhys Glover, IT Dept." "Yes?"

"I've got you on speaker," Rhys said. "Quinn's here. Uh…we have some information."

"Then spit it out," he growled. With his free hand he shooed Emily out of his office, not even caring how much of a prick he must seem.

Nothing mattered more than finding Addison as soon as possible.

"We can't track her phone. It looks like it's been turned off or at the very least disconnected from the internet, so there's no location data being sent," Rhys said.

After a short pause a throat cleared on the other end of the line. "And the IP address for the Comrade Real Estate domain registration matches the one we've been tracking for Michael Zetta," Quinn said.

"Christ!" he roared. "I thought we were supposed to have eyes on that bastard."

It was useless taking the frustration out on his IT team since security detail wasn't their responsibility, but the curse words spewed out of him without restraint. He slammed the phone down and jabbed at the intercom button. "Emily? Tell Aiden and Owen to get their asses in here now."

A moment later, the two men walked into the office. Aiden had a perplexed look on his face. "We've got eyes on Zetta, Logan. I promise, he *doesn't* have Addison with him."

"Then where the fuck is she?" He glared pointedly at Owen. "You were supposed to be watching her."

"Hang on a minute." Owen held his hands up. "She was in the office. Did you expect me to sit on her shoulder like a deranged fucking parrot?"

"If you had, she wouldn't be missing right now." Logan felt the rage boiling away inside him, threatening to burn everything in his wake.

"That's bullshit and you know it." Owen shook his head. "Instead of playing the blame game, we need to figure out what's happened to her. What information do we have?"

Logan filled them in on what Rhys and Quinn had uncovered. "But if Michael Zetta hasn't got her, then who has?"

Two blank faces stared back at him, mirroring the anger and concern that clutched at his own heart. If they didn't think of something soon, he might never get to tell Addison how he felt.

ADDISON TRIED TO suck in a breath, but instead she gagged on something clogging her mouth. Whatever it was, it tasted disgusting—like chemicals and dust and something sweetly metallic that turned her stomach. Her head felt like it weighed a ton and she could barely seem to hold it up.

"Ah, the little princess is *finally* awake." A voice

echoed around the room, the sound bouncing around so much that Addison couldn't tell where it originated. "Did you have a good sleep, my dear?"

Her tongue moved against the material in her mouth and she coughed. If she'd wanted to respond, the sound would have been muffled beyond comprehension anyway. So she stayed quiet.

"It's rude not to answer a question."

Pain blinded Addison as something hard connected with the back of her head and white-hot flashes exploded behind her eyelids. A wet trickle snaked down her skull; she was sure it was blood. She craned her head, trying to see who was behind her.

"You want to look at my face, do you?" The man who'd greeted her with his clipboard came around into her field of vision. "There you are, get your fill."

He didn't look dangerous. His suit was neat, although not flashy, his black hair styled. So ordinary, unassuming. But a gun rested in one of his hands, a telltale smear of blood on the grip.

Danger comes in many forms, her dad had once said to her. She tried to swallow against the rising tide of fear in her throat.

"I should reintroduce myself," he said, his ice-cold eyes piercing in the dull, dusty light.

Addison tried to glance around without letting him out of her peripheral vision. They seemed to be in an abandoned building. Broken windows let in shafts of light; a few pieces of office furniture sat unused and covered in dust.

How far had he taken her?

"You know me as Richard James, but that's only part of the story. I'm Richard James Zetta." Her face must have registered the name, because his lips twisted into a catlike smile. "So you *do* know me. Very clever, Ms. Cobalt. Too bad your security company doesn't seem to be so quick. I believe they've been tailing my brother."

A chill ran through Addison's body. His brother... Michael Zetta. How had they missed that? Logan's team would be following the wrong man, which meant no one would know where she was.

Cold fingers clutched at her heart.

"My stupid, stupid brother. All he cares about is suing the prison." Richard shook his head. "Money doesn't equal justice. It's an eye for an eye! But he's spending everything he has on fancy lawyers and he'll probably lose the lot. But you—" he pointed at her with the gun "—you can help me get justice for my father."

She tried to speak, but the words were lost in her gag. Her voice sounded muffled and her throat burned.

"Shh." He held up a finger. "It's not your turn, Addison. I'm sure you're not used to having someone tell you what to do, but you're smart enough to understand how this works. You do what I say and I don't shoot you. Got it?"

She nodded, shivering at the cold grip of fear's bony fingers wrapping around her spine.

"Now, we're going to have a little game of show-and-tell. I show you your bank's website and you tell me how to access your accounts." He cackled at her confused look. "Money doesn't equal justice for me, but I don't want my brother going broke trying to pay legal fees. I figure you can help us both get what we want."

The money didn't matter to her, but it was clear that nothing she handed over would save her. She struggled against the restraints, trying to get a better view of the room. Trying to see if there was some way she could escape.

"And before you start thinking that your employees might turn up looking for you, don't bother." Richard held up a broken device that appeared to be her smartphone. "I made sure no one would be able to track you."

Her stomach sank. How the hell was she going to get out of this?

"WE'VE MISSED SOMETHING," Logan said as he faced the best and brightest of his team. Rhys, Quinn, Aiden and Owen all looked among one another, but no one seemed to have any ideas. "What is Zetta's current position?"

"He's at work," Aiden replied, tapping away at the laptop in front of him. They all sat around the boardroom table with their computers, desperately clutching at anything that might help them find Addison. "I've checked in with our eyes on the ground and he hasn't left the building so far today."

"He must be working with someone else," Owen said. "What about a relative of his father? Have we seen any other names come up in the court case against the prison?"

"Not that I could find," Quinn replied, blowing a stray strand of hot-pink hair out of her eyes. "We looked into the mother, but I found an obituary for her. Maria Zetta died last year. I also went through a bunch of articles about the case and the only person listed was Michael Zetta."

"And there were no other relatives listed in the obituary?" Logan asked.

"Let me bring it up. I don't remember seeing anything else." Quinn cocked her head. "All it says is that it was written by the 'Zetta family.'"

"Maybe there's another obituary?" Rhys said, leaning over to read Quinn's screen.

Soft clicking filled the room as they searched, the minutes ticking away faster than Logan could stand. "Here we go," Quinn said. "There was another obituary posted a few days later. It says, 'Maria is survived by her two sons.' So Michael must have a brother."

"Find him," Logan growled. "Aiden, get in touch with your man on the ground and tell him that we may need to approach."

Aiden nodded and left the room, tapping at his phone as he walked.

"Look for school records," Rhys said to Quinn. "We might be able to find the brother's name through school sporting teams or academic achievements."

The room was suddenly a flurry of activity, everyone suggesting ways to find the other Zetta brother. A few seconds later Quinn gasped. "I found something. Michael Zetta played tennis for his high school all the way until his senior year."

"And his brother played, too?" Logan asked.

"No." She glanced up, her hazel eyes wide. "But someone from Cobalt & Dane did."

She turned her laptop around to show an old photo of a boy and girl in tennis whites. They had matching jet-black hair and confident smiles. The names printed under the photo were Michael Zetta and Emily Facinelli.

Logan's heart twisted in his chest as he stared at the photo. She looked much younger in the photo, but he would recognize his assistant anywhere.

"Everybody clear out," he said, trying to keep his voice from shaking. "Emily and I need to have a chat."

17

"WHERE IS SHE?" He braced both hands on the surface of the table, more to stop himself from trembling with rage than to intimidate his pint-sized assistant, Emily.

Right now, controlling himself was taking up all his mental energy, which left little for dealing with this situation calmly.

"I don't know what you're talking about." She stared up at him with large eyes. Her lips were pulled taut and her hands were folded in her lap.

"You're telling me you have no idea where Addison is currently?"

"Why would I know where she is? I don't take care of her schedule." She picked at the hem of her black pencil skirt, her brow crinkled. "Ask Renee."

"Okay, fine. Let's try this." He showed her the copy of the photo from earlier. "Who are the people in this photo?"

"That's me," she said, her voice suddenly wavering. "And that's my best friend, Michael. We play mixed doubles together." She paused. "Why do you have an old photo of me?"

"Does Michael have a brother?" The pieces were starting to fall into place, his body buzzing with the possibility that he could make it all right again. That he could save Addison.

Emily nodded. "Yes, he has a brother named Richard."

"And where does Richard work? It's important that you tell me, Emily."

"Umm." She bit down on her lip. "He was doing some cleaning work for a real estate company. Something to do with building maintenance... I'm not quite sure."

"Was the company called Comrade Real Estate?"

"I don't think so." She shook her head. "But I can't remember the name. It was one of the big companies, I think. He was excited when he got the job because he'd been looking for work on and off for over a year without much luck."

"It's very important I find out where he works, Emily. Could you call Michael and find out?"

"Why? What's going on?" She shook her head. "I don't see what it has to do with Addison."

"We think he's kidnapped her and may intend to harm her." Saying the words caused his throat to tighten, a lump lodging in his windpipe and blocking anything further from coming out.

"Oh God." She pressed her hand to her cheek.

Logan nodded and swallowed slowly, taking back control of his body. Now was not the time to let emotion take over; he had to treat this like any other assignment. Stay calm, stay focused. Get the client out alive.

But this wasn't any other client. This was the woman he loved. And he would get her out alive.

"Okay, of course I'll call Michael." Emily jumped up from her chair. "I'll do it right now."

REGRETS RIOTED IN Addison's mind. She should have taken that first email more seriously; she should have listened to Rhys and Logan. She should have at least told someone where she would be. But the chances of anyone finding her now…well, they were wafer-thin.

"I have to confess, this is so much more satisfying than I thought it would be." Richard Zetta looked her over, his eyes gleaming in a way that made her skin crawl. He had a laptop resting on an old desk and he typed with one hand since his other hand was occupied by the gun. "I can only hope there is an afterlife so your father can see what he's done to you."

Her eyes watered as she tried to scream through the cotton gag. It was useless, of course, since they were alone in a big, empty building. But she couldn't go down silently. She *wouldn't*.

"Do you think I wanted to do this?" Richard asked, his eyes wide and bulging. "No, I wanted my father home. He would never have hurt anyone. He was taking from rich people who had more money than sense so he could pay for my brother and me to go to college."

Addison squeezed her eyes shut, willing the plastic ties binding her to fall away. But as she wriggled, they burned into her skin. The harsh edges cut her, leaving her skin raw and probably bleeding.

"Don't shut your eyes!" He hit her again, this time across the cheek, and her head whipped back as the chair rocked.

It teetered and then fell. But there was nothing she could do to brace her fall and she landed hard against the concrete. The pain stole her breath as it shot up her arm like fireworks. Her whole body was ablaze.

"You're not allowed to ignore me." He kicked her in the rib cage, piling on more hurt. More pain. "No one is allowed to ignore me anymore because *I* am the one avenging my father."

Her throat prickled, warm tears seeping out the edges of her eyes as she lay there bound and immobile. If this was going to be the end, she hoped it would come swiftly. And she hoped, more than anything else, that Logan would somehow know how she felt about him. That she loved him and had done so ever since she was a besotted teenager.

Richard continued to rage at her, but Addison blocked out the sound. She may not know the right way to get out of zip ties, but her mind was her best feature. In that aspect, she was stronger than most. She wouldn't crumble. She had to *think*.

Her tongue worked at the gag, trying to push it out of her mouth. Or at the very least, slip it over her lip so that she could get some words out. Without the ability to speak she was at a disadvantage. Rubbing her face against the ground, the fabric rolled out of her mouth.

"Richard, please." She managed to say the words but her voice was weak and croaky. How long had she been out? "This isn't going to bring your father back."

"It's not about bringing him back," he snapped. "It's about doing what's right."

He seemed to calm down and refocus. From her angle on the ground she could see him move back toward the desk, and a moment later the clicking of keys resumed.

"And you think hurting me is going to make you feel better? News flash, it won't." She glared up at him from her curled position on the floor.

"Oh it will." He looked down to her. "Okay, we're going to start with your customer identification number."

A sharp, stabbing pain started radiating outward from her arm and midsection. Something wasn't right, a broken bone, maybe. Bruising, possibly internal bleeding. She forced down the swell of nausea in her stomach.

The second she gave him her banking account details she was as good as dead.

"Nothing will ever make those feelings go away," she said, stalling. "Do what you will, but I promise you that even if you kill me it won't make the pain and guilt and grief any better. And I'm guessing you know that already."

He crouched down, resting the gun inches from her head. She could see straight down the black barrel, like it was some rabbit hole into another life. As she waited for the beginning of the end, Addison's heart pounded hard in her chest. Fighting to stay alive, fighting to fuel her with energy that she had no way of expending.

"Richard Zetta!" His name echoed through the empty room, like a gunshot bouncing off the walls. "Step back and keep the gun where I can see it."

For a moment Addison wondered if her imagination had taken over and dreamed Logan into existence. Her white knight, as much as she'd always resented him for trying to play that role, was here for her. His footsteps sounded slow and steady as he approached. She even recognized that about him, the careful way he walked. With purpose, with intent.

Richard gripped the gun tighter, his knuckles white. "Well, well, if it isn't Logan Dane."

"I don't have any beef with you," Logan said in calm, soothing tones. "But I can't let you hurt her."

She still couldn't see him, but his presence filled the air. It breathed hope into her lungs.

"I'll shoot her if you come any closer." Richard waved the gun around but it was clear he'd been spooked. Obviously he had no contingency plan for being discovered. He was alone, whereas Logan would definitely have backup.

"Do I need to call my team in here or will you let her go?" Logan's voice was honey smooth, as calm as if he were ordering a drink at a bar. No aggression, no fear. He'd done this before and he knew that unnecessary emotion wouldn't help. He'd told her that once.

"This is not your place," Richard spat, and he moved to point the gun at Addison.

There was a *click*, footsteps. More people had entered the room. "We'll take you down before you even get a shot off, Richard. Lower the gun and we can all walk away." Logan stepped closer, his boots coming into Addison's line of sight.

She tried to move but pain engulfed her and she muffled a cry.

"Are you okay, Addi?" he asked as he stepped forward. His boots were covered in the dust that coated the floor, which now lined her throat and lungs.

She coughed. "Yeah, mostly."

"Fuck both of you," Richard screamed. "I know who you are, and you're as bad as she is."

"We're just doing our jobs," Logan said calmly. "Put the gun down."

In the distance Addison could see another set of feet moving quickly, quietly. Like a ninja. *Owen.* Richard hadn't noticed anyone coming up behind him because

Logan had his full attention. They must be hoping not to shoot him by catching him unawares.

"You think I won't pull the trigger?" Richard aimed the gun back down at Addison and she instinctively cringed, clamping her eyes shut. "You think I won't kill her?"

"If you'd wanted to kill her you would have done it already." Logan took another step and then another. "I know you're angry and grieving. But this isn't the way to fix that."

Before Richard had the chance to respond, Owen sneaked up behind him and got one bulky arm around his throat. With his other hand he directed Richard's hand away from her. A shot went off, shattering a window. Glass flashed as it fell to the ground in twinkling shards, the sound echoing around the room.

Aiden rushed Richard and retrieved the gun from him, disarming him and immediately dumping the cartridge out onto the floor with a loud *clang*.

"Are you hurt?" Logan dropped to the floor in front of her, his hands smoothing over her face.

"My arm." She cringed as the pain intensified. "And my head."

Now that Richard was no longer a threat, all the pain came back in full, vibrant feeling. Her head pounded like someone was taking a sledgehammer to the inside of her skull. Each breath was like jabbing a thousand needles into her lungs.

Logan gingerly slipped his hands under her arms and helped to lift her off the ground, setting the chair down first. He dug a Swiss army knife out of his pocket and cut the ties from her wrists, then her ankles. While he worked, she saw a billowing anger in his eyes. The

dark brown depths—usually so warm and sensual—
were wild.

"The police are on their way," Aiden announced.
"We'll hold Richard here until they're ready. Paramedics should be here shortly."

Addison twisted her good wrist, not daring to even try
to move her other arm. "How did you find me, Logan?"

"*We* found you. It was a team effort." He grabbed her
hand and wrapped it over his arm, bracing her as she
stood slowly. "But I can tell you right now, I would have
ripped through every building in this city to find you."

He filled her in on the connection between the Zettas
and Emily as they walked slowly out of the building.
Apparently Michael had given her the name of the
company Richard was working for, as well as the fact
that his brother been assigned to clean an abandoned
building—it had sounded like the perfect spot to commit
a crime. Addison didn't even want to think about what
might have happened if they'd gone to the wrong place.

For now, she needed to focus on something other than
her pain and fear lest she collapse in an emotional heap.
It wouldn't do to let the team see her as some damsel in
distress, even though that's exactly how she felt.

"We're a good team, you and I," he said as they
stepped out of the gloomy building and into the fading sunlight.

"Why, because I always need saving and you have a
hero complex?" she quipped. Jokes were easier than the
truth right now, although what she'd said was certainly
colored with experience.

"It was a general observation." He brushed the hair
back from her face and she felt the grit of dirt and dust
slide along her scratched-up skin. "We've built a good

company together. We've taken what your father started and made it stronger. Better."

The last thing she needed right now was a guilt trip about her decision to leave. This event hadn't changed her mind. If anything, it only made her more determined to strike out on her own. Life was short and psychos were aplenty.

She had to live her life to the fullest, corny as it sounded. She could see that now. There was no point holding back, no point being fearful. Because even the most cautious people could get caught up in danger.

"I was wrong not to listen to you," she said as they sat on a stone wall outside the building, waiting for the ambulance to arrive. Her arm throbbed and she cradled it against her chest. "This could have been avoided if I'd taken your advice."

"And I could have been less of an asshole about it." He leaned his head against her, the familiar scent of his soap cutting through the grime clogging her throat and nostrils. Even with all that filth, she could still feel him. Sense him.

No matter how at odds they were, his presence was a comfort.

"This could have ended very differently," she whispered, realization creeping into her mind. "You could have found me with a bullet between the eyes."

"I know." His hand found her good one, his fingers interlocking with hers.

"I don't want to play games anymore, Logan." She blinked as a wave of emotion crashed over her, threatening to pull her under its dark, endless depths. "I want us to be real with each other. No more power struggles, no more cat and mouse."

"I kind of like the cat and mouse." A smile tugged on his lips.

"I'm still leaving Cobalt & Dane."

The wail of sirens filled the air, growing louder with each passing second. Soon she would be patched up, shiny as new. But she wouldn't forget today—what she might have lost. What she might have thrown away because of her own stubbornness.

"I understand," he said, his head bobbing. "And I support you no matter what."

18

When Addison woke, her eyes felt like they were filled with grit. She lifted a hand to rub them, but her arm refused to move and pain shot straight up to her shoulder. That's when she noticed the plaster and sling.

Oh right, the doctor had said she had a broken arm. Bruised ribs. Stitches. Possible concussion.

The last one must have been okay since she'd woken up from her sleep. She blinked, trying to bring the room into focus. White on white on white. Her stomach roiled.

"Goddamn hospitals," she muttered, though her voice was merely a croak.

She hadn't set foot in one since her father had passed away. Something about the smell seemed to bring the memories rushing back, and with it feelings of hopelessness and despair. She'd never felt more useless in all her life than she had when she'd sat at her father's side and watched him slowly die.

Tears pricked at her eyes but she didn't even have the energy to cry. Her head sank back into the pillow. The room was silent. Everyone from Cobalt & Dane mus have gone home, but she'd been hoping that Logan might still be here.

That he might care enough to be by her side when she woke, even though she'd told him she still planned to leave.

A hot, wet droplet fell onto her cheek and rolled toward her jaw. Her throat tightened as she tried—and failed—to stem her emotions. As she shut her eyes, a scent caught her attention. Something sweet...familiar.

Reaching with her good hand, she found the remote for the bed and pushed the button that would help her sit up. That's when she caught sight of them.

Yellow roses. Everywhere.

Not just one pretty bunch in a vase, but multiple bunches. The room was a florist's dream. There were bright blooms the color of lemon rind, rich bold bursts of gold, and pale muted petals in tones of butter and early-morning sunshine. Some sat in boxes, ringed with delicate white baby's breath, and others were left alone, allowed to shine all by themselves.

A sob caught in her throat. Logan.

He was carrying on a tradition, letting his actions speak louder than his words. A smile tugged at her lips and, as if on cue, he walked into the room. Another box of flowers bundled up in his arms.

"What on earth are you doing?" She brushed the fallen tears away with her good hand.

"I had to pick these up," he grumbled, setting them down on one of the few free spots remaining. "They called me last minute to tell me the delivery guy was sick."

"Did you buy all of them?" she asked, although she

already knew the answer. When he nodded she laughed. "Why?"

"I have a lot of things to apologize for." The statement was matter-of-fact, spare. Logan was a man who owned his mistakes and she respected him for that. "I got one lot of flowers for every apology, since I figured I'd already fallen behind by not saying anything for the past few years."

"Let's hear it then." She patted the bed. "I won't say no to an apology."

"You're one of a kind, you know that, right?" His dark eyes gleamed. The bed creaked under his weight as he sat, his large frame encased in an inky black T-shirt that looked harsh against the clinical white furnishings. "Addi, I'm sorry for being such a jerk."

He reached for her hand and ran his thumb over her knuckles. The gentle touch sent a shiver rocketing through her, blanking out everything else—the pain, uncertainty. Grief.

"I respect that you want to be independent and that you want your space." His eyes seemed to look past her. "I've had too much of a hand in your life where you didn't want me."

"I do want you in my life," she said, squeezing his hand. "But I want to be my own person at the same time."

"I get it." He nodded. "It's just that the thought of anything happening to you…it fucking terrifies me. The world is so much better with you around. *I'm* so much better with you around."

"What are you trying to say?"

When he glanced up, every bone in her body melted under the intensity of his gaze. There was a raw openness in his expression that she'd never seen before.

"I want us to be Cobalt & Dane again."

Disappointment clutched at her heart like a tight fist. "What happened doesn't change my plans, Logan. I want to go out on my own and try to make it. I want to build something and see if it survives. I want—"

"Stop." He shook his head. "What I meant is that I want us to be together again. Not as a company but as a…" He swallowed. "I don't know, just…us."

"You mean, like in a relationship?" A smile melted across her lips. "An exclusive relationship?"

"I mean forever." He reached out and brushed a thumb over her cheek, touching one of the cuts there. The gesture was so soft, so tender. "With a ring and everything. I don't want to keep pretending that you're not the best thing in my life because I'm scared to lose you."

They were the words she'd longed to hear from him, words that he whispered to her in the quiet corners of her dreams. But this wasn't a dream.

Her hands found his face; they traced the rough angle of his jaw—now coated in stubble—and the high planes of his cheekbones. She wanted to memorize him with her hands, capture this moment in her mind so that she could replay it over and over and over.

"I'm not going anywhere. Scout's honor." She saluted him and he chuckled.

The room hummed around them. Machines beeped, footsteps rushed past, and the hustle and bustle of the hospital crackled in her ears like white noise. None of it mattered—not her broken bones or her scarred heart. Not all their collective fears and mistakes.

They were together now and they were laying themselves bare.

"I get that you might leave me." He nodded, his eyes

down as if he were sorting something out in his head. She brushed her fingers through his hair. "You might get sick or I might get sick. It might happen unexpectedly but…that's not a reason to keep us apart."

"Or we might grow old and gray and wrinkly together. That's an option, too."

"I'd like that." His eyes shone as he lifted them to hers. "But only if you promise you won't stop wearing all that sexy underwear, even if we do get old."

She grinned. "You have my word."

He leaned forward to kiss her, being careful not to put pressure on her injured arm. But right now, Addison couldn't care less about her scars. About her pain. She had Logan, and that was all that mattered.

As his lips brushed hers the world melted away. Her body sang at his touch. His kiss was better than any medicine, any drug. He was hers, and now she was whole.

"I love you," she said as they pulled apart, his taste still lingering on her lips. "And I have for a very long time."

"Couldn't resist my brooding charms, eh?" He flashed her that roguish smirk that she loved so very much.

"Not even a little bit." She touched his kiss-bruised mouth. "No matter how frustrated I got with you poking around in my life, I could never stay away from you. You've got a good heart, Logan. You're a good man. *My* man."

"I love you, too." He cupped her face. "You're my family, Addi. You're my best friend, my voice of reason."

"Your future wife," she whispered.

"My future everything."

Epilogue

Three months later

LOGAN STOOD TO the side of the room, trying to figure out how to get the beer up to his mouth without splitting the too-tight fabric of his costume around his biceps. Addison had insisted that the Batman costume should fit like a second skin, otherwise the fantasy would be ruined, apparently. And since she was pouring herself into a latex Catwoman costume, it was only fair that he come to the party—both literally *and* figuratively.

"You been working out, Logan? Looks like you're about to Hulk out of that costume." Owen said as he sauntered over with Aiden, looking free and breezy in what appeared to be a white bedsheet. Gold leaves glinted against his blond hair, and a thin rope cinched in his waist. "Do I need to be on wardrobe malfunction watch?"

"Very funny," he grumbled. "At least I'm wearing a costume."

"What's that supposed to mean?" Owen looked down at himself. "This is a genuine Roman-era bedsheet."

"Genuine, huh?" Aiden tugged at the care label sewn into the fabric knotted at his friend's waist.

"Totally." Owen grinned. "Besides, this is the perfect costume for me."

"Because you like easy access?" Aiden tossed his head back and laughed.

"Because I like history. What does your costume say about you?" He gestured to Aiden's bright blue overalls and comically fake mustache.

"It's an inside joke." Aiden adjusted the red cap on his head, which had the letter *M* emblazoned on it. "She was supposed to dress up as Princess Peach, but we agreed that Lara Croft suits her better."

They looked over to where Quinn stood in the iconic costume, her pink hair hanging in a long braid down her back. She was laughing at something Rhys had said. He and his girlfriend, Wren, were dressed as *Big Bang Theory* characters.

"This whole thing is so Quinn, isn't it?" Owen commented. "Of course she would have an engagement party that resembles a nerd convention. But I still can't believe she said yes to you."

"Why wouldn't she?" Aiden puffed out his chest, which only served to make him look even more ridiculous in his Super Mario outfit. "We're perfect together."

"Someone pass me a bucket," Owen joked, slapping Aiden on his back. "You make me sick."

Logan shook his head and forced the beer up to his lips, cringing when the seams of the Batsuit protested. In front of him, the room was filled with people in colorful costumes. It was hard to recognize most of the people, although his eyes were inexorably drawn to Addison's slim body encased in a reflective black catsuit. A head-